PRAISE FOR "DRIVING QUESTIONS"

"Joe Giglio has pulled no punches nor spared any sacred cows in calling for a new transportation vision. He raises good questions—questions that, whether you agree with him or not, need to be addressed." –Robert L. Darbelnet, President and Chief Executive Officer, AAA

"Joe Giglio is no newcomer to innovative thinking. I have read his work on privatization and transportation since the 1980s. In his new book, *Driving Questions*, don't expect to ride in the passenger seat. Joe puts the reader squarely behind the wheel in an insightful ride through the problems facing America's transportation system. Hold on. The ride's not pretty… but there is light at the end of the tunnel." –Tom Beasley, former CEO, Chairman, and founder of Corrections Corporation of America

"From FDR's 'War Plan Orange' to defeat the Japanese Imperial Navy, to management guru Peter Drucker's admonition that the purpose of enterprise is to create 'customers,' Joe Giglio has challenged us with the urgent need to develop a national transportation strategy. To do so, he says we need to focus more on 'content' and less on 'form.' I believe he is right in that distinction, and right to point to the need for a new national strategy." –John Horsley, Executive Director of the American Association of State Highway and Transportation Officials (AASHTO)

"Dr. Giglio brings clarity to approaching complex problems that makes one think in fresh ways about how to solve them. With this book he does it again." –Bill Millar, President of the American Public Transportation Association

"Once again Professor Giglio has looked at how we should deliver the transportation services in the U.S. through the lens of integration and alignment—the alignment of vision, funding, modes, and the interests of users. In the game of transportation, he sees the entire board and beyond." –Patrick D. Jones, Executive Director, International Bridge, Tunnel, and Turnpike Association

Also by Joseph M. Giglio

Fast Lane to the Future: The Privatization Route
(Hudson Institute, 1996)

Mobility: America's Transportation Mess and How to Fix It
(Hudson Institute, 2005)

Driving Questions: Developing a National Transportation Vision
(Hudson Institute, 2007)

JUDGES OF THE SECRET COURT

**A contemporary novel about two
rogues with compelling ideas**

JOE GIGLIO

HUDSON INSTITUTE
Washington, D.C.

Copyright © 2008 Hudson Institute, Inc. All rights reserved.
Printed in Washington, DC, by Kirby Lithographic Company, Inc.
ISBN: 978-1-55813-163-7

For information about obtaining additional copies of this or other Hudson Institute publications, please contact:

Hudson Institute Fulfillment Center
P.O. Box 1020
Noblesville, IN 46061
Toll Free: 888-554-1325
Fax: 317-913-2392
Or visit Hudson's online bookstore at www.hudson.org.

For media and speaking engagement purposes, contact the Hudson Institute at 202-974-2400, or email at info@hudson.org.

About the Hudson Institute
Hudson Institute is a nonpartisan policy research organization dedicated to innovative research and analysis that promotes global security, prosperity and freedom. We challenge conventional thinking and help manage strategic transitions to the future through interdisciplinary and collaborative studies in defense, international relations, economics, culture, science, technology, and law. Through publications, conferences, and policy recommendations, we seek to guide global leaders in government and business.

Since our founding in 1961 by the brilliant futurist Herman Kahn, Hudson's perspective has been uniquely future-oriented and optimistic. Our research has stood the test of time in a world dramatically transformed by the collapse of the Soviet Union, the rise of China, and the advent of radicalism within Islam. Because Hudson sees the complexities within societies, we focus on the often-overlooked interplay between culture, demography, technology, markets, and political leadership. Our broad-based approach has, for decades, allowed us to present well-timed recommendations to leaders in government and business.

For more information, visit www.hudson.org.

To all my children

Contents

Author's Note

You are reading my literary obituary. You will be grateful to learn that after three books in three years on transportation, I have decided to wise up and step around the subject and kick the habit. I know it's a shock but try to be brave. This book is the coda to put the trilogy to rest.

Writing about transportation is a tough habit to break, but enough is enough. I don't want to earn the award for Indecent Repetition. Also, my backlog of other things I want to do looks like the National Debt. Finally, I promised the New York Knicks I will play point guard for them next season. That I can be so flip about this decision gives you some notion of the ruthlessness of the person you are reading.

In my previous books, articles, and speeches, I've discussed at considerable length the basic ideas that must drive our thinking about transportation. I've been gratified by the positive response to these ideas among transportation mavens. But at the same time, I've been left with the same uneasy feeling that the math professor has after he's crammed his students full of enough Calculus to pass the final exam—and knows they'll promptly forget everything after the course is over.

That is the problem with trying to explain difficult concepts like transportation principles (differential equations) through the medium of academic prose. You can wear yourself out coming up with colorful metaphors to keep your readers on the edge of their seats. But in the end, this prose is no different from one of those brilliant Hong Kong martial arts movies starring Jackie Chan or Michelle Yeoh. Irresistible while you're watching it because of the compelling action sequences. But totally forgettable after it's over.

In short, academic prose may grab your mind while you're reading it. But it doesn't grab your gut, which is the secret of being truly mean-ingful and having the kind of staying power that can make a difference down the line. So it ends up being a classroom exercise that's too soon forgotten.

The alternative is to use an entirely different medium to explain these things, letting the chips fall where they may. One that we call the Novel. Which ostensibly focuses on presenting fictional human beings in dra-matic circumstances that grab us by the gut and make us care about them. So they set up house in our minds. Often (if their names are Cap-tain Ahab or Jay Gatsby) for the rest of our lives.

But these fictional people can have ideas, iridescent ideas. Insights and beliefs about things that both relate to, and transcend, their personal lives. And if they talk about them, we're going to pay attention in ways that we don't if the same ideas, insights, and beliefs are explained to us in abstract academic prose. Which means that they grab us by the gut and stay with us. And maybe (just maybe) end up influencing our own ideas, insights, and beliefs in ways that three-foot stacks of academic tomes could never do. (Remember when you read John Steinbeck's *The Grapes of Wrath* for the first time, and realized that the world could never look the same to you again?)

That's why I've decided to go out on a limb and make my last book on transportation a novel rather than a traditional nonfiction treatise. A novel about two lively people with an unconventional way of looking at familiar things. And personal lives that force them to confront ideas we're not likely to find in the *New Yorker* or in polite intellectual circles. Reminding us again there is no such thing as a saint without a past and a sinner without a future.

I want to thank the following for helping me get smart on the issues and for their friendship: William Ankner, Michael Ascher, Coby Chase, Charlie Chieppo, Jonathan R. Davis, Dan Dornan, Mike Doyle, Jane Garvey, Stan Grayson, Butch Eley, Pat Jones, Kevin Kiley, Dick Mudge, Ken Philmus, Kathy Ruffalo, James Simpson, and Laurie Slosberg.

Special thanks to Martin Capper for always asking the right questions. As always, if there are errors technical or otherwise, the fault is with these people. I'm tired of being the fall guy. (Just kidding.)

A nod of gratitude to Grace Terzian for her untiring and good-humored support along with that of her colleagues Rachel DiCarlo Currie and Mitzi H. Pepall. Finally, I want to thank Anne Himmelfarb for her able and timely efforts as editor.

I hope you enjoy the walk on the wild side.

Chapter One
Two Guys from Brooklyn

The digital clock on my dashboard blinked eight fifteen sharp that Sunday morning when I drove my secondhand Corolla into the federal prison's parking lot.

Plenty early for my scheduled visit with investment banker Elijah Stern. Who was serving a term in the prison's minimum security unit for Insider Stock Market Trading.

I found a parking space near the Visitors Building, shut off the engine, and started going through my two lists.

This wasn't the first time I'd visited a prison inmate, so I knew the general drill. I also had the Visitor Instructions pages that I'd copied from the prison's web site. They gave me exact details about what I could and couldn't bring with me on my visit.

I began going through my A-list, which covered things visitors were allowed to bring into the prison.

My California driver's license.

Check. I dropped it into the outside breast pocket of my navy blue blazer.

My newspaper's photo-ID press card encased in clear plastic with a black fabric lanyard attached so I could wear it around my neck.

Check. I slipped it over my head and let it dangle.

Nineteen dollars in loose quarters for the Visitors Building vending machines, split between two clear plastic Ziploc bags.

Check. I placed one bag in each side pocket of my blazer.

Two throw-away ballpoint pens.

Check. I clipped them to the left inside pocket of my blazer.

My car keys.

Check. I slipped them into the right outside pocket of my blazer.

Then I turned to the B-list, which covered things I couldn't bring into the prison.

My wallet containing the usual credit cards, eighty dollars in twenties, and various other personal items.

Check. I laid it on the passenger seat beside me.

My cell phone with its built-in digital camera.

Check. I placed it next to my wallet.

My pocket tape recorder.

Check. Most reporters regard tape recorders as essential tools of their trade. But a tape recorder intimidates a lot of people. So I had trained myself to listen carefully and remember what I heard. In any case, prison rules specified no tape recorders. I laid mine on the passenger seat next to my cell phone.

My reporter's notebook.

Check. Spiral bound like a steno pad, but narrow enough to slip easily into the side pocket of a jacket. No mention of anything like this in the Visitor Instructions. But I knew from past experience that most prisons regard any kind of writing pad as a no-no. So I laid mine on the passenger seat.

A small leather case containing my apartment and office keys, plus an extra car key for emergencies.

Check. I added it to the neat row of items on the seat next to me.

Assorted pocket change.

Check. I dumped the coins into the door's open storage pocket next to my Auto Club map of the central California coast.

That completed everything on my B-list.

I folded up the two lists, plus the print-out of Visitor Instructions, and slipped them into the right inside breast pocket of my blazer. If I had to write down anything during my visit, I could use the backs of these pages.

Then I leaned over and pulled open the drawer hidden under the passenger seat. Inside was an insulated plastic portfolio that I took out and unzipped. There was just enough room inside to hold all the no-no items I'd laid out on the seat.

I zipped the portfolio shut and placed it back in the drawer, which I closed and locked with my car's ignition key. Hopefully, the portfolio's insulation would protect my cell phone and tape recorder from the heat inside the car that the strong sun was bound to generate during the hours to come.

I opened the car's two front windows about an inch to provide some ventilation. Got out of the car and locked it. Then walked to the open front door of the one-story Visitors Building and went inside.

* * *

I found myself in what looked like a standard-issue school room. With off-white walls and a dozen rows of armless plastic chairs that held a scattering of other visitors. At the far end of the room was a counter behind which two uniformed prison guards stood fumbling with papers. On the wall behind them was a big sign labeled *Rules For Visitors*.

As the sign directed, I walked up to the counter and began filling out a one-page *Visitor's Application* form with one of my ballpoint pens. The guard nearest me stopped fumbling with his papers and eyed me without moving. The black plastic name tag just above his left breast pocket read *T. Joad* in white letters, and I obviously wasn't the first prison visitor with a black face he'd ever seen.

But I couldn't help wondering what he thought of the nonblack clothes I was wearing. The well-worn navy blazer with its slightly tarnished brass buttons I'd bought at J. Press during my junior year at Harvard. The button-down blue dress shirt from Land's End, with no tie and the collar open. The khaki pants from Brooks Brothers, laundered so many times they looked as soft as napkins in an upscale Manhattan restaurant.

My standard reporter's uniform ever since graduate school at Columbia. And I sensed that many nonurban Californians were confused by it. Apparently, they expected all blacks to wear cliché ghetto garb. Grey sweat pants with the crotch down around my knees. Long-sleeved hoodie with the hood lying loose around the back of my neck. High-topped black Keds sneakers with the white laces flapping loose….

Oh sure. Like I was going on stage for a modern minstrel show.

I finished the application form, and Joad immediately moved over to me. Took the form and started reading it slowly.

After nearly a minute, he stopped reading and looked at me.

"You Wesley Graham?" he said.

"Yes, Officer Joad," I answered, remembering that prison guards always liked to be addressed as "Officer." With a very large capital "O."

"Everything you wrote on this form is the truth?"

"Yes, sir."

"You have photo ID?"

"Yes, sir. My newspaper's press card."

"That thing around your neck?"

"Yes sir."

"All right, Wesley. Hand it to me, please."

I slipped my press card over my head and handed it to him. He compared its photo with my face several times. Then placed it on the counter.

"Any other photo ID?" he said.

"My California driver's license."

"Hand it to me, please."

I took my license from the outside breast pocket of my blazer and handed it to him. He glanced at it briefly, then placed it on the counter next to my press pass.

"Now tell me, Wesley." he said. "Do you have any controlled substances on your person?"

"No, sir."

"Any illegal drugs?"

"No, sir."

"Any prescription medicines?"

"No, sir."

"Any over-the-counter medicines?"

"No, sir."

"Any coins or bills?"

"I have nineteen dollars in quarters. For the vending machines. Two clear plastic bags in the side pockets of my jacket. Would you like to see them?"

"Yes."

I took out the bags and laid them on the counter.

It was easy to imagine that Joad was cross-examining me this way because I was black. But I knew the reality was much simpler. The main concern of prison guards is security. So the memorized questions he was asking were simply part of the prescribed drill some higher-up had written out in the interests of security.

Joad reached under the counter and pulled out a plastic tray about the size of a school notebook.

"Please empty the contents of your pockets into this tray," he said.

I did so, and he stirred the items with his thick fingers. Then handed me back my two lists and page of Visitor Instructions when he saw what they were.

"You can keep these papers on you," he said.

"Thank you, Officer Joad."

"But leave everything else in the tray until you get inside the Visiting Room. It'll be easier going through the metal detector that way."

"Yes, sir."

He reached to his left and dragged a large ledger-like book into the counter space between us. It was open to a fresh page. Since all reporters learn how to read upside down, I could make out the contents of the page.

It was divided into two columns. The outside column contained three-by-five-inch peel-off labels. Each one had the words AUTHORIZED VISITOR in large black letters across the middle. Printed in red across the top of each label was a four-digit serial number. I knew from previous visits to prison inmates that one of these labels would be my visitor's pass.

Next to each label on the page's inside column was a box headed by the label's red serial number with blank spaces below for information to be filled in.

"Now then, Wesley." Joad said, looking straight at me. "Have you read all the information on the Visitor Instructions?"

"Yes, sir."

"Do you agree to abide by all its terms and limitations?"

"Yes, I do."

"Do you understand that any violation of these terms and limitations will constitute grounds for immediate termination of your visit? And possible bans on future visits?"

"Yes, Officer."

"Good. Now I'm going to issue your visitor's pass."

I watched him print my name in black under the red serial number on a fresh label at the top of the page, then print Elijah Stern's name across the bottom of the label. He also printed my name and Stern's name in the spaces provided in the box next to the label, and added a brief description of my two photo-ID items just below. Then he spun the ledger around so its page was right side up to me.

"Please read the information in the box and sign it at the bottom," he said, handing me his ballpoint pen.

I scanned the box quickly. Above the space for my signature were several lines of tiny print stating that I agreed to abide by the terms of the Visitor Instructions. I quickly scrawled my signature and handed back the pen.

"We'll keep your photo ID items here at the counter," Joad said, spinning the ledger back around to him. "You can pick them up when you leave."

"Yes, sir. I understand."

He took a worn plastic bag from under the counter and placed my press card and driver's license inside. The bag was labeled C-19, and he wrote this ID on my visitor's pass next to my name. Then peeled off my pass from the ledger page and handed it to me.

"Stick this on your jacket," he said. "Keep it visible at all times during your visit. Turn it in here at the counter when you leave and you'll get back your photo-ID items."

"Yes, Officer Joad. Thank you."

"Okay, Wesley. That's everything. Take a seat. We'll call you."

"Yes, sir."

* * *

I had run across Elijah Stern's name on the Internet while researching material for a possible magazine article about stock market fraud. According to the Internet entry. he'd been a managing director in a large investment banking firm in New York. Had pleaded guilty to Insider Trading and received a two-year prison sentence. Was currently assigned to the minimum security unit of a federal prison complex about an hour's drive down the coast from the small city where my newspaper was located. Close enough for me to interview him if he was willing to see me. Worth checking out.

After finding his prison mailing address on the U.S. Bureau of Prisons' Web site, I wrote him a two-page letter explaining who I was, why I wanted to see him, and the nature of the magazine article I was doing. Since there was no way he could check this, I also mentioned that the editor of the *Atlantic* had expressed considerable interest in my article.

Three weeks later, I got a letter from Stern stating that he'd be pleased to have me visit him at the prison. Suggested a Sunday would be the best day. Hoped he would be able to provide me with helpful information.

Interestingly, he suggested I make the arrangements for my visit through his wife Susan since they were in daily telephone contact. He gave me her home phone number, and I noticed that it had a Brooklyn area code. I phoned her that night and found that Stern had already told her about me. She promised to arrange all the details, gave me her email address and cell phone number, and asked for mine so we could keep in touch. Very cooperative. The ball seemed to be rolling.

Doing these freelance articles for issue-oriented magazines back East seemed like the best shot for rehabilitating my journalism career. Otherwise I'd be stuck forever scratching out a living as a beat reporter on small-town newspapers that couldn't care less about the scandal I'd caused in Washington. Just so long as I turned in my copy on time, kept my expense account under control, and didn't upset any of their advertisers.

* * *

I spent the next half hour squirming in my too-small plastic chair waiting for the guards to call my name and reviewing my strategy for interviewing Stern. Given what little I knew about him, the best approach was probably the simplest. Get him talking about whatever he wanted to. Then try to guide him around to the subject of Insider Trading. Play it pretty much by ear and see what developed.

Finally Officer Joad began calling our names. Five at a time. Instructing us to line up at the far end of the counter opposite a closed green door that had a small square glass window. Every few minutes, the door was opened from the inside. The waiting visitors walked through and the door closed behind them.

My name was called second in the fourth group of five. I lined up with the others in front of the green door, each of us clutching the plastic tray containing our personal effects. The door opened and we filed inside.

I found myself in a medium-sized room dominated by an airport-style metal detector manned by two guards. We went through the metal detector one by one and were directed to wait in front of another green door just beyond. After all of us had been checked out by the metal detector, one of the guards opened the door and we walked through. Into what was obviously the main visitors' room. About three times the size of the waiting room outside and with clusters of the same plastic chairs.

The inmates stood facing us in a long rank across the width of the room. They were all dressed the same. Cheap khaki pants. Blue work shirts. Heavy brown work shoes. I noticed they were all white-skinned. Probably meant they were serving terms for white-collar crimes.

I scanned the rank of inmates looking for someone who might be Elijah Stern. Then I noticed a medium-sized, middle-aged man with a close-cropped iron-grey beard wearing steel-rimmed glasses and a black yarmulke. I walked over and saw that he had the kind of face I'd always associated with the landlords who came once a month to collect apartment rents in the Brooklyn neighborhood where I grew up.

"Excuse me, are you Elijah Stern?" I said after stopping in front of him.

"You bet," he answered with a welcoming smile. "And you're Wesley Graham?"

"Yes. Thank you for agreeing to see me."

We shook hands formally. As if meeting for the first time at a business lunch in one of Manhattan's better restaurants. Then his smile widened into a broad grin.

"Wow," he said. "You weren't kidding my wife about your height. How tall are you, anyway?"

"Six-five."

"You played basketball?"

"I grew up in Bedford Stuyvesant. If you know my community, you know the answer."

"I know Bed-Stuy. I'm from Borough Park."

"The Orthodox Jewish community?"

"Right. Were you any good at basketball?"

"Well, Lincoln High School tried to recruit me in my last year of junior high."

"Sure. The big Brooklyn basketball high school on Ocean Parkway. Is that where you went?"

"Actually, arrangements were already in place to send me to Phillips Exeter Academy. That's a New England prep school."

"I've heard of Exeter. That's what led you to Harvard?"

"How do you know I went to Harvard?"

"It was in the *Time* magazine story about you."

"Along with a lot of less flattering things."

"You certainly seem to have upset a lot of people. Was the *Time* story accurate?"

"More or less. Of course, there can be a great difference between accuracy and truth."

"Tell me about it. What are you doing in California?"

"I work here."

"Yeah, I know. I've been reading your newspaper stories."

"About the latest Chamber of Commerce lunch and so on? Real exciting."

"At least they give you a byline."

"We all have bylines. Along with our newspaper email addresses. The publisher thinks it helps personalize the news for our readers."

"I see."

"To answer the question you're too polite to ask, the newspaper here was the only one that would give me a job after they got finished chewing me to pieces back East."

"Yeah, I can imagine."

"But I'm still a good reporter. You can trust me not to misrepresent anything you tell me. That's why this magazine article I'm doing...."

"Let's get to that in a minute. Would you like some coffee?"

"Sure. I brought plenty of quarters for the vending machines."

"Good. They're over against that far wall. Come on. I'll show you."

* * *

Stern was clearly a highly skilled talker, even for somebody from Brooklyn. He seemed able to direct the conversation any way he wanted and induce you to talk about things you didn't intend to get into. In fact, he was probably better at it than I was, despite my years as a Washington reporter for a major national newspaper. So I had to be on my guard. And work extra hard to persuade him to talk about the things I wanted to cover.

We got two black coffees from the vending machine. Then he led me to a corner where there were two plastic chairs on either side of a small plastic table. We sat down opposite each other and took cautious sips from our coffees. He swallowed, made a face, and placed his coffee on the table.

"Tastes like shit, doesn't it," he said.

"Not exactly Starbucks. Is all the food this bad?"

"Pretty much. Since I'm Orthodox, I can insist on kosher meals. Not that it does any good. You know Jewish food?"

"Who doesn't in Brooklyn?"

"Well I'm convinced the prison dietitians here are all closet anti-Semites when it comes to Jewish food."

"Maybe not so closet."

"You could be right, Wesley. May I call you Wesley?"

"Most people call me Wes."

"Then Wes it is. You can call me Elijah."

"Like the prophet?"

"It has its advantages. He was a major noodge, after all."

"Do you also discredit pagan gods on the side?"

"Interesting you should ask. You seem pretty well-read."

"I sang in the choir at prep school. We did Mendelssohn's oratorio one spring. To show off our new ecumenical spirit."

"Anyway, at least I can escape the coffee in this place."

"By being a noodge?"

"My wife sends me regular packages of wonderful green teas from the Chinese stores on Eighth Avenue."

"I didn't know Jews were into green tea."

"My wife's Chinese."

"But when I talked to her on the phone...."

"I know. She sounds like a Jewish woman from Queens. That's be-cause she grew up in Flushing. So most of her friends in school were Jewish and Irish. Which is why she doesn't have a Chinese accent. But she's as fluent in Cantonese as I am in Yiddish. She's also a secular Bud-dhist. Just like I'm a secular Jew."

"I thought you were Orthodox."

"Oh I still am, Wes. I study the Talmud every day. Observe all the holidays. Wear a yarmulke."

"But how could you marry a woman who isn't Jewish? I thought Or-thodox Jews...."

"We found a way my family could live with. Of course, the Orthodox sect I grew up in still excommunicated me for marrying a shiksa."

"Excommunicated you?"

"Declared me to be a nonperson. As far as they were concerned, I no longer existed."

"That must have been terrible for you."

"I actually found it liberating. Freed me from being bound by all that antique bullshit about what you can eat and so on. So I could concen-trate on the true moral core of Judaism, which is what really matters."

"Then you don't hate the Jewish religion?"

"No, I love Judaism. It's God I can't stand."

"You don't like God?"

"I think he's a Nazi."

"You're kidding."

"No, I'm not. Read the Books of Moses, Wes. What you goys call the Old Testament. Read the story of Abraham and Isaac. Then visit Dachau or one of the other death camps in Europe. That'll put it all in perspec-tive for you."

Was I talking to a total nut? I'd never before heard anyone say such things. Not even the most rabid atheist. Had prison done something to his mind?

15

He watched my face as I struggled to make sense of what I'd just heard. Then he took a breath and smiled.

"Sorry if I shocked you," he said. "Let me try to explain."

"By all means."

"Suppose, just for the sake of illustration, it's 1944 and you and I have arrived at a German death camp somewhere in Poland."

"Just for the sake of illustration?"

"You'll see what I mean."

"Okay."

"Now one of the things we notice is the inmates have arranged themselves into three groups. One group consists of scientists, engineers, university professors, writers, and so on."

"Camp intellectuals."

"Pretty much. And they keep telling each other that the camp commandant doesn't actually exist. After all, has anybody ever seen him? No. So what proof is there that he exists?"

"Who do they think runs the camp?"

"It pretty much runs itself."

"How?"

"Well, there's a whole library full of operating manuals in the administration building. In typical German fashion, they're very well organized and cover every eventuality. Whenever the guards have questions about something, all they have to do is look at the right operating manual. The answers are there in black and white. So there's no need for a commandant. Or so the members of this group keep telling each other. You with me so far?"

"I think so. They're like atheists on the issue of the commandant's existence."

"Right. Now the second group of inmates is by far the largest one. And they absolutely believe in the existence of the commandant. But they keep telling each other that he's really a very decent guy at heart. Does everything he can to make life easier for the inmates. He's even come up with a plan to resettle them in a New Israel far beyond the reach of murderous goys. That's why he has the guards select a certain number of inmates each day to be taken to the showers on the other side of the camp. So they'll be nice and clean for their train trip to the New Israel."

"What about the third group?"

"They're the smallest. They also believe the commandant exists. But they insist there's no point in kidding themselves about what he's really like. Because they're convinced he's a dedicated Nazi. Eager to do anything he can to torment the inmates as much as possible. And so on."

"You really believe all this?"

"Does that surprise you?"

"It's ... not exactly what I expected."

"I can imagine. You come here to talk about Insider Trading and I hit you over the head with some off-beat religious concepts."

"Well...."

"So let's talk about Insider Trading. A Great American Dream. Like having your own private copy of tomorrow's *Wall Street Journal* delivered this afternoon in time to place your trades before today's markets close. Is it any wonder most people find the whole concept irresistible?"

"You tell me, Elijah. You're the maven."

"Okay. You ready?"

"Ready."

* * *

He leaned back and fixed his eyes at the empty space over my head. As if trying to organize his topic points. But I suspected he already had them in good order in his mind.

Then he abruptly leaned forward and looked straight at me.

"Let's assume, purely for the purposes of illustration, you go to work for a large investment banking firm in New York," he said.

"Doing what?"

"Doesn't matter. Something to do with generating new business for the firm, maybe."

"Okay."

"Now one of the things you're going to find out fairly quickly is that you've become part of a very special world."

"Special in what way?"

"Three ways. First, everybody talks to everybody else about what they're working on."

"Water cooler gossip?"

"More like trying to prove who has the biggest cock. But some of that talk can have great potential dollar value."

"How so?"

"I'll get to that in a minute. The second way this world is special is that it's extremely competitive. Each guy's trying to get ahead of the next guy."

"Sounds like journalism."

"Probably. Now the third way this world is special is that your career matters more than the welfare of the firm you're working for."

"Okay."

"A year from now, you may be working for an entirely different investment bank. Five years from now, you can find you've worked for three or four different firms."

"People tend to move around, in other words."

"Right. Change is a constant. But another constant is staying in touch with the people you've worked with in the past. Today, you're working closely with several guys in the same firm. In a year or so, you've all moved on to different firms. But you stay in touch with each other."

"Like a brotherhood?"

"Exactly. A brotherhood that keeps growing in size. One of the reasons your Rolodex gets fatter every year. So you're part of what amounts to an informal network. Whose members make it a point to exchange favors. You see what I'm getting at?"

"I think so."

"Good. Now let's come back to the talk you keep hearing at whatever firm you happen to be working for. The other guys can't help bragging about the deals they're working on at the moment. And it doesn't take you long to realize that some of these details have the potential for moving up the stock price of the company in question. Once they become public, that is."

"Inside information."

"Right. Inside information you can make a profit trading on. In theory, that is. If you buy the company's stock before the information becomes public. And if the information causes the stock price to move up. You with me so far?"

"I think so."

"Sure, it's simple enough in theory. But in practice, it's more complicated. For example, suppose you hear about a proposed merger deal from a guy in your firm who's working on it. You realize it's bound to affect the stock prices of the companies involved. But you can't trade on it yourself."

"Why not?"

"Because it's inside information. According to the Federal Securities and Exchange Commission. And trading on inside information is technically illegal. So if you trade on information about a deal your firm is working on, it could raise suspicions. And you want to avoid raising suspicions at all costs."

"Which leaves me where?"

"It leaves you making a personal phone call to somebody in your network. A securities lawyer maybe. Or an investment banker who works for another firm that has nothing to do with the merger deal. He can trade on that information without raising any suspicions. The profits he makes will simply look like a matter of luck. Nobody can prove any wrongdoing."

"And the person I pass this information on to will do the same for me?"

"Absolutely. Next week or next month, you'll get a phone call from him. About a deal he's working on that your firm has nothing to do with. That's how the network operates. Colleagues doing favors for each other. Personal favors. Highly lucrative favors."

"Sounds like a perfect system."

"Not quite. There's another important wrinkle I haven't explained yet."

"But you're going to."

"Of course. I want you to get the whole picture."

"Okay."

He paused for a moment, as if gathering his thoughts. More showmanship, I figured.

"Suppose you make your trades through personal accounts here in the U.S.," he said. "That means your profits are subject to federal and state taxes. So you have to report the details of each trade on IRS Schedule D. The date you made the buy and how much you paid. The date you sold and how much you received. The profit you made. Right?"

"Sure."

"So there's a record of your trades on file with the IRS and the state tax bureau. And it's going to show you made a profit on every trade. Every single trade. That can be like a red flag to the SEC."

"But I thought income tax records were confidential."

"Yeah sure. Like I'm the tooth fairy."

"That bad?"

"Believe me, nothing's confidential as far as the feds are concerned. And your tax records are going to show a lot of consistently profitable trades. How do you explain that all these trades are kosher as far as SEC regs are concerned? You can't. Not convincingly."

"Suppose I don't report the trades?"

"Too dangerous. Comes under the heading of failing to report taxable income. Which is a felony. Much worse than Insider Trading."

"So what do I do?"

"Very simple. You make all your trades outside the U.S. in ways that don't have to be reported to the IRS. You set up confidential offshore accounts and run all your trades through them."

"You mean like Swiss banks?"

"That's one possibility. But there are better ones in places besides Switzerland. More secret. More secure."

"Okay. But how do I get the profits back into the U.S.?"

"You don't. Not ever. Not if you're smart."

"But...."

"Your goal is to build up asset value offshore. Lots of asset value. Enough asset value so you can eventually invest it outside the U.S. to produce an entirely kosher seven-figure income for yourself. Which can be paid to you in the U.S. if you want to continue living here. And be reported to the IRS as taxable dividends or consulting fees or whatever without raising any suspicions. Get the picture?"

"I think so. Sort of like your own private 401k plan."

"Not a bad analogy."

"But not entirely legal."

"Well, not the Insider Trading part. Not according to the SEC."

"What about the moral issues? Making trading profits by using information not available to the general public?"

"Ah. Now we're getting to something really interesting."

"I assume you have some opinions about the moral aspect."

"You bet. But do me a favor first."

"Sure. What."

"I'm thirsty from so much talking. Can you get me a cold soda from the vending machines?"

"Of course. I'm a little thirsty, too."

"I'd get it myself. But you're the one with the quarters. And they don't like us to handle money."

"No problem. What's your pleasure?"

"Regular Coke. Nice and cold."

"Sure."

"I'll hold the table for us."

"Be right back."

* * *

I got us two cold cans of Coke from one of the vending machines. Elijah took two long swallows from his, then gave a satisfied sigh.

"Hard to beat, isn't it," he said.

"You're right. The other sodas taste like cheap mouthwash by comparison."

"You know the story of Coke?"

"How it once contained real cocaine?"

"Back in the late nineteenth century. When it was marketed as an over-the-counter patent medicine. Good for whatever ailed you."

"Because its cocaine gave you a nice high."

"And entirely legal. Until Congress passed a law making the sale of cocaine a crime. Does that suggest something to you?"

"You mean, the arbitrary nature of so many laws?"

"Yes."

"Are you telling me we can't judge an action merely by whether or not it's legal?"

"Absolutely."

"So the true rights or wrongs of Insider Trading have nothing to do with laws?"

"Not unless you're a defense lawyer. Or a prosecutor."

"Then where does that leave us?"

"With a simple question. Does Insider Trading hurt anybody? When you think about it, the question of whether an action hurts somebody else is the whole basis of morality. That's what the Talmud's really all about."

"So you're arguing that the rights and wrongs of Insider Trading depend on whether it hurts other people."

"Right. And a lot of entirely respectable mavens insist that it doesn't.

22

Milton Friedman, for example. He was as decent a human being as you could find, regardless of whether or not you agree with his economic ideas."

"About the blessings of capitalism?"

"Unrestrained free-market capitalism. The solution to all our problems, according to free-market economists like Friedman. Let the free market decide everything and we'll all be home free."

"So I've heard."

"You've studied economics?"

"I took one of those survey courses at Harvard. It had a lot about free-market capitalism."

"Did it get into something called Entrepreneurial Discovery?"

"That doesn't ring a bell."

"I'm not surprised. Most introductory courses miss it. But it happens to be a key concept in free-market theory."

"Can you fill me in?"

"Sure. Remember those supply and demand diagrams from your economics course? You know, the two curved lines crossing each other? And where they cross marks the equilibrium price?"

"I think so."

"Professors love to draw them on blackboards. They act like they're giving you the Secret of Life. But they're missing a very large point."

"What do you mean?"

"They always draw the curves in heavy solid lines. Creating an impression of permanence. But they should really draw them in dotted lines."

"Why?"

"Dotted lines would imply that supply and demand are always changing. Which is usually the case."

"So?"

"If they're always changing, the equilibrium price is a moving target. One a market keeps chasing but rarely catches. And holds onto only briefly when it does. See the significance?"

"Not yet. Sorry if I seem slow-witted."

"Don't apologize. Most professional economists don't see it. Or act as if they don't."

"But you're going to explain it to me."

"I'm working up to it. Now listen carefully."

"I promise."

"If equilibrium's a moving target because supply and demand are always changing, doesn't it follow that the first buyers and sellers who see these changes have an edge?"

"Makes sense."

"We call these sharp buyers and sellers entrepreneurs. They're able to cash in before the others on important market developments. So they make the most profits. For the record, we call the whole thing the Process of Entrepreneurial Discovery."

"So you're saying Insider Trading is nothing more than an example of Entrepreneurial Discovery."

"I admit it sounds like a pretentious term for acting on information picked up around the water cooler. But the parallels are there. The price of a common stock is a moving target. Because the supply and demand for its shares in the stock market are always changing. So acting on information that can influence those changes helps make the market more efficient more quickly."

"Not to mention generating profits for those who get there first."

"Absolutely. You trade on information not yet public and you can make nice profits. But sooner or later, the information becomes common knowledge and the best trading opportunities disappear."

"Which I guess is inevitable."

"Always. That's why economists like Milton Friedman believe Insider Trading is a good thing. Part of the Entrepreneurial Discovery process that makes securities markets more efficient."

"So Insider Trading's morally okay because it improves the efficiency of the stock market and doesn't hurt anybody."

"Maybe."

"Maybe?"

"There are different kinds of Insider Trading. Some kinds hurt people. Other kinds don't. Shall I give you an example?"

"By all means."

"Suppose, purely for discussion's sake, you're the CEO of a company that trades on the New York Stock Exchange. You've just had a bad quarter. Sales are way down. Earnings have tanked. And now it's time for you as CEO to publicly report the bad news. Which you know will cause the company's stock to go down. Costing your existing stockholders money. At least on paper. Follow me so far?"

"I think so."

"Now as CEO, you're in a position to quietly place bets against your company's stock before you make the bad news public. By selling the stock short. Buying put options. And so on. In other words, trade as an insider on information not yet public. You'll make a nice profit when the bad news is announced. But how much profit depends on how the market responds to the bad news. And as CEO, you're in a position to influence that response."

"By what kind of spin you put on your announcement of the bad news?"

"Very good. You can imply in your announcement that the bad quarter was no big deal for the long term. Or, you can imply the bad quarter may indicate a fundamental change in the company's long-term outlook. The second implication will obviously mean a bigger profit for you because the company's stock will fall a lot farther. But it'll also mean more pain for your existing stockholders."

"So if I'm in a position to influence the outcome and I can't resist the temptation...?"

"Exactly. Greed triumphs in the worst possible way. People get hurt. So your Insider Trading is morally wrong."

"But suppose I'm not able to influence the outcome?"

"You mean, suppose you're simply a member of the auditing team provided by the company's independent accounting firm?"

"I guess so. I know how bad last quarter was before the news becomes public. I know this will mean the company's stock will fall when it's announced. So I trade on this inside information. What then?"

"You can't influence how much the stock will fall, right?"

"Right."

"Which means you have no control over how much pain existing stockholders will suffer. No matter what you do."

"Then my Insider Trading is morally okay?"

"Why not?"

"But what about the idea of a level playing field? Don't Inside Traders have an advantage over other investors?"

"Of course. That's the whole idea behind free markets. People exploiting temporary advantages. That's what promotes market efficiency. Or so the advocates of free markets claim."

"Do I sense that you're not entirely convinced?"

"Don't be put off by my attempts to be objective. Life's more complicated than it may seem. Why do you think I study the Talmud?"

"In any case, you pleaded guilty to Insider Trading."

"Yes."

"Even though you apparently believe that your kind of Insider Trading was morally okay. Because it didn't hurt anybody."

"Yes again."

"Then why did you plead guilty? If you don't mind my asking."

"It's a perfectly legitimate question. But you seem to be getting fidgety."

"Sorry. Not out of boredom, believe me. Your ideas are fascinating. But these chairs must have been made in Japan."

"Not exactly suited to tushes your size. We could take a little walk if you'd like."

"Around the room?"

"No. Outside."

"It's allowed?"

"Oh, yes. There's lots of room. This is a minimum security facility. So there aren't any fences."

"Okay, fine. Let's walk a bit."

* * *

We walked through an open door next to the vending machines and found ourselves in a large grassy area ringed by trees that shaded wooden benches. I assumed that Elijah was going to talk to me about something he regarded as confidential and didn't want to be overheard.

But instead, he went off on another of his speculations.

"Give me three reasons why somebody would plead guilty to Insider Trading," he said.

"Three reasons."

"Go ahead. Take a shot."

"All right, let's see. Reason Number One. He knows he's done something wrong. Feels guilty about it. So he confesses and seeks atonement."

"Guilt, confession, atonement. You're not Roman Catholic, are you?"

"No. Oh, well, my mother brought the usual Anglican religious concepts with her from Trinidad."

"Anglican's sort of like Catholic without the Pope, isn't it?"

"Pretty much."

"Did you buy into its religious concepts?"

"Mom tried to teach me. But they didn't take. Didn't seem relevant to what I saw around me on the streets of Bed-Stuy."

"I can imagine."

"I had to come up with my own sense of what was right and what was wrong."

"Very pragmatic. I suppose that makes you an existentialist."

"Nobody uses that term anymore."

"Maybe because they're too busy living it."

"Could be."

"Okay. Guilt, confession, atonement. Possible. But only in a small minority of cases. Most people who do Insider Trading don't think of it as wrong. Just illegal."

"You know better than me."

"Does that suggest a second reason why somebody would plead guilty to Insider Trading?"

"Oh, I think I see what you're getting at. If your Somebody knows Insider Trading is illegal but not necessarily morally wrong, then any charges brought by the SEC are simply nuisances. To be disposed of as expeditiously as possible."

"Which means?"

"Your Somebody pleads guilty and accepts minimal penalties just to put the whole business behind him and move on."

"You think a prison term qualifies as a minimal penalty?"

"Maybe the prison term came as a surprise."

"There aren't any surprises in guilty pleas. Your lawyer negotiates every detail. Including the penalties."

"Okay. Then it's simply a matter of who your Somebody is."

"Maybe. Now what about the third reason?"

"You've got me on that one."

"Come on, think. You've been to the movies and watched crime shows on television. What's the most common reason why the hero pleads guilty to a crime he didn't commit?"

"He's trying to protect somebody?"

"Right. Somebody. Or something."

"Are you telling me you pleaded guilty to Insider Trading to protect somebody? Or something?"

"Let me tell you a little story."

"I figured you wouldn't give me a straight answer."

"Now don't take it that way. Remember, I'm a student of the Talmud. One of our shticks is using hypothetical stories to illustrate our arguments. Makes things clearer."

"Okay. Tell me the story."

* * *

We had reached the far end of the grassy area and sat down on a wooden bench under one of the trees. Other inmates were strolling around the area with their visitors or sitting on benches. But there was no one near us.

"Don't any of the inmates just … walk away?" I asked Elijah curiously. "There aren't any fences. And no guards in sight."

"They don't see the point."

"The point in walking away?"

"This is a minimum security facility. The inmates are here for white-collar violations. Or nonviolent drug crimes. Or they're nearing the end of their sentences for more serious crimes. Their next step is transfer to a halfway house near their families for the last few months of their sentence. What's the point of screwing things up by deliberately violating prison regulations?"

"Okay, if you say so."

"Anyway, let's get on to that story."

"I'm all ears."

"Now the first thing to keep in mind is that investment banking firms provide their clients with various important services. One is underwriting issues of debt and equity to provide clients with more capital. You with me so far?"

"I think so. And the firms make money how?"

"By charging investors more for the debt or equity issues than they pay their underwriting clients. Slightly more in percentage terms. But it can still mean big dollars. It's like the bid-and-ask spread for a broker who makes a market in a particular stock."

"The broker pays less to somebody who wants to sell the stock than he charges somebody who wants to buy the stock. Is that it?"

"That's it exactly."

"And what's another service?"

"Providing financial advice to clients. For a fee."

"Acting as a financial consultant, in other words."

"Right. Now consider the hypothetical case of a certain Managing Director in an investment banking firm. He runs a unit that provides financial advisory services to state and local governments. For annual fees. Very lucrative."

"Is there anything in investment banking that isn't lucrative?"

"I've never run across it. But such fee-based services can be especially profitable because they need so little capital. Also, there can be some interesting angles to exploit."

"I can imagine."

"Anyway, one of this hypothetical unit's clients is the government of a major industrial state. It's just elected one of its hotshot congressmen as governor. And everybody knows the new governor wants to make a run for the White House. Now what does that suggest to you?"

"The governor wants to use his office to help position himself as a high-profile presidential candidate?"

"Right. Build up his image as a pragmatic, take-charge guy. Somebody who can get things done. Solve problems. Isn't afraid to try new approaches. Just what the country needs in the White House."

"So if our hypothetical Managing Director can come up with a new financial approach…?"

"Now you've got it. That's the angle he can exploit. All he needs is the right opportunity. And as it turns out, such an opportunity exists."

"Okay."

"The state government's been trying for several years to get a major capital project off the ground. Something everybody seems to want. But very expensive. Too expensive to be financed in conventional ways. So the project's stalled."

"And the Managing Director comes up with a new way to finance the project?"

"A radical new way. Something that can change the whole approach for financing such projects. I won't confuse you with the details at this point. The important thing is our hypothetical Managing Director has developed a radical new way to finance the project so it can finally move ahead."

"Which I assume pleases the governor."

"Absolutely. It's just the kind of thing he's looking for to build up his political image. So he embraces the project completely. Makes it his own. Puts the full weight of the state's government behind it. Gives speeches about how he's solved the problem of financing this major capital project. Gets favorable coverage in the national media even."

"So everything's fine."

"On the surface."

"But something happens?"

"Yes. An obscure lawyer working for a Washington lobbying firm pleads guilty to tax evasion. Starts naming names. One of whom is our Managing Director."

"I don't see the connection."

"Several years earlier, this lawyer was doing securities work for a law firm in New York. Hoping to make partner."

"So?"

"He was a member of the same informal network of investment bankers and securities lawyers the Managing Director was part of. They were passing inside information back and forth. Just like I explained before."

"Insider Trading?"

"Yes. Anyway, the lawyer didn't make partner. So he moved on. Went off on his own. But that can be expensive, especially when you have a family to support. Which caused him to start repatriating some of the Insider Trading profits in his offshore accounts."

"You said before that could be very dangerous."

"Right. The IRS got word of this and came after him for tax evasion. The lawyer panicked. Pleaded guilty. Promised to cooperate. Named names. Which the IRS shared with the SEC. And one of these names was our hypothetical Managing Director."

"So the SEC came after the Managing Director?"

"They apparently felt they at least had to go through the motions. So they charged the Managing Director with five counts of Insider Trading. Based on information they got from the IRS. Am I going too fast for you?"

"No, I think I've got it. And the Managing Director pleaded guilty."

"That's what it came down to. The Managing Director's lawyers thought the SEC's case was weak. They thought they could win if they went to trial."

"Then why…?"

"A trial and its discovery process can open many cans of worms. About that big capital project, for example. The Managing Director's connection with it. And with the governor who's planning a run for the White House."

"But I still don't see.… "

"The Managing Director naturally assumes the governor will back away from the project if it gets mentioned in a trial. Remember, the governor's only interest in the project is how it can enhance his political image. Which it obviously can't do if it gets tainted by being mentioned in a criminal trial."

"So the Managing Director pleads guilty to protect the governor?"

"No. To protect the project."

"Sorry, that seems pretty far out. I guess you're going to have to confuse me with more details."

"All right. I'll try to make it as simple as I can. Don't be afraid to interrupt me if you have trouble understanding anything."

"Don't worry."

"Would you like to walk some more?"

"Okay."

* * *

We got up from the bench and began strolling around the grassy area again. And this time, Elijah got right to the point.

"The hypothetical capital project we've been talking about happens to involve building a new highway between the state's two most important metropolitan regions. Do you know how major highway projects are financed in the U.S.?"

"No. You'll have to educate me."

"You may find some of this hard to believe."

"Try me. I'm pretty gullible."

"Okay. A standard way to finance large highway projects is for the state government to apply for a federal capital grant. That's money the state never has to pay back."

"So it's like free money."

"In effect. And the amount of the grant is supposed to be enough to cover 80 percent of the highway's construction cost. In theory."

"Where does the rest come from?"

"The state government has to come up with it. Usually by issuing general obligation bonds that are paid off over a number of years."

"By the state?"

"Yes. Each year's payment of bond interest and principal comes from the state government's operating budget. Which means it comes from taxes paid by state residents and business firms."

"Okay."

"Now the federal grant comes from something called the Highway Trust Fund. It's able to make grants because it gets revenue from federal fuel taxes. This is the arrangement Congress set up back in the mid-1950s when it created the Interstate Highway Program. Worked okay for a while. But now there are problems."

"I guess I shouldn't be surprised."

"Not if you're as smart as I think you are. Here's a basic problem.

Fuel tax revenue flowing into the trust fund isn't nearly enough to cover all the grants that should be made to upgrade the nation's transportation systems."

"Why?"

"Several reasons. One is that the rate per gallon of the federal fuel tax hasn't kept pace with inflation. In fact, it hasn't been increased since 1993. Too many senators and congressmen have convinced themselves that voting to raise taxes is a worse turnoff for voters than getting caught in a motel room with an underage girl. So after you adjust for inflation, the growth rate of revenues flowing into the trust fund is slowing down."

"Okay."

"And this is made worse because the nation's cars and trucks are becoming more fuel efficient on average. Plus, fuel additives like ethanol aren't taxed at all, which cuts into the tax take from each gallon sold. So even though the annual miles driven by cars and trucks are increasing, fuel tax revenues are increasing much more slowly. You know what that means?"

"The trust fund's being starved for revenues, especially with soaring fuel prices causing a decline in vehicle miles travelled."

"Exactly. While at the same time, the need for more grant funds is exploding. Because of the growing backlog of restoration and expansion projects. Because the unit costs of concrete and steel are skyrocketing as nations like China and India increase their spending on infrastructure. And because various environmental regulations make project planning and design take much longer than they used to. More time always means higher costs."

"Sounds like a perfect storm."

"That's what some people call it. But the basic issue is the federal fuel tax has ceased to be a reliable funding source for transportation. Its day has passed. We need to replace it with something better."

"Is that why there's been so much talk about toll roads?"

"I see you've been doing some reading."

"Just in passing. Toll roads seem to have become a popular topic in the media. Especially on slow news days when editors are looking for something to fill their space."

"Yes. Popular. Also controversial."

"I guess that's inevitable. Is that the new wrinkle our Managing Director came up with for the highway project?"

"Part of it. But let's talk about some basic principles first."

* * *

We reached the far end of the grassy area and Elijah guided us around a neatly trimmed bush so that we started back the other way. He looked at the ground and was silent for a moment. Then glanced towards me.

"You go to the movies?" he said.

"Sure."

"But you're not the movie critic for your newspaper?"

"No."

"So you have to pay to get in."

"Just like everybody."

"Naturally. You have to pay an admission price when you want to see a movie. How is that different from paying a toll when you want to drive on a highway? Isn't paying a toll basically the same as buying a movie ticket?"

"You're logic is overwhelming."

"Glad you see the connection. And isn't there a similar connection with most other things we need or want? Books, food, housing, clothes. You name it. We have to pay for them up front."

"Unless we use credit cards."

"Same difference. We're still incurring an obligation to pay for what we want."

"I was just being flip."

"You're entitled. The point is, we have to pay directly for what we want. Why shouldn't the same principle apply to traveling on highways?"

35

"Makes sense when you put it that way."

"Sure it does. And the tolls we pay generate a revenue stream to cover the cost of building and operating the highway. No need for federal grants. Or fuel taxes. Or construction bonds that have to be paid off by a state's taxpayers. The people who drive on the highway pay for the highway. What could be simpler?"

"And this is the new concept our Managing Director comes up with?"

"That's where it begins. Our hypothetical Managing Director repackages the stalled highway project as a toll road. Able to cover all its costs with toll revenues. No longer dependent on grants from the Highway Trust Fund. Because it's entirely self-supporting. Just like a movie theater."

"Sounds great."

"But he doesn't stop there. To give the project added sex appeal, he has the toll highway include separate lanes for car and trucks. So they don't get in each others' way. Plus a pair of railroad tracks that can be rented to private freight railroad companies wanting to run trains between the two metro regions. That's sexy because it allows more freight to be moved by rail rather than in trucks on the highway. Which the environmental crowd's going to love."

"Seems like he's covering all the bases."

"He's getting there. He even leaves space in the corridor to add a pair of tracks for passenger trains between the metro regions. Because there's been talk about giving the people traveling between the two central business districts the option of going by train instead of driving. Something else that has great sex appeal to environmental types."

"Not to mention the governor."

"Oh, definitely. Because now the project isn't just a highway, which can be a downer to many people. Now it can be called a 'Multi-Modal Transportation Corridor.' Something modern and innovative. Just the thing to build up the governor's image on the national political scene."

"I can see why."

"But our hypothetical Managing Director doesn't stop there."

"There's more?"

"You bet. It involves control of the project."

"I thought it was a state project."

"There has to be more to it than that. Another new angle."

"What kind of new angle?"

"Some other states have toyed with the concept of building new toll highways. And as soon as they see the revenue implications, they jump at the idea of selling a long-term concession to a private company to build and operate the highway as a profit-making venture. Texas and Indiana have been the pioneers. Bring in private-sector capital. In return for a big up-front cash payment to the state government for the concession."

"That's what they call privatization, isn't it?"

"Exactly. Let the private sector do it. Unleash the alleged miracles of free-market capitalism to solve all our problems. That's what made America great, right?"

"Do I detect a certain note of cynicism in your voice?"

"Cynical? Me? I'm just a barefoot boy from Brooklyn trying to make sense of the world."

"Oh, sure."

"Of course, our hypothetical Managing Director knows this version of privatization can't possibly fly. Certainly not in the state we're talking about. The public will never buy it."

"Why not?"

"Look. One of the requirements of a free market is many buyers and sellers. Enough so no individual buyer or seller can control the price. You know Canal Street in Manhattan's Chinatown?"

"Sure."

"That's a free market. Or pretty close. All those stalls lining the sidewalks. Selling the same cheap knockoffs of Breitling watches or Mont Blanc pens or Vuitton handbags. All those buyers milling around with twenty-dollar bills in their pockets. Eager to hondel, get the lowest possible price from the stall operators. Economics 101 in action on a real-world stage."

"With the NYPD making periodic raids to close down the stalls for selling illegal knockoffs."

"Of course. To help convince the German and Scandinavian tourists standing by of the bargains that must await them. But that's not the toll highway corridor."

"What's the critical difference?"

"The toll highway isn't free-market capitalism. It's Monopoly Capitalism. Or quasi-monopoly, at least. Like having the only food store in town."

"Yeah, I guess that's true."

"You think the public's going to sit still for turning that monopoly over to a private firm? Not likely. Because they know a business firm's natural instinct is to maximize its profits. By charging the highest toll rates the market will bear and providing the least service it can get away with."

"Capitalist greed in action."

"You can imagine the rest. Noisy legislative hearings. Local politicians falling all over themselves to denounce the project as a rip-off of the public. With the governor backing away as fast as possible because his political campaign doesn't need that kind of flack."

"But can't the state government set up some sort of regulatory commission? Like they have for utility companies?"

"Another paper-generating bureaucracy? Kiss of death for customer-oriented managers. Anyway, our hypothetical Managing Director has a better answer. Because he's already anticipated the problems from trying to use the standard concession model."

"Okay."

"He proposes having the state government set up an independent commercial corporation to build, own, and operate the transportation facilities in the corridor. And to be entirely self-supporting from highway tolls and other revenues."

"With the state owning the corporation?"

"I'm getting to that. He further proposes the state solicit bids from private investor syndicates to buy shares of equity ownership in the corporation. In return for annual dividends paid by the corporation. That brings private equity capital to the corporation's balance sheet. Reducing the amount of debt capital it has to issue. You with me so far?"

"I think so. But...."

"Don't worry. I'm going to deal with your 'but' right now."

"Okay."

"You wondering about the natural instinct of private investors to push for corporate policies that maximize profits. Right?"

"Yes."

"So their representatives on the corporation's board of directors will argue for high toll rates and minimum services?"

"Only natural."

"Of course. But our hypothetical Managing Director's ready for that. Which is why he proposes that the state government also have equity ownership in the corporation. Now what do you think the state government wants to maximize?"

"I don't know. Votes maybe?"

"Good for you. Like all governments, its natural instinct is to maximize votes for its elected leaders. And in terms of the corporation, what's the best way to accomplish that?"

"Lots of transportation service, and low toll rates?"

"You've got it. See how the government's vote-maximizing instinct can balance the profit-maximizing instinct of the private investors?"

"Yes. But...."

"Another 'but'? Tell me."

"Can't this lead to stalemates among the board members? Low tolls versus high tolls? More service versus less service?"

"You have to anticipate that. Which our hypothetical Managing Director certainly does. That's why he proposes a third class of owners for the corporation."

"A third class?"

"In addition to the private investors and the state government. A class of owners whose natural instincts make them automatic referees between private investors and the government."

"Now you're losing me."

"Think for a moment. Think about large companies that do most of their business in the two metropolitan regions. Local banks, for example. Utility companies. Retail chains. The list is a fairly long one."

"Yeah. So?"

"Since most of their sales revenue comes from the two metro regions, shouldn't they want to see the economies of these regions become more prosperous? After all, more prosperity for the regions means more sales revenue for them. And more sales revenue means higher profits."

"The new transportation corridor can make that kind of difference?"

"You'd be surprised. And the companies we're talking about know it. Now imagine what happens when some of them buy equity ownership in the corridor corporation. Enough to give them strong representation on the board of directors. Aren't they going to push for corporate policies to improve transportation in ways that increase their sales revenue?"

"I guess so."

"And aren't they going to want the corporation to be financially secure in the long run?"

"Of course."

"So doesn't that translate into toll rates that make sense from a financial standpoint as well as market standpoint? And service levels that meet public needs in a financially responsible manner?"

"Our Managing Director understands all this?"

"Absolutely. That's why he knows his whole concept represents a true breakthrough. Not just for the state and its politically ambitious governor. But for meeting transportation needs all over the country. Especially in our metropolitan regions. They're the most important."

"Why?"

"We're an urban nation now, Wes. Something like two-thirds of all

Americans live in the top one hundred metro regions. And they generate a good three-quarters of our Gross Domestic Product. So our future prosperity depends on keeping them healthy. Not letting their economies choke to death on traffic congestion."

"I guess you're right. It's like a big fat super-rich pastrami sandwich."

"With lots of spicy mustard. You sound like a patron of the Carnegie Deli."

"Only when I'm in town. Which seems like a lifetime ago."

* * *

We were starting to get hungry and Elijah suggested we tap the vending machines for whatever might pass as lunch.

I fed quarters into several of the machines as he directed. We came away with a couple of luke-warm hot dogs that didn't exactly taste like Nathan's. Plus a pair of tuna sandwiches on cotton-soft white bread slathered with something masquerading as mayo. Topped off by ice-cold Cokes, which no vending machine could screw up.

The Visiting Room wasn't yet full of the lunchtime crowd, so our table in the corner was empty.

"I've got a question," I said when we began eating.

"Only one?"

"It may lead to several others."

"Go ahead."

"You said one of the best things about our Managing Director's plan is how it opens up a new way to finance transportation improvements."

"Right."

"And this is something with national implications. Because it can theoretically be used all over the country."

"Especially in major metropolitan regions."

"To which we can expect Mr. Average Guy to respond with a big 'So what?'"

"Ah."

"Isn't Mr. Average Guy bound to wonder why transportation is so important?"

"Inevitably. But let me ask you this. Is he bound to wonder why greater national prosperity is so important?"

"I guess he takes that for granted."

"Of course he does. More jobs for more people. But think of what that means."

"I don't follow."

"Don't those additional people have to commute to and from those additional jobs?"

"Sure."

"So more jobs for more people inevitably means more people commuting to and from more jobs."

"In other words, you're linking transportation volume to economic activity?"

"The link is there whether we recognize it or not. Economic activity generates demand for transportation. More economic activity increases that demand."

"Yeah, I see what you're getting at."

"Think of it this way. A factory produces more widgets to take advantage of rising demand. Doesn't it have to hire more workers to make those widgets? Don't those extra workers have to commute to and from the factory? Doesn't that mean more transportation volume?"

"Naturally."

"Also, the factory has to ship those additional widgets to market. Doesn't that mean more transportation volume, too? And the factory needs to have more raw materials delivered to make those widgets. Doesn't that mean still more transportation volume?"

"I get the picture. Increased production of widgets increases the demand for transportation."

"It's automatic. And inevitable. But consider what can happen if transportation capacity is already saturated. The factory can't hire more workers because they can't commute to and from the factory. It can't ship more widgets to market or have more raw materials delivered...."

"...So it can't produce more widgets to meet rising demand."

"Right. Lack of enough transportation capacity where it's needed can impose a ceiling on the number of widgets the factory can produce. An artificial ceiling. One that has nothing to do with how many widgets customers actually want to buy. As if government imposed an arbitrary maximum on the number of widgets the factory was allowed to produce."

"Isn't that what used to happen in the Soviet Union and other Eastern European countries?"

"More or less. What do you think the result is?"

"Something like rationing?"

"Absolutely. And how do you think such rationing works?"

"The price of widgets goes up?"

"That's what happens under so-called free-market capitalism. If there's a shortage of widgets relative to consumer demand, the price of widgets rises. It rises until enough potential consumers are discouraged from wanting to buy widgets. So the available supply finally matches actual demand. That's what we call Price Rationing. But there's an alternative. It's called Time Rationing."

"Time Rationing?"

"Think back to the days when Eastern European countries practiced the Leninist brand of Communism. Remember the stories we used to hear about long lines of people waiting to buy consumer goods?"

"Sure."

"Prices were set at arbitrarily low levels, so virtually everybody could afford to buy. But you had to wait in long lines to buy anything."

"Which discouraged enough people from wanting to buy...."

"Exactly. That's called Time Rationing. It has the same end result as Price Rationing. Eventually, available supply matches remaining demand. The difference is, Time Rationing gives the edge to people who place a low value on the time they spend waiting in lines. While Price Rationing gives the edge to people rich enough not to care how much they spend."

"Which obviously raises the issue of fairness."

"Fairness?"

"I know that's not exactly a fashionable topic these days."

"Fashionable, shmashionable. It's a relevant point. Go ahead and raise it."

"As you said, rich people don't have to worry about what things cost. If they want it, they buy it. But with Price Rationing, poor people may have to go without."

"Are you saying Time Rationing levels the playing field?"

"Well, doesn't it?"

"But what if rich people can pay poor people to stand in line for them?"

"You mean, like personal shoppers?"

"That's the polite term these days. Poor people may not think their time's worth much. But they can sell it to people rich enough to think their time's worth too much to spend it shopping. Make a profit on their low-valued time, in other words."

"Well...."

"Anyway, we've gotten off the point."

"My fault. Sorry."

"The fairness issue's nothing to apologize for. It's obviously important when you have shortages. How do you allocate an inadequate supply of widgets? Who do you favor? Those who are rich with money? Those who are rich with time? Or is there a third way?"

"You mean, increase the supply?"

"Right. Produce enough widgets so there's enough for everybody. But...."

"But?"

"Producing more widgets generates a demand for more transportation."

"I think I get the picture."

"Sure you do. Now I'm going to give you some interesting numbers."

"Okay."

"One way to measure transportation volume is by VMT. Short for Vehicle Miles Traveled."

"That's one vehicle traveling one mile?"

"Right. Moving people or goods. Now between 1980 and 2005, VMT for cars in the United States increased 94 percent. For trucks, the increase was 105 percent. So we're talking about VMT roughly doubling over twenty-five years."

"Okay."

"But how much do you think the number of highway lane-miles increased?"

"Less?"

"Much less. Would you believe 3.5 percent?"

"That little?"

"A whole 3.5 percent."

"Wow."

"In other words, transportation demand increased roughly thirty times as much as highway capacity."

"All because of funding problems?"

"They're the key. When you have enough money, other problems tend to go away. Or so most people think."

"And that's why our Managing Director thought his new approach to financing could be a breakthrough for transportation all over the country?"

"Right. A breakthrough for transportation. And for unleashing the ability of the nation's economy to grow faster in the future. Which we're going to need if we want to solve some of our major problems."

"You mean like health care?"

"That's obviously one. We're the only major industrial country without a comprehensive national system to finance health care. And the results are piss-poor. We spend a larger percentage of our national income on health care. But by all objective quality measures, we rank way down the list. So we pay more and get less compared to other industrial countries. That's no way to stay competitive in the world."

"True."

"Also, we have this crazy practice of making health insurance dependent on jobs. So we've saddled all our widget-making companies with being in the health care business, too. That's a business most of them don't want to be in. Can't afford to be in any longer. Not when their offshore competitors reside in countries with the sensible practice of making health care a national responsibility rather than a private-company responsibility."

"So what's the solution?"

"Simple enough. Remove the minimum age limit on Medicare."

"Make Medicare the health insurance system for everybody?"

"That's what other countries do. Those that spend less than we do and get more for it."

"And reduce the private insurance companies to a fringe role?"

"More like eliminate them completely. They're a big part of the high cost problem."

"How?"

"Their administrative costs are huge compared to Medicare. Because they insist on cherry-picking the market to screen out potential customers who may already be sick. Have what they like to call 'preexisting conditions.' Costs a fortune to do that."

"So there could be important cost savings."

"Sure. But let's not kid ourselves. Having Medicare cover everybody's going to be expensive, no matter how efficiently it's run."

"How does the country pay for it?"

"Well, we have three options. One is politely called 'Managing Supply.'"

"You're talking about rationing care."

"Sure. The Triage System. Minimal care to those who are going to get well anyway. Or die no matter what you do. So you can concentrate your available resources on patients where the amount of care makes all the difference. Or on patients who are supposedly 'worth more.'"

"Worth more?"

"You know, have higher incomes. By paying them more, American society's obviously saying they're worth more. So they get more health care."

"You'll pardon me for saying so, but that's disgraceful."

"Just another reality of free-market capitalist principles. Which we already practice in health care, if you look beneath the surface. Not so much in Brooklyn maybe. But certainly in other places."

"It's still disgraceful. And you think so, too. I can tell by your eyes."

"Well, it wouldn't affect me personally. Investment bankers and their families don't usually wind up in charity wards. Even with a prison term or two behind them."

"Tell me the other options."

"Option Two is to have enough health care for everybody. So rationing's unnecessary."

"To each according to his need?"

"The old socialist motto. Very humane and idealistic. Of course, paying for it could mean skyrocketing tax rates for everybody. Accompanied by lots of screaming. Except among those winding up in hospitals. That's why Option Three really makes the most sense."

"And Option Three is…?"

"Growing our national economy faster. Fast enough to generate the tax revenue needed to buy adequate medical care for everybody. With no increase in tax rates."

"Yeah, I see what you're getting at."

"More prosperity doesn't just mean being able to buy more luxuries like Hawaiian vacations or seven-dollar gas for our SUVs. It means being able to solve our real problems."

"Like health care."

"That's clearly one. The retiring Baby Boom generation is another. Bigger and more thorny. But don't get me started on that."

"And transportation's the key to solving all that."

"One of them. How can the national economy grow fast enough if we hold it back with all kinds of transportation bottlenecks? Especially in metropolitan regions. You can even argue that none of the other keys matter much if you lack the transportation key. And we sure as hell don't have it right now."

"So if I read you correctly, you advocate spending more money on transportation. But mainly in metropolitan regions."

"That's where the action is. As far as future prosperity is concerned."

"A lot of Americans will give you an argument about that."

"Of course. Because they're still lost in a Jeffersonian fairyland."

"You're referring to *Thomas* Jefferson? The Founding Father?"

"And Number One colonial schnorrer. You know the word schnorrer?"

"It means beggar or sponger, doesn't it?"

"Yes. In broad terms, somebody who lives off the sweat of somebody else's brow."

"That's what we used to call landlords in my old neighborhood."

"I don't wonder."

"But I don't see the connection with Jefferson."

"He was born rich. Son of a Virginia plantation owner. With a full set of slaves to do all the work. So he never had to do a serious day's work in his life. All the money he spent was produced by his slaves. Which makes him a classic schnorrer."

"Yeah, I see what you mean."

"And being a rich aristocrat affected how he saw the world. That's why his vision for America was a land of independent farmers living prosperous lives on land worked by their slaves. So naturally he hated cities. They were 'un-American' as far as he was concerned. Since he was a card-carrying resident of his own private rural fairyland."

"And you think this is the Great American Hang-up?"

"Look at the evidence. The instinctive national image for too many of our fellow citizens is the rural small town surrounded by pastoral farms."

"I guess you can make that argument."

"But they refuse to face a critical fact. Those small towns are losing their young people at a furious rate. As soon as they're old enough, kids flee to the cities as fast as they can. Because they know that's where the action is. Cities have always been doorways to the future."

"Yeah."

"Yet too many Americans can't come to terms with that reality. Just like Jefferson couldn't come to terms with the reality of Sally Hemings."

"Wasn't she the slave woman he…?"

"The most important person in his life, from what we now know. Theirs was a Great American Love Story, Wes. And a sad one. Because he could never bring himself to free her from slavery, no matter how much he loved her. Ditto the children they had together. Too much a prisoner of his rural fairyland dreams."

"All of which supposedly explains why we don't concentrate more transportation investments in metropolitan regions."

"Call it the Sally Hemings hang-up. Sorry if that sounds like mixing the sacred with the profane."

"It's not always easy to tell where one ends and the other begins."

"Matter of interpretation, I guess."

"Yeah. But listen, Elijah."

"What."

"Aren't the Green types going to have problems with all this emphasis on economic growth?"

"Which Green types do you mean?"

"You know. The ones who talk about how more economic growth means more pollution."

"But those people aren't really concerned about the environment. They just want to piggyback on a hot topic to push their private agendas."

"Such as?"

"Look. Suppose, through sheer luck, you're born rich with all the right connections and everything handed to you on a silver spoon. Society works fine for you, and you want to keep it that way. But economic growth creates opportunities for other people to move up in the world. The wrong kind of people, as far as you're concerned. Blacks. Hispanics. Immigrants from Asia and Eastern Europe. People you want to keep confined to what you like to call the servant classes. But economic growth can open too many doors to make this possible. So what do you do to hang onto your privileged status?"

"You're saying they jump on the environmental bandwagon? As a socially respectable way to piss on economic growth? So they can preserve the status quo?"

"That's what these Marie Antoinette types think. They figure it's their best shot for closing the flood gates against the barbarians. So they do whatever they can to block new economic development projects, public or private. By claiming they'll be bad for the environment. That's become a surefire way to win arguments."

"Interesting idea."

"Then we have the professional schnorrers, as we call them in Borough Park. Their classic shtick is to show up as uninvited guests at social events like weddings and bar mitzvahs. Passing themselves off as visiting rabbis. Hitting up the other guests for a few dollar bills each. Contributions to some high-minded charity in Israel, they insist. You'd be surprised what good livings they make. Do you see the connection?"

"With environmentalists?"

"Look at it this way. We're always going to have career con artists looking for any angle that can line their pockets. They don't care what the angle is, just as long as it can produce money."

"And environmentalism is such an angle."

"You bet. It's a socially respectable issue. Lots of publicity. So all they have to do to get attention is speak out in favor of the environment. In the most radical way possible. Which usually means opposing anything to do with economic development. That gets their names in the papers. Attracts supporters. Generates contributions. Most of which they skim to live like kings."

"Like leaders of religious sects."

"Same principle."

"So you're saying the environmental movement is totally corrupt."

"Not at all. The Marie Antoinette types and professional schnorrers are just a self-serving fringe. Using environmentalism to push their private agendas. Nothing to do with serious mainstream Greens."

"And you can spot serious mainstream Greens because they favor economic growth?"

"They're not dummies. They know prosperous societies always do better by the environment than poorer societies."

"You really believe that?"

"Look at the evidence. Mexico City has the worst air pollution in the world. Brazil's cutting down the Amazon rain forests like there's no tomorrow. Argentina's poisoning the sea water around Buenos Aires with toxic waste from chemical plants. The list goes on."

"So more economic growth is the key to saving the environment."

"If you're smart. And serious mainstream Greens know it."

"Which brings us back to transportation."

"Inevitably. But that happens to be my personal shtick."

"Looks like I should learn more about transportation if I'm going to hold up my end of our conversation."

"Wouldn't hurt. It's all on the Internet."

* * *

By the time we finished eating, our energy had begun to flag from so much talking. We obviously needed another meeting and decided on the same time next Sunday. Then shook hands and parted.

I walked outside to the visitors' reception area. Turned in my pass. Recovered my driver's license and newspaper press pass. Then went out to my car.

Needless to say, it was like a furnace inside my car from the strong midday sun. I started the engine and cranked up the air conditioner to

High. Fortunately, the insulated portfolio in the drawer under the passenger's seat had kept my cell phone and tape recorder from overheating too badly. So I took out my tape recorder, held it to the side of my mouth, and pressed the record button.

But no words came. That seemed odd since I was overflowing with information. I made a few more stabs, but nothing meaningful came out. I was too full of information to articulate anything meaningful at that point. It was all inside me but apparently needed time to jell.

This was a new experience for me. I shook my head and put the tape recorder down on the seat beside me. Then drove out of the prison parking lot and started for home.

But as I drove along the back road that twisted through the ragged mountains, an interesting thought struck me.

Despite all his elaborate stories about that hypothetical Managing Director, Elijah still hadn't explained very clearly why he had to plead guilty to Insider Trading charges he probably could have beaten in court.

He naturally wanted to protect his highway project. But how could that be threatened by a public trial involving something so unrelated as Insider Trading? There had to be more to it than he'd told me so far. I'd have to try and dig it out of him at our next meeting. If I was clever enough.

Had I stumbled across something considerably more than a source of technical information about Insider Trading? Useful fodder for an article or two that might impress professional intellectuals back East and help rehabilitate my career?

Maybe I'd uncovered one of those special Brooklyn mystics like Pete Hamill. Who had penetrated the heart of the world's true reality. And emerged on the other side dripping with truths about what the whole megilla was really all about?

Why was I using the Jewish word "megilla" to express something that, in Bed-Stuy, had always meant the *Whole Shmear*? Was I being sucked in by Elijah's Talmudic showmanship? Not to mention his highly articulate Brooklyn dialect, whose racy excitement I'd been separated from far too long?

Did this mean I should really be focusing on an article about Elijah's ideas? Or several articles? Maybe even an entire book? Which could, conceivably, overwhelm the intellectuals back East and bring me home in some kind of triumph.

When I got to my apartment, I fired up the computer on my desk in the living room. Spent the rest of the afternoon and all night surfing the Internet. Trying to get smart about American transportation issues. Which seemed to mean so much to Elijah.

Once I noticed how light it was getting outside my apartment windows, I shut down my computer. Took a hot shower and shaved. Made coffee and reheated the Chinese take-out food left over from yesterday. Then lay down to take a nap after setting my alarm clock for 11:00 a.m.

So I'd be on time for any big excitement at the Rotary Club lunch my newspaper had assigned me to cover.

Chapter Two
After the Biblical Scribes

Three nights of surfing the Internet had made me feel like something of a maven about transportation issues. Especially when I was able to play back the mass of information I'd dug out from various Web sites against what Elijah had told me to give it all some context.

So I took a shot at trying to summarize the main points in some crude notes that I saved in a Word file. They seemed to make reasonable sense when I read them over on my computer screen.

TRANSPORTATION FACT SHEET #1
What Are The BASIC REALITIES?

• *Economic activity generates demand for transportation. This is inevitable. Workers have to commute to and from their jobs. Factories have to ship their products to market. Raw materials have to be shipped to factories. Salesmen have to call on customers. Etc.*

• *So more economic activity inevitably means more demand for transportation.*

• *Economic growth means increased economic activity. Generally regarded as a good thing (more jobs, etc.).*

- *But economic growth increases the demand for transportation.*

- *Economic activity is measured by Gross Domestic Product (GDP). Numbers for GDP are available for the nation, for each state, and for each metropolitan region (at least the main ones).*

- *Transportation volume is measured by Vehicle Miles of Travel (maybe in other ways too). Can VMT also be used to measure transportation demand? Maybe so. Check with Elijah.*

- *Transportation capacity concerns the ability of roadways and other facilities to accommodate transportation demand. How is capacity measured? By **potential** VMT? Discuss with Elijah.*

- *The nation's economic activity is concentrated in the 100 largest metropolitan regions. With only some 12 percent of the nation's land, they generate 76 percent of its Gross Domestic Product. House about 65 percent of its citizens (including about 74 percent of the best educated). Generate 77 percent of its "knowledge economy" jobs. Are the targets for 84 percent of its immigrants (who are the world's "natural elites" and therefore should be highly prized—because they have the energy and risk-taking initiative to come here in search of better lives, and these are the most important human skills for building a more prosperous country).*

What Are The IMPLICATIONS?

*Transportation capacity is one of the things that can impose a **ceiling** on the rate of economic growth. Too little capacity limits economic*

55

growth to something less than it could be. We can't afford that. The country needs all the economic growth it can get.

- *So ideally at least, the **only** meaningful determinant of the rate of capacity growth is the desired rate of economic growth (subject to whatever constraints are imposed by other factors).*

- *What is the relationship between (1) the growth rate of the economy, and (2) the growth rate of transportation capacity? Has it been quantified? If No, can it be? Is the relationship a straight line or some sort of curve? Does Elijah have any sources of information about this?*

- *Given all this, annual spending on transportation should ideally be **what is needed** to accommodate the desired rate of economic growth. So the availability of transportation funds should be driven by need. Economists who buy into this would presumably argue that transportation spending should rise so long as each additional dollar spent on transportation generates **at least one additional dollar of GDP**. (That's the theory at least.)*

- *But that's not the way it works in practice. All the evidence suggests that the U.S. grossly underinvests in its transportation systems. So we're living off what our grandparents built and adding very little new to the mix. That's like burning your inherited furniture in the fireplace to keep warm in the winter after your antiquated home heating system has collapsed from neglect. Eventually, you run out of furniture.*

- *In 1968, the average American was delayed about 16 hours per year because of traffic congestion. Today, such delays approach 8 days per year in the 13 largest metropolitan areas alone. The* cost of these delays (in the time people waste traveling, fuel wasted by idling engines, extra wear and tear on motor vehicles, etc.) is estimated at about $78 billion per year. And who benefits? The guys selling cut flowers to motorists stuck at jammed intersections? (Those are very expensive flowers.)

• Since 1960, the privately owned freight railroad industry has abandoned about half its track mileage "to save money." But the total tonnage of goods to be moved keeps increasing as population and economic activity increase. So lack of track capacity forces more and more of this tonnage to be moved in trucks on already-crowded roadways. That makes goods-movement trips take longer. And the people-moving trips these trucks delay take longer, too.

• Waste is a key feature of our transportation systems. Waste on a grand scale. Like the 2.9 billion gallons of fuel per year wasted due to traffic congestion—enough to fill 58 supertankers. Or the 42,000 lives lost in traffic accidents each year and the 2.7 million people injured. And the thousands of cubic miles of air poisoned each year by greenhouse gas emissions (28 percent of which is pumped forth by transportation).

What Is The PRESENT SITUATION?
(At least for roadways.)

• Right now, roadways are theoretically funded like public parks (excluding toll roads). They're supported by society as a whole rather than only by those who use roadways. Why? Can it be argued that most of their benefits are **indirect** (accruing to the general public) rather than **direct** (accruing only to drivers)? Weak argument.

- *In practice, much roadway funding comes from fuel taxes (semi-earmarked) levied by federal and state governments. Plus from general revenues of state and county governments.*

- *Do fuel taxes establish a link between how much drivers pay for roadways and how much they use them? Maybe yes in theory. But maybe not in the minds of drivers. Because taxes are hidden away in the price per gallon, so drivers aren't aware of how much tax they're paying.*

- *On the one hand, drivers use roadways for travel. On the other hand, they buy fuel periodically under circumstances where the taxes they pay for each tank of fuel aren't apparent. So there's no clear connection in their minds between using roadways and paying for them.*

- *Fuel tax revenues depend on two things: (1) total VMT, and (2) the tax rate.*

- *Total VMT is rising, so revenues rise too. But at a slower rate because the nation's motor vehicle fleet is gradually becoming more fuel efficient. Also because additives like ethanol aren't taxed. Therefore, fuel tax revenues are rising more slowly than VMT. And more slowly than inflation.*

- ***Increases in VMT** determine how much roadway operators must spend to maintain roadways properly, how rapidly roadways wear out and must be rebuilt, how soon and how much new capacity is needed to accommodate increases in VMT. So fuel tax revenues should rise at least as fast as VMT.*

- ***Inflation** reduces the **purchasing power** of each million dollars*

58

in fuel tax revenues. So fuel tax revenues should rise at least as fast as inflation.

- *Traditionally, tax rates are set at so many **pennies per gallon**— not at so many **percentage points of the price per gallon**. So there's no **automatic** link between fuel tax revenues and the price of fuel. Instead, elected officials must periodically take deliberate action to raise the pennies-per-gallon tax rate if they want the growth rate of revenues to match the growth rate of VMT and inflation. Which they don't want to do because they're convinced that "tax increases" offend voters. So fuel tax revenues rise more slowly than VMT and inflation.*

- *Because fuel tax revenues rise more slowly than roadway use and inflation, there's a growing gap between the **need for funds** and the **availability of funds**. This gap means that roadway capacity can't keep pace with economic growth (which generates travel demand).*

- *In effect, fuel taxes are losing their viability as the main source of roadway funding. They need to be replaced with something better.*

- *A better alternative may be to charge **drivers** for roadway use. This means tolls, which electronic toll collection has made a practical proposition. In other words, replace fuel taxes with user charges (tolls).*

- *This is how we pay for water, electric power, communications services, and most other things we need or want in a capitalist society. You want, you pay. The more you want, the more you pay. The buyer determines how much he really wants based on how much he's willing to pay. Makes sense if you accept the traditional Adam Smith view.*

What Is ELIJAH'S MODEL?

- *Applies these capitalist principles to funding roadways. Drivers pay to travel on toll roads. Toll rates are set at rates that generate enough revenues to cover all roadway costs (building, operating, maintaining, replacing, expanding). So roadways become **self-supporting**. His model also sets up a structure to make this work.*

- *A state government establishes a corporation to build and operate a toll road as a self-supporting commercial enterprise.*

- *The corporation issues debt to raise funds to build the road. Debt is secured by toll revenues.*

- *To reduce the amount of debt that it has to issue, the corporation sells equity shares to private investors. They are attracted by the promised dividend stream from toll revenues.*

- *As owners, these investors want to maximize their dividends. So they want the corporation to charge the highest tolls possible while keeping costs low by providing the least service possible.*

- *To offset this, the corporation allocates equity shares to the state government (and maybe local governments in the toll road's service area), in exchange for the various government concessions, zoning changes, etc. that the toll road requires. The natural instinct of these government owners is to win favor with the public. So they want the corporation to provide lots of service and keep tolls low (maximizing votes for their elected officials).*

- *To avoid policy stalemates between these two classes of owners, the corporation sells equity shares to a third class of owners. These are private companies whose revenues depend mainly on the amount of economic activity the region generates (i.e., local banks, utilities, major retail chains, etc.). Their natural instinct is to have the corporation help boost regional economic activity by providing good service at acceptable toll rates. So the interests of this class of owners are most closely aligned with the public interest.*

I read through the notes a second time. Somewhat jumbled and repetitious, obviously. But at least they contained some clear threads of logic.

Yet something was missing. An important gut factor that made the whole argument truly compelling. Hinted at here and there maybe. But why pussyfoot? Why not come right out and say it in plain terms?

I thought for a few minutes. Then heard some words begin to jell in my brain and resumed typing.

CAN AMERICA SAVE ITSELF?

- *The nation faces some big problems. Expensive problems. And time is running out to solve them if we're going to survive.*

- *But the only way we can afford to solve these problems is to grow our economy fast enough to generate the resources needed. Otherwise we'll end up eating our tail. Doing that will bankrupt us just as surely as if we ignore these problems.*

- *Growing the economy fast enough requires that we unleash our transportation systems so they become growth boosters. We must end the folly of allowing transportation to limit economic growth.*

- *Better transportation may not assure our survival all by itself. But better transportation is the price of that survival.*

I had to smile to myself as the familiar pattern of these last words struck me. They paraphrased a key point in the dramatic policy debate at the heart of what was probably the most sophisticated movie ever made about World War II.

It was the 1949 MGM film *Command Decision*. With Clark Gable as commander of the Eighth Air Force's bombers in England during 1943. Trying to convince his boss Walter Pidgeon to let him finish bombing the three German factories producing the Luftwaffe's spectacular new jet fighters during a rare break in the weather, even though bomber losses would probably be high. While Pidgeon, as head of the entire Eighth Air Force, insists that the key to ultimate victory in bombing Germany lies in convincing Washington to allocate them enough bombers in the long run. Which means keeping current loss rates as modest as possible by avoiding high-risk raids. Needless to say, the Gable character wins the debate.

Not exactly historically accurate, of course. But very dramatic. And full of rare insights about the higher political and strategic realities of fighting a major backs-to-the-wall war against the Forces of Darkness.

One advantage of choosing history as my undergraduate major was that it taught me how the U.S. and its allies won World War II. For better or worse, that's what made the world we live in today. And that victory still has much to teach us about truly critical issues.

So I continued adding new ideas to the notes on my computer screen.

BIG PROBLEM #1: HEALTH CARE

- *The U.S. spends a larger portion of its national income on health care than other industrial nations. But gets less for it, according to all objective health measures.*

- *Obvious difference is that other industrial nations fund health care for everyone through a single-payer system managed by the central government. Experience shows that this is both cost-efficient and very effective in terms of maximizing overall performance.*

- *But the U.S. insists on going its own way. Relying on a horse-and-buggy approach to health care that can't cover everyone, imposes high overhead costs, buries health care providers under mountains of bureaucratic paperwork, and too often leaves patients lost in the shuffle.*

- *Elijah's solution makes sense. Eliminate the minimum age limit on Medicare so it can become the single-payer system for everybody. Stop subcontracting health care coverage to the high-cost private insurance industry. Stop imposing on American companies the extra cost burden of having to provide their employees with health care coverage, which their offshore competitors aren't saddled with. (Increasing numbers of American companies are already discarding this burden as unaffordable. Leaving only the wallets of hard-pressed employees to pick up the slack.)*

- *How do we pay for all this? Raise tax rates across the board to generate the necessary extra revenue for an expanded Medicare system? Not practical. Nor desirable.*

- *Grow the economy faster, so the same tax rates as today can generate more revenue from a bigger pie? The only practical approach.*

- *How do we grow the economy faster? Improving transportation is an important factor. Make transportation a growth generator.*

BIG PROBLEM #2: BABY BOOM RETIREMENT

- *After World War II, American's Greatest Generation went on an uncontrolled breeding binge. This produced the huge demographic bulge we call the Baby Boomers. And we've been stuck with the consequences ever since.*

- *First the Baby Boomers swamped the nation's public school systems. So we had to spend huge amounts of money building more schools.*

- *After that, they swamped the higher education system. Demanding another costly round of new construction.*

- *Then they swamped the job market. Forcing those who couldn't find decent entry jobs to drop out and too often become the source of various expensive social problems.*

- *Like an oversized mongoose swallowed by an unwitting snake, the Baby Boomer generation has crept its slow way through the writhing body of the society struggling to digest it.*

- *Now the Baby Boomers are retiring in ever-increasing numbers.*

Swamping the nation's rickety complex of too many thousand private pension systems. Most of which are so mismanaged, underfunded, and generally patched together with Scotch tape that they can't begin to keep their cavalier promises of decent living standards for the elderly in the so-called Golden Years.

• *Once again, this is an example of how America ignores what the rest of the industrial world does. Insists on going its own way. And ends up wallowing in deep do-do. Just as with Health Care.*

• *Experience in other countries shows that the best arrangement is a comprehensive National Pension System managed by the central government. Like Social Security with a nationwide monopoly. Providing defined benefit pensions for everyone that are indexed to inflation so they protect the purchasing power of retired people. Not just a safety net but a truly decent living. Eliminate private pensions entirely. But encourage people to save during their working years if they can afford to.*

• *Fully fund this pension system so there's no question of it being secure. Prudently invest its trust funds in a broad array of bonds, stocks, mortgages, you name it. So these trust funds become one of the largest sources of investment capital for the American economy. Like in Finland (and maybe in other Scandinavian countries too—more info needed).*

• *Obviously, the transition to a National Pension System is going to be costly. But much of this money may have to be spent anyway as private pensions collapse and force the taxpayer to support their victims through some form of quasi-welfare.*

65

- *Best solution is to grow the economy fast enough to cover these transition costs without big hikes in tax rates on the nation's labor force and private companies. (Or do we just borrow the money from China?)*

- *Growing the economy brings us back to the transportation issue again. Shows how critical it is to make transportation a true growth generator.*

BIG PROBLEM #3:
PROTECTING THE ENVIRONMENT

- *Clear link between economic prosperity and improving the natural environment. Rich societies take care of the environment. Poor societies may have little alternative to doing things that ruin the environment. So more prosperity equals a better environment.*

- *Examples: Severe air pollution in Mexico City. Amazon rain forest destruction in Brazil. Ocean pollution around Buenos Aires from dumping industrial waste. Poisoned brownfields in former Leninist countries of Eastern Europe. (Get more examples. Many available.)*

- *Therefore, economic growth is an essential tool for improving the environment. Also, a clean environment helps promote economic growth. Mainstream Greens know this.*

- *But the issue is clouded by what Elijah calls Marie Antoinette types and professional schnorrers. They push their self-serving agendas by opposing economic growth as BAD for the*

environment. Which is a flat-earth assumption that isn't sup-
ported by the evidence. But it gets them a lot of attention and
confuses the public.

• *More details and insights needed here.*

That was better. A top-down, macro perspective on the problem. High-lighting the basic issues more clearly. Providing some essential orientation.

So I sent the notes to Elijah's wife as an attachment to an email asking that she try to get them to him before our upcoming Sunday meeting. She emailed me back the next day, saying they were already on their way to him by FedEx and she thought he would find them very inter-esting.

But the same old question kept nagging at me. Why had Elijah really pleaded guilty to Insider Trading? He claimed it was to protect the toll road project, to keep certain things from coming out at the trial.

But what things? Nothing he'd told me so far seemed to threaten the project. The counts of Insider Trading he'd pleaded to had happened years ago and had no apparent relation to the project.

He was one of those people who could throw a lot of words in your di-rection without actually communicating much of anything, when that served his purpose. I would have to try a more point-blank approach with him.

* * *

My intent was to get right to it when we met that Sunday. But he insisted on talking about my transportation notes first.

"You seem to have learned a lot in a very short time," he said.

"The Internet makes it easier than in the old days, when you had struggle with libraries."

"That's one of the things I miss most in here."

"You don't have access to the Internet?"

"Not in ways that matter. That's why I had to mail my wife a handwritten letter with my comments about your notes. She'll scan the letter and send it to you as an email attachment."

"You think I'm on the right track?"

"Oh, definitely. There's some perceptive analysis in your notes. I like your ideas about a national pension system."

"You hadn't already thought of that?"

"Not to the extent you obviously have."

"Gee. High praise."

"But your notes also suggest something else."

"Yeah? What."

"You seem to be moving beyond the idea of one or two articles about Insider Trading."

"I'm keeping my options open."

"To include maybe a full-fledged book about transportation issues?"

"Looks like somebody needs to write one."

"And if you become that somebody, it could be a big step in your career rehab?"

"I won't deny it. But there's a problem."

"What."

"My credibility."

"Because of what happened in Washington?"

"Partly. But also a more basic problem. Nobody sees me as a transportation guru. So why should they pay attention to any book I might write?"

"You could do some articles first. Build your credibility."

"Possibly."

"Or, you could team up with somebody who already has credibility."

"Does that include you?"

"It could."

"You'd really be willing to work with me?"

"Maybe."

"A transportation book by a pair of self-confessed rogues? Come on, Elijah."

"Might be an effective marketing ploy for a publisher smart enough to run with it."

"Especially if we can find a way to incorporate stories about our past sins as dramatic color."

"Good credibility booster. You know how Americans love to slobber all over former sinners. That's something religious sects hang their hats on."

"But there's still one thing I'm confused about, Elijah."

"What's that."

"Why you pleaded guilty to acts of Insider Trading that presumably took place years before your toll road project got off the ground."

"Are you referring to our hypothetical Managing Director?"

"Who else? You said he did it to protect the project. But I don't see the connection. The Managing Director had nothing to conceal when it came to the project."

"Everybody has something to conceal."

"Isn't that Sam Spade's line?"

"From *The Maltese Falcon*. John Huston's film version."

"When Sam tells off the district attorney."

"Right."

"So you're implying there are things you haven't told me."

"I didn't want to confuse you with too much detail at first."

"But instead you left me confused with too little detail."

"So it seems. My apologies."

"Can you unconfuse me?"

"I'll try."

* * *

We'd been sitting at that corner table in the Visiting Room. Elijah had brought along some of the Chinese tea his wife regularly sent him. Green tea with jasmine blossoms. He had me get us two Styrofoam cups of hot water from the vending machines. Then poured the tea leaves into the hot water. After a few moments, the leaves sank to the bottom of the cups and began giving off an interesting aroma.

We began sipping the hot tea. Its taste was an odd mixture of bitterness and floral sweetness. But as it cooled, I noticed how the bitterness diminished and the sweetness became stronger. It was the first time I realized how the taste of tea can change with its temperature. Could that subtly influence the flow of conversation among tea drinkers? Did it help explain why Asians made such a big deal about tea-drinking rituals?

"Come on. Let's walk a bit," Elijah said finally when we had finished our tea."

"Okay."

We went outside and began walking across the grass.

"What do you know about the underwriting business?" he asked me abruptly.

"Investment banking firms buy new issues of stocks and bonds. Then turn around and sell them to private investors. Hopefully, at a profit."

"Better than hopefully. But the details are interesting."

"I'm all ears."

"Think of it this way. A commercial fishing boat enters the harbor full of a fresh catch of fish. Which the captain wants to sell for the highest possible price."

"Okay."

"Waiting on the pier are half a dozen fish wholesalers, ready to place bids for the entire boatload of fish. Each one has his own sense of the current price retail customers are willing to pay for fish. At restaurants, supermarket chains, and neighborhood fish stores. And each one has his own sense of how much markup these retail outlets need to charge to make a profit. Which determines how much they can afford to pay to buy fish from the wholesalers."

"So they sort of work it backwards in their minds?"

"Pretty much. Each wholesaler computes how much money he can expect to get by selling the boatload of fish to the retailers he normally does business with. That tells him the maximum price he can afford to bid for the boatload of fish. You with me so far?"

"I think so."

"Good. Now remember, each wholesaler has his own sense of what the current economics of the fish business are like. So each wholesaler is likely to submit a different bid to the fishing boat captain. Who naturally accepts the highest bid."

"Which means that the wholesaler submitting the highest bid gets all the fish and therefore earns all the profits from reselling the fish to retailers?"

"That's it exactly. Leaving the other wholesalers out in the cold. Waiting for the next boat."

"Okay. I get the analogy. But instead of fish, we're talking about new issues of stocks and bonds."

"Which is what traditional underwriting in the investment banking industry is all about."

"But I gather our Managing Director came up with a new wrinkle."

"Yes, indeed. Now, remember what business his unit is in?"

"Providing financial advice to state and local governments for an annual fee."

"Right. And an important chunk of that advice involves issuing bonds for capital projects. But traditional underwriting usually means arms-length competitive bidding. That limits his clients to plain vanilla debt issues. And that's not the best way to produce the lowest borrowing cost, which is the primary goal of government clients."

"What's the alternative?"

"Something called Negotiated Underwriting."

"Which is what?"

"Go back to our fish analogy. Suppose a smart fishing-boat captain sits down with a particular fish wholesaler before he sets out on a voyage. They agree on a mutually beneficial deal. The wholesaler will pay the captain an agreed price for his next boatload of fish. No competitive bidding after the fishing boat returns to port, in other words."

"Which means that the captain will sell his fish only to the wholesaler for the agreed price?"

"Right. And the wholesaler, based on his up-to-date knowledge of the fish market, will tell the captain what kinds of fish to go after and how much of each kind to catch. This helps the captain get the highest possible price for his next boatload of fish. And, not so incidentally, guarantees the highest profit for the wholesaler."

"I can see why you like the fish analogy. Are there really so many ways to structure bond issues?"

"As many as there are fish in the sea. Or at least, the species of fish in the sea."

"So the Managing Director's play is to convince his government clients to forget competitive-bidding underwriting and adopt Negotiated Underwriting?"

"Right. He shows them how this can produce lower borrowing costs on their debt issues. And he reminds them that private corporations have been using Negotiated Underwriting for years. These days, showing governments how they can apply private-sector practices gets of lot of favorable attention."

"Justifiably?"

"Sometimes. But it's the perception that counts."

"Okay. Our Managing Director convinces his clients to use Negotiated Underwritings. That's it?"

"Just the beginning."

"I should have known."

"One of the financial advisory services he provides is helping government clients select the right investment banking firm to work with on a Negotiated Underwriting."

"So he makes recommendations?"

"Right. Now obviously, he can't recommend his own firm. That would be seen as a clear conflict of interest. He has to give clients a list of other firms they can invite to make sales pitches. The usual list consists of three investment banking firms."

"And he helps his clients evaluate their pitches?"

"Absolutely."

"Which means he can effectively steer a client to one of the firms."

"That's how it usually works out. But there's a larger issue. A more interesting one."

"What."

"It has to do with how our hypothetical Managing Director selects the firms to recommend to his clients. Obviously, the firm that gets the deal stands to make big dollars."

"We're talking about Pay to Play?"

"You pick up fast."

"My years in Washington."

"Of course, we're not talking about anything so crude as straight kickbacks. Our Managing Director has something more elegant in mind. With less danger of negative repercussions."

"Why am I not surprised?"

"He goes to the head of his firm and suggests they make a significant equity investment in a hot, young, closely held management consulting company. Which will then offer special consulting services to investment banking firms wanting to increase their Negotiated Underwriting business with state and local governments. These services generate lucrative fees for the management consulting company. Which increase its profits and therefore the dividends it pays to its shareholders. One of which is the Managing Director's firm."

"And all the investment banking firms he recommends to his government clients are clients of the management consulting company?"

"More or less. To make things look kosher, he usually includes one nonclient investment bank on his list of recommendations. But since he's in a position to influence the government's choice of a firm for the Negotiated Underwriting...."

"And that's what happened with the toll road project?"

"No, that was an exception."

"An exception?"

"Our hypothetical Managing Director wanted to make sure that this deal would seem really glatt kosher. So none of the investment banks on his recommended list were clients of the management consulting company. There was no connection at all."

"Then where's the problem?"

"The governor threw out the Managing Director's list. And substituted his own choice of an investment banking firm. Which happened to be headed by one of his major political fund-raisers."

"The governor was that stupid?"

"What do you think, people who run for office are rocket scientists?"

"I guess not."

"Anyway, you know how it is. The two of them were old friends. Drinking buddies, as the saying goes. Lots of unspoken trust between them. Not all that uncommon."

"Yeah, I suppose so. But wait a minute, Elijah."

"What."

"You said the Managing Director has a Pay to Play arrangement when it comes to recommending investment banking firms to his government clients."

"That's right."

"But he didn't use this arrangement for the toll road project."

"Right again."

"Then where's the danger to the project if the Managing Director goes to trial on the Insider Trading charges? Even if the prosecutor's able to raise the Pay to Play issue in his case, how can this be linked to the project? As you said, the Managing Director's recommendations don't include any firms that are clients of the management consulting company."

"It's not a matter of what the prosecutor can prove. It's what he can ask questions about during a trial. Leading questions."

"Yeah, but…."

"Look at it this way. Our hypothetical Managing Director has to believe the project's going to come up in the prosecutor's case. And even if there's no question of the project being linked to Pay to Play, the fact that it's mentioned at all in a criminal trial can raise a red flag to the governor's political enemies. Who start looking into the project for something to embarrass the governor. "

"Like his choice of the investment banking firm?"

"Our Managing Director has to expect that. Causing the governor to backpedal as fast as he can. Put on a great show of outrage that somebody in his office arranged to give the deal to a firm headed by a major fund-raiser. Without his knowledge, of course. Announce that he's canceling the deal. Welcomes a full investigation by the state legislature. Effectively shoves the project onto a back burner and tries to move on."

"I suppose that's possible."

"Remember. The governor has no particular commitment to the project except as one more thing that can make him look good politically. But not if it turns out to have a bad smell."

"So the Managing Director has to lean over backwards to make sure the project never gets mentioned in a criminal trial?"

"And the best way to do that is to avoid a trial completely. By pleading guilty. Even if that means some jail time in a so-called federal country club prison like this one. Doesn't that seem logical?"

"Maybe so. I'm going to have to think about it."

"Think away. Meanwhile, let me ask you a question."

"What."

"That *Time* magazine article about your so-called scandal was pretty skimpy on details. Just some allusions about falsifying sources for some of your stories. I'd like to know more."

"Sort of a quid pro quo?"

"If you want to put it that way."

"Okay. You've been forthcoming with me. In your own roundabout way, at least. Let me take you through the details."

"I'm listening."

* * *

We were sitting on a wooden bench under the trees at the far end of the grassy area. This was the first time I'd ever gone into my case with someone who wasn't a hungry lawyer angling to represent me in a discrimination case against the newspaper that fired me. So it took me a few minutes to get my thoughts together.

"Let's consider the hypothetical case of an ambitious Young Journalist with all the right credentials," I said finally.

"I see you're learning."

"From a master. Anyway, our Young Journalist graduates from a prestigious journalism school and gets hired by the Washington bureau of a major national newspaper."

"Is that the usual pattern?"

"No. But as I said, our Young Journalist has all the right credentials. Which includes some influential names in journalism willing to make phone calls on his behalf."

"Secular rabbis. Really big machers."

"The biggest. So he gets hired and is assigned to cover several federal agencies. Routine stuff. Recycling the usual agency handouts. Nothing his newspaper would ever bother running. Just to ease him into the flow of things, as it were."

"But that's not the way things work out, I gather."

"Well, it works okay at first. While our Young Journalist is learning the ropes of his new job. You know how it is."

"And then something happens?"

"Yes. One day, our Young Journalist reads a standard handout from one of the agencies he covers. It's a routine announcement of a contract award to a private consulting firm he's never heard of. And something about it strikes him as funny."

"Funny?"

"Odd. Phony, even. He has a certain instinct about such things. What seems phony and what doesn't. Nothing he can ever put a finger on. Just a feeling."

"Because he grew up in Brooklyn?"

"I don't have to tell you that Brooklyn teaches you a lot about what's real and what's phony."

"Comes with the territory."

"Naturally. But there's another thing. Our Young Journalist knows from experience that the English language is, among other things, one of the greatest con artist tools ever invented."

"Ah."

"You can communicate things in English without ever leaving a word trail. Or, you can use lots of words that sound great but don't actually say anything. It all depends on how clever you are with the language. And what you're trying to accomplish. But I don't need you tell you this."

"You think I'm a journalist all of a sudden?"

"Yeah, sure. What else could I mean?"

"Never mind."

"Anyway, our Young Journalist's very sensitive to this because he's become pretty good at it himself."

"By going to Harvard?"

"After growing up in Brooklyn. Nice mixture of form and content."

"And all this caused our Young Journalist to wonder if the agency handout might be trying to cover up something?"

"Right. I won't bore you with the details because they don't matter. The important thing is, our Young Journalist decides to run with his instincts. Starts making phone calls. Asking innocent-sounding questions. Getting people into conversations where they end up saying more than they originally intended to. Our Young Journalist is quite good at this."

"Why am I not surprised?"

"Yeah. But remember, Elijah. This is just a hypothetical story. To illustrate certain things."

"Of course."

"Anyway, the bottom line is that our Young Journalist decides he's run across a case of fraud involving that contract. Not major fraud because the contract's a small one. But fraud nonetheless. So he takes the story to his editors."

"They're properly impressed?"

"Well, they're certainly impressed by his initiative and insights. They make a big fuss over that. Though they don't think this particular story is big enough to be worth running. But they encourage him to do more of the same."

"Become an Investigative Journalist, in other words."

"More or less. Though they don't use that term."

"Naturally."

"But there's one other thing they tell him."

"What's that?"

"In the nicest possible way, they remind him to provide lots of documentation for his future stories. The newspaper has a big thing about documentation. Everything in a story has to be linked to a documented source. Like a person. Another newspaper story. Some other secondary source. Complete with dates and page numbers. You get the idea."

"Sounds like they want PhD dissertations."

"Pretty much. Which is a real pain for our Young Journalist because his mind doesn't work that way. It goes back to his undergraduate days, when he was too lazy to take notes in class."

"Lazy? I thought he played basketball."

"Of course. Basketball's the ideal game for a lazy man."

"Come on, Wes. You're kidding."

"No, I'm not. Think about it. You don't have to memorize a lot of complicated plays like in football. You don't have to study the elaborate science of getting on base, like in baseball. In basketball, you look for opportunities and run with them. Spur of the moment opportunities."

"Interesting analogy."

"Sure. And accurate. A basketball team is like a jazz combo. Each player has to be ready to take off with his own improvisation on a moment's notice."

"I think you've convinced me."

"Okay. So as an undergraduate, our Young Journalist was too lazy to take notes in class. You know what he did instead?"

"What?"

"First: he did all the assigned reading ahead of time. Religiously. To get a good idea what the lecturer would be talking about. Because most lecturers simply recycle what the readings cover. Second: he listened very carefully in class. Thought about what the lecturer was saying as he went along. Put it into his own words. Made it meaningful. Part of him. Which made memorizing it more or less automatic."

"I guess that's the whole purpose of taking notes in class. So you don't have to memorize."

"Right. But our Young Journalist was too lazy to take notes. Instead, he sat there comfortably in his chair and listened. Listened and thought and remembered. Because his brain worked much faster than his hand. Faster and in a nonlinear manner. Like a computer. Able to randomly access information from the readings or what the lecturer had said half an hour ago. More or less instantly. As needed."

"Novel approach. I wish I'd known about that when I was going to graduate school nights after working all day."

"Which graduate school?"

"Baruch. Part of New York's City University."

"What was your major?"

"Finance. What else?"

"Figures. Sorry, I seem to be getting off the point."

"You were explaining how your hypothetical Young Journalist was struggling with his newspaper's documentation requirements."

"Right. And you can see how these requirements were incompatible with the way his mind worked. Just like in his undergraduate classes, he'd rather listen and think. Not wear himself out taking lots of superficial notes that got in the way of thinking. Be ready to run with a theme, like a jazz musician. Improvise."

"So what was his solution?"

"Again, he drew on his undergraduate experience. In this case, the papers he had to write for his classes. The approach he came up with was to do a lot of reading about the subject. Seemingly, disorganized reading. But his brain did its own organizing. Until he understood the subject in a way that made sense to him. Gave him a point of view for the paper. Which he then proceeded to write as if the subject was part of his own experience rather than something he'd simply read about. Know what I mean?"

"I think so. But didn't he have to present documentation?"

"Oh sure. Lots of footnotes. His professors insisted on that. And his solution was a simple one."

"Yeah?"

"After he wrote the paper, he'd go back to his readings and find stuff he could use as footnotes. Stuff that matched his ideas. Or could be made to match them with the right kind of editing. That way, the final draft of the paper could have lots of footnotes. Which his professors liked to see but never bothered to check out. So he was home free."

"In other words, his shtick was to do enough reading to develop his own understanding of the subject. Then write the paper. Then go back and find enough footnote material to satisfy his professors."

"Right. And he did the same thing when he wrote for the university's student newspaper. That happened to be one of the most prestigious extracurricular activities on campus. And it got him interested in journalism as a career. So after graduation, he managed to get himself a job as a junior reporter for a daily newspaper in a rundown industrial town."

"Like the newspaper you're now working for?"

"They're a dime a dozen around the country, Elijah. So it's nothing special. Anyway, the editor assigned our hypothetical Young Journalist to the police beat. Which none of the more established reporters wanted to cover because it was too routine. You know. The usual bar fights where somebody winds up getting stabbed or shot. Youth gang rumbles over drug sale territories. Muggings. Occasional murders. The endless parade of meaningless street crimes that people think defines urban America."

"And he brought his own special reporter's shtick to this?"

"The police beat was made for it. I mean, all he ever had to write down was the right names and addresses. Who got charged with what crime. Simple facts like that. So he had lots of time to hang out in police precincts. Watch what was going on. Get to know cops and listen to their war stories. Think about what he saw and heard."

"Until he developed his own insights?"

"That was inevitable. He began to see patterns. Like how today's big street mugging related to so many others over the past six months. Until he was able to color each of his stories with insights about the larger picture. Not in any obvious way, of course. But enough so his stories began to present the underlying truths of street crime in a minor industrial town left behind by the rest of America. Truths that meant something rather than facts that meant nothing. If you get the distinction."

"It's hard to miss the way you put it."

"Now just for the record, there's nothing very new about this. It dates back at least to the old tabloid era. Long before reporters started calling themselves 'journalists' and switched from cheap whiskey to white wine. In those days, it wasn't so much a matter of getting the facts correct. The big thing was giving the stories an angle."

"An angle?"

"Like a shtick. Something that made the story stand out. Made it human to readers. Explained things. Want an example?"

"By all means."

"You know the old movie *His Girl Friday*? With Cary Grant and Roz Russell?"

"Directed by Howard Hawks?"

"Right. With everybody talking as fast as possible. Because that fit the popular image of reporters in the tabloid era. Now. Remember a

81

sequence towards the middle of the movie? Hildy Johnson—that's the Roz Russell character—wangles herself an interview with Earl Williams, who's waiting on death row to be executed for shooting a cop."

"I remember."

"She's looking for an angle. One that'll give readers a clear sense of why Earl shot that cop. So she gets him talking about what he was doing before the crime. Finally he remembers listening to a street corner radical haranguing a crowd."

"That's right. The radical was going on about.... what was it? Oh yeah, 'Production for Use.' The old anarchist mantra."

"Which Earl remembers. And Hildy immediately picks up on. She asks him whether that's what could have been going through his mind when he was holding the gun and the cop was coming towards him. Production for Use."

"And Earl doesn't disagree."

"Right. He doesn't really know. But he's willing to let Hildy put words in his mouth. Giving her the angle she needs for her story. To help readers understand how a total nebbish like Earl could wind up shooting a cop."

"And that's the kind of thing our Young Journalist did as a police reporter?"

"Well, it was a little more elegant. And he always tried to put an upscale spin on his angles. Laced them with popular sociology and so on. But yeah, he basically followed Hildy's example. And those crime stories were a big plus that got him admitted to a super-star graduate journalism school."

"Like Columbia?"

"That's as good an example as any."

"Which led to his job in the Washington bureau of that major newspaper."

"Right. Where he had to adapt his police reporting approach to meet his editor's insistence on lots of documentation."

"But I assume he found this easy enough to do."

"Pretty much. It was mostly a matter of writing the story first, then going back and coming up with documentation that seemed convincing. Like statements from people who, quote, couldn't allow their names to be used because they weren't authorized to speak for their agencies, unquote. Needless to say, there were lots of those. Plus citations from stories in obscure small-town newspapers that he could edit to make them say whatever he wanted. Even books sometimes."

"But all made up."

"Well, mostly. Some of it was legit. In any case, he was able to fill up thick file folders full of so-called documentation. All neatly labeled and stacked prominently on his desk. Which delighted his editors."

"And that frees our Young Journalist to do the kind of stories he wants."

"Absolutely. His specialty becomes stories exposing cases of Waste, Fraud, and Abuse in federal agencies. Readers love that sort of thing. In a few cases, the stories are so embarrassing the White House has to force the political hack in charge to resign. So our Young Journalist's career is moving ahead by leaps and bounds."

"Until it all blows up in his face."

"I guess you can call that inevitable. Or maybe he just got careless. In any case, he did a series of stories about problems in a particular agency. Really serious problems, not just penny-ante stuff. So the White House decides that the political hack running the agency has to resign."

"So he can spend more time with his family."

"Not in this case. Just a one-sentence letter. Because it turns out that this political hack has another agenda."

"Which is?"

"He sues the newspaper for libel."

"Ah."

"Big bucks libel."

"Naturally."

"Of course, the newspaper's being sued all the time by the usual cranks and so on. It even keeps a specialty law firm on retainer just to deal with these suits. So nobody pays much attention. Until the law firm examines the Young Journalist's files, as part of its standard due diligence."

"And finds his documentation for the stories in question has a bad smell?"

"It's mostly phony. No basis for a legal defense against libel. So the law firm has no choice but to advise the newspaper to offer the political hack a big settlement. Which it does."

"And the newspaper then hangs our Young Journalist out to dry."

"That's what it comes down to. The newspaper's top management pisses all over its Washington bureau for costing it so much money. By not supervising our Young Journalist properly. Letting him run wild. While the head of the Washington bureau is deeply embarrassed and concerned about keeping his own job. So he pisses all over our Young Journalist."

"Fires him?"

"More than just fires him. Our Young Journalist happens to come from a high-visibility minority group. One that's not exactly overrepresented in the journalism community."

"Of course."

"The head of the Washington bureau felt that he had leaned over backwards to give the Young Journalist every opportunity to do well. Become the kind of star who would reflect well on the bureau. And, quote, A Credit To His Race, unquote."

"Like Joe Louis."

"The old boxer? Is that where that line came from?"

"Sports writers always used that line about Joe Louis. But that was probably before your time."

"Maybe that's why I never made it as a basketball star."

"Is that your excuse?"

"Well, it didn't exactly help that I wrecked my right knee in my last year at Exeter."

"No doubt."

"Anyway, the head of the Washington bureau was convinced our Young Journalist had betrayed him. This filled him with so much outrage he couldn't help swearing vengeance."

"Beyond just firing him?"

"Absolutely. He wanted to drive him out of the profession. Make sure he never worked again. Not in the Eastern Establishment media, at least. So he leaked all kinds of stories to his colleagues in Washington. How our Young Journalist was mentally unstable. Bordering on crazy. Couldn't be trusted. Possibly on drugs. Had his own sick agenda. A threat to the credibility of reporters everywhere."

"Full-court press, in other words."

"Right. Needless to say, there was no shortage of people in the world of journalism ready to gulp down these stories. With predictable results."

"He finds himself unable to get a job on any other newspaper?"

"Not a major one. Or even an also-ran. So he swallows his pride and takes what he can get."

"On a nothing paper in a nowhere town far from the big leagues."

"What else can he do? Become a total Uncle Tom and get a dishwashing job someplace? With half a pint of cheap vodka in his back pocket to help him get through the day? Mine the old cliché for all it's worth?"

* * *

I barely got these words out before I realized that my heart was pounding away like mad as the old rage and frustration boiled up inside me.

So I forced myself to stop babbling, and we sat there in silence. Until I had calmed down enough to suggest that we walk some more. In a voice that could halfway pass for normal.

"I guess I haven't given you a very flattering picture of our Young Journalist," I said finally as we walked across the grassy area."

"Oh, I don't know," Elijah said.

"I mean, it's not as if he was involved in your kind of Insider Trading and didn't hurt anybody. He hurt lots of people."

"Who?"

"Well, the people who believed in him, for example. People who did favors to help his career. They must have gotten hurt."

"Maybe. On the other hand, he may be in better company than you think."

"Yeah? How?"

"You know about the scriptures?"

"What scriptures?"

"The Bible. The Books of Moses. The Old Testament. Whatever you want to call them."

"I don't see the connection."

"You know where the scriptures came from?"

"Not really."

"From people like your Young Journalist. Who saw fundamental truths about things. Made up stories to illustrate these truths. And put together whatever documentation they needed to get people's attention."

"Sorry. I'm having trouble following you."

"Look, Wes. Every society has its myths and fables. People accept them as illustrating important truths without worrying too much about their factual accuracy."

"Like George Washington and the cherry tree?"

"That's one example. Probably didn't actually happen. But that doesn't matter to most Americans. The important thing is, it illustrates an essential truth about an historical figure who was crucial to establishing the thirteen colonies as an independent nation."

"Okay."

"In fact, the basic *idea* of George Washington has become so universally accepted that a lot of contemporary historians informally refer to Ho Chi Min as 'the Asian George Washington.' Saves a lot of tiresome explaining because it immediately makes clear what Ho was all about."

"That much I can understand. Despite the obvious irony."

"Never mind ironies. Myths and fables aren't concerned with ironies.

Otherwise, we could find ourselves referring to George Washington as 'the American Ho Chi Min.' Just to cloud the issue."

"That'll be the day."

"Now most people in a society accept its myths and fables without asking a lot of questions. But those who make their livings as professional intellectuals often stake their entire careers on asking questions. Like how certain myths and fables actually got started. This can open up some serious cans of worms. Especially in societies that have continuous histories measured in centuries."

"You mean, societies whose myths and fables started out as stories told around the proverbial campfires."

"That's it exactly. Jewish society is an example. It claims to be at least five thousand years old, give or take. And that's important. Among other things, for better or worse its myths and fables laid the groundwork for Christianity. Mostly worse, if you accept the argument that Christianity has set the record for inflicting more misery on the human race than any other religion."

"I guess that's true."

"Admittedly, Islamic fundamentalism seems to be running hard to catch up. It's already destroyed the great Arab civilization that gave the world its modern number system. I mean, can you imagine trying to add and subtract using Roman numerals?"

"Pardon me for asking, Elijah. But isn't your Jewish chauvinism showing?"

"The point is, Jewish society's so old its myths and fables predate the ability to write."

"You're talking about the so-called Oral Tradition?"

"Right. That's where these myths and fables got started. Among glib talkers telling stories about past heroes like Abraham and Noah and Moses to anyone who would listen. Stories that got passed down from one generation to the next. With a certain amount of inevitable editing along the way."

"Why inevitable?"

"So each storyteller could make a particular story reflect his own shtick. Illustrate the moral lesson he wanted to impress people with. Make the story more entertaining so he'd be invited to more free dinners."

"You're embarrassing me."

"Sorry. I was just trying to make my point clear."

"It's okay. I was only kidding."

"Anyway, you see how the process works. I mean, there's no evidence people like Abraham, Noah, Moses, and the others actually existed. The stories about each of them are more likely mixtures of stories originally about a lot of separate people. But really clever storytellers combined and streamlined them as happening to a single person. Because they found this helped emphasize their particular shtick. Not to mention making for better dinner entertainment."

"Like Margaret Mitchell writing *Gone With the Wind* by mixing to-gether fairy tales she'd heard from her grandparents and their friends about how the Old South was ruined by the Civil War and Reconstruction?"

"Sure. And telling the whole story from the perspective of Scarlett O'Hara. Who happens to be an especially compelling person. But no more real historically than Moses."

"Aren't you leaving out the question of divine inspiration?"

"You're talking about two different things. The inspiration part has to do with how you take various stories and combine them into some-thing you claim is the life of Scarlett O'Hara. Or Moses."

"And the divine part?"

"That's just a marketing ploy. You convince people that Scarlett O'Hara—or Moses—was a real person by citing God as your source. In a world riddled by fear and ignorance, who's going to challenge that?"

"I suppose it makes a certain amount of sense. In a twisted way."

"Sure it does. The problem is, different storytellers have different shticks. So the stories are always being edited. Revised. Changed completely even. Until the day comes when they're written down. Then you have to decide which oral version to use for each story. Or maybe you finesse the question by combining several versions and trying to smooth over the inconsistencies. And, of course, you inevitably have your own shtick to emphasize. Which is bound to be different from your grandfather's. So it goes."

"And that's how we ended up with the scriptures?"

"Doesn't it make sense?"

"Well...."

"Look. Let me try another example. Maybe this will work better for you."

"Okay."

"This one may seem a little far-out. So bear with me."

"If it's that far-out, maybe we should sit for a while."

"Sure."

* * *

We sat down on another bench under shade trees. Elijah seemed especially anxious to tell me this new story and began talking as soon as we were settled.

"You're familiar with the early parts of Genesis?"

"You mean, God creating the earth in six days and all that?"

"Right. This particular story begins with God busy populating the earth with living creatures."

"Like Adam and Eve."

"Not yet. He's still working on the other animals. And he realizes he hasn't yet developed a really effective serial killer. I mean, he's already done the shark and the barracuda and the piranha. But these are sea creatures. And he wants his ultimate serial killer to be a creature that roams the earth's land areas."

"But why a serial killer?"

"I told you last time. God's a Nazi."

"Come on, Elijah. I thought you were kidding about that."

"You'd rather I carry on like those death camp inmates? Telling each other the commandant is really a very decent guy at heart?"

89

"I should have known better than to raise the issue."

"Anyway, God marshaled all his creative powers and set to work. And after much extensive R&D, he finally came up with the greatest serial killer of all. Which we call … the cat."

"The cat? A serial killer?"

"Have you ever seen a cat capture a mouse or bird or baby squirrel? And proceed to torture it to death by slow degrees as his eyes glitter with sadistic glee? Then start hunting for the next victim for his terrifying claws and teeth? His whole life seems to be devoted to torture and murder. At least while he's awake."

"You must really hate cats."

"On the contrary. They're my favorite animal."

"But…. "

"I live with five cats at home. Each one of them came in off the street as strays, full of arrogance and attitude. Making it clear that my family and I were being adopted, so we'd better get used to it. And in the process, handing me a golden opportunity to change their destiny."

"Change their destiny?"

"As serial killers. By lavishing them with lots of love and rich food. I've succeeded with two of them so far. They won't even bother going after flies or cockroaches now. Their killer instincts seem to have entirely disappeared. So in my small way, I've managed to frustrate God's will."

"You'll pardon me for saying so, Elijah. But this sounds a little crazy."

"I can see why you might think so. But you may change your mind when you hear the rest of this Genesis story."

"Okay. I'll reserve judgment."

"Now once God had created the first cat, he immediately realized that this was his masterpiece among the earth's living creatures. So he proceeded to develop many more versions of cats. Ranging from tiny felines of little more than a few pounds each all the way up to nine-hundred pound Siberian Tigers, the most fearsome animals on earth. All of them endowed with the physical and instinctive characteristics needed to function as world-champion serial killers. And when God had finished this monumental undertaking, he was so pleased with what he'd done he decided to award himself a prize."

"You've got to be kidding."

"You don't think God has an ego?"

"All right. If you insist. What was the prize?"

"The prize was Eve."

"Eve? You mean, Adam's Eve?"

"Well, Adam wasn't around yet. Just Eve. A remarkable creature who embodied all the grace and mystery inherent in cats. And after admiring this self-awarded prize for a while, God placed Eve in the earth's Garden of Eden for safekeeping while he went off to clean up some loose ends on the planet Jupiter."

"This gets better and better."

"But Eve, like all women, had her own ideas about things. And one of those ideas involved having a bigger, stronger, more-or-less mirror image of herself. To take out the garbage, mow Eden's lawns, bring her armloads of fresh fruit, and fill her nights with ecstasy. So all by herself, while God's back was turned, Eve conceived Adam and brought him into the world to be her companion. End of story."

"I can see why you said it might sound a little far-out."

"But when you think about it, doesn't it seem consistent with what many scientists tell us actually happened when human beings first began appearing on earth? As gradually evolving mutations to which less evolved females gave birth? In metaphorical terms, of course."

"I guess so."

"Certainly more consistent than the traditional version. With God creating Adam first. Then taking one of Adam's ribs to create Eve. I mean, come on. What kind of fairy-tale horseshit is that?"

"But why is the traditional version the only one we ever hear?"

"Ah. Good question. Who wrote Genesis?"

"I don't know, various prophets and scribes?"

91

"Right. All of whom were men."

"Yeah. So?"

"So being men, weren't they instinctively terrified of women? Who remain forever beyond their understanding?"

"That's certainly a possibility."

"Look at the record. Haven't men always used their greater physical size and strength to develop male chauvinist societies in a vain attempt to make women seem less intimidating? Denying them basic human rights? Restricting their freedom?"

"Abusing them physically."

"Why not? But always seeking justification in the actions of God. Who they define as the ultimate male sports hero. And who, among other things, imposed on women the increasing physical discomfort of pregnancy. Culminating in the screaming agony of giving birth. So if it's okay for God to abuse women...."

"That's pretty extreme. But I see what you're getting at."

"In which case, wouldn't an Eve-first version of Genesis be a real problem for these men? Enough of a problem for them to develop their own version? An Adam-first version? And then invent a lot of fairy tales to blame women for all the troubles in the world? Remember what they insisted Adam said when God asked him why he had eaten the forbidden fruit from the Tree of Knowledge? 'The woman made me do it.' Right?"

"And these are the men you think I'm in such good company with?"

"They gave us the scriptures, didn't they?"

"A collection of silly fairy tales, to use your own term."

"Admittedly. But they also contained some profound truths. Moral truths. Presented in the form of fables striking enough to stick in the craws of the people they were trying to influence."

"Yeah, I suppose so."

"And the originators of these fables didn't let themselves be held back by concerns about factual documentation. Because the moral truths were what mattered. Not mundane facts that might be nothing more than matters of opinion anyway. Just like in your newspaper stories."

"Okay, you win. Maybe I'm in better company than I thought. But if push came to shove on the matter of credibility, at least they could claim that God whispered these truths in their ears."

"God can take many forms. A burning bush. Or a published book by a recognized maven. A vivid lighting storm. Or a Deep Throat who meets you late at night in a parking garage. Even a mysterious somebody who can't let his name be used because he isn't authorized to speak for his agency. Take your pick."

"You mean, we make God up as we go along?"

"That's putting it too crudely. Let's just say that inspiration can have many sources."

"So God may really be whispering in our ears?"

"Or maybe we're whispering in his. Assuming he's paying any attention."

* * *

We went inside for lunch, and the food was just as bad as it had been the previous week. But I shouldn't have been surprised since it tasted like warmed-over versions of last week's food.

By the time we finished eating, the room was getting crowded and noisy. So we went back outside and resumed walking.

"I want to come back to something," Elijah said after a moment.

"What."

"In your transportation notes, you talked about applying capitalist principles to roadways."

"I got that from you. Plus from some of the stuff I read on the Internet."

"It's a popular concept these days. Price access to roadways the same way that we price access to seats in a movie theater. But it's important that you understand the alternative."

"You mean, operating roads like they were public parks?"

93

"It goes farther than that. Let me tell you a story."

"Naturally."

"Oh, this isn't one of my stories."

"No?"

"I heard it from an Irish kid when I was in graduate school. He was from Hell's Kitchen."

"Tough neighborhood."

"Used to be before it started getting gentrified and people insisted on calling it Clinton. Anyway, this Irish kid wanted to be a writer."

"What was he doing at Baruch if he wanted to be a writer?"

"He thought a writer should know something about money, since that's what makes the world go round. He was an extension student and enrolled in the same economics class I was taking. That's how I met him. We got friendly enough to start eating dinner together in the cafeteria after class. And that's when I began to realize what a remarkable mind he had."

"How so?"

"Irish writers are often touched by a certain magic that eludes the rest of us."

"Like Betty Smith?"

"Who?"

"She wrote *A Tree Grows in Brooklyn*."

"Oh, right. Actually, she was of German descent."

"You're kidding."

"No, it's true. But she grew up in the Irish ghetto of Williamsburg before World War I. That's what she wrote about. So I guess she qualifies as at least proxy-Irish. With that same touch of magic. You read her book?"

"Most kids in my neighborhood did."

"Interesting."

"It was like she was writing about all of us. Except for skin color. Which we forgot about after the first few pages."

"A definitive tale of Brooklyn ghetto life. That's why it's such a masterpiece."

"I've read it a few times. There's always something new in it."

"Anyway, this Irish kid from Hell's Kitchen was writing a novel when I knew him. He used to talk about it while we were eating dinner. Its title was *The Island of Plenty*."

"Nice title. Was it ever published?"

"Unfortunately, it never even got written. He was run down and killed by a car a block from his apartment a few months after we met. Random accident as far as anybody could tell."

"My God.... The same thing happened to my mother."

"Really?"

"She was walking along Madison Avenue, near where she worked. And a taxi driver trying to beat the light lost control of his cab. Ran up on the sidewalk and plowed into a group of pedestrians. One of them was my mother."

"I'm sorry. She was...?"

"Killed instantly, as far as I know."

"Just like the Irish kid. But it tells you something, doesn't it."

"What do you mean?"

"One of the great fears of New Yorkers is some stranger coming out of nowhere to kill or injure them. Of course, the probability of that happening is very low. But if it does happen, the stranger's more likely to be behind the wheel of a car than the barrel of a gun."

"I never thought of it that way."

"We're always afraid of the wrong things. The Irish kid's big fear was getting caught in the crossfire of a gang fight in his neighborhood. It was Westies turf."

"Yeah, I've heard about the Westies. Throwback to the old days of fighting street gangs."

"Extremely violent."

"You said the Irish kid told you a lot about his novel."

"The beginning, anyway. It starts on a luxury cruise ship. Nearly a thousand passengers and crew are sailing an unnamed ocean far from any known land. But the ship gets caught in a violent storm. Gets blown way off course. Finally hits an uncharted reef and begins to sink. Fortunately, the ship has enough lifeboats to hold everybody."

"No *Titanic*, in other words."

"Right. Everybody's saved. And there's this handy island nearby for them to land on. Fair-sized island. About as big as Manhattan. And subtropical, with lots of fruit trees. Small animals like rabbits. Lush meadows where something that looks like wild corn grows. Streams full of fish, and so on. But no people."

"Uninhabited?"

"Uninhabited. Uncharted. Far from the shipping lanes. So there's no reason to expect anybody's going to be able to find them."

"They don't have radios? You know, two-way radios so they can send out distress calls?

"All that went down with the ship."

"So they're marooned."

"Like a big group of Robinson Crusoes. And it looks like they're going to stay that way for the foreseeable future."

"Okay."

"Now after a few days of exploring the island, it's clear they're not going to starve. Because they're marooned on what's truly an island of plenty. But it's also clear that they can't expect to be rescued. Certainly not anytime soon. So what's their next step?"

"Try to organize something like a society? To guide their lives?"

"Right. And there's lots of discussion about what kind of society. At first, it's mostly based on the idea of everybody taking care of himself. You know. Stake out a parcel of land. Feed yourself with fruit from the trees on your land. Maybe cultivate some of that wild corn if there's enough space. Build yourself some sort of hut to live in."

"Every man for himself, in other words."

"In effect. But it has a more sophisticated twist than the usual jungle example. For instance. there's this guy going around telling everybody who'll listen about how they can trade with each other. You know. Somebody whose parcel of land has lots of fruit trees but no room to grow corn can trade his excess fruit to somebody whose land parcel has relatively few fruit trees but lots of space to grow corn."

"Fruit in exchange for corn."

"And vice versa. So both are better off."

"Sounds like the guy must have been an economics professor back home."

"How did you guess? Anyway, he insists people will automatically start trading with each other. Because trading's a natural human instinct. It doesn't have to be organized in any formal way. Just let nature take its course. And it'll leave everybody better off. Or so the professor claims."

"Market capitalism. Straight out of Adam Smith, isn't it?"

"Pretty much. And there's lots of real-world evidence this is what human beings naturally gravitate to if you throw them together in situations where they have to sort things out for themselves. Each person pursues his own self-interest, as the saying goes. And the end result benefits society as a whole."

"Do you really believe that?"

"Not quite. Anyway, just because something's natural doesn't automatically make it good. Take cancer, for example."

"Cancer?"

"Or diseases in general. Pain and suffering. The big eat the small and are eaten by the still-bigger. Death on a grand scale. God's filled the universe with all kinds of natural things we find morally abominable."

"God again."

"Or Ma Nature. If you find the traditional male sports hero concept of the Deity too chauvinistic. It's all the same."

"You're saying God's bisexual?"

"Why not? Can't you picture him dressed up in a cocktail gown and high heels? We've had at least one mayor who did that. Not to mention a famous cardinal."

"I thought a Gestapo uniform would be more his speed."

"Can't God have more than a single clothes fetish?"

"Did the Irish kid get involved with this kind of religious stuff in his book?"

"Sorry, Wes. That's just me editorializing again."

"I figured."

"The Irish kid's concern was the alternatives we have to choose between in organizing human society."

"One of which is what we might call Natural Capitalism."

"Right."

"And the other?"

"Ah. Here's where his book gets really interesting. On the one hand, he's got this economics professor running around pitching Natural Capitalism to anybody who'll listen. But he's also got somebody else pitching something quite different. A society built around human cooperation rather than competition."

"I guess that was inevitable."

"Maybe so. The idea was that everybody should work together instead of pursuing their own self-interest. Cooperate in ways that assure the best life for all concerned. With all the land on the island owned by society as a whole rather than individually in separate parcels. One for all and all for one."

"No 'I' in team."

"Absolutely. And the person pitching this concept happened to be a very articulate and compelling woman. Who was accompanied by a group of equally articulate and compelling women."

"Okay."

"Do you see anything significant about this?"

"Significant?"

"About her being a woman."

"Significant how?"

"Ever watch nature films on PBS?"

"Occasionally."

"Ever see any about lions?"

"I suppose so."

"Do you recognize the link?"

"What link?"

"With the person pitching the idea of a cooperative society. The fact that she's a woman rather than a man."

"No, I...."

"Come on, Wes. You're almost there. What is it about lions that really stands out?"

"Stands out? Oh, wait. Are you talking about the way female lions form what you might call sisterhoods?"

"You've got it. Now go ahead and run with it."

"Let's see. Female lions work together cooperatively. They hunt together. Share the food they catch. Raise their cubs communally. Take care of each other. Protect each other. Form a true community."

"Right. And the key word is female. They're the ones who organize these cooperative societies. Males aren't involved, except for reproductive purposes."

"Are you saying women are more likely to prefer cooperative societies than men?"

"It's an interesting point. There must be a reason why the Irish kid choose to have a woman push the argument in favor of a cooperative society. Unfortunately, I never got around to asking him before he got killed. But you have to admit, it seems credible to have a woman take the lead."

"I agree. What happened next?"

"Well, the concept had great appeal to most of the people. Cooperation. All for one and one for all. Much better than leaving everybody to fend for himself."

"So that's what they adopted?"

"No."

"No?"

"Most of them thought it was a great idea. In theory, that is. But when it came to deciding how to put it into practice, there were all kinds of problems. Like, how do you actually organize such a society? Who makes the day-to-day decisions for the group? That sort of thing."

"They couldn't come to some sort of agreement?"

"All they could do was debate what amounted to abstractions. Possibly this. Possibly that. You know how these things go. So in the end...."

"They adopted Natural Capitalism by default?"

"That's about it. Because Natural Capitalism doesn't require any complicated agreements about who should make decisions for the group. Everybody just does his own thing, and it all sort of works out. Most of the time, anyway. Certainly in the beginning."

"Sounds pretty messy."

"Only on the surface. Like Canal Street on a busy day. But under the surface, there may be more structure than people realize. In fact, some economists insist that markets tend to organize themselves."

"Is that what the Irish kid thought?"

"I don't think he ever got that far. Remember, he was a novelist. Or at least. that's the way his mind seemed to work. His main interest was telling stories about people. Not proving or disproving social science theories."

"So what happened after his people choose Natural Capitalism by default?"

"His intention was to tell a series of stories about people responding to the consequences of that decision. Some of them prosper. Grow rich and powerful because of their ability to exploit the free-market process. End up running the society. Others fall by the wayside. Most just muddle along. Until the Revolution."

"He saw Natural Capitalism inevitably leading to revolution?"

"That seemed to be his general vision. Because it couldn't help evolving into Monopoly Capitalism. A society where a few people, by hook or crook, gain control of everything that matters on the island. Including the market process, which ceases to be free."

"And sooner or later, the Proletariat gets sick of this and rebels? Uses their superior numbers to overthrow the Elite by force and take control?"

"One of the classic stories of human history."

"And the Revolution implements a different model for the society?"

"Of course."

"The Cooperative model?"

"Their version of it, anyway. With all decisions for society made by the leaders of the Revolution. Who become the new Elite and end up making the same mistakes that the old one did."

"Fidel Castro all over again. Couldn't the Irish kid conceive of some kind of middle ground?"

"The Irish aren't exactly famous for going after the middle ground."

"So in his eyes, the people on that island of plenty were doomed."

"Probably. But as you've probably realized by now, he thought of his book as a modern fable."

"I guess so."

"And fables aren't all that concerned with Reality. Certainly not in the sense that *A Tree Grows in Brooklyn* is."

"Maybe that's why people stopped paying attention to fables."

"Could be."

"Well, the literary world may have lost an interesting book when the Irish kid got killed by that car."

"Not just the literary world."

* * *

As I was driving back to my apartment later, it occurred to me that there might never have been an Irish kid from Hell's Kitchen at all. Elijah may simply have been following the advice of George Burns, who knew so much about getting people's attention that he was a natural to play God in his final movies.

"If you really want to get good laughs from your latest joke, don't let the audience think you made it up yourself. Tell them you heard it

from Groucho Marx or Bob Hope. They'll find it a lot easier to laugh if you do that."

Just like me in Washington.

Except for the laughs.

Chapter Three

Enter the Dragon Lady

Late next Saturday afternoon, I got back from my weekly trip to the supermarket to find a message from Elijah's wife on my answering machine asking me to phone her when I got in. She left the name and number of a motel. And I noticed that the motel had the same area code as Elijah's prison.

"Hello, Wesley," she said after I dialed the motel and they put me through to her. "Thank you for returning my call so quickly."

"Just got back. You're here in California?"

"I fly out most Fridays to spend Saturdays with Elijah."

"Oh."

"Anyway, I'm afraid he won't be able to see you tomorrow. He's under the weather and they have him in the prison infirmary."

"Anything serious?"

"Just a touch of food poisoning. I visited him today and he seems fine. But they want to keep him in the infirmary for the rest of the weekend."

"Okay."

"But he looks forward to seeing you next Sunday as usual."

"Yes, fine."

"Meanwhile, you and I could have lunch tomorrow. If you'd like."

"Sure. That would be great."

"Good. Why don't you meet me at my motel around twelve thirty."

"Okay. Let me write down the address."

* * *

I reached the motel a few minutes early on Sunday and found Susan waiting for me in the lounge area next to the registration counter.

We had talked on the phone often enough in recent weeks to be on a first-name basis. But that scarcely prepared me for the stunning Asian beauty who glided towards me. With an elegant smile lighting up a face that clearly belonged in a major art museum.

Could that be why she looked so familiar in a way I couldn't quite define?

"Good to meet you at last," she said in a smooth mezzo voice as she shook my hand. "Elijah's told me so much about you. You've obviously made quite an impression on him."

"He's a very remarkable man."

"You don't know the half of it."

"Is he better today?"

"Oh, yes. I was with him all morning, feeding him chicken soup."

"Jewish penicillin. That figures."

"In this case, Chinese penicillin. From a local restaurant. It always works when he gets these attacks of food poisoning."

"It happens often?"

"Well, more than I'd like. The prison kitchen isn't exactly a paragon of sanitary practices. That's why they insist on calling what he has an intestinal virus. They think it lets them off the hook."

"No doubt."

"Anyway, now that I've managed to ruin your appetite, why don't we decide where to have lunch?"

"I see you're something of a wit. Did you get that from Elijah?"

"Could be. But I come from a Cantonese family. Elijah thinks Cantonese and Yiddish share a common tradition of earthy wit."

"He speaks Cantonese, too?"

"I taught him. While he was teaching me Yiddish. Part of the grand plot we developed to convince our families to accept our relationship."

"Sounds like an interesting story."

"It was to us."

"I'd like to hear it."

"Let's decide about lunch first."

"Okay."

"Do you like Chinese food?"

"Didn't Elijah tell you I grew up in Brooklyn?"

"I should have known."

"Or you could say you were just being polite."

"I see I'm going to have to watch out for you. Anyway, I've managed to find a surprisingly good Chinese restaurant downtown."

"Sounds good to me."

"We can go in my car, since I know the way."

"Okay."

* * *

The restaurant was on a side street near the railroad tracks. Nondescript outside and in. The large round tables in the center were filled with Chinese men in open-necked shirts eating large plates of steaming food with stamped aluminum forks.

"That's one of the two ways you can tell a restaurant's main clientele is Chinese workers," Susan whispered, nudging me.

"What do you mean?"

"Notice they're all eating with forks and spoons. Not a chopstick in sight."

"Oh."

"Just like the restaurants along Canal Street in Manhattan."

"I've often wondered about that."

"There are several small apparel factories nearby. They work seven days a week. This is where many of their workers eat lunch."

"What's the other way you can tell if a restaurant's main clientele is Chinese?"

"They only serve white rice. No brown rice. It's a cultural thing."

"Like Europeans insisting on white bread?"

"Yes. Interesting, isn't it. Especially since so many educated Americans prefer brown rice and dark bread. Or say they do."

An elderly waiter in a white apron approached us with a welcoming smile. Susan said something to him in Cantonese, and he seated us in a booth along the side wall. She motioned to him to wait, then turned to me.

"Shall I order for both of us?" she said. "I know most of their specialties."

"Fine."

"Is there anything in particular you'd rather not eat?"

"Well, no chicken feet."

She laughed brightly. Then turned back to the waiter and began a lengthy conversation with him in Cantonese. Finally he nodded, scribbled some Chinese characters on his order pad, left the pad's top sheet on our table, and walked back to the kitchen.

"Will they bring us chopsticks or do we have to ask?" I said.

"Oh, don't worry about that. I always come prepared."

She opened her shoulder bag and took out a flat wooden box about eight inches long. Laid it on the table and opened it. Inside were two sets of jade green chopsticks inlaid with Chinese characters. She handed one set to me.

"Don't let the color fool you," she said. "They're not real jade."

"They look very elegant."

"Elijah picked them up on a trip to Hong Kong a few years ago. At the Jade Market in Kowloon. That's the best place to buy fake jade items. You can tell they're fake because of the low prices."

"Real jade is expensive?"

"You have no idea. And so easy to counterfeit. That's why you must never buy real jade unless you're sure that the jeweler is truly kosher."

"Kosher?"

"You know what I mean. See this pendant I'm wearing?"

It was hanging from a thin gold chain around her neck. She slipped the tip of a chopstick under it and held it forward so I could see it more clearly. It was a flat green carving of a seated cat, about the size of a quarter.

"That's real jade?" I said, catching a whiff of her exotic perfume that made my head spin.

"Yes. Burmese jade. Do you see the difference? Compared to the chopstick, I mean."

"To be honest, no. But I'm scarcely an expert."

"That's the whole point. Even an expert can't tell the difference just by looking. You need ultraviolet light and other specialized equipment. That's why most of the jade tourists buy in upscale Hong Kong stores is fake. To be sure of buying real jade, you have to be introduced to the store owner by someone he knows. Assuming the someone isn't a shill."

"But Kowloon's Jade Market is different?"

"Oh, yes. Because the stall operators make it clear by their low prices that they're only offering jade reproductions."

"Counterfeits, in other words."

"Well, 'reproductions' sounds better. That's all they sell. Reproductions of jade, pearls, old silver coins...."

"Silver coins?"

"Old ones. From the days when Chinese currency was based on silver. In Hong Kong, too. Silver coins the size of U.S. dollars. From Mexico, Peru, Spain, other European countries occasionally. The whole Chinese commercial world was linked to silver as money. You should see the magnificent reproductions of silver coins Elijah bought in the Kowloon Jade Market when he got these chopsticks."

"He collects coins?"

"Anything to do with money."

"Why am I not surprised?"

* * *

The waiter brought us a large pot of hot tea. Then noticed Susan's chopsticks, said something to her in Cantonese, and returned a few moments later with a second pot.

"Why did he bring us two pots of tea?" I asked her.

"The second pot is for washing our chopsticks."

"Washing them?"

"Old Chinese custom. Or ritual, if you prefer. I'll do the honors. Give me your chopsticks."

I watched as she dipped one end of a paper napkin in the second teapot, washed down my chopsticks, and handed them back to me. She did the same with her chopsticks.

Then she poured out two cups of tea from the first pot and handed one cup to me.

"Let this cool for a few minutes," she said. "I think you'll find it quite different from the little bags you buy at the supermarket."

"I can imagine."

I took the steaming tea cup from her and placed it on the table next to my chopsticks.

"Elijah's concerned about you," she said abruptly.

"Me? Why?"

"He thinks you're being too hard on yourself. About that Washington business."

"Well, he told me I'm no worse than the guys who wrote the Bible."

"Could he be right?"

"I'd like to think so. But it's more complicated."

"Complicated how? If you don't mind my asking."

"No, that's all right. It's complicated because I was born with a gold spoon in my mouth."

"Don't you mean a silver spoon?"

"No. A silver spoon is when you're born into a rich WASP family with all the right social connections. So you're a trust fund baby who's guaranteed to inherit all kinds of things without having to work for them. Like unearned wealth. A nice living in whatever profession you choose. Admission to an Ivy League university without regard to your school grades or SAT scores. Club memberships. Ready-made friends with the same background. You name it."

"And a gold spoon?"

"That means you're born the kind of person everybody automatically likes. Wants to do things for. Makes excuses for you if you slip up. Plus you're born with an instinctive sense of how to exploit these benefits. In a supposedly upward mobile society like America, that's worth a lot more than any silver spoon. You can start without a dollar in your pocket, and you'll be a success in life. Guaranteed."

"Interesting. I've never heard it explained that way before."

"Look at me, Susan. I'm tall and well-coordinated, physically and mentally. I managed to turn myself into a pretty decent basketball player in the local school yard. Which made me a dime a dozen in Bed-Stuy. So what's the best a guy like that can normally look forward to?"

"Tell me."

"Maybe get recruited by Lincoln High School where I could refine my basketball skills in a high-visibility sports environment. If I was lucky and helped my team win the city's PSAL championship, get an athletic scholarship to one of those universities down south you only hear about during basketball season. Keep my fingers crossed that maybe I'd get drafted by an NBA team, where the serious money is. But that's a real long shot. So I'd probably end up coming back home with a meaningless degree in Physical Education. Looking for a way to make a decent living that was at least reasonably legal."

"Elijah's right. You really are hard on yourself."

"No, I'm not. Because the guy I just described isn't me. He wasn't born with my gold spoon. And that makes all the difference."

"Does it?"

"Look. I didn't end up at a Southern basketball college. As Elijah must have told you, I went to Harvard. And before that, Exeter. Not Lincoln High School. Why? Because I was born with that gold spoon in my mouth. You want the details?"

"They might help."

At that point, the waiter arrived with our food. Two large platters of beef and bean sprouts with brown gravy, steaming away on a high mound of white rice.

"You probably expected something more elaborate," Susan said. "But once you taste it, you'll understand."

"I'm sure...."

"This is the kind of food working-class Chinese live on. In Hong Kong as well as the United States. Simple and hearty. Let it cool for a few minutes so the flavors have a chance to mix."

"It smells wonderful. I can hardly wait to dig in."

"Patience, young man."

* * *

I couldn't very well just sit there staring at my platter of food. Especially since Susan's oddly familiar beauty was so unsettling. So I cleared my throat and decided to plunge ahead with the conversation.

"When I was growing up in Bed-Stuy, my mother worked as a house-keeper for an aristocratic couple who lived on their inherited wealth in a townhouse on East 73rd Street in Manhattan," I said, trying to sound as if I was writing a term paper for a sociology class back at Harvard.

"Husband and wife?"

"Yes. Both loaded. So there wasn't any question of having to work for a living. They could devote all their time to the right kind of social events. You know, hosting fund-raising receptions for the Metropolitan Museum and the New York Public Library and the Metropolitan Opera. That sort of thing. Fashionable nonprofit institutions whose boards they were on, and who live off Manhattan's super-rich."

"What about children?"

"No, all their charities were culture-related."

"I meant, did they have children?"

"Oh. None that I ever heard about. Just socially fashionable charities. And me."

"You?"

"I used to go to their house a lot in the afternoons to bring my mother home. So she wouldn't have to ride the subway alone."

"Like a good son. And you got to know the couple?

"That's where my gold spoon went to work."

"Ah. Your gold spoon."

"It automatically made people like me. Like that East Side couple. I was able to make them think I was somebody special. Just by talking to them when I went to their house to pick up my mother. Saying the right things in the right way. Something that was second nature to me. They seemed to enjoy talking to me."

"I can imagine."

"Obviously, it helped that they were flaming rich liberals who wanted to see black people have a chance to rise from the ghetto. Because of my gold spoon, I was able to make them think I was a special kind of black guy. Who could make them all proud, given half a chance. They virtually adopted me. Especially after Mom died."

"So they arranged to send you to Harvard."

"Exeter first. It was the guy's prep school. He made a few phone calls to get me in. Paid for everything, including the right kind of wardrobe from J. Press. Whatever I needed. They told me I should consider myself one of the family."

"And you learned fast."

"You bet. After Exeter, Harvard was more or less automatic. Followed by a master's from Columbia's journalism school."

"All because the couple liked you."

"Well, it did occur to me that the guy might have had a thing for my mother."

"Ah."

"Like many women from Trinidad, Mom was very good-looking. And no dummy. They depended on her to manage their entire household. No small accomplishment for a day worker."

"Day worker?"

"She usually went there early in the morning and left at the end of the afternoon. And I suppose that's something I could have wondered about. No live-in servants for such a large house."

"Interesting."

"Just day workers like my mother. A cook. A daily cleaning staff supplied by a commercial cleaning company. Mom arranged all that. Along with a catering service for their receptions. Plus a black car service to drive them where they wanted to go."

"Everything outsourced."

"That's about it. Anyway, this turned out to be an example of how my gold spoon made all the difference in my life. And what did I ever do to deserve it? It wasn't as if I was being rewarded for being some sort of moral paragon in a previous life. Or in this life, for that matter. Simply a matter of good luck."

"How refreshing."

"Refreshing?"

"Most people insist on attributing their success to lots of hard work. And sacrifice. The usual virtues. Good luck is what makes other people successful."

"I don't try to kid myself. Not now."

"After you blew it in Washington?"

"If you want to put it crudely."

"The question is, did you blow it on purpose or was it just an accident?"

"What are you, some kind of psychologist?"

"Actually, I'm an economist."

"Is that why you wound up married to Elijah?"

"You mean, did it give us interests in common?"

"Something like that."

"No, it was more elemental."

"Elemental how?"

"I thought he smelled good. Better than any man I'd ever known."

I couldn't think of a suitable response to such an earthy revelation. So

I finessed it by digging into the plate of food in front of me. Which tasted fantastic. Unexpectedly so, considering how far I was from Canal Street.

*　*　*

We ate in silence for a long minute or two.

"This food's terrific," I said finally, to break the silence.

"I thought you'd like it. By the way, I'm familiar with the standard theory."

"About what?"

"You know. How women are supposedly attracted to men who seem able to give them superior children."

"Oh, that."

"When they're adolescents and their sensibilities are still undeveloped, that means physically superior. Handsome. Muscular. Sports-hero types."

"Yeah."

"But when they get older and more sophisticated about things, 'superior' means able to make money. Lots of money. That's what matters most in our society."

"So the old cliché about the beautiful young blond hanging on the arm of the ancient billionaire…?"

"She's not necessarily a gold digger at all. She may truly be sexually attracted to him. Because of his obvious ability to make lots of money. And give her children who can make lots of money."

"That certainly applies to Elijah."

"But not when we first met. He was just another Jewish guy from Brooklyn going for his MBA at Baruch nights while working full-time. It wasn't until ten years later that he got into investment banking and began making serious money."

"Are you saying the standard theory went out the window as far as the two of you were concerned?"

"I told you. He smelled good to me. And he thought I smelled good. Very mystical, if you want to get poetic about it."

113

"But how…?"

"I'd been an undergraduate math major at Queens College. Mainly because it seemed more promising than being a cashier in my uncle's restaurant in Flushing. In my senior year, a guy I was dating told me economics was becoming increasingly math-oriented. That sounded like a better alternative than teaching math in the public schools. So I went to graduate school at Baruch, hoping I could make it all the way to an economics PhD."

"Where you met Elijah."

"We had a class together. Sat next to each other, in fact. When he found out I'd been a math major, he asked if I could teach him calculus so he could bypass regular math classes and move directly into advanced courses in finance."

"He learned quickly?"

"You have no idea. He's very bright and disciplined. In less than a month, I had him solving first order differential equations."

"Sounds pretty hairy."

"It usually takes a solid year of calculus to get that far. We'd meet in an empty classroom so I could use the blackboard. That's when I realized how good he smelled. It actually made my head swim."

"Which led to marriage."

"In time, yes. But first we had to overcome some major family problems."

"Because Orthodox Jews aren't supposed to marry non-Jewish women?"

"His family was horrified by our relationship. And my family was just as bad."

"Your family?"

"Does that surprise you? Chinese families can be just as tradition-bound as Jewish families. Having a daughter marry a man who's not Chinese is unimaginable to them. Worse than her dying a virgin."

"Couldn't you just … go your own way? Marry privately and let your families come around in their own time? That's what a lot of couples do these days when they come from different ethnic cultures."

"Abandon our families?"

"Temporarily. Until they came to terms with your marriage."

"No, we couldn't consider that. We wanted their blessings for our marriage up front. However reluctant. This sort of thing may be outside your experience, but...."

"As a matter of fact, I understand completely. Something like that happened to me."

"Wanting to marry someone from a different ethnic culture?"

"Yes."

"How interesting. Can you tell me about it?"

"We met at Harvard. She was a Jewish girl from a rich Great Neck family. Something clicked between us, and it wasn't long before we were finishing each others sentences. If you know what I mean."

"Of course."

"Her father was the problem."

"Ah."

"Highly successful businessman who came from nothing. Made a fortune through sheer brilliance and hard work and his ability to manipulate people."

"Sounds like another man born with a gold spoon."

"That's why we got on so well together. Really liked each other. Had long talks about world affairs and so on."

"Then what was the problem?"

"He wanted his only daughter to marry somebody born with a silver spoon. That would be his greatest achievement in life. Marry off his daughter to a man who was automatically accepted in all the best circles. Because of what he'd inherited rather than what he'd accomplished."

"An old story. Self-made tycoon marrying off his daughter to an aristocrat."

"More or less. Anyway, he showed up in Cambridge one day. Invited me to dinner. Told me he'd taken Sarah out of Harvard and sent her to

Israel for a year. To work in a kibbutz teaching children. We would never see each other again. Nothing personal, he insisted. He thought I was a great guy. Very bright and destined to be successful in whatever I did, and so on. But I wasn't going to marry his daughter. Period."

"How did you react to that?"

"Naturally, I was devastated. I tried to tell myself it was because I was black. But that didn't work. So what could I do except face reality?"

"And your definition of reality was…?"

"It took a while. But gradually I came to realize there were probably lots of women I could marry and find happiness with. So why not follow the course of least resistance?"

"How rational. And how sad."

"Yeah, I guess so."

"Did it work out the way you expected?"

"Did I ever marry? Not so far. Just a few temporary girlfriends along the way. Here and there. Between career moves."

"That wouldn't have worked for Elijah and me. We had to get our parents' blessings."

"So what did you do?"

"We worked out a plan. A rather intricate plan, as it turned out."

"Is that the story you alluded to earlier?"

"Yes."

"Are you going to tell me about it?"

"I suppose I am, since we've come this far."

* * *

She gazed down at her half-eaten platter of food. Then placed her chopsticks neatly across the side of the platter and looked at me with those exotically slanted Asian eyes. So vast and dark and shimmering it was easy to believe they were truly the windows of her soul.

But that could simply have been my imagination. Or the fact that she looked so familiar.

"It was a three-part plan," she said. "Very detailed and carefully thought out."

"With Elijah, how could it have been anything else?"

"The first part involved him teaching me Yiddish and me teaching him Cantonese. So we could talk with our respective grandparents."

"Your grandparents?"

"As I said, both of our families are very tradition-oriented. Among other things, that means taking seriously the views of the most senior members of the family. Our grandparents."

"So you began by charming both sets of grandparents?"

"It wasn't an easy process and took more time than we expected. Months of carefully structured Sunday visits. In Borough Park with his two sets of grandparents, and in Flushing with my two sets. Alternating visits week by week. Conversing entirely in Cantonese with my grandparents and entirely in Yiddish with his. Exhausting, to say the least."

"Sounds very Old World."

"Yes. But it meant a lot to our grandparents to see how we were willing to respect Tradition. And we had one other thing going for us."

"What was that?"

"Our grandparents were survivors of traumatic historical events. All four of mine lost everything in Chairman Mao's revolution and had to flee to Hong Kong with nothing but the clothes on their backs. Start new lives in one of those awful shantytowns built on a hillside just north of Kowloon. That's where they met."

"My God."

"Elijah's grandparents were Holocaust survivors. The only members of their respective families to make it alive out of the German death camps in Poland. Those terrible monuments to fifteen hundred years of European Christianity."

"Monuments?"

"Elijah thinks the death camps tell us more about the true meaning of Christianity than all of Europe's great cathedrals and religious paintings."

117

"Is that why he thinks God's a Nazi?"

"Oh, he's told you that."

"Couple of times."

"Well, he's a little crazy about certain things."

"He always seems perfectly lucid."

"Have you ever heard a sane man call God a Nazi?"

"Is that supposed to be a non sequitur?"

"Could be. In any case, all of our grandparents survived these traumas to meet and marry afterwards and find good lives in New York City."

"The real Jerusalem."

"Not only for Jews. Don't forget the countless other New Yorkers who've survived all manner of traumas in Asia and Europe and Africa. Not to mention in Mississippi and Iowa and other places west of the Hudson."

"But how did this end up working for you?"

"Survivors like our grandparents know that the world can change in terrible ways. But as long as there are children, there's hope for the future. So the wishes of children have to be respected."

"Ah."

"That awareness finally enabled them to accept our wish to marry after they had gotten used to seeing us together. Talking with them in their own languages. So they communicated this to our parents in no uncertain terms. Who, being tradition-oriented themselves, had to accept the wisdom of their elders."

"Bravo."

"Elijah must have sensed this all along. He's something of a con artist, in case you haven't noticed."

"On him it looks good."

"So having gained the blessings of our grandparents, the first part of our plan had been completed."

"And Part Two?"

"We had to arrange for our fathers to get to know each other."

"Sounds reasonable."

"In families like ours, fathers are the primary decision makers."

"Of course."

"My father was what you might call a restaurant impresario. Always looking for fresh opportunities to open new restaurants. Elijah's father was the rabbi of a small congregation in Borough Park. Leader of his flock, as it were. So both were in the habit of making decisions about things. If they could agree to our marriage, our mothers would go along. Especially since our grandparents were on board."

"So your fathers had to size each other up."

"Yes. Fortunately, Elijah's father liked Chinese food. And it happened that a business colleague of my father owned a kosher Chinese restaurant near the Diamond District in Midtown Manhattan."

"Neutral ground between Borough Park and Flushing."

"Ideally so. And we arranged a dinner for the four of us there on the first available Sunday evening."

"It went well?"

"Very well. After a few minutes, our fathers were talking away in New York street English like old friends. I think the real icebreaker was when Elijah's father mentioned that his community needed a kosher Chinese restaurant on Fort Hamilton Parkway.

"And your father picked up on this?"

"Oh, immediately. He was intrigued by the possibilities. In fact, it became their primary topic of conversation during the rest of the dinner."

"Not your marriage?"

"Much better that way. They were able to become comfortable with each other discussing something that didn't involve the issue of our marriage. Elijah's father knew some local real estate agents who could help find suitable storefronts. And my father was plugged into various sources of Chinese money in Flushing. All Elijah and I had to do was sit and listen. And eat."

"The old New York magic."

"Magic?"

"Two guys from radically different ethnic backgrounds start talking about something that can make money, which is a favorite topic in New York. And pretty soon, they discover interests in common. Which turn out to be a lot more important than any ethnic differences."

"We economists like to call that the Power of the Marketplace."

"I guess New York is the world's largest collection of marketplaces."

"Very true. And once people experience the pleasure of making money together, all the Old World hang-ups about ethnic differences seem too unimportant to worry about."

"Did the restaurant ever open?"

"Oh, yes. In a matter of months. On Eighth Avenue rather than Fort Hamilton Parkway, because the rent was cheaper. That was before the days when Eighth Avenue became the spine of a new Chinatown in Brooklyn. But it may have helped to start the ball rolling."

"And your marriage?"

"It almost became a side issue to our fathers. After that first dinner, they had many meetings concerning the restaurant. In the course of which, both of them came to accept the idea of our marriage. Unconsciously. Without the need for any formal agreement."

"So you and Elijah were home free."

"Not quite."

"Not quite?"

"Our fathers may have accepted the idea that we would marry. Someday. But it wasn't the same thing as turning our mothers loose to start planning a wedding. You know, setting a date. Interviewing caterers. That sort of thing. So Elijah and I had to precipitate it."

"Part Three of your plan?"

"Yes. As it turned out."

"Which involved what?"

"Arranging for me to get pregnant."

"You're kidding."

"Not at all. It wasn't as if our relationship had been exactly chaste. After all, we loved each other. And we belonged to a generation that didn't have the old hang-ups about sex. So it was simply a matter of our ceasing to use birth control for a while. Until I was pregnant."

"That's not … very conventional."

"Our marrying wasn't conventional, as far as our families were concerned. So we had to move the decision about a wedding to the front burner. Elijah had already gotten his MBA by that point and had gone to work for New York City's Office of Management and Budget. There was no question of our being able to afford marriage. Not to mention a child."

"And it worked?"

"Oh, yes. Naturally, there was a lot of screaming and crying in our respective households when we told them I was pregnant. But we expected that and knew it would pass. Which it did. So our mothers got to work planning the wedding. Actually, we had two ceremonies."

"Two?"

"One was a Jewish ceremony, which a rabbi friend of Elijah's father conducted in Borough Park."

"You two were able to marry Jewish?"

"Elijah and his father found a way. It involved having me go through a Reform conversion. You know about Reform Judaism?"

"Like the other end of the theological scale from Orthodox, isn't it?"

"More or less. Very modern and open. I could become a Reform Jew and then we'd have a Reform wedding. Elijah's father convinced his family to go along. He may have been a rabbi, but he was no innocent about the ways of the real world."

"So you two had a Jewish wedding."

"If you put quotation marks around it."

"What was the other ceremony?"

"A Buddhist wedding in Flushing. For my family. Conducted entirely in Cantonese. But Elijah's family was very impressed, even though they couldn't understand a word."

"Which left the two of you well and truly married."

"Yes, indeed."

"Then why was Elijah excommunicated by his sect?"

"Because they only accepted Orthodox conversions as valid. As far as they were concerned, I was still a shiksa. So the sect leaders ruled that Elijah had violated Orthodox Jewish law by marrying a non-Jewish woman. That's why they excommunicated him. Meaning he was a non-person as far as the sect was concerned."

"He told me it was a liberating experience."

"That's what he's always claimed."

"You don't agree?"

"It may been liberating to him intellectually. But not emotionally, if you know what I mean."

"Is that why he seems like such a … a renegade?"

"It certainly helped. But I think he would have become an Orthodox renegade anyway. Sooner or later. He doesn't exactly have a conventional mind."

"That's putting it mildly."

"Also, his intellectual hero is Moses Maimonides. You know Maimonides?"

"The big hospital in Borough Park?"

"They named it after him. He was a famous Jewish scholar and physician from Spain. He made unconventional thinking seem conventional."

* * *

We had finished as much of the food as we had room for. The waiter came and took the platters away, and we sat there sipping tea.

"You're flying back to Brooklyn today?" I said, mainly to make conversation.

"Tonight. I always fly in and out through Santa Barbara. The connections are good and it's only about an hour's drive from here."

"Right."

"So we still have lots of time to talk. If you're not busy."

"That's good. Because I wanted to ask you about Elijah's toll road project. I assume he's discussed it with you?"

"Oh yes. We've had lots of discussions about it. Especially late at night when we're.... Excuse me, why are you smiling?"

"Sorry. It's the image of you and Elijah lying in bed discussing cosmic transportation issues."

"Don't be impertinent, young man. We're an old married couple with four children. We discuss all kinds of things late at night."

"Including the toll road project."

"Of course. Have you any idea what a breakthrough it can be?"

"It seems very impressive. And radical. I mean, the concept of drivers paying directly for the roads they use."

"That's only the beginning. It's even more radical in other ways."

"Yeah? How."

"Its pricing policies, for example. Do you know the standard way most toll road authorities set their toll rates?"

"I guess it has something to do with generating enough revenue to cover their costs."

"Right. Political considerations aside, they need enough revenue to cover operating and maintenance costs. Plus interest and principle payments on their outstanding debt. Plus a little extra for what they like to call a reserve fund."

"Okay."

"In other words, their pricing policies are driven by their costs."

"Makes sense."

"Not much different from the approach most private business firms use to price their products. Costs plus a markup. Entirely consistent with classical free-market price theory. Do you know about that?"

"Let's see if I remember from my undergraduate economics class. Umm … the minimum price for a product sold in a free market has to be high enough for sellers to cover their costs and earn a fair profit. Otherwise they won't supply the product."

"Close enough."

"So I get an 'A' for paying attention in class?"

"In effect. Now suppose you were the CEO of a company making widgets...."

"Widgets."

"It's an economist's favorite product, Wesley."

"I know. But what exactly is a widget?"

"It's closely related to Alfred Hitchcock's MacGuffins."

"You're into classic movies?"

"If they're old enough."

"Old enough?"

"You know. All the actors dead. Or at least, long retired and living quietly in Manhattan."

"Like Olivia de Havilland."

"Perfect example. Anyway, we were talking about you being CEO of a company making widgets. Wouldn't you set their price high enough to cover all your costs? Including allowance for a fair profit? Which is the return on your invested capital."

"Maybe."

"Not certainly?"

"Suppose I'm a hired-gun CEO. I don't own the company, though I may have some stock options."

"All right."

"As a hired-gun manager, the basic size of my income package generally depends on how big the company is. With big being measured by its annual sales in dollars. So don't I want to set a price that generates the most sales?"

"Now you're talking like a sociologist."

"Maybe so. But that's the gut reality for hired-gun managers in big companies. Especially if their stock's publicly traded. Not maximizing shareholder value or any of those other ivory tower B-school concepts. They want to maximize sales revenue. Because that's what really determines how much they get paid."

"Toyota and other Japanese companies even made that respectable. They called it 'gaining market share.'"

"Right. And the sales-maximizing price is likely to be lower than the profit-maximizing price, isn't it?"

"Probably."

"So we go after sales and forget about profits. At least for a while."

"Which gives us three ways to set prices. Cover costs, including a fair profit. Maximize profits. And maximize sales."

"Seems right to a non-economist like me."

"But there's a fourth way, Wesley."

"There is?"

"It's called Value Pricing."

"That's one I've never heard of."

"Let's consider an example. Suppose you're a buyer for Macy's."

"Okay. Not that I actually know what a buyer is. I mean, I've heard the term before. But...."

"He's sort of a product manager. With profit responsibility for a product line."

"I get it."

"You're a buyer for Macy's. And you've just received an order of one hundred designer cocktail dresses from your supplier in Hong Kong. You know what the total cost of the order is. So what price do you set on the dresses?"

"You tell me."

"You start out setting a price that reflects Macy's highest markup for such dresses. Then you put them on the racks and see how many you can sell at that price."

"Okay."

"Now most women are going to look at the price and decide the dress isn't worth it to them. But a certain number of women are going to be okay with the price. They need a new cocktail dress for an event this Saturday. Or they always want to have the newest style. Whatever. The

125

point is, those women are going to decide that the value to them of being able to buy the dress today is worth the posted price. You see?"

"I think so. But aren't you still left with a lot of dresses?"

"Of course. So after a few weeks, you cut the price by 10 or 15 percent and put big 'Sale' signs on the racks. And you see how many dresses you can sell at this new lower price."

"Which more women are going to find is worth it, right?"

"Right. For these women, the value of being able to buy the dress today is now worth the discounted price."

"And you sell all the remaining dresses?"

"Probably not. But you may sell most of them. And after a few more weeks, you cut the price another 10 or 15 percent and put big 'Close-Out' signs on the racks. You're still making a profit on each dress. But it's a lot smaller than what you made at the original price. Then you stand back and watch the bargain hunters make your dresses disappear. Because those close-out prices represent good value to them."

"And what you don't sell this way, you unload on Loehmann's or some other close-out place for whatever you can get."

"That's the usual practice."

"Okay, let's see if I've got this. You can sell a certain number of dresses at the original high price. But you don't know how many. So you put all of them on the racks at that price and see how many you sell. And some women are going to consider that a fair-value price because they want the latest style today."

"That's the idea."

"Then you discount the price on the rest of the dresses. And more women are going to consider that a fair-value price. Finally, you put a close-out price on what's left and wait for the bargain hunters. Because the fair-value price to them is always the close-out price. After which, you unload the rest on Loehmann's."

"That's it exactly. And then you can calculate your profit on the entire order of dresses. Because that's what counts. Can you imagine how that's done?"

"I'm not great with numbers. You'd better take me through it."

"Let's assume you've received an order of a hundred dresses that cost you $50 per dress. Which amounts to $5,000 for the whole order. Needless to say, these are simplified numbers."

"Simple I can follow when it comes to numbers."

"You mark up the dresses 100 percent. That's an original price of $100 per dress. Assume you sell twenty-five at that price. Your total sales volume so far is $2,500. Then you cut the price to $85 and sell another fifty. The sales volume on them is $4,225. Which brings your total sales volume so far to $6,750. So you've already covered the cost of the order and made a nice little profit."

"You did all that in your head. I'm impressed."

"Comes from being an undergraduate math major. Anyway, you've still got twenty-five dresses left. So you mark them down with a closeout price of $70 and sell twenty. For a sales volume of $1,400. Raising your total sales volume to $8,150. The remaining five dresses you sell to Loehmann's for $250—just what you paid for them. So you finish with a total sales volume of $8,400."

"That's total sales. What about the profit?"

"Subtract the $5,000 you paid for the order. And your total profit is $3,400. That amounts to 68 percent of the order price. Nice?"

"No wonder people want to be in the retail business."

"It doesn't always go that smoothly. But you get the idea."

"I must say, for an economist you're very savvy."

"I'll take that as compliment. Even if it does insult my profession."

"Well, you know most economists. On the one hand this, on the other hand that. You never get a straight answer."

"Many people don't really want straight answers."

* * *

She sat back and took a sip of tea. Which was almost room temperature by now.

"Have you noticed how the flavor of tea changes with its temperature?"

"Elijah clued me in to that. He brought some of your tea with him at our last meeting. But listen...."

"Yes?"

"I have a question."

"Ask away."

"Value Pricing the Macy's way. Isn't that like a backwards version of the routine airlines use to set fares?"

"You're referring to what they call Yield Management?"

"Right. If you order your ticket well in advance, you get a big discount. But the longer you wait, the less the discount. And if you want to buy a ticket at the last minute, you pay full price."

"Ever meet any airline managers?"

"Not yet."

"Well, let's say they don't exactly seem like the brightest kids in class."

"You're saying they've got the Macy's approach backwards?"

"What do you think?"

"No wonder their companies are mostly basket cases."

"But you see why the Macy's approach is a correct application of Value Pricing?"

"You mean, because some women are going to buy dresses at the original price if they think the value of having the latest style today is worth the price? While others are willing to wait a few weeks until the price falls to rock bottom? Because the most important thing to them is getting a bargain, even if they have to wait for it?"

"In this case, it's a trade-off between price and time. Some women will pay a high price to save time in being able to wear the latest fashion. Other women will spend time to get a bargain price. Each woman makes her own choice. Consumer sovereignty, in other words."

"I never thought about it that way. But what about the seller?"

"In his case, it's all involved with a classical concept called Economic Rent. Do you know about that?"

"No."

"Take the case of a college basketball player. He's been playing the game most of his life and loves it. He'd rather play basketball than do anything else. And he'd be absolutely delighted if he could make a decent living playing basketball as a full-time job."

"How do you define a 'decent living'?"

"Let's be generous and say a salary of $100,000 a year, plus good medical benefits and a guaranteed pension. A reasonable upper-middle-class income for a college graduate."

"Okay."

"But NBA teams will pay him much more than that if they think he's talented enough to hire."

"I'll say."

"How much more? Ten times as much?"

"Maybe a hundred times as much, if he's a real star."

"All right. That amounts to $10 million a year. For playing basketball. Doing something as a full-time job he'd be willing to do for $100,000 a year. Now. What's the dollar difference between those two amounts?"

"You want me to do it in my head?"

"Come on, Wesley. You can't be that math-challenged. Even if you did go to Harvard."

"You're as bad as Elijah."

"I hope you meant that as a compliment."

"What else? Okay. Let's see. The difference is ... umm, $9,900,000. Right?"

"Yes. An NBA team will pay him $9.9 million a year *more* to play basketball professionally than he'd be willing to do it for full-time. And that extra amount is what we call Economic Rent. Which is...."

"Hold on a second, Susan. Let's see if I've got this. Economic Rent is the difference between the minimum salary somebody requires to do a job and the higher salary his employer is actually willing to pay him, for whatever reason. Am I right?"

"Absolutely. But the concept of Economic Rent isn't limited just to salaries. It can be applied to many other things. Such as the difference between a seller's cost-based price for a product and the higher price that buyers are actually willing to pay because of its value to them."

"Yeah, I can see how that follows."

"But the key is always value. The value to buyers. In other words, to consumers of the product. And the product can just as easily be a service as a good."

"Okay."

"Economic Rent is a good thing if you look at it from the perspective of buyer value. After all, are professional basketball teams compelled by federal law or some other outside force to pay such high player salaries?"

"Not so you'd notice."

"They pay those salaries because of their perception that good players are worth it to them. Worth it in terms of helping them win more games. Which attracts more spectators and leads to more lucrative television contracts. In other words, paying high salaries to players enables basketball teams make more money."

"Makes sense."

"Of course it does. And the same principle applies to a toll road. Drivers who use it can make their trips in less time. Time savings have value to drivers. Value they're willing to pay for, in the form of tolls. And the amount they're willing to pay has nothing to do with the toll road operator's costs."

"It can be higher, in other words."

"Sometimes much higher, if the toll road serves a corridor that has lots of travel demand."

"So the toll road operator can earn what you call Economic Rent."

"Yes."

"And in this case, Economic Rent is the extra revenue the operator earns by setting tolls at levels that reflect the value of time savings to drivers rather than just enough to cover his costs? Assuming there's no political pressure to keep toll rates artificially low."

"That's it exactly."

"And this is the sort of thing you and Elijah talk about in bed late at night."

"Well, not exclusively."

"Sorry, Susan. I didn't mean to be snide."

"You're forgiven."

"Okay. Let's see if I understand this. Political realities aside, there are three ways a toll road operator can set toll rates."

"No. Two ways."

"Then why do I see three ways?"

"I don't know. Let's go through your list."

"The first way is cost-based. The operator's only concern is enough revenue to cover his costs."

"Yes."

"The second way is value-based. The operator sets tolls at levels that reflect the value to drivers of the time they save using the toll road. That's likely to produce higher revenues."

"And the third way?"

"Congestion pricing. You know. Higher toll rates during rush hours. So you can keep volume down to the level you need to maintain free-flowing traffic."

"Ah. But isn't that just the flip side of Value Pricing?"

"How?"

"Think about it, Wesley. With congestion pricing, the toll road operator wants to keep traffic volume low enough to avoid stop-and-go traffic. In other words, he wants to maintain a fairly high average traffic speed. Which will maximize the number of vehicles passing a given point on the toll road."

"That's how Elijah explained it."

"And how does the operator do this? By setting tolls at levels that are *higher* than the value of the time savings to *some* drivers."

"Some drivers?"

"In other words, to drivers who are making what they regard as lower-priority trips. Low enough for them to accept the longer travel times on congested toll-free roads. Or by making their trips at times of day when travel demand on the toll road is low. So its toll rates are low enough for the time savings to have positive value to drivers making lower-priority trips."

"I think I see what you're getting at. Congestion pricing works because it's actually a version of Value Pricing. Same principle as those women in Macy's deciding whether buying a dress today is worth the price being charged. Which might be lower next week."

"Yes. In which case...."

"Okay. That answers my next question."

"Which would have been?"

"How you determine the actual Value Price. And you're implying it's done empirically. By finding the congestion price that reduces travel demand enough to assure free traffic flow. Even during rush hours and other high-volume travel periods."

"You learn quickly."

"But why didn't Elijah explain it this way?"

"He was probably trying to bring you along in easy stages. Remember, he's used to dealing with people who aren't as quick-witted as you are."

"Didn't grow up in Brooklyn."

"If you want to put it that way."

"Sorry if that sounds...."

"... Elitist?"

"That wasn't the word I was looking for, but it'll do. It's just that my experience with most people from other places is they're like two sentences behind when you talk to them."

"Yes, I've noticed that. Their lives seem more slowly paced."

"So they get a lot less living done than we do."

"True."

"Anyway, I've got another question about Value Pricing."

"Go ahead."

"What does the toll operator do with all that extra revenue?"

"His Economic Rent?"

"Yes. He doesn't need it to cover his costs. So aren't people going to say he should return it to the public?"

"That's probably inevitable, given political realities."

"Then...?"

"The question is, how?"

"You tell me, Susan."

"Remember what Elijah told you about including new tracks for freight trains in the toll road corridor?"

"Yeah."

"Those tracks allow freight to move through the corridor by rail rather than in trucks on the toll lanes."

"Right."

"That improves service to auto drivers, who hate trucks. Improved service enhances the value to auto drivers of using the toll road. Which the AAA crowd should love."

"Are you saying that the operator uses some of his extra revenue to subsidize the freight tracks?"

"That's certainly a possibility."

"But Elijah said the private railroad companies would have to pay to run trains on the tracks."

"Yes. Track tolls, in effect."

"So the tracks would be self-supporting."

"They could be, in theory. But remember what the operator is trying to accomplish. Shifting freight from trucks to rail. Among other things, that means less wear and tear on the toll lanes from heavy trucks. Resulting in lower maintenance costs. In addition to better service for auto drivers."

"Trucking companies are going to love that."

"They will if it means faster trip times for their trucks. Because faster trip times save them money."

"Okay."

"But to shift enough freight from trucks to rail, you may need to provide incentives to freight shippers and railroad companies."

"Oh, now I see where you're going. The operator uses some of his extra toll-lane revenues to subsidize the costs of operating and maintaining the freight tracks. Which allows lower tolls on the tracks. Low enough to make their use sufficiently attractive to freight shippers and railroad companies."

"Yes. And let's not forget about passenger rail service in the corridor. Elijah told you about that, didn't he?"

"He said something about making provisions for it."

"The social value of moving people by rail far exceeds its direct value to passengers. But there's no practical way to charge passengers for social value. Fares would have to be too high."

"So the operator subsidizes passenger rail service with his extra revenue."

"Exactly. In other words, we're talking about a Multi-Modal Transportation Corridor where the toll road mode subsidizes the rail modes. In order to provide the most efficient balance of travel volume among the various modes."

"I can see why you call this a radical new idea."

"Radical, yes. But not new."

"No?"

"It's been done in New York City since the 1960s."

"You're kidding."

"You know about the Metropolitan Transportation Authority, don't you?"

"The MTA? Yeah. Subways and buses and commuter railroads."

"But the MTA also runs the toll bridges and tunnels that connect the five boroughs together."

"Like the Verrazano Bridge and the Battery Tunnel?"

"That's right. Most revenue produced by those toll crossings is used to help cover the operating costs of the subways, buses, and commuter railroads."

"I never knew that."

"In other words, cross-subsidies. Which many libertarian economists consider a dirty word. They think everything should pay its own way in the most simple-minded terms imaginable."

"The free-market guys."

"Many of them. Not all. For example, economists of the free-market Austrian school believe that markets are inherently self-organizing. Because, to a great extent, market participants tend to be more interdependent than independent."

"And that justifies cross-subsidies?"

"Those are real-world applications of that concept. Look at the pharmaceutical companies. They continue to sell low-priced medicines long after their patents have expired simply to maintain a customer base for new high-priced medicines. Whose sales revenues help subsidize their low-priced medicines. So the cross-subsidy concept has a respectable pedigree."

"Will wonders never cease. I can see why Elijah was attracted to you."

"Because I smell good?"

"No, no, Jesus.... I mean, I wasn't trying to.... I never.... "

"Relax. I was just being flip. We've been covering some very heavy ideas."

"Yeah."

"You seem so grim sometimes."

"I know. Sorry if I jumped to any wrong conclusions."

"That's all right."

* * *

Having lunch with Susan was a delightful experience. She was so beautiful and charming. With such an exciting mind. Why had I made such an ass of myself? I could taste my embarrassment.

135

She was the kind of woman any sensible man would look for. She and Elijah must have great times together. On many levels. I couldn't help wondering if I'd ever be able to find a wife like her.

Maybe that's why she seemed like somebody I'd known for years. But couldn't quite place.

"There's another thing we should talk about," she said abruptly, leaning towards me again. "Possibly the most critical thing."

"Yeah? What."

"Let's go back to classical free-market theory again."

"Okay."

"Among other things, it says that the selling price for widgets is a given. Because it's set by the marketplace."

"Right."

"So if you want to make and sell widgets, you have to keep your costs at levels low enough to fit within the market price."

"Yeah."

"Therefore, your entire focus has to be on producing widgets as efficiently as possible. And if you do that well enough, the world will presumably beat a path to your door. Because in a free market, you can sell all the widgets you can make."

"Sure."

"Does that remind you of something?"

"Oh. You mean, the traditional business concentration on Production?"

"Exactly. Make steel. Make automobiles. Make any number of things. Because your main business activity is Production. Efficient Production. If you're efficient enough, everything else presumably takes care of itself. And you earn profits."

"Business the old-fashioned way. But I thought that was pretty much obsolete now."

"Yes, indeed. Because in the real world, most business firms don't operate in true free markets. They operate in warped markets. With only some of the characteristics of a true free market. And that means a lot of them may find they can't sell all the widgets that they make if they just sit back and wait for buyers to come to them. So what do you do if you're in that position?"

"Advertise?"

"Ah. An obvious solution. Hire a Madison Avenue advertising agency full of creative people to prepare catchy television commercials and prints ads. You're still making the same car. But advertising tries to give it a more compelling image. It's not just reliable transportation anymore. Now it's a status symbol. Buy it and other people will look up to you. Think you're a better and more successful person. So you can feel superior by owning it and driving it. Even though it's still the same car."

"Pure puffery, in other words."

"Yes."

"But that's so old-hat now."

"Of course. It belongs to the era of the 1950s. When advertising was Manhattan's most prestigious industry, like investment banking is today. And when intellectuals were writing books about how Madison Avenue was committing terrible sins by manipulating consumers into buying things they didn't really need."

"The Good Old Days."

"People always make that mistake, don't they, Wesley. The past was somehow better than the present. It's the 'Remembrance of Things Past' syndrome."

"Thank you, Marcel Proust."

"You've read him?"

"Only bits and pieces back in college. Does anybody ever read more than that?"

"No one I've ever met. But let's come back to you, the manufacturer of cars. Sorry to have switched metaphors in midstream."

"Better than widgets. At least I know what a car is."

"You want to sell more cars. So these days, what do you do?"

"I don't know. Maybe a full-court Marketing press?"

"Marketing? You mean like when we were children and our mothers talked about going to the supermarket to buy groceries?"

"No, no.… What are you…?"

"Now you're looking grim again."

"Sorry. But that came out of left field."

"I'm trying to make a point."

"By confusing me?"

"A little. Because 'Marketing' is a confusing term. It's like me pointing to a tall wooden plantlike thing on a hillside with leaves on its branches and calling it a refrigerator. All that does is confuse normal people. Because the term 'refrigerator' already belongs to the kitchen appliance we keep food cold in. Just like the term 'Marketing' instinctively reminds us of our mothers going to the supermarket."

"I'm assuming all this will eventually become clear to me. If I'm patient enough."

"Bear with me a little longer, Wesley. I'm getting there."

"Okay."

"Now back in the late 1950s, some very sharp business theorists came up with a dramatic new concept to guide the design of products. Instead of designing the product according to your own private ideas about what buyers want, they said you should go out and ask potential buyers what they *actually* want. What features are most important to them. And what they'd be willing to pay for these features."

"Market Research, in other words."

"Right. Which, in this case, has nothing to do with comparison shopping in a supermarket."

"I think I'm clear about the difference now."

"But most people aren't. The business theorists who developed this concept may have been very sharp. But they certainly weren't poets. In fact, they weren't even middling good when it came to expressing themselves in clear English. So they made a major blunder when they named their concept 'Marketing.' And that confused too many people."

"Including sales types in business?"

"Them most of all, in ways that counted."

"Interesting."

"Think about it, Wesley. What you really have to do is ask your potential customers what price they'd be willing to pay for a given set of product features. Then act accordingly."

"Give them what they want. Get them down on all fours and look at it from the customer's perspective. Makes sense."

"But notice how I've switched terms?"

"What do you mean?"

"Price and Features. I've put Price first. Why? Because Price is the critical strategic element. Everything flows from Price. So that's where you should start. But because the word 'Marketing' confuses so many people, the importance of Price tends to be forgotten. The emphasis is mainly on a product's Features."

"And that holds true for a toll road operator."

"Oh, definitely. Do you understand why?"

"Let's see. As a toll road operator, I produce a product that has various features. Features involving transportation. Saving time. A more comfortable ride. No stop-and-go traffic. Whatever. And I charge drivers a price to travel on my road so they can take advantage of these features."

"No."

"No?"

"You have it backwards. Remember, Price comes first. It's the most important strategic element."

"Right. Let me try it again. As a toll road operator, I charge drivers a price to travel on my road. And they're willing to pay that price because the value to them of the transportation features I offer is worth it."

"Just like women shopping for dresses in Macy's."

"So I have to research my customers to find out which transportation features they want."

"Want in terms of being willing to pay for."

"And I find that out how exactly?"

"As a toll road operator, you have an advantage. All that new technology. To monitor average traffic speeds. Count the number of vehicles passing a given point during a given time period. Change the toll rate per mile from one minute to the next if you wish. Tell drivers at each entry point what the current toll rate is, and what average traffic speed you guarantee them. You know, by using those signs with all the lights."

"Variable Message signs?"

"Yes."

"With everything linked to a computer that's probably no bigger than the ones we have at home."

"Of course. So you can sit at the keyboard and input, for example, the average traffic speed you want to have on the road. Go on, Wesley. Give me a speed."

"How about fifty miles an hour."

"Fifty miles an hour it is. The computer instantly translates that into the number of vehicles passing a given point per minute. If the actual traffic speed is lower than fifty miles per hour, the computer starts raising the toll rate. Which shows up on the Variable Message signs at the toll road's entry points. And it keeps raising the toll rate until the number of vehicles entering the road is no greater than the number needed to achieve your desired traffic speed."

"So you're screening out drivers who decide the value of saving time at a guaranteed fifty miles per hour isn't worth the posted toll rate, is that it?"

"Yes. And that tells you how many drivers think the value of the time they save at fifty miles is worth the price you're charging. To them, your price is the Value Price. Which can change hour by -hour on any given day. And from day to day. You see?"

"I've read stuff about that on the Internet. But it was all sort of general and abstract."

"It helps to go through it step-by-step. That makes it seem real."

"I'll say."

"And the software that does all this is simpler than the software we use to write and send emails. As easy to use. Transparent, in other words. You don't have to be a math nerd to do this kind of customer research."

"Sounds a lot easier than trying to find the Value Price for a new car you want to design."

"Less expensive, too. You can experiment at the keyboard to your heart's content. And by finding the Value Price for different average speeds and other factors in the real world, you obtain information about what product features matter most to your customers. But it all begins with Price."

"Is now the time for me to cut loose with a big 'Wow'?"

"Not quite. There's an important complication you need to be aware of."

"I should have known."

"In the old days, a driver wanting to use a traditional toll road had to stop at a toll plaza, rummage in his pocket for cash, and hand it to the attendant. Just like buying a ticket at a movie theater."

"Okay."

"In other words, the act of buying was directly linked to the act of paying."

"Like on the Verrazano Bridge before E-Z Pass."

"Right. But today's electronic toll collection technology eliminates all that. You don't have to stop or even slow down. The little transponder on your windshield is read electronically when you enter and leave the road. The computer calculates your total toll and charges it to your account. You're not even aware that it's happening. Can you appreciate what that means?"

"Tell me, so I'll be sure."

"It means that the act of buying is entirely divorced from the act of paying."

"So?"

"Years ago, department stores like Macy's stumbled onto that concept and realized they could use it to increase sales. That's the main reason why they started issuing charge cards to their customers. This was long before American Express and MasterCard. Shall I give you an example of why it made such a difference?"

"By all means."

"Assume you go to Macy's to buy a shirt. But while you're there, you see other things that catch your eye. There's a belt that's on sale. Or a pair of very nice gloves."

"There's certainly no shortage of things to catch your eye in Macy's."

"But if the only way you can buy them is by paying cash on the spot, you have to think about how much cash you have in your pocket. And maybe that means you decide to pass up buying the belt or gloves. Some other time, maybe."

"I think I see. But if I can buy them with plastic...."

"Then what you buy isn't determined by the cash in your pocket. You simply hand the clerk your credit card. And the cost of the belt or gloves gets added to the statement you receive at the end of the month. Which you pay with a single check. Or a simple cash transfer done on your computer. So the act of buying that belt or pair of gloves is totally divorced in your mind from the act of paying for them."

"Which means that I tend to buy more."

"Absolutely. And on a modern toll road, the same principle applies. Because of electronic toll collection, the act of buying access to the road is totally divorced from the act of paying for it."

"Does that mean that my perception of the Value Price is different?"

"Isn't that logical? If you have to dig cash out of your pocket, the Value Price to you is likely to be lower than if you can drive straight through without stopping."

"But isn't that going to screw up congestion pricing?"

"Well, it means the toll rate needed to achieve a particular average traffic speed is likely to be higher than it would be with old-fashioned cash toll plazas. Probably much higher."

"And much higher means more toll revenue."

"Exactly. More Economic Rent to the toll operator."

"My God, you're more than just an economist."

"Is that another attempt to insult my profession?"

"No, seriously. You've got what might be called a strategic mind."

"Or at least a practical mind. Most women do. Men tend to focus on abstractions. Theories and so on. I suppose that's why we have so many wars."

* * *

We left the restaurant soon after that. Drove back to Susan's motel so I could pick up my car. Said goodbye in the afternoon sunshine. Which made her compelling beauty shimmer in a most unsettling manner.

But as I was driving home, it occurred to me that Elijah could have set up the whole thing. Pleaded illness so he could send his wife to meet with me in his place. Hoping she might be able to find out things about me that he couldn't. Or thought it better to find out indirectly. I wouldn't put it past him.

Well, she'd given as good as she'd gotten. All that stuff about their marriage and how they had conned their families into accepting it. Not to mention other personal information.

But maybe that was part of his plan, too. Making sure that I knew things about him without having to tell me himself. Using his wife as a convenient go-between. Who was too beautiful and charming to resist.

He was nothing if not devious.

Of course, all that had certain advantages. For both of us. Just like his use of hypotheticals and stories to reveal things without leaving any verbal footprints. After all, it wasn't as if I hadn't occasionally used the same trick myself as a reporter. Elijah had simply raised the whole process to something like a high art.

But it still couldn't help leaving me with a certain sense of confusion.

143

* * *

I reached home late in the afternoon and found myself at something like loose ends. There was no serious work I could think of to do. So I finally ended up sitting in front of the TV set, idly watching a golf tournament.

Not that I had any passion for golf. I'd never played the game in my life and didn't expect to. The whole thing had all the excitement to me of Chinese Checkers.

But in their pursuit of showmanship, the TV guys had come up with a live coverage feature that struck me as at least borderline hilarious. It involved the TV announcers speaking in hushed whispers. Especially when one of the players was trying to sink a putt. As if they were trying to quiet the whole world so there'd be nothing to disturb the putter's concentration. The polar opposite of other spectator spots, where crowd noise was part of the action. The louder the better.

Whenever I watched this silliness unfold on my TV screen, I'd sit there laughing to myself. Unable to avoid daydreaming about someday sneaking into a golf tournament. Positioning myself in the crowd around an important hole. And as the requisite hush fell over the crowd when one of the players got ready to putt, removing a miniature bullhorn from inside my coat. Placing it to my mouth. Pushing the bottom. And letting out an ear-piercing screech that turned everything to chaos. Then running for my life from the enraged crowd. Laughing with glee at having desecrated their holy sanctuary.

That afternoon, I had just reached the point in my irresistible daydream where I was removing the bullhorn from inside my coat. When an incredible thought struck me from way out in left field.

I suddenly knew why Susan had seemed so familiar to me.

She looked just like the Dragon Lady. Milton Caniff's remarkable character who had lit up his daily comic strip *Terry and the Pirates* during the 1930s and '40s.

I remembered her gazing at me across the table at the Chinese restaurant. It was all there, just like in the comic strip. Her slightly triangular face with its vivid cheek bones. The way her dramatic eyebrows arched grandly up and down as she spoke. The vastness of her dark, slanted eyes that revealed so little even when she seemed to be saying so much. Her black hair, wound in a tight bun behind her head. Her perfect ears and lush mouth and elegantly sculpted chin. Everything.

She was a living incarnation of the Dragon Lady. Facing me across the years and miles and whatever else was hidden away in some treasure chest of my brain. Stirring images that flickered in the hazy twilight of memory.

No, this was crazy. She was Elijah's wife. That's all. An agelessly beautiful Chinese woman with an imperious mezzo voice and matter-of-fact Queens accent. Sitting in for him on this particular Sunday. Talking quite openly about a variety of things that he and I hadn't yet gotten around to discussing. Nothing else.

I took a deep breath and shook my head several times. But that sense of her failed to disappear. It remained as strong as ever. In the air all around me.

Susan was the Dragon Lady.

* * *

I stood up and walked across the living room. Stopped at the crowded bookshelves standing against the far wall. On the leftmost end of the third shelf from the bottom stood twenty-five slim volumes containing reprints of the complete 1934 to 1946 run of *Terry and the Pirates* comic strips, just as they had appeared in daily newspapers of the time.

I had bought them on a whim when I was at Columbia. From a comic book store off Herald Square where I'd taken refuge from a sudden thunderstorm. Stumbled onto the volumes quite by accident as I browsed mindlessly around the store while waiting for the storm to let up. Began idly paging through them to pass the time. Became entranced by Caniff's drawing style and dialogue and characters. Bought the complete set before the rain stopped and lugged them back to my apartment near Columbia. Where I spent the rest of the day and most of the evening reading them from beginning to end.

Which is how the Dragon Lady first entered my life.

I took down Volume One from my shelf and opened it. A group of folded typewritten pages slipped out from inside the front cover, but I managed to grab them before they fell to the floor. They contained an essay about the Dragon Lady I'd run across on the Internet by accident and printed out. It was by somebody whose name I'd never heard of, who identified himself as a "literary critic of classic American comic strips."

I unfolded the pages and began reading them. For what must have been the hundredth time.

The Dragon Lady is surely one of the great characters in American literature. Unfortunately, her real significance has become obscured by the passage of more than half a century since she starred in Milton Caniff's comic strip TERRY AND THE PIRATES, which he set in turbulent China during the 1930s and '40s and which is now regarded as something of a masterpiece.

It began as a standard newspaper comic strip that followed the adventure-story traditions of its time. Terry Lee was a plucky adolescent able to run around China (instead going to school back in the U.S.) under the watchful eyes of his adult mentor Pat Ryan. Pat was a two-fisted Black Irish soldier-of-fortune who was assumed to be an appropriate guardian for Terry because he smoked a pipe, talked in terse ambiguities, played football in college, and never displayed any discernable sense of humor. In short, an ideal comic strip for kids of all ages.

But all these conventions went out the window when the Dragon Lady appeared on the scene.

These days, most people think of her as the quintessential

Asian temptress luring men to perdition with her irresistible female wiles. Embodying in full-blooded glory all the primal male fears of women, which they have woven into elaborate horror stories to tell each other in locker rooms or sports bars or their equivalent ever since the Old Testament scribes insisted on rewriting the real story of Adam and Eve.

Naturally, many contemporary Asian (and non-Asian) women find this bound-foot stereotype offensive, and rightly so. But it has nothing to do with the remarkable character that Caniff created. Unfortunately, newsprint is highly perishable. So few people today are able to see for themselves what the Dragon Lady was really all about.

Yes, she was awesomely beautiful. But she never let this genetic accident define her character. Never sat for hours in front of a mirror admiring her dramatic cheekbones. Or worrying about age lines. Or experimenting with different ways of doing her hair. Unlike most women of the 1930s, she paid no attention to the standard male view that a woman's physical appearance is the most important thing about her.

Yes, she spent most of her life engaged in various illegal activities. But this was more an expression of her clear-eyed pragmatism than evidence of some moral depravity inherent in her female nature. From her perspective, living outside the law gave her more freedom to be her own person than she could ever have enjoyed in any of the conventional roles assigned to women. In those days, women in polite society were expected to define themselves entirely in terms of what men wanted them to be. But the Dragon Lady had no patience with this.

Yes, she didn't try to hide her forthright sexuality. But she never used sex as a weapon. Or as a bargaining chip. Or as a means of obtaining a comfortable life for herself. She enjoyed good sex the way she enjoyed good food. As one of life's fleeting *pleasures. To be savored with a gourmet's passion whenever the right opportunity arose.*

She was a brilliant and sophisticated woman, whose Chinese-English ancestry had made her an outcast to both societies. Highly educated in the cultures of both East and West. Wise in the ways of the world and the frailties of its people. Most of all, choosing to live entirely by her own existential set of moral principles that gave no quarter to anyone. Which made her more than a match for Caniff's extensive set of irredeemably wicked multiethnic villains.

He first brought her on stage in 1934 during the strip's initial story, as the strong-willed leader of a pirate gang preying up and down the South China coast. This kind of dominating executive role in command of an all-male crew was scarcely common among female characters in American literature of the time. But Caniff made it seem like the most natural thing in the world by emphasizing her cool intelligence, emotional toughness, and Wall Street trader's ability to balance risks against rewards....

I put down the essay and opened Volume One. Began rereading the first story. Following the familiar action as Terry and Pat are captured by the Dragon Lady's pirate gang and taken on board their junk. Where the Dragon Lady sizes them up with an appraising eye. Decides that Pat is a handsome (if infantile) stud and well worth bedding. So she has him brought to her cabin in order to seduce him.

"Why are you so cool to me?" she whispers to him in a silken voice as she smoothes back his hair while they sit together on her couch. "I am not without charm. But you ignore me."

"Well—uh.... You see.... Miss.... I.... ah...." Pat mumbles, obviously not accustomed to a woman being the sexual aggressor.

"You stammer like a school boy. I can make you rich. Be my partner and together we will rule the China Sea," she goes on, caressing his cheek as she plies him with the kind of phony inducements that endless legions of male seducers have used since time immemorial.

But Terry has been listening just outside her cabin door. And as Pat sinks helplessly into total confusion, he bursts in full of adolescent enthusiasm.

"Hey, Pat," he cries out excitedly. "I just learned how to pronounce the names of your wife and ten children in Chinese. Ain't that swell?"

Pat grins in relief. And the Dragon Lady is outraged. She turns on Terry and threatens him with dire punishment. But he stands up to her.

"We may be your prisoners," he tells her pugnaciously. "But you can't make a sea-going gigolo out of my pal Pat."

She gazes at him in surprise. Perhaps seeing in his adolescent face glimmerings of the kind of man she has never encountered before. So she orders her guards to take Pat back to his cabin, but asks Terry to stay and have tea with her.

As she prepares tea for the two of them, she tries to charm him with words that she imagines will melt his antagonism. But Terry isn't buying. And when she offers him a steaming cup of tea, he turns it down.

"Drink, I say," she insists. "I am not accustomed to having my hospitality spurned."

"Hospitality, my eye," he replies. "I saw you drop poison into this cup."

(Or maybe it was just a sleeping drug to dissolve his resistance so she could enjoy him sexually. Remember, this was 1934. When the outer boundaries of progressive literary fashion allowed such things to happen,

149

even if they couldn't be clearly alluded to in popular comic strips. But Caniff was always willing to take chances.)

In any case, their confrontation was interrupted by a sudden attack from a rival pirate gang. Which sinks their ship, captures everyone, and imprisons Terry and Pat with the Dragon Lady in the hold of their junk. But clever Terry persuades her to lend him the mirror from her bag by promising that he and Pat will help her escape.

Their plan is to use the mirror to signal a passing ship of their plight. It works, and soon a U.S. warship is on its way to rescue them. But once the three of them are ashore at the naval base in Hong Kong, the Dragon Lady becomes convinced that they're going to betray her.

"So this is the way you keep your promise to help me escape,"
she says bitterly to Terry and Pat. "After I gave you the mirror
with which to signal for aid. You liars!"

But just then a naval base police officer asks them about the
Dragon Lady."

"And the Chinese Lady?" he says. "Is she a member of the
pirate gang?"

And Terry quickly replies:

"Why, ah ,,,, She was captured and taken aboard Fang's
ship at the same time we were."

Which satisfies the police officer, who walks away with the
wrong impression. Then Terry and Pat turn to the Dragon Lady
with reproachful smiles.

"You see, Miss?" Pat says to her. "We are not exactly liars."

"I am not used to apologies," she replies contritely. "But I am
grateful. You have saved me from being hanged. I do not forget."

And she goes on her way, unmolested by the naval base po-
lice. Leaving Terry and Pat wondering whether they were be-
witched by her compelling charm into making an unwise
decision.

"Maybe we're a couple of saps to let her get away," Pat says. "She's a dangerous gal."

"Yeah. But we kept our word," Terry reminds him. "And somehow, I gotta hunch we're not going to regret it."

Terry's fateful words hang over the entire rest of Caniff's great comic strip. Especially where he is concerned. For despite his adolescence, he seems to sense that he's just gotten to know the most remarkable woman who will ever pass through his life.

I pushed Volume One aside and continued reading the essay.

> *In subsequent stories, the Dragon Lady turned up as a leader of other criminal gangs. Not to mention free-lance spy and masterful con artist. She was usually an antagonist for Terry and Pat. Though sometimes she formed alliances of convenience with them.*
>
> *But after the invasion of China by Japan, she still found time to organize and lead a guerrilla army against the Japanese. Showing a command of military tactics and leadership skills that Chairman Mao would have been proud of. In fact, her rousing speech in 1938 to rally dispirited bandits whose warlord leader had just been discredited as a coward has all the inspirational fervor that Shakespeare's version of Henry the Fifth managed to summon up at Agincourt on Saint Crispin's Day....*

I went back to the bookshelves and took down Volume Six of the strip's reprints. Found the panels showing her standing on a box addressing the bandits. Resplendent in black riding boots, tan jodhpurs, and a dark blouse whose open V-neck plunged down between her breasts nearly to her navel. As Terry looks on with wondering eyes.

And as I read, I could hear her ringing mezzo voice rise from the page into the clear air of war-torn China.

"Men of China!" she declaims, raising her long arms towards them. "You have just renounced a leader who has proved himself a coward! The Dragon Lady speaks to you now! Give ear. These are important words!"

Now she separates her arms, as if to embrace them.

"You were held together as bandit soldiers by Klang," she continues. "You plundered and robbed both sides on the fringe of the War. But you did the greatest harm to your own people—with no profit to yourselves. Now the most selfish Klang no longer guides your destinies. And unless a competent leader holds you together you may scatter as autumn leaves in the wind. I, the Dragon Lady, bid you acclaim me as your Master!"

"Listen to that Dragon Lady go," Terry murmurs to those around him. "She's got old Klang's mob swinging on every word."

"You are a well-trained unit of fighting men," she tells the bandits. "But your ability has been dissipated in futile murder of helpless peasants by the coward Klang."

She lowers her arms and leans towards them.

"No one has ever accused the Dragon Lady of drum-beating patriotics," she says in a softer, almost pleading, voice. "But at this moment the soul of China is being ravished by an invading horde. It is no matter of individual feelings, but the preservation of your racial heritage."

Now she raises her right arm to them.

"I entreat you, Men of China, to follow me—and throw your skill and bravery against the iron heel of the foreign transgressor!" she cries out, her voice ringing forth sternly again. "If the blood of Genghis Khan still flows in your veins, answer Yes!"

"Dragon Lady want us to fight invader!" one of the bandits says to the man next to him.

"Always she pirate. Now patriot!" the one next to him replies.

"We live by plunder long time," a third bandit says in a louder voice that reaches the Dragon Lady's ears. "How now make living?"

"You won't make a living!" she answers candidly. "You may starve! You may freeze! But wouldn't you rather do that than relinquish your birthright as a people?"

Now she raises her left fist at them.

"China has borne the world's mockery and exploitation for centuries because our civilization was too ancient to be disturbed by petty passions," she reminds them in a stirring voice. "If this vast land is conquered, we will become a lost people. We will be swallowed by the all-enveloping culture of mingled West and East. I ask you to die that your descendants may not lose face!"

"Dragon Lady speak true words!" one of the bandits shouts.

"She brave leader! We follow!" another calls out.

"Dragon Lady is new master!" a third announces.

"Done!" she cries out in triumph. "Then prepare to march! We move up at once!"

And amid the cheers of her new army, the Dragon Lady steps down from her bully pulpit as Terry approaches her full of admiration.

"Boy. I gotta hand it to you," he says. "You sure sold those guys a bill of goods."

She responds with something like a conspiratorial smile. Then places her left hand alongside her mouth to make sure no one but Terry can hear her.

"Do not be so naïve, my erstwhile friend," she tells him in a low voice, as if concerned that he may be getting the wrong idea about her. "The Dragon Lady has not changed her scales. If the invader conquers China, such bandits as I will be wiped out by highly organized military police. I must fight to keep the country helpless so that I get the spoils of war."

153

Or maybe Terry was seeing the real truth about her, I couldn't help thinking as I reread this sequence for the umpteenth time. She had a great talent for deliberate ambiguity. Which an increasingly savvy Terry had learned to take with a grain of salt.

I closed Volume Six and went back to reading the essay.

One of the strip's highlights was the Dragon Lady's evolving relationship with Terry. During his early adolescent years, when he and Pat were sometimes battling her and other times were temporarily allied with her, she developed an oddly protective maternal fondness for him that expressed itself in some interesting ways. And as he matured into a young man with decent human instincts whom she found sexually attractive, there are frequent hints that she came to regard him as one of the few adults whom she could wholeheartedly admire and respect. Possibly because of his nonjudgmental acceptance of her on her own terms. And because of his ability to bring out the best in her when they were together.

The transition between these two phases of their long and complicated relationship occurred in Hong Kong during 1939, when Terry unexpectedly rescued her from a gang of assassins one night and hid her in rooms over a nearby Wan Chai dive to recover from her superficial wounds. When she had recovered sufficiently to ask what she could do for him in return ("the Dragon Lady always pays her debts"), he swallowed hard and haltingly asked if she could teach him to dance. So he could impress the honey-tongued Southern belle his own age with whom he had become hopelessly infatuated.

There follows a remarkable series of panels that show the Dragon Lady teaching Terry to dance. And to mouth the polite romantic phrases that were supposed to delight young women in those days....

I went back to the bookshelves to get Volume Nine, which contained this sequence. Took it back to the table and paged through it, looking for it.

There it was.

> *"I never knew anyone could be as completely graceful as you are,"* Terry says, *getting into the spirit of things as they dance together in her living room to the music of a record player on the table.*
>
> *"Why, thank you, sir," she replies demurely.*
>
> *"It seems that the time and the place and the music have combined to form a setting for the precious jewel that is you."*
>
> *"Ah, you are adept at the pretty speech."*
>
> *"I don't think life could ever hold a moment as exquisite as this."*
>
> *"Aren't you being a bit flattering?"*
>
> *"I mean it.... We've been through a lot together—and we've had quarrels.... But right now, I know you're the most wonderful person alive."*
>
> *"You are too kind!"*
>
> *"Oh, darling. You're too beautiful to share with other people! Let's get away—where we can really be alone!"*
>
> *The record ends and they stop dancing.*
>
> *"Very good," the Dragon Lady says, smoothing back her hair as Terry mops his brow. "But when dancing with your young miss—say the speeches more as if you just thought of them—not just as the Dragon Lady taught them to you."*

I picked up the essay again and continued reading from where I had left off.

> *As they parrot these clichés while they dance together, it becomes apparent that they're really expressing their growing*

awareness of how important they've become to each other. As frequent antagonists. Occasional allies. Almost proxy mother and son. And now, undeniably, Man and Woman.

This is wonderfully passionate storytelling, with Caniff merging words and pictures into compelling images of complex human feelings. There on the edge of the South China Sea....

I felt the same thrill of emotion that always grabbed me each time I read this sequence. It seemed even stronger this time. Could that be because I found myself half believing I'd just had lunch with the real Dragon Lady?

I stared out the window next to the table where I sat. Into the gathering night racing towards me from Brooklyn and all the other things that really mattered in the world. And realized something profound and disturbing.

I must have been unconsciously searching for the Dragon Lady ever since that rain-soaked night at Columbia when she had first seduced me in my imagination. Now, at long last, I had found her.

And she was the wife of a man I was coming to respect more than anyone else I knew.

God help me. Even if he was a Nazi. Not to mention a cross-dresser. And who knew what else.

I was in no position to be choosy.

Chapter Four
Five-Star Turmoil

It would have been easy for me to spend all my time obsessing about Susan as an incarnation of the Dragon Lady. Spinning out the usual elaborate fantasies, in which something somehow happens to make the impossible possible. Even better than in the comic strip. With me being magically transformed into a blond-haired, pink-skinned Terry.

Yeah, sure.

Fortunately, I wasn't so far gone as to bow to this crazy temptation. At least, not completely. Instead, I forced myself to think about something more down-to-earth.

Like doing a book on the national implications of current transportation issues.

The more I thought about it, the more convinced I became that a readable book along these lines had good potential for getting published and attracting favorable attention.

If I could do such a book, it would go a long way towards letting me kiss goodbye the dreary business of covering Rotary Club luncheons for a nothing newspaper in a nowhere town and claw my way back into the big leagues of serious journalism. Where I knew I belonged.

It was certainly better to arrive home in triumph on the back of a successful book. Rather than bow to the temptations dangled in the occasional letters I still received from eager lawyers seeking to represent me in a discrimination lawsuit against the newspaper that had fired me.

The most a lawsuit could bring me was a fat cash settlement. Plus a token job at a nice salary. Writing safe, dull articles for a prestige Eastern newspaper whose editor buried them in back pages if he ran them at all.

Which was tantamount to chrome-plated retirement and irrelevancy as the world passed me by.

But I was too young and hungry to settle for that. Not while I had that gold spoon I'd been born with.

Through sheer luck.

And that I still had done nothing to earn.

* * *

Obviously, the key to getting the kind of book I needed off the ground was a high-impact sales pitch. In the form of a carefully crafted Book Proposal. Compelling enough to grab the cojones of mainstream publishers in New York and get me at least one solid offer.

Just as obviously, an effective sales pitch didn't have to worry too much about truth as far as the book itself was concerned. The main thing was making it sensitive to the instinctive biases of my target customers. Senior editors at mainstream publishers. Guys who decide what books get published.

What were their instinctive biases concerning a book like mine? Simple enough.

First: they naturally assumed all businessmen were crooks ready to sell their mothers if the price was high enough.

Second: all elected officials had sold their souls to various Special Interests.

Third: all government employees were incompetent drones whose only concern was staying out of trouble until their pensions kicked in.

How did I know these things?

Because one of my colleagues on the *Harvard Crimson* was an English major who'd gone into book publishing after graduating. And was so horrified by what he found that he fled to the pop music industry after several years because he considered it to be "more couth." So he had a nice repertoire of war stories about publishing to regale me with at occasional lunches during my days at Columbia.

All that made it easy for me to picture the scene in some New York publisher when my Book Proposal arrived.

It would land on the desk of an Assistant Editor. Probably a borderline anorexic with an English degree from Brandeis or NYU. Proud of her rapidly developing ability to suppress her literary sensibilities beneath an aggressive commercial sense.

If she liked it, she'd take it to her Senior Editor. A loud-voiced burley type who liked to talk on his feet while he strode up and down the length of his cluttered office. He would allow the Assistant Editor to talk for about fifteen seconds before leaping to his feet.

"Wesley Graham? I know that name," he'd interrupt as he began to stride.

"Former Washington reporter," the Assistant Editor would say.

"Right. Black guy. Got himself in big trouble a couple of years ago. Something about faking news sources. They threw him out of journalism."

"That's him."

"He wants to do a tell-all memoir about his experiences? I can see sales potential in that if it's done right."

"Actually, he wants to do a book about the Crisis in American Transportation."

"What crisis?"

"You know. Traffic congestion. The Minneapolis bridge that fell down. Proposals to put tolls on highways."

"Who wants to buy a book about that?"

"I feel the same way."

"Can he write?"

"Oh, yes. Fast-paced prose style. Colorful metaphors. Easy reading."

"Think you could switch him to doing a tell-all memoir?"

"I haven't contacted him yet. His Proposal just came this morning. I wanted to...."

"Okay. Talk to him. See if you can switch him to the memoir. If he's really hung up on the transportation book, dangle the possibility of a two-book deal. We'll publish his transportation book if he gives us the memoir, too. Who's his agent?"

An agent was the second key. You need a literary agent to get publishers to take you seriously. But agents only want new clients sent by people they know.

So early the next morning, to take advantage of the time difference, I phoned my old roommate Tim at his New York office.

His family name was one of the most notorious of the old Robber Baron era, and his parents and grandparents had devoted their lives making up for that through their well-known foundations devoted to problems like Third World hunger. But Tim and his numerous cousins preferred to keep a lower profile and play behind-the-scenes roles in their Good Works.

Obviously, Tim's family name would open any door in the world for him. But his greatest asset was his distinctly unpretentious physical appearance. He had a face like a bullfrog. With watery blue eyes and a faint stutter. Plus an awkward, undersized body that made the most expensive clothes look like Salvation Army castoffs on him. So most people felt instantly at ease in his presence, an advantage he learned to exploit with consummate artistry.

We got to know each other during our final year at Exeter and became roommates at Harvard, despite our radically different interests. After graduation, our paths diverged as he went down the street to MIT for a PhD in environmental science while I went into journalism.

But he showed up on my doorstep two days after the storm broke over me in Washington. Insisted on taking me to dinner. Where he kept asking what attracted me to basketball as a kid. How I learned the game. What it was like to be a star player at a top prep school. How I felt when my shattered knee ended my sports career.

After that, he phoned me almost every night to talk about anything but my scandal. He was the only person who stuck by me through those terrible months when my world came to an end. Even to the point of telling me, almost as an aside a few weeks before my unemployment payments were scheduled to run out, about a small California newspaper that was looking for an experienced reporter. And it didn't dawn on me until much later that he'd probably checked out the newspaper ahead of time and even recommended me to the publisher.

So naturally Tim was the first person I thought of calling about an agent.

"Sure, Wes. I know somebody you might want to talk to," he said after I'd filled him in on my book project. "Got to know him last year when one of our guys had a Global Warming manuscript he wanted to find a home for. Did a great job for us. Want his number?"

"I'd be very grateful."

"Okay. Give me a minute while I look."

I could picture him leafing through his Rolodex. Enormously fat because he knew almost everybody worth knowing in the world. Not hard when you have a family name like Tim's.

After a few moments, he came back on the line with the agent's name and phone number.

"Give me a chance to call Ralph first," he said. "So he can expect to hear from you. Can I phone you later?"

"I'm covering a Lions Club lunch for my newspaper. Can you leave a text message on my cell phone?"

"Sure. Let me check if I have your current number."

* * *

Tim's text message was on my cell phone when the Lions Club lunch ended shortly after two. Lots of useful detail. But the bottom line was that Ralph was looking forward to hearing from me and would be in his office until six. So I phoned him from my car in the parking lot.

He acted delighted to hear from me. Asked how I knew Tim. Wanted to be filled in on the details of my book. Sounded encouraging, and wondered how soon I could send him a Proposal. I told him a day or two so I could go over the final draft one more time. He acted pleasantly surprised.

We rambled on for a while trying to impress each other. Then he pleaded running late for cocktails with a book editor across town and asked if we could talk further tomorrow. I told him sure, since I knew nobody drank cocktails anymore in New York. He ended our conversation by asking me to give his best regards to Tim.

As I drove back to the newspaper, I formulated the Lions Club lunch story in my mind. I knocked it off in an easy fifteen minutes when I arrived. Then mentioned a possible story idea I needed to follow up on. Left the office and drove to my apartment. Where my computer stood waiting patiently on my desk.

I knew an effective Book Proposal needed a distinctive angle. Something fresh and eye-catching. Promising a book on an important topic. Written in a catchy prose style that would make it a compelling read. And tickle the biases of Senior Editors at mainstream publishers. Not to mention the literary agents who lived off them.

So I sat down at the keyboard and started writing. Spilling forth ideas that had been percolating in my mind for longer than I realized. Turning out the Introduction in a nonstop blaze of inspiration. Being pleasantly surprised when I read it over on the screen.

BOOK PROPOSAL
Introduction

It's the same old debate that's waxed and waned ever since the thirteen original colonies transformed themselves into the United State of America.

- *Should we let GOVERNMENT take care of our problems?*

- *Or should we rely on PRIVATE ENTERPRISE?*

By **GOVERNMENT,** *do we mean:*

- *Today's collection of time-serving bureaucrats who never had a fresh idea in their lives? Mindlessly shuffling papers on their desks while they wait for their pensions to kick in?*

- *Working in agencies headed by political hacks who have trouble finding the Men's Room?*

- *Administering programs passed by elected politicians? Who campaign for votes by pandering to the biases they assume have replaced sound judgment among the voting population? With their pockets stuffed full of dollars from the K Street lobbyists and trade associations that are their only real constituents?*

All of which has brought us such proud government triumphs as the New Orleans recovery from Hurricane Katrina. The collapse of the Minneapolis bridge. Stalemated overseas wars that can be neither won nor abandoned. You get the idea.

By **PRIVATE ENTERPRISE,** *do we mean:*

- *Large corporations run by hired-gun top managers? Who talk glibly about "enhancing stockholder value" while they quietly manipulate corporate cash flows to feather their own nests?*

- *Or businessmen like jewelry king "Mad Max" Bloom? Who get more thrills by ripping off the public for ten dollars through chicanery and fraud than by earning a hundred dollars legitimately?*

- *Or the super-couth Boy Scout leader types who carry on end-lessly about the importance of being "good corporate citizens"? While they secretly cook their company books to hide the cash they've diverted to off-balance-sheet enterprises that they just happen to own?*

All attracted to the institutionalized greed of Private Enterprise. Giving us such disasters as Enron, WorldCom, and countless other American companies looted into Chapter Eleven by their top managers.

This Great Debate ranges across the entire spectrum of the American economy as we struggle to figure out how to handle the megaproblems of a rapidly aging population. Not to mention providing all Americans with effective, affordable health care. And correcting the environmental mess we've made of the planet.

The list goes on. And it's a long one.

But nowhere is this debate sharper than in transportation, which provides essential support services for the nation's entire economy.

Take our roadway systems, for example. They're the primary component of the nation's transportation complex. And the only component able to offer direct door-to-door service for moving people and goods.

Since the 1930s, roadways have been the near-exclusive preserve of Government.

But since 1980, their lane capacity has only increased by little more than 3 percent. While travel demand has doubled.

With numbers like these, is it any wonder that traffic congestion has reached gridlock levels in our most important metropolitan regions as average travel speeds plummet? While existing roads prematurely wear out at skyrocketing rates because of inadequate maintenance, as state and local governments seek to "save money"?

All of which forces commuters to spend more time traveling to and from their jobs. Not to mention increasing the costs of moving goods, which we all have to pay for in higher prices for everything we buy.

The effect of both being to turn our roadway systems into constraints on economic growth rather than growth boosters.

*Government's traditional mantra has always been that "**roads should be free.**" Supported by taxes. Just like public parks and swimming pools.*

- *But fuel tax revenues at existing rates can't begin to keep pace with the ever-rising costs of roadway construction and maintenance as the nation's motor vehicle fleet becomes increasingly fuel efficient and additives like ethanol remain untaxed.*

- *Meanwhile, elected government officials refuse to adjust tax rates to reflect inflation. Because they're convinced that tax increases are a greater voter turnoff than being caught in a motel room with an underage girl.*

*So government roadway operators are caught in a bind between high-growth costs and slow-growth revenues. Which converts the football coach's old half-time pep talk about "**doing more with less**" into the more depressingly real "**doing less with less.**"*

The roadway funding crisis has become so critical that it's actually stirred new interest in supplementing fuel taxes with tolls.

Crazy? Sure. As crazy as charging people for admission to movie theaters.

But isn't this how we acquire most of the goods and services produced by Private Enterprise? You want, you pay. The more you want, the more you pay. Why should roads be any different?

Charging tolls on a few roads, bridges, and tunnels has been a small part of the transportation scene since the New Deal. Small, but very successful.

- *Tolls charge individual travelers (not taxpayers in general) for access to these transportation facilities according to how many trips they want to make on them.*

- *The revenues that tolls generate are better able to keep pace with roadway construction and operating costs. So toll facilities can be properly maintained to assure long working lives and smoother rides for motorists. Plus new capacity to meet rising travel demand.*

- *Today's electronic toll collection technology eliminates the need to stop at crowded toll plazas. Dig money out of your pocket. Hand it to the attendant or drop it in a basket. Now you can drive straight through without stopping. So the potential for widespread use of tolls has moved out of the economics class-room and into the real world.*

Funding our roadway systems with tolls ("user charges" as stained-glass academic types like to call them) means adopting one of the most effective principles of Private Enterprise. And it opens the door to applying other sensible Private Enterprise principles to managing our roadway systems more effectively. Even to the point of forming creative partnerships between government agencies and private corporations to build and operate toll road systems truly able to cope with the demands of the 21st Century.

But is greater reliance on Private Enterprise really the best way to solve current transportation problems?

Not if the Airline Industry is any example.

Airlines are another vital component of the nation's transportation complex. And the most effective way to move people and time-sensitive goods over distances of more than a few hundred miles.

But since the domestic airlines were freed from government regula-tion in 1978, they've managed to turn themselves into Third World basket cases.

- *Collectively, they've set an astonishing record for losing more money than they've ever made.*

- *Most of them have been in and out of bankruptcy at least once. And in the process, they've squandered the billions of dollars in private equity capital invested in them over the years. While making a few "vulture capitalists" who knew how to exploit the bankruptcy laws immensely rich.*

- *Today, they stumble along with aging fleets of inefficient airplanes while subjecting passengers to cattle-car conditions in overcrowded cabins. Losing their baggage in unpredictable ways that seem to have become one more hidden cost of flying. Not to mention travel delays that have increasingly become the norm.*

- *Most of their top managers aren't even smart enough to hedge the future cost of jet fuel with today's highly flexible derivative tools. Then wonder in surprise why their rosy profit projections get swallowed up in red ink as petroleum prices rise.*

- *These same managers cling blindly to their superglitzy "yield management" programs. These are supposed to generate higher revenues by giving discounts to passengers who reserve early and charging top fares to those who show up at the last minute. But isn't that like Macy's increasing the price of a cocktail dress the longer it remains hanging on the rack? Oh yeah, smart.*

From a purely business standpoint, most domestic airlines seem to have turned into conduits for funneling revenues generated by air passengers and air cargo shippers into the maws of service and supply firms that circle them like hyenas. Firms that lease them outdated airplanes. Clean their cabins (if you don't look too closely). Sell them corner-cutting main-tenance services. Anything to make a buck.

Could Government really do any worse?

Things have gotten so bad in the domestic airline industry that experts have largely given up trying to devise solutions.

Oh sure, some people still talk about reregulating the airlines so air travel can be as nice as it was in the Good Old Days. Or crafting intri-cate new financing plans to provide airlines with the modern plant and equipment they need to make decent profits. Or devising new economic models for airline operations that are supposed to solve everything.

But nobody really takes these panaceas seriously. Instead, they hold their breaths waiting for a total collapse that may be just around the corner.

The magic of Private Enterprise in action? Come on.

Well, who cares?

Aren't we like a passive TV audience watching a pair of networks knock themselves out trying to save two former hit shows in the same time slot now dying of old age? One may make it. Or both. Or neither. No cash out of our pockets in any case. There's always something else to watch.

Except that we can't afford to be passive where transportation is con-cerned. Not when the outcome can effect how much cash we'll have in our pockets tomorrow. We have to get involved. At least pay attention. Know what the options are.

What options? Here they are. All four of them.

- **OPTION ONE. Do nothing. *Forget about spending huge sums of money to build the new transportation capacity our econ-omy needs. Learn to live with what we've got. Stop bellyaching about bottlenecks that diminish our mobility. Leave earlier in the morning to accommodate a more time-consuming trip to work. Have dinner an hour or two later in the evening. Make fewer discretionary trips. Spend more time at home watching***

*TV. Muddle through. At least we'll get to keep a bigger propor-
tion of our income in our pockets instead of paying it out in
higher prices and taxes to transportation providers.*

*Of course, this assumes our income won't shrink as transporta-
tion bottlenecks choke off economic activity. Leaving a smaller
pie to be divided among more people. Not to mention forcing us
to pay higher prices for consumer goods and services because of
the added transportation costs imposed on producers. Which
we try to offset by buying less. Lowering our living standards.*

  *Needless to say, some sharp businessmen will make out like
bandits as they learn how to exploit the decline of our society.
Remember what Rhett Butler told Scarlett? There are as many
fortunes to be made from the decline of a society as from building one. So let's keep our fingers crossed that we can be among
these few lucky individuals.*

- **OPTION TWO.** *Have the Federal Government move aggressively to shrink the nation's economy to a level where its transportation needs can comfortably be met by existing capacity.
  The assumption is that formal "Planned Shrinkage" programs
  can spread the resulting pain more equitably among the American people.*

*Obviously, the main focus of these programs will have to be the
nation's 100 top metropolitan regions because that's where most
of the economic action is. They generate three-quarters of the nation's Gross Domestic Product and are home to two-thirds of its
population. Their dominance as economic engines means the effect
of shrinking their economies will spill over to the rest of the country. Placing all Americans on a low-cal diet of reduced living standards. (Except, of course, the very rich.)*

We can expect these federal programs to include strict regulations that bring immigration to a screeching halt. Limit the number of children women are allowed to have so the size of the nation's population is effectively frozen. Impose residency rules directing where people can live, to achieve "rational" population density levels according to the dictates of federal planners. Ration health care services to favor the nation's most productive workers and their families, while limiting services to the elderly and other dependent members of the population. You get the idea.

All this may sound like one of those contemporary graphic novels (which is what intellectuals like to call comic books these days to justify their high prices) depicting the End of America in properly shocking terms.

On the other hand, think of all the money we'll save by not having to pay for elaborate new programs to increase transportation capacity. Even if most of these savings quickly run through our fingers to pay the extra costs imposed by a declining society.

- **OPTION THREE. *Convert our top 100 metropolitan regions into true 24-hour societies so we can make use of existing transportation capacity now lying idle during the nighttime hours when most people are asleep.***

By spreading economic activity in these regions more evenly across all hours of the day, we effectively acquire new capacity that would cost multibillions of dollars to build from scratch. So we make more efficient use of the transportation capacity we already have. Just like factories that operate three shifts per day. So the money invested in the buildings and their production equipment is always generating profits.

Of course, the social engineering needed to accomplish this is scarcely trivial. Roughly half the people living in each of these metro regions would have to switch from living during the day to living at night. Working. Commuting. Going to school. Shopping. Patronizing restaurants and movie theaters. All the other human activities that compose the normal business day. No doubt some fairly heroic government regulations would be necessary to assure the right balance between the daytime and nighttime populations.

But think how cheaply we could acquire additional transportation capacity this way.

- *OPTION FOUR. Do the unthinkable and move aggressively to acquire the new transportation capacity we need. Marshall the best resources of Government and Private Enterprise to get it all done in sensible ways. Shame them into it, if necessary. Face up to the cost and figure out clever new ways to fund it. Act like Big Kids for a change.*

Political commentators who like to think they're as witty as Groucho Marx will smile droll smiles and tell us this is the worst option—except for all the others. Well, let them have their fun. It's a small price to pay as long as they get on board.

For years the Federal Government has told us "We can't build our way out of congestion."

Of course we can. And we have to if we expect our children to live better than we do.

Otherwise we're looking into an Abyss of Lost Dreams.

That's why this book will concentrate on the Great Debate concerning Government versus Private Enterprise as it affects how we can solve our problems in transportation.

But in the process, it can illustrate solutions that apply to the whole American economy.

Stay tuned.

* * *

Better than I'd hoped.

Of course, it still needed a couple of sections full of facts and figures. And some creative ideas. Headed with punchy titles like "The Challenge" and "The Game Plan." Just to demonstrate that I knew the territory. But the Introduction would do most of the selling. In fact, it was as far as most Senior Editors would read.

So I emailed a copy of the Introduction to Ralph in New York with a cover note explaining that I was still wordsmithing the follow-up sections. Emailed another copy to Susan so she could get it to Elijah. And emailed one to Tim.

Then I saved the whole file. Turned off the computer. Went to bed and fell asleep immediately.

* * *

The night before my next meeting with Elijah, I had a remarkable dream.

I was lying on a canvas stretcher. Being carried by two Chinese guerrilla soldiers through the nighttime darkness. Towards an unmarked DC-3 that sat on an airstrip somewhere in rural China during World War II.

"Be careful with him," I heard the Dragon Lady say to the soldiers from somewhere close behind me. "His knee is injured."

"Yes, Madam," one of the soldiers replied.

I remembered the sequence from the comic strip, which I'd read many times.

But this time something was different. Something I couldn't put my finger on.

Then the Dragon Lady moved into my field of vision alongside the stretcher. She was dressed in military combat clothes. And the difference immediately became clear.

"Wait a minute. There's something wrong," I said to her. "You're the one who should be lying on this stretcher."

"There's nothing wrong with my legs."

"I'll say. They're the greatest legs in China."

"Don't be impertinent, young man. We have to get you on that plane and fly you out of here."

"Are you coming, too?"

"Of course. I'm not going to let you make the trip alone."

"What if I try to escape?"

"No chance of that. Your knee is too badly injured. Besides, I'll be with you the whole time."

"That's some consolation."

"No doubt. Now lie still."

It was happening just like in the comic strip. Except that our positions were reversed. I was the injured one lying on the stretcher. Not her. Why? What did it mean?

As the soldiers raised my stretcher to load it onto the plane, its jostling movements made me aware of a throbbing pain in my right knee. The one I had wrecked at Exeter playing basketball.

But that hadn't happened until years after World War II.

More confusion.

The DC-3 had been converted to a cargo carrier so there were no seats inside. The soldiers carried me to the middle of the cabin and gently placed my stretcher across two wooden crates that may have been used to carry ammunition. The Dragon Lady seated herself on a third crate facing me.

"How did I injure my knee?" I asked her. "I forget."

"Casualty of war. It doesn't matter now. The plane will take off in a minute."

"Where are we going?"

"Chungking. It has hospitals to treat your knee. You deserve all the honors due a hero. You helped to save us from the Japanese."

"Including you?"

"Of course. This isn't the first time. The Dragon Lady always pays her debts."

"Yeah, I've heard that from you before."

"Haven't I always kept my word?"

"In a roundabout sort of way."

"Never mind. We're ready to take off. Hold tight to my hand."

"Aren't you getting a little chummy?"

"Don't get the wrong idea. I don't want you to fall off the stretcher."

"I should have figured."

"Not that I don't find you pleasing, young man. But you already know that."

"And how."

I took her hand. It was slim but surprisingly strong. And I thought I could feel something special passing between our fingers. But that could have been my imagination. Or because of the throbbing in my knee.

She continued to hold my hand as the plane roared down the runway, took off, and climbed rapidly to its cruising altitude.

When it finally leveled off, she let go of my hand. Then abruptly stood up and began unbuttoning the front of her combat jacket.

"Hey. What are you doing?" I said in surprise.

"It's cold at this altitude."

"I know, but...."

"I have to protect my investment."

"Wait a minute. That's a line from a movie I've seen. *Trading Places*, I think. Jamie Lee Curtis...."

"Never mind movies. We have a long history of doing favors for each other. I want that to continue."

I was sweating when I awoke from that incredible dream. With soaked pajamas and bed sheets. Clinging instinctively to its thrilling immediacy.

But finally, inevitably, it died away. And I was left alone in the darkness of my bedroom. Gasping for breath. My heart pounding.

Then the entirety of the dream hit me like a sledgehammer. Making my stomach turn over sickeningly.

I was supposed to meet Elijah in a few hours.

But I had just made passionate love with his wife in the dream world of that World War II airplane. Which had flown us into an eternity of bliss from which there could be no return.

And I could hear in my mind the sing-song street verse chanted by school kids in my old neighborhood.

What is Right
And what is Wrong?
And how do I tell
The Difference?

Oh Susan, Susan.... What's to become of us?

I was afraid to let myself go back to sleep. So I got up and turned on the bedroom light. Put on fresh pajamas. Walked into the living room and turned on all its lights. To drive away any hint of the darkness and whatever else had given birth to my dream. Sat down at my computer and fired it up. Resumed wordsmithing the Book Proposal with mindless intensity. Trying distract myself from what I knew mattered more than anything else in the world.

What was it the poet said? In dreams begin responsibilities?

Yeah, right.

* * *

I tried to think of a reasonable-sounding excuse to postpone my meeting with Elijah until the following week. But there wasn't enough time to get word to him. I had no choice but to keep our scheduled meeting.

As I walked through the green door into the Visiting Room and saw Elijah waiting for me, I felt like a guilty kid with his hand in the cookie jar. And even though he couldn't possibly know how I had betrayed him in my dream a few hours earlier, my guts still clenched and churned.

"How are you feeling?" I managed to say as we shook hands.

"Fine, fine. Thanks for asking. Just a touch of food poisoning. No big deal."

Yeah, sure. Probably didn't even happen. A ploy to send me Susan in his place. To find out things about me. Taunt me with her uncanny resemblance to the Dragon Lady. Put me at a psychological disadvantage.

But I couldn't let him get away with it. I had to turn the tables on him.

What was it the guy said about the best defense being a good offense?

"Listen," I said as we sat drinking Susan's green tea at the table in the corner. "I still have questions about why you pleaded guilty."

"I already explained that."

"No, you didn't. All you did was give me a lot of hypothetical bullshit about that phony Managing Director. And it doesn't add up."

"That bad?"

"You've got to trust me, Elijah. Tell me the truth. I swear not to tell anybody else."

"You look so grim. Is it really that important?"

Why did he have to use Susan's phrase about me looking grim, after she had left me babbling with that comment about smelling good? Had she told him every detail about our lunch at the Chinese restaurant? Including how I reacted to the things she said?

Of course she had. She was no dummy.

But neither was I.

"Come on, Elijah. Level with me. One Brooklyn street kid to another."

"Yeah, okay."

"You'll tell me?"

"Sure. What's to lose?"

"And no hiding behind hypothetical fairy tales or other Talmudic tricks this time?"

"No, no. Plain language. I promise."

"Good."

He took a long sip of tea. Then placed his cup back on the table and looked straight at me.

"You remember what I said about the toll road corporation selling equity shares to private investors?" he said.

"Yeah."

"Well, private equity tends to be expensive. In terms of the investment return it demands, I mean. But to make the project look really exciting from a financial standpoint, I had to find bargain-priced equity."

"Okay."

"Bargain-priced equity usually exists in foreign companies that have piled up a lot of U.S. dollars offshore. Underground dollars. Dollars they want to convert into kosher income streams in the United States."

"You're talking about money laundering?"

"That's what some people call it. Anyway, I made some phone calls to people I knew at various banks. And one guy thought his firm's London office had some clients who might be what I was looking for. So I phoned his contact in London and flew over that night for some confidential meetings."

"Sounds like a spy movie."

"Better. This is the real world where serious money is involved. The clients in question were a group of Arab companies. They had a big pile of offshore U.S. dollars from acting as middlemen for Afghanistan poppy growers.

"Poppy growers?"

"You know, opium poppies. Afghanistan's biggest industry."

"Jesus...."

"So I offered them a deal. They'd form a consortium with a U.S. company, which would act as their American front. The consortium would buy equity shares in the toll road corporation. With poppy cash supplied by the Arab companies. In return for a glatt kosher income stream in the U.S. composed of yearly dividends paid from the toll road corporation's revenues."

"From roadway tolls."

"Mainly. But they'd have to sit still for a lower-than-normal investment return from their dividends. So the toll road corporation would have bargain-priced equity."

"Dividends paid from the corporation's yearly toll revenues?"

"Right. Which the Arab companies were okay with, since their goal was to convert their offshore poppy cash into a kosher U.S. income stream. Clear so far?"

"I think so. But why were they willing to accept a low dividend rate?"

"Six of one, half a dozen of the other. If you know what I mean."

"Sorry. You've lost me."

"Most ways of laundering offshore dollars aren't going to give you a hundred cents on the dollar."

"Less?"

"Usually much less. But my way offered them a hundred cents on the dollar in the U.S., so long as they were willing to accept a lower dividend rate. In the end, they'd make out better with my deal."

"So they accepted it."

"They did the deal. But they wanted a guarantee to cover their risk."

"What risk?"

"Normal business risk. Like the toll road corporation not being able to pay dividends for some reason. Not likely, of course. But Arabs are very conservative when it comes to such things and I wasn't going to argue. So I told them my firm would give them a private put on their investment. You know what a put is?"

"Some kind of financial option, isn't it?"

"Yes. In this case, the Arab companies would have the right to sell their equity investment to my firm anytime in the next ten years for a price equal to its original value. Payable in U.S. dollars in New York. Guaranteed by my firm. Backed by a line of credit from the bank whose London office would be the broker of record for the deal. So either way, the Arabs would achieve their goal of laundering their poppy cash. And we had a deal."

"But was it legal?"

"Legal? You mean, legally enforceable?"

"I guess so."

"Sure. We even got formal letters of opinion from a New York law firm and a London law firm stating that the deal was legally enforceable under the laws of our respective countries. Capish?"

"Why are you going Italian on me all of a sudden?"

"Slip of the tongue. Borough Park's just north of Bensonhurst, after all."

"Are you suggesting the Mafia was involved?"

"Italy's Mafia certainly. They run the business of refining raw opium. In Sicily mostly."

"And New York's Five Families?"

"They're involved in everything. But usually behind the scenes. It wasn't something I had to worry about. We know how to stay out of each others way."

How could I expect to stand up to a mind like Elijah's? He could probably run rings around anybody in the world.

But I had to keep on trying.

"Sounds like you were home free," I said.

"More or less."

"Then why did you have to plead guilty?"

"Don't you see? If I went to trial, the prosecutor was bound to bring up the toll road project."

"So?"

"With Arab companies supplying the equity capital? To launder their opium poppy profits? Plus the possibility of the Five Families hanging around the edges? Come on, Wes. You know the media. They'd have a field day with all that when it came out. Wouldn't you do the same thing if you were still working in Washington?"

"Yeah, I suppose so."

"The only way I could protect the toll road project was to stay as far as possible from a courtroom. That meant pleading guilty."

"No matter what the cost."

179

"What cost? I paid a hundred thousand dollar fine. That's pennies to any reasonably successful investment banker."

"Plus jail time."

"Yeah, jail time. But it was worth it. I couldn't sit still and see the toll road project go down in flames, could I?"

"Okay. Now it's all clear. I believe you."

"Thanks a lot."

"But not entirely for the reasons you've just given."

"What do you mean?"

"Wasn't it also to protect your family?"

"From what?"

"Look, Elijah. In Brooklyn, the ultimate sin is to be a canary."

"Yeah, the old Abe Reles story. Like all canaries, he could sing but he couldn't fly."

"That's something we learned at our mother's knee. We don't even have to think about it."

"So?"

"So I don't have to remind you of the reputation Arabs have for vengeance against people who rat on them. And as for the Five Families. . . . "

"I told you, their involvement was ... peripheral."

"Yeah, sure. Don't try to tell me you weren't concerned about protecting your family. I've met your wife. And I can imagine what your children are like. Am I supposed to believe you wouldn't do anything to keep them safe?"

"I pleaded guilty, didn't I?"

"But without agreeing to testify against anybody else, right?"

"Naturally. . . . "

"Yeah, naturally. And look what it cost you to keep your mouth shut. In prison time and fines."

I actually had him squirming. He looked at me, then quickly looked away. Tried to say something, but no words came. Finally composed himself and looked at me with a slow smile.

"Either I taught you too well or you're smarter than I thought," he said with what had to be a trace of admiration in his voice.

"Whatever. But it obviously sounds better to say you were simply trying to protect the toll road project. Which is okay by me. I'll tell it that way to anybody who asks, if that's what you want."

"Fine. Now can I ask you a question?"

"Shoot."

"It's about your book proposal. Especially the Introduction."

"What's wrong with it?"

"Do I detect a certain tone of what might be called a knee-jerk liberal bias against Private Enterprise and free markets?"

"Come on, Elijah. It's just a sales pitch. Playing to the prejudices of New York book editors. You know what they're like,"

"A lot of people aren't going to read it that way. Your Introduction implies that Government is basically okay as an institution. The problem is that it's been taken over by too many klutzes."

"Yeah, so?"

"But you go on to imply that Private Enterprise as an institution is inherently evil. That's why it attracts so many crooks and connivers like Mad Max Bloom."

"I don't recall using the word 'evil.'"

"Maybe not. But that's what comes through. Reflecting your liberal biases."

"Because I went to Harvard and worked for the Liberal Eastern Media?"

"I have no opinion about the source. Just your Introduction's tone."

"I.... Look, do you mind if we talk about this outside? I need some fresh air."

"Me, too."

* * *

As I followed him across the lounge and out the door into the yard, I noticed for the first time that he walked with a slightly uncoordinated waddle. Which made me feel better. I was an athlete and he wasn't. I could spot him fifty points on any schoolyard basketball court in Brooklyn and still beat him handily. Assuming he could even play basketball.

With Susan watching us through the chain link fence while I ran him into the ground. Making her forget all about how good he smelled.

My God, what was wrong with me? I was turning into a monster.

But I couldn't help it. He held Susan a prisoner in marriage. And I wanted her so much it was turning my guts inside out.

"Look," Elijah said as soon as we were outside. "I've worked both sides of the street, so I know what I'm talking about. After I got my MBA, I spent nine years working for New York City. In the Office of Management and Budget. That gave me a good sense of Government at its best."

"And?"

"High moral standards were taken for granted. Oh sure, we had occasional crooks. But very few considering the enormous number of people in City Government. Just enough to keep the media happy. You know how they love to drool over government scandals. But the basic culture was one of high moral standards."

"So why did you switch to investment banking?"

"The money, obviously."

"Oh come on, Elijah. That's too pat."

"You think so? The firm that recruited me thought there was big money to be made offering governments financial advice for nice annual fees. They knew about me because I was active in various government finance trade associations and had a reputation. So they figured I had a nice fat Rolodex they could exploit. And when they saw how fast I returned their phone call.…"

"You were that hungry?"

"I had two kids, with a third on the way. Even students of the Talmud know there's a real world out there. What do you want from me, Wes?"

"But there must have been other possibilities."

"Like those traditional White Shoe investment banking firms maybe? Where everybody went to Princeton after prepping at Lawrenceville? And they take each other to lunch in their private Manhattan clubs? To talk about the latest America's Cup sailboat races? And oh-so-politely allude to next year's bond issue? Which should obviously be placed with the most socially acceptable life insurance companies? Where we just happen to have 'Friends on the Board'? Can you remotely, in your wildest imagination, picture a firm like that wanting to recruit me?"

"Their loss."

"Yeah. Nice of you to say so. But they're dying anyway. You know the informal motto of the firm that recruited me?"

"What."

"You eat what you kill."

"That's ... awful."

"Is it? What do you suppose makes the world turn?"

"I know, but...."

"Call it Cultural Darwinism at its worst. Call it whatever makes you feel better. It's today's Reality."

"Even in what you call White Shoe firms?"

"Oh, they can pretend it's a totally couth gentlemen's game. By only doing deals with their former Princeton classmates and social equals. But that customer base isn't large enough these days. Not with so many hungry firms out there run by Big Swinging Dicks from the trading floor. You know what a trader's like?"

"I guess not."

"He's a wild animal, Wes. A complete predator. Looking for every opportunity to pounce, kill, and devour. Just like a Siberian Tiger, the most fearsome animal on earth. What chance does a White Shoe firm stand against that kind of competition?"

"And one of those firms recruited you."

"Absolutely. Now, remember what I told you about Insider Trading at our first meeting?"

"Sure. The moral standards were much lower."

"Not just lower. Nonexistent. There was no culture of morality at all at my firm. It was taken for granted you'd grab every chance to line your pockets. Just don't get caught."

"You sound like a witness for my defense."

"You're missing my point. In City Government, there are surprisingly few opportunities to cheat for personal gain. Mainly because Government isn't a commercial undertaking. But in Private Enterprise, such opportunities are all around you. Because the whole megilla is commercial."

"So you agree that Private Enterprise is inherently…."

"Neither institution is inherently anything when it comes to morality. It all depends on the people they attract. Take the Mad Maxes of this world. You mentioned them in your Introduction."

"Right."

"You defined them as getting more satisfaction out of making ten dollars by ripping off the public than making a hundred dollars by behaving like Boy Scouts."

"You don't agree?"

"It's an interesting insight. How did you come up with it?"

"I read an article about Max Bloom on the Internet. Its theme was how a Bad Guy finally got caught and sent to prison for securities fraud. Lots of detail about how he finagled the books of his retail jewelry chain before taking it public. Stuff like that."

"Yeah, I know the article."

"The writer seemed to have lots of facts."

"Sure. Like that *Time* magazine article about your Washington scandal."

"At least they had the facts straight. More or less."

"But didn't we agree that facts and truth are two different things?"

"Are you saying the Mad Max article may be kind of anemic when it comes to truth?"

"More than kind of. That's why your insight is so interesting."

"Chalk it up to my former police reporter's instinct."

"Whatever. In any case, it catches the essence of Uncle Max."

"Uncle?"

"By marriage. Only by marriage."

"Jesus...."

"He married my mother's youngest sister."

"I didn't know he was Orthodox."

"He was whatever he had to be to get what he wanted."

"So he put on a show?"

"If my aunt had been Irish Catholic, he would have joined the Holy Name Society and claimed Bloom was a fine old Irish name. Just like Caruso."

"As bad as that."

"Worse. That's why he had a job waiting for me when I graduated from Brooklyn College with my accounting degree."

"You went to work for his jewelry chain?"

"Nothing so transparent. The job he had for me was with a medium-sized accounting firm in Manhattan. Where his jewelry chain happened to be the largest client. I was supposed to be his mole."

"Mole?"

"That's what it amounted to. I was like a junior gofer on his account. Checking numbers and routine stuff like that. But it put me in a position to hear what the senior partners were saying about how to handle certain items in his books. So I could report any problems to him."

"I thought accounting was pretty cut and dried."

"Anything but. A lot of it comes down to a matter of opinion. Wide open, in other words."

"Like what happened with Enron?"

"Enron's a perfect example of how the presumably objective and staid Science of Accounting can be turned into a con artist's tool. Let me give you an example."

185

"I figured that was coming."

"Just pay attention. Assume you own a company whose fiscal year ends on December 31."

"Okay."

"Now assume that one of your customers accepts delivery from you of $100 worth of widgets on December 15."

"Signs a receipt and everything?"

"Everything. And at the end of December, you bill him for the hundred dollars. In the normal course of things, he pays you sometime in the next thirty days. Since your fiscal year ends on December 31, that means you receive the cash sometime in January of your next fiscal year. Clear?"

"Yeah."

"Now for the key question. In which fiscal year do you report that hundred-dollar sale of widgets? This fiscal year when the customer accepts delivery? Or next fiscal year when he sends you a check?"

"This has to be a trick question. It sounds too simple."

"Of course it's a trick question. That's what Accounting is all about. Come on, Wes What's your answer?"

"Okay. I report the sale in the next fiscal year. When the customer sends me the cash."

"That's a perfectly reasonable answer. But not to your accountant. He insists you report the sale in this fiscal year."

"That sounds crazy."

"To a normal person, yes. But your accountant insists you have to report the sale in this fiscal year. Because that's when the Economic Event took place."

"The what?"

"The Economic Event. In this case, the customer accepting delivery of the widgets. That's the whole basis of accrual accounting. The timing of Economic Events is what matters."

"So I report the sale in this fiscal year because the customer accepted delivery in December?"

"Right."

"But what happens to the hundred dollars the customer still owes me?"

"You simply add that to an asset category on your balance sheet. Called Accounts Receivable. That's a list of the money people still owe you at the end of the fiscal year. In accrual accounting, cash owed to you has the same asset status as cash you have in the bank."

"That's … mind-blowing."

"Just like Uncle Max's TV commercials. Remember the statuesque blonde wearing the long black blouse screaming at the top of her lungs: 'Our diamond prices can't be beat'? But that's how accounting works in the real world."

"Why not report everything on a cash basis?"

"Not allowed."

"By who?"

"Something called the Financial Accounting Standards Board. Popularly known as FASB."

"That's a government agency I've never heard of."

"I'm not surprised. FASB isn't a government agency."

"It's not?"

"The accounting profession is self-regulated. In the best American tradition of giving the fox the keys to the henhouse. FASB is a collection of private academic klutzes. Mostly accounting professors from leading business schools. And they have a horror of cash. To them, cash is like shit. Something you can't talk about in polite company. So they insist that everything has to be reported on a strict accrual basis. And business firms have no choice but to comply."

"So you're saying the financial statements released by business firms…?"

"Fairy tales. Whatever top management wants to show to con you into buying their stock. Within very broad limits set by something called GAAP."

"Gap? You mean, like the gap between Reality and Fairyland?"

"That's good, Wes. Very good. I should know better than to give your Harvard wit such an obvious opening."

"You did say gap, didn't you?"

"That's G-A-A-P. Short for Generally Accepted Accounting Principles."

"Accepted by whom?"

"The accounting profession. Not to mention top managers seeking to cook their books. And, of course, the suckers they want to con. Want an example?"

"Yeah. Assume I'm like some idiot who's always thought the earth was flat being confronted by the possibility it's actually round."

"That's how you learn. Now pay attention."

"Yes, yes."

"Suppose you have a customer who signs a contract with you on December 15. And the contract obligates him to accept delivery of a hundred dollars worth of widgets from you each month from January through next December. You with me?"

"Yes."

"That's twelve hundred dollars worth of widgets during your next fiscal year."

"Okay."

"Now. In what fiscal year do you report that twelve hundred dollar chunk of sales? In this fiscal year, when the customer signs the contract? In the next fiscal year when the customer accepts delivery of the twelve shipments of widgets? Some combination? What?"

"Oh my God...."

"You see how open-ended it is? GAAP lets *you* define when the so-called Economic Event took place. Did it take place on December 15 of this fiscal year? When the customer signed the contract? In which case, you can report the entire twelve hundred dollars as sales revenue for this fiscal year. Or did it take place during each of the next twelve months beginning in January? When the customer accepted delivery of the widgets? Which lets you report the twelve hundred dollars as sales revenue for the next fiscal year. It's up to top managers to decide. Based on how they want to twist GAAP around to serve their private agendas. And FASB will bless their decision."

"So where does that leave the poor slob who wants to Invest in America?"

"Oh, he gets fucked. Naturally."

"Naturally?"

"The pros sucker him into the equity markets to provide the grease for stock manipulations. The pros know he doesn't have a clue about the reality of things or he'd stick to nice safe Treasury securities and bank CDs. They figure he's greedy for a big score. So they sucker him in with all kinds of promises. Then strip him naked and leave him bleeding by the side of the road. Figuring his greed got him just what he deserved."

"Blame the victim, in other words."

"No. Blame the victim's foolish greed. He wants something for nothing. So they give him something. A few weeks of cheap thrills watching his stock go up. Then leave him with nothing."

"Then it really is a cesspool."

"It's certainly no Boy Scout summer camp. Now let me ask you a question."

"Go ahead."

"Why do you suppose professional athletes are forbidden from betting on any games they play in?"

"That's easy. So they won't be tempted to make their bets pay off by shaving points and so on."

"Makes all the sense in the world, doesn't it?"

"Sure."

"And yet we allow top managers to bet on the games they play in."

"By buying stock in the companies they run?"

"Sure. We even encourage that kind of betting. We shower them with stock options."

"While they can manipulate the final score by the way they cook the books to drive up the price of the company's stock."

189

"All strictly according to GAAP."

"Yeah, I see what you mean."

"So shouldn't we *prohibit* managers from buying and selling stock in their companies? Just like we prohibit professional athletes from betting on the games they play in."

"Makes sense when you put it that way. How would you pay them?"

"Give them big cash salaries. Plus generous bonuses depending on how well their companies do."

"I guess that would work."

"And link the size of their bonuses to how profitable their companies are over several years. Five years maybe. As an incentive for them to manage their companies wisely."

"So their bonuses would be deferred?"

"Of course. That's what you want. To encourage them to really and truly manage for the future."

"Not to mention removing the incentive to cook the books."

"That goes without saying."

"And where would this leave the Max Blooms of this world?"

"Oh, they'd still have an edge. Remember. Uncle Max's business was retail jewelry."

"What difference does that make?"

"The big advantage of retail is it's mainly a cash business. Or can be if you're clever."

"So?"

"So in a cash business, who knows whether you did a million dollars in sales last quarter? Or only half that much? Depends on what you report. And you ultimately pay income taxes on your reported sales volume, after the usual business deductions for expenses."

"You're talking about skimming."

"Of course. That's the beauty of retail. The more cash business you do, the more you can skim. Uncle Max turned it into something like an art form. Remember the commercials? 'Mad Max is selling one thousand brand new diamond rings this Sunday at prices that'll blow your mind. So bring your wallets. Don't miss out on these incredible bargains.'"

"But aren't most of those wallets full of credit cards? Especially when you're buying something like jewelry?"

"Sure. And most customers expected to pay with plastic when they walked into one of Uncle Max's stores. It was the salesman's job to turn them into cash buyers."

"How?"

"First, Uncle Max paid his salesmen big commissions for cash sales. Paid them in cash and off the books. To motivate them."

"Yeah, but the customer...."

"Second, Uncle Max let his salesmen offer big discounts. Amazingly big discounts. Like nothing the customer's ever seen before. But only on all-cash sales. Uncle Max even put private ATM machines in all his stores."

"I'm beginning to get the picture."

"Sure. It's not that complicated. And at the end of the day, each store manager would bring Uncle Max a plastic bag full of cash from his sales. Plus another plastic bag filled with handwritten receipts for those sales."

"And they'd count the cash?"

"On the dining room table in Uncle Max's big apartment in Midwood. You know Midwood?"

"Near Brooklyn College?"

"Just south. They'd count the cash and divide it into three piles. The smallest pile would be cash for the salesmen's commissions. The store manager would take that with him when he left. The next pile would be cash for sales that Uncle Max would report. Accompanied by sales receipts covering the amount, to keep things kosher. The store manager would take that with him too and deposit it in the bank."

"And the third pile?"

"That was the skim. After the store manager left, I'd help Uncle Max hide it in his proverbial dropped kitchen ceiling."

"You?"

"Who do you think was keeping score during the counting?"

"But.…"

"Uncle Max considered me Family. I was just doing what I was told."

"Following orders. The old German excuse."

"You're right. I don't deny it. So technically, I was an accessory to income tax evasion. If anybody could prove I knew what was happening to the cash."

"The cash you helped Uncle Max hide in his kitchen ceiling. That's the usual hiding place for skimmed cash."

"Ever wonder why dropped ceilings are so popular in Brooklyn?"

"Because it has so many small retail businessmen?"

"Great places to hide skimmed cash until it can be taken out of the country."

"To banks in Israel?"

"Why does everybody assume Israeli banks are into money laundering?"

"I just figured.…"

"Uncle Max used Asian and African banks mostly. And some Latin American banks. He liked them better. For reasons he never explained."

"Okay."

"Anyway, every few months Uncle Max would get on a plane for some foreign destination. Sometimes his wife would go along. Both with carry-on bags loaded with cash from his kitchen ceiling. In those days, there was no airline security. You just walked right on board with your bags."

"Yeah, but how much cash can you move that way? I mean, even if it's all in hundred-dollar bills, you can't be talking about more than.…"

"You're right. That's why Uncle Max converted the cash first."

"Into what?"

"You know about U.S. Treasury Bearer Securities?"

"You'll have to educate me."

"Treasury is always issuing new debt. To pay off old debt and to fund the budget deficit."

"Yeah, so?"

"In those days, a lot of that debt took the form of elaborately engraved pieces of paper called Bearer Securities. About the size of a typewriter page and full fancy writing. With the key phrase being 'Pay to the Bearer on such-and-such date the sum of, say, ten thousand dollars.' And you know who the Bearer is?"

"No."

"Whoever happens to have that piece of paper on the date specified. If you have it, then you're the Bearer. And Treasury will pay you the ten thousand dollars. No questions asked. If you sell it to me first, then I'm the Bearer. Get the picture?"

"You mean, it's just like a hundred-dollar bill."

"For practical purposes. Except that it's worth ten thousand dollars, not a hundred dollars. So with ten of those pieces of paper, you've got a hundred thousand dollars. And with a hundred of them, you've got a million dollars. In a stack no thicker than a copy of *Playboy* magazine. Which doesn't take up much space in a carry-on bag."

"Wow."

"It's a lot less noticeable than trying to carry a million dollars in hundred-dollar bills. In ten thousand individual hundred-dollar bills, to be precise."

"I'll say."

"So Uncle Max could walk into any Asian or African or Latin American bank where he did business and increase his account balance by a million dollars just by handing them that thin stack of Treasury securities. Nice?"

"And that's what drove him to do all those things in his retail chain?"

"No. That was simply one of the mechanisms he used to make what he wanted to do anyway pay off big."

"But...."

"You put your finger on it before. Because of the meshugana way his brain was wired, he got more kicks from being a crook than he could ever have gotten from being a Boy Scout. Economists like Susan call that Psychic Income."

Susan again. He had to remind me. Clenching my guts into a painful knot as the image of her flared up in my mind. Forcing me to breathe as slowly and evenly as I could.

"Now," he went on, seeming not to notice my physical distress. "There are millions of people like Uncle Max in America. Actuals or wannabes. And where do you think they naturally gravitate? To Government? Or to Private Enterprise?"

"To Private Enterprise, naturally."

"Right. And once they reach a certain critical mass in any business firm or industry, they determine its moral culture."

"But doesn't my Introduction imply…?"

"Readers are going to assume you're saying that the *institution itself* determines whether its people behave like saints or sinners. Government or Private Enterprise. But that's exactly backwards. It's the people collectively who determine the moral culture. And which institution do the Mad Maxes of the world naturally gravitate to?"

"I see what you're saying. It's just a question of wordsmithing."

"Wrong. It's a question of your instinctive biases. They unconsciously determine what words you use and how you arrange them."

"So because I went to Harvard and worked for the Liberal Eastern Media…."

"Look, we all have our irrational biases. That's okay. But we have to learn not to take them seriously. We have to focus on Reality. Use our intelligence and reasoning ability to understand the truth of things. Do you see?"

"I guess so. But doesn't what you've been saying undercut the whole idea of public-private partnerships?"

"How?"

"By enabling Private Enterprise types to corrupt Government.

"Not if we're smart enough to make their corruption work *for* us rather than *against* us."

"And how do you do that?"

"First of all, by not assuming that saints are automatically dumber than sinners."

"Easier said than done."

"Could be. But listen. Are you getting hungry? It's getting close to lunchtime."

At that point, food was the last thing my uneasy gastrointestinal system wanted. The soft-boiled eggs and toast I'd managed to stuff down a few hours earlier still lay in my stomach like so much indigestible garbage. In fact, I could contemplate with relief the prospect of never eating again.

"Sure," I felt compelled to say. "Let's beat the crowd for lunch."

* * *

Elijah ate his vending machine food like somebody stuck with a bad habit. I took a couple of bites of mine and managed to swallow them with sips of Coke.

Finally he stopped eating and looked at me.

"The first thing we have to realize is that public-private partnerships are as American as handguns," he said.

"Does that make them good, bad, or indifferent?"

"That's another discussion. Obviously, the attitude about handguns in Brooklyn is different from what it is in the rest of America. The same goes for public-private partnerships."

"But Brooklyn isn't America, Elijah."

"Well, America certainly isn't Brooklyn."

"Or maybe Brooklyn is the *real* America. I mean, in terms of cultural diversity and democratic ideals and all those things politicians like to talk about in their Fourth of July speeches."

"What are you trying to do, Wes? Confuse me?"

"That'll be the day."

"The point is, partnerships between Government and Private Enterprise are a fact of life in America. Like handguns. They're the Reality. Sometimes formal. Mostly informal."

"Because Government can't possibly produce all the goods and services it needs in-house?"

"That's as good a reason as any. A Government has to buy lots of stuff in order to function. And who does it buy from? Other governments? Not likely. It buys from private business firms. Lots of them. So it depends on Private Enterprise in order to function."

"Okay."

"So isn't that dependency a form of public-private partnership?"

"Maybe."

"Only maybe?"

"Private business firms also have to buy stuff from other business firms. Do you call those relationships private-private partnerships?"

"No. There's a distinction."

"Yeah? What?"

"Government and Private Enterprise have fundamentally different goals. And those goals color their reasons for buying stuff."

"In what way?"

"Government's goals involve delivering services to the public. And covering the costs of doing that with tax revenues collected from the public at large. Without reference to how much services any particular member of the public consumes."

"Okay."

"But the goals of Private Enterprise involve making profits. Mainly, by pricing what it sells at a higher level than its costs. And its sales revenue from each customer depends on how much he consumes at what price. Do you see the difference?"

"I see *a* difference. I don't know whether it's *the* difference."

"All right, think of it this way. Don't your goals color your attitudes about what you buy?"

"Why?"

"If your goals involve profits, doesn't that give your attitudes about what you buy a … a different color than if your goals involve service to the public?"

Maybe it was my imagination, but his normally articulate logic about things seemed weaker than usual. Anyway, it was worth pressing the point.

"Suppose I agree," I said. "Then what?"

"Since Government's main concern is service to the public, its *reasons* for buying stuff are bound to be different from Private Enterprise. Whose main concern is profits."

"That's just another way of saying the same thing you said before. Something's missing."

"Let me try it again. Now…. General Motors has to buy steel to make cars, right? Oh come on, Wes. Why are you shaking your head?"

I had seen an opening and plunged right in.

"Bad example," I said.

"Bad example how?"

"General Motors isn't really Private Enterprise."

"No? What do you think it is?"

"In terms of its true role in American society? GM is simply a Jobs Program."

"What an interesting idea. Tell me more."

"Think about it, Elijah. Is GM on the cutting edge of automotive technology and innovation?"

"Not so you'd notice. It's always playing catch-up ball."

"And if GM stopped making cars, would that create a crippling shortage in the automotive market?"

"No, I guess not. The other car companies could fill the gap quickly enough. Even if they had to go on three shifts per day for a while."

"Then what's left? The jobs that GM produces. Right? Jobs for American workers. Paying decent salaries and providing good benefits."

"You may be on to something."

"Okay. Let's take it one step further. If GM is mainly a Jobs Program, what should its primary management goal be? Not to maximize profits, but to maximize the number of domestic jobs. Not so?"

"Sure."

"But it's not doing that. Most of the new jobs GM creates are in other countries. Not in the United States. In fact, the number of GM domestic jobs has been falling in recent years. So where does that leave us?"

"Are you going to argue that Government should nationalize GM?"

"All right. Let's consider the implications of that. Reverse privatization, you can call it. The Federal Government buys controlling interest in GM. Installs a new Board of Directors. Whose mandate is to maximize the number of domestic jobs. Hires ace managers to do this as effectively as possible."

"Sounds very European, Wes. Airbus all over again."

"Why not, if that's what it takes? Don't forget. To the average guy, Capitalism is a failure if it can't provide him with a decent living. He doesn't give a shit about economic theory. That's why the standard American model of Capitalism is being rejected in so many parts of the world."

"And how does your government-owned GM support all these domestic jobs it's mandated to produce?"

"Oh, it still makes and sells cars."

"Even if they need government subsidies to be competitive in the marketplace?"

"If necessary. That becomes a public policy issue. Because those subsidies are really intended to support the General Motors Jobs Program. In the national interest, naturally."

"Naturally."

"But isn't that the American way, Elijah? Don't a great many private-sector jobs receive government subsidies? In one way or another?"

"You're talking about Agriculture."

"That's just the most obvious example. But it goes far beyond the usual farm welfare programs. I'm willing to bet a surprisingly large proportion of American jobs are subsidized to some degree. Usually indirectly. In hidden ways. Through special tax breaks for certain kinds of businesses. Government construction projects. Incentive programs run by state and county governments. The whole Defense establishment. And so on."

He pursed his lips and was silent for a long moment.

"You've obviously given this a lot of thought," he said finally.

"Well, I didn't exactly come up with it on the spur of the moment."

"Where did you get the basic idea? At Harvard?"

"Yeah, sure. Like you learned to study the Talmud at Lincoln High School. Before basketball practice."

He couldn't help laughing at this.

"I guess I left myself open for that," he said with a friendly grin.

"It wasn't exactly something I could resist."

"But we did play basketball at my Yeshiva."

"Where you were the star, I presume."

"Actually, chess was more my speed. But come on. I think we need to walk some more."

"Okay."

* * *

We walked across the lawn outside in total silence. It was obvious my General Motors example had taken Elijah by surprise and he was busy thinking. So I didn't disturb him.

Our silence also gave me a chance to appreciate the odd sense of exhilaration I felt. The rest of my body may have been totally whacked-out, but my brain was functioning just fine. Better than fine, in fact. And it couldn't have been the few bites of vending machine food I'd managed to choke down.

But when we reached the far side of the lawn, my knees started to get weak again. So I plunked myself down on a handy bench. Elijah sat down next to me. Still thinking.

Finally he turned to me with something like a twinkle in his eyes.

"You realize, of course, that most academic economists would piss all over your ideas," he said. "About job subsidies, I mean."

"So?"

"They have this big thing about rational use of economic resources. Including Labor."

"What's rational to a middle-aged auto worker in Detroit whose job's been moved to China? Where people supposedly work for next to nothing. And if they get sick, they're free to go off and die. Because a lot of other poor slobs are waiting to take their places on the assembly line."

"A temporary condition, presumably. In the long run...."

"But people don't eat in the long run, Elijah. They have to eat every day."

"Thank you, Lord Keynes."

"I'm not totally illiterate. Even if I did go to Harvard."

"If Susan was here, she could explain all this a lot more clearly than I can."

Susan, Susan.... Why did he have to keep mentioning her? My stomach turned over with an agonizing jolt.

And I abruptly became aware of something going raving mad inside me. A terrible sickness. Tearing at my guts. Coursing rapidly through my arms and legs. Making me sweat all over.

Then it was rising up my throat. Setting off all kinds of alarm bells.

"Oh, Jesus...." I moaned.

"Wes? What's wrong?"

I spun around on the bench and leaned over the back just in time as my whole stomach erupted.

"HOOAAAGGGG.... HOOAAAAGGGG.... Uh, uh, uh.... HOOAAAAAAGGGGGG.... "

"My God, Wes.... "

I was dimly aware that Elijah had leaped to his feet. But I couldn't have cared less. I was too busy throwing up over the back of the bench. Feeling my shirt becoming drenched with sweat. Praying that my tortured heaves wouldn't knock the bench over backwards and dump me into that steaming yellow puddle I was making in the grass.

Finally I was empty. Able to turn around weakly and wipe my mouth with my pocket handkerchief. Struggle to my feet and drop the sodden handkerchief in the grass. Aware that Elijah was facing me from a safe distance.

"You okay now?" he said.

"I guess so. Just … a little food poisoning."

"Like I had."

"Yeah. Lot of that going around these days."

"You look terrible. You're as.… "

"White as a sheet?"

"At least you haven't lost your sense of humor."

"That'll be the day."

I felt my knees sagging and sat back down on the bench. Elijah remained standing and mumbled things about how disabling food poisoning could be. How quickly its effects could overtake you. The usual. I mumbled words of agreement.

But I knew it wasn't food poisoning. Nothing so simple. It was the old story of my gastrointestinal system reacting to a major emotional trauma by going crazy. Something I'd been cursed with all my life.

Then I felt Phase Two getting ready to kick in and stood up quickly.

"Is there a bathroom handy I could use?" I said.

"A bathroom?"

"Yes, yes. Right away."

"There's one in the Visiting Room."

"Can you show me? Hurry."

"Follow me."

I made it onto the john without a moment to spare as my large intestine exploded a stinking mass of runny wet shit into the water of the bowl.

Wrenched agonizingly and exploded again.

Once. Twice. Three times.

Alternately wrenching and exploding until I was pouring forth nothing but streams of hot sewer water like a fire hose.

Making my asshole burn with excruciating pain.

Sitting there gasping aloud as my tormented bowels purged themselves.

But I knew from experience it couldn't last forever. And finally, at long last, it was over. My bowels relaxed. Shut down completely. Left my burning raw asshole in peace. As tears coursed down my cheeks.

Oh Jesus, Susan.... Look what you've done to me.

Chapter Five

Agonies and Ecstasies

For the next several weeks, I found it impossible to eat much of anything. Or sleep without leaving the light on in my bedroom.

Because my craving for Susan so ravaged my body that it had stopped working normally.

If I'd been your average American drinker, I probably would have walked around all day in an alcoholic haze from the vodka or gin or scotch I gulped down to take the edge off the pain.

But instead, I was enduring the whole thing stone cold sober.

Whenever I glanced at my apartment phone or felt the lump of my cell phone in my pocket, I was overcome by an irrational urge to call her. As if we were lovers struggling with an illicit affair in the real world instead of just in my imagination.

Fortunately, I was always able to stop myself from doing something so totally idiotic. Sometimes just in time after dialing the first few digits of her number in Brooklyn.

If I could have sat in local bars at night with other tormented souls, I would have poured out my heart about her to any strangers willing to listen. Endlessly and in agonizing detail. Until they made an excuse to go to the men's room and were careful not to come back.

But I had no one to talk to about Susan. Not even the most uninterested of strangers.

All I could do was force myself to concentrate on the dullest and most mechanical physical activity imaginable. Like basketball practice in the local school yard. Shooting foul shots. Focusing on the tips of my fingers gripping the ball. Trying to feel the movement of my arms as they cocked and shot. Cocked and shot. Over and over like some automaton. Until the hot pressure in my groin finally died away from sheer boredom.

My dreams were the worst torture. Three or four of them a week. Full of such excruciatingly vivid detail that I would wake up ejaculating wildly.

In some of them, she was clearly the Dragon Lady and we were making passionate love in the fictional China of Milton Caniff's comic strip....

In others, she was clearly Susan and we were throwing all caution and good sense to the winds in her motel room near Elijah's prison or my old apartment in Washington....

* * *

But one thing I kept forcing myself to do was show up for my Sunday meetings with Elijah. Religiously. As if nothing had changed between us in my tormented mind.

Except, of course, our discussions of intellectual issues became more like impassioned arguments. As we faced each other with fists metaphorically clenched, bent on winning personal victories. Certainly the case with me.

Oddly enough, the sexual frustration ravaging my body seemed to sharpen my mind. Whenever I saw Elijah, I became like a tiger confronting a rival male. Instantly alert. Pacing this way and that. Probing for the slightest weakness. Ready to kill. With the words of William Blake ringing in my ears.

> *Tiger, tiger, burning bright*
> *In the forests of the night.*
> *What immortal hand or eye*
> *Dare frame thy fearful symmetry?*

* * *

"You can't say that, Elijah," I exploded during one of our arguments.

"Why not?"

"Big corporations are only interested in their bottom lines. They'll sell their mothers for the bottom line. Everybody knows that."

"Everybody? You mean every upscale idiot at Harvard and the Eastern Establishment media who carries on like a flaming liberal?"

"Don't try to beat up on me with...."

"I'll beat up on you with whatever it takes to make you see things sensibly. You're a Brooklyn street kid, just like me. You're too savvy to be led into intellectual perdition by their wine and cheese bullshit."

"Intellectual perdition? Wow."

"Sorry, Wes. I guess that was kind of off-the-wall."

"Kind of. But don't mind me. I've been a little tense lately."

"From all the weight you've been losing?"

"What weight?"

"You don't think I've noticed?"

"I ... I went on a diet. My blazer was getting too tight. That's been my weight guideline since college."

"Yeah. Well, don't overdo it. A big guy like you needs lots of calories."

"I know."

"Anyway, all I was trying to say was there's a lot more naked greed in the private sector than in Government.

"Gee. Really? What a surprise."

"Come on, Wes. You know what I'm trying to get at. If public-private partnerships are going to work, we have to figure out how to make private-sector greed work for us."

"Why not simply make it impossible for them to cheat?"

"You're talking about elaborate oversight procedures?"

"I guess so."

"That never works. Oversight's just a fancy way to spend a hundred dollars to keep some private firm from ripping you off for ten dollars. Where's the percentage in that?"

"But...."

"On the other hand, suppose you start by assuming that private firms are going to cheat. Part of their nature, as the Scorpion said to the Turtle."

"The what?"

"You never heard that story?"

"Sorry. I went to Harvard, remember?"

"Okay, here goes. A Scorpion and a Turtle are sitting on the edge of a river. And the Scorpion says to the Turtle: 'Let me ride on your back while you swim across the river.' To which the Turtle answers: 'But how do I know you won't sting me while I'm swimming?' And the Scorpion replies: 'Would that be a rational thing for me to do? If I sting you, we'll both drown.' Which makes sense to the Turtle. So he agrees to let the scorpion ride on his back. You with me so far?"

"Yes."

"Good. So the Scorpion climbs on the Turtle's back and the Turtle starts swimming across the river. But when they reach the middle, the Scorpion abruptly stings the Turtle in the neck. Which paralyzes the Turtle so he can't swim. And as they're both sinking beneath the water, the Turtle manages to say to the Scorpion: 'But you said it wouldn't be rational to sting me while I was swimming.' To which the Scorpion replies: 'I know it wasn't rational. But it's my nature.'"

Despite the story's appalling cynicism, I couldn't help laughing. Even though laughing worsened the usual pain in my gut.

"Just like Mad Max Bloom, in other words," I managed to say.

"In a manner of speaking. And what did all that cheating and conniving get him? Eight years washing dishes in federal prison for securities fraud and tax evasion. Not to mention fines up the wazoo. But if he had it to do over, would he behave any different? Like a Boy Scout maybe? Not likely. Because it was his nature to cheat and connive."

"All right. So we begin by assuming that any private firm is going to cheat. Then what?"

"We structure our contract to make it easy for the firm to cheat in ways we can monitor. Then use the evidence from our monitoring to force the firm to deliver some benefits for us that aren't in the contract. Of course, we have to be clever about it."

"Clever how?"

"By including some obvious opportunities to cheat. So obvious the firm figures they're set-ups and avoids them. Instead, it looks for less obvious opportunities. Which we make sure the contract provides. In semi-subtle ways. You want an example?"

"Go ahead."

"Let's take a real simple case. You contract with a firm to deliver you reams of copy paper for a fixed price. A thousand reams per month, let's say. On ten pallets, to make them easy to handle. One hundred reams per pallet. Now what's the most obvious way for the firm to cheat?"

"Deliver less than a hundred reams per pallet?"

"Right. Load the pallets so each one contains only ninety-five reams. So each delivery is short-weighted by fifty reams."

"But that's so pat."

"Of course it is. And the firm steers clear of that opportunity because it looks like a set-up. So it looks for more subtle opportunities to cheat."

"Which I provide."

"If you're smart. Like including a provision in the contract that lets the firm package each ream in its own proprietary wrapper. You know, with its company name and logo on the outside."

"So the firm can short-weight each ream?"

"Or every other ream. Or every third ream. Whatever it thinks works best, all things considered. You get the idea."

"Yeah. But how do I monitor this without spending a fortune checking each ream?"

"You use standard statistical sampling. Same thing auditors use. So the cost of monitoring is modest. But it still gives you the evidence you need."

"Which I use to beat up on the firm so it'll throw in some extra goodies at no cost."

"That's one possibility."

"There are others?"

"Suppose you plan to renew the contract when it runs out."

"Why would I want to, if I know the firm's cheating?"

"Maybe you figure it's better doing business with a devil you know. Because its deliveries are reliable, for instance. So you never have to worry about running out of paper. And it doesn't short-change you on paper quality. Remember, this is business. Your goals are decent quality paper and reliable deliveries at an acceptable cost you can keep an eye on."

"Okay, I renew the contract. Then what?"

"Now remember. Your statistical sampling is giving you pretty good probabilities on how much the firm is short-weighting you on each delivery. So you can figure what your true cost per sheet of paper is. Right?"

"Yeah."

"Well, in your negotiations for the new contract, you make sure the firm knows that *you* know what this cost is. In a polite way, of course. Because you're not trying to embarrass anybody. You just want to hondel and get a better price."

"In other words, I want the firm to share with me some of its cost savings from cheating."

"What could be fairer than that? After all, the firm doesn't have to pay taxes on the money it saves by short-weighting deliveries. Cost savings are tax-free."

"Then the price written into the new contract isn't the *real* price."

"Simply the price of record. And you and the firm couldn't care less about it. What matters to both of you is the *actual* price per sheet you're paying. Which will be less than you paid on the old contract. And some of it will be tax-free to the firm. So everybody wins, as the old saying goes."

"But won't the firm look for new ways to cheat?"

"Probably. So you anticipate that by building into the contract the right kind of opportunities. The kind you can monitor without spending a lot of money."

"Jesus…"

"Needless to say, this is an oversimplified example. Just to give you an idea how these things work. But the same principles apply in real cases that are bound to be more complicated. Like contracts to build something. A new highway overpass maybe. Or installing and operating a whiz-bang new traffic light system for a downtown street network. Or entering into a partnership to create and run a self-supporting toll road with all the trimmings. If you're savvy enough, you can always find ways to make private greed pay off nicely. So long as you don't insist on everything being glatt kosher."

* * *

It took me a few days to get my mind around all this because it sounded so radical. But then I saw a connection with something that seemed to make it clear. And I laid this on Elijah at our next meeting.

"Forgive me for saying so, but you made the whole business about contracts with private firms sound like a Poker game," I said.

"What's to forgive?"

"Then you agree?"

"Of course. It's a good analogy."

"Do you play Poker?"

"Sure."

"Is that like 'Sure, doesn't everybody?' Or is it more like 'Sure, it's more exciting than Chess?'"

"The first."

"You're saying everybody plays Poker, in one way or another?"

"Of course. But only a tiny percentage of people are aware they're playing."

"How so?"

"Poker's a game of managing Risk based on incomplete information. You know what Risk is?"

"You mean, the definition?"

"Yes."

"I guess it has to do with the chances of getting your ass handed to you."

"Very well put. Much better than what B-school finance professors teach."

"How do they define Risk?"

"You're going to find this hard to believe. So listen carefully."

"Okay, I'm listening."

"They define Risk as, quote, 'the Standard Deviation of investment returns around the Mean in a Normal Distribution,' unquote."

"You're not smiling, so I assume you're serious."

"Dead serious, Wes. I had to learn all that cold in my Finance classes at Baruch. From masters, no less. One of whom won the Nobel Prize in Economics for coming up with such horseshit."

"Is there an English translation?"

"Sure. It basically means the chances of getting your ass handed to you are matched by equal chances of winning the New York State lottery."

"But I'm only worried about getting my ass handed to me."

"You and every other normal person."

"Except Finance professors."

"They're a special breed. Maybe a mutant breed. They like to point to the Empire State Building and call it a subway train. Which doesn't do a lot to advance the art of communication."

"So my definition of Risk makes sense?"

"Of course it does as far as normal people are concerned. And isn't Risk what life is all about? You get up in the morning to face a day full of risky decisions. Some big. Some small. Some where you have lots of information to help you minimize Risk. Or think you do. Some decisions where information's in short supply. Some you can put off for a while if you want. Some you can't put off if you're going to get out of bed and do anything. All kinds of decisions. Which you have to make in ways that avoid getting your ass handed to you."

"Life's a Big Casino, in other words."

"But with an importance difference."

"Which is?"

"You walk in the door of a casino in Atlantic City or Vegas, and right off the bat you have to make a basic choice. Are you going to play House games like Roulette or Craps or Blackjack? Or are you going to head for the Poker rooms?"

"I'll take your word for it. I've never actually been inside a casino."

"Don't kid yourself. You've never gotten out."

"What's that supposed to mean?"

"You'll see in a minute. Let's talk about your choice first."

"Okay."

"If you choose to play Roulette or Craps or some other House game, you're going to lose in the long run."

"Because the House cheats?"

"Nothing so simple-minded. You're going to lose because you're playing against the House. And game payoffs are structured to give the House an edge, percentage-wise. With the smiling approval of the state gaming commissions that regulate them. So all you can do is choose the game with the smallest House edge. Like Baccarat, for instance. It doesn't mean you'll win in the long run. Just that you'll lose more slowly."

"Sounds like a sucker's game all around."

"Not necessarily."

"No?"

"Look at it this way. Some people play the stock market or bet the horses primarily for the excitement. Deep down, they expect to lose. But that's simply the price they're willing to pay to get in on the excitement. Which they find entertaining."

211

"Casino customers are the same?"

"Most of them, even if they don't realize it. Why do you suppose casino operators keep saying they're in the entertainment business? They're not talking about the glitzy nightclub shows they put on. It's the table games and slot machines. Where most of their customers expect to lose but enjoy the excitement of gambling. Which they're willing to pay for by losing to the House."

"But Poker's different, I suppose."

"Absolutely. If you choose the Poker rooms when you walk into a casino, you're not playing against the House. You're playing against other Poker players. So there's no built-in House edge to worry about, like in Roulette. The House simply hosts the game. Supplies the rooms and tables and dealers and decks of cards. And takes a small cut of each pot for its trouble."

"And that means you can win in the long run?"

"If you're good enough compared to other players so you don't get your ass handed to you. If you can make the right decisions most of the time about how to play the cards dealt to you. If you know how to fake out the other players. If you can figure how much of your stake to bet and when. All based on incomplete information, of course."

"How did you learn so much about Poker?"

"Susan taught me."

I felt my stomach turn over. Why did he have to mention Susan? It was almost as if he knew what we'd been doing in my dreams and was taunting me with it.

But that was impossible, I kept telling myself over and over. Absolutely impossible.

Wasn't it?

"You know how crazy Asians are about gambling," he went on. "And since Susan grew up in Flushing rather than Manhattan's Chinatown, Poker's her game. Texas Hold'em Poker, to be exact. She thought it would relax me."

"I guess most people think of Poker as a man's game," I managed to say in a super-calm voice.

"Why? Upper body strength isn't a factor. There're some great female Poker players. Ever hear of Jennifer Harman?"

"No."

"One of the best, male or female. You want to see a great Poker brain at work, read the chapter she wrote for Doyle Brunson's latest book."

"They write books about Poker?"

"You bet. Some of them very advanced. Susan has most of them."

It didn't occur to me until later that maybe she'd been playing me like a Poker opponent at our lunch in the Chinese restaurant. I was too busy trying not to let my emotions show.

So I swallowed hard and rushed to change the subject.

"Are you trying to tell me God's the ultimate casino operator?" I said in as arch a tone as I could muster.

"Let's just say he hosts the ultimate Poker room. With no gaming commission looking over his shoulder. Because nobody can regulate God."

"Why should that matter?"

"Like I said, he hosts the game."

"So?"

"One of the things a game host does is supply decks of cards."

"Okay."

"Which means he can stack the decks."

"But he's already getting a cut of each pot. Why should he stack the decks?"

"It's his nature. Like in the story about the Scorpion and the Turtle."

"Oh come on, Elijah...."

"Remember what you wrote in your Book Proposal about the Mad Maxes of this world? It's their nature to prefer getting ten dollars by cheating than getting a hundred dollars by playing fair and square."

"Are you saying that Mad Maxes are the true Sons of God?"

"Makes sense, when you think about it."

"So in addition to being a Nazi and a cross-dresser, God's also a card shark."

"Why not?"

"And we spend our lives in his Poker rooms. Whether we realize it or not."

"Right. So we'd better learn how to play if we want to survive."

"And how do you do that?"

"Well, as far as Poker's concerned, you start by learning the rankings of the various hands. You can find that in any basic book about Poker."

"Then what?"

"You learn the probabilities of each hand being dealt. Or filled out once the initial cards have been dealt. That's in the books too."

"And you have to memorize all that?"

"It's easier than you think, once you start playing."

"Sounds like an expensive education."

"Not necessarily. These days, you can practice on various on-line sites without having to lay out any actual money."

"And once you learn all that, you can win?"

"Not very often."

"But...."

"You still have to learn when it makes sense to bet."

"You mean, by knowing whether you've got a good hand?"

"That's only part of it. Suppose you've got a pair of Jacks between your hole cards and what's lying on the table. But it'll cost you fifty dollars to call a bet one of the other players makes. If there's five hundred dollars in the pot, calling the other guy's bet may make sense. You're risking fifty dollars on a chance to win five hundred. That's a ten-to-one ratio. Not bad. But if there's one hundred dollars in the pot, that's only a two-to-one ratio."

"In which case, I fold?"

"Probably. Unless you think your hand's really good compared to other players. Like a pair of aces in your hole cards with a third ace on the table. Then you may want to raise, say, another hundred dollars. To see how many of the other players you can shake out."

"Get them to fold?"

"Right. Psych them out with your raise. Something else you have to learn."

"Psyching out the other players?"

"It's called bluffing. Very important part of Poker. Remember, it's a game of incomplete information."

"Yeah, I see what you mean."

"You don't actually know what cards the other players are holding. But they don't know your cards either. So you have to use your best judgment."

"Like when you're negotiating a deal with a private firm."

"Absolutely. Putting together any kind of public-private partnership is simply a big Poker game. Whether it's a complicated deal like a toll road or a simple deal like buying copy paper. But there's one other thing you have to remember."

"What's that?"

"If you play Poker at a casino in Atlantic City or Vegas, you can depend on the decks of cards being kosher. Not stacked to favor any particular player."

"But that isn't true in the real world, I suppose."

"You can't depend on it. Not with God hosting the Poker room."

"But didn't Einstein say something about God not playing dice with the Universe?"

"Even Einstein wasn't right about everything."

"So God really does play dice with the Universe."

"You have to assume that. And he plays with loaded dice. It goes along with supplying stacked decks in his cosmic Poker room."

"And which players do his stacked decks benefit?"

"Oh, the other guys, naturally."

"I should have figured. So where does that leave us?"

"When it comes to public-private partnerships?"

"Among other things."

"Not as badly off as you might think. If we assume the decks are stacked, we can adjust our thinking accordingly. About probabilities, I mean."

"How do we do that?"

"Remember, even a stacked deck has a probability distribution. Not the so-called Normal Distribution you have with a purely random deck, of course. Another kind."

"Now you're losing me. I never studied statistics."

"But you know about the bell-shaped curve?"

"Well, yeah. The curved line shaped like the Liberty Bell, isn't it? With the peak in the middle and the two tails trailing off equally on each side?"

"Right. A symmetrical curve, they call it. That's the shape of the Normal Distribution. You use it to determine the probability of drawing, say, a Jack from a purely random deck of cards."

"Okay."

"But a stacked deck has a different-shaped curve. Not symmetrical. The right tail can be longer than the left, for example. So you can use that nonsymmetrical curve to determine the probability of drawing a Jack from a stacked deck. Which can be higher."

"I think I'm beginning to see what you mean. Everything has a pattern. But not necessarily the same pattern."

"That's basically it. Of course, they don't let you bring your laptop to the table in a casino Poker room so you can calculate probabilities on an Excel spreadsheet. You have to develop a gut sense about these things. Be tuned in to the patterns."

"But if I'm negotiating a deal with a private firm, I can use a computer."

"Sure. But you still have to be tuned in to the patterns. Which is something you can learn."

"So that's what you meant when you said we shouldn't automatically assume saints are dumber than sinners."

"You remember everything, don't you."

"Better than relying on tape recorders. The batteries don't give out."

"Okay. So assume you're going to do a toll road deal with a private firm. Or a consortium of private firms. What categories of Risk do you worry about?"

"Corruption has to be one."

"Right. We've already talked about that. But just to review, you start by insisting on an open and transparent process for arranging the deal. Not that it'll do much good necessarily."

"Then why bother?"

"The private guys expect it. They may think you're trying to put something over on them if you don't make a big deal about openness and transparency. And you don't want that."

"Yeah."

"You're Government, remember. A bona fide saint. So they'll naturally assume you're dumber than they are. Which can work to your advantage if you play it right."

"So openness and transparency means competitive bidding."

"That's what the public feels most comfortable with. But sole source can produce just as good a deal, and a lot faster. That's why private firms would rather negotiate sole source deals. However, they don't have to worry about the public."

"Just stockholders."

"But they're used to getting screwed by top management anyway."

"So once you've got your potential partners. . . ."

"Then the hands have been dealt and you start playing your cards."

"Negotiating the contract."

"Which we've already talked about. You carefully build in opportunities for your partners to cheat. But in ways you can monitor and profit from."

"Talk about cynical...."

"Not cynical, Wes. Realistic."

"Yeah. Like Hedonist is what a Stoic calls an Epicurean."

"That's good. Something you learned at Harvard?"

"Where else?"

"Okay. Now remember. It's not possible to totally eliminate corruption. So you want to minimize it. Isolate it and make it work for you."

"Whatever. As long as you can find enough potential partners."

"Which brings us to another category of Risk. A thin market base of deal partners."

"Yeah. Can you find enough to do all the public-private partnerships you seem to think are necessary?"

"And that Risk category's turning out not to be a problem."

"Why?"

"Investment bankers are always looking for ways to increase their deal flow. They see public-private partnerships as a hot new source of deals. So they're working overtime organizing infrastructure investment funds. Scaring up potential partners for new consortiums among domestic and foreign companies in construction, pension funds, and so on. They're even looking at having existing public authorities with toll road experience join the party."

"But doesn't that defeat the whole purpose of privatization?"

"Recruiting existing toll authorities?"

"Yes."

"Not necessarily. Some of them can bring a lot of worthwhile experience to the table. They know how to run toll roads on a day-to-day basis. They've been dealing directly with toll road customers. They may even have back-office operations already in place to handle electronic toll collection. Some of them may well be interested in joining the consortiums investment banking firms are creating."

"But if they're so good, why would they want to join a consortium?"

"Two reasons. Want to guess what they are?"

"Come on, Elijah. Don't start that again."

"Okay. Reason Number One. If a public authority gets a concession from the state for a new toll road on its own, it's going to be subject to the same old political control over toll rates. You know what that means."

"The politicos insist on low tolls. As low as possible."

"Which effectively rules out Value Pricing. And its flip side, Congestion Pricing."

"Yeah, I guess so."

"But if the authority's simply one equity partner in a commercial corporation doing the new toll road...."

"Like your toll corridor project."

"Right. Ownership of the corporation is divided among the various equity partners. The state government. The existing toll authority. Private investors who are only in it for the annual dividends. Various business firms, including the regional firms we talked about earlier. All with representation on the corporation's board of directors."

"Which sets toll rates, among other things."

"Absolutely. Since it's a *commercial* corporation, it has to have independent pricing power. That's what makes Value Pricing and Congestion Pricing possible."

"But with the state government influencing toll rates through its board members. To protect the public from getting ripped off by the private investors."

"And the state can count on the toll authority's board members for support. Because it controls the authority. Indirectly."

"Very intricate."

"Like the subway system. Part of its charm."

"Have you been sneaking these ideas out of prison?"

"I'm allowed to have visitors."

"Yeah. But they can't bring tape recorders with them. And some of your ideas are so complicated...."

"Well, the key guys in these things all know Susan. She's been to their conventions with me and turned on the charm. So they return her phone calls and pay attention to her emails explaining things. You know how it is."

"She's sort of like your partner?"

"Isn't that what a marriage is supposed to be?"

"Yeah."

The possibility of Susan being his intellectual and business partner was something I'd never though about before. And it brought me up short.

"Anyway, that's Reason One," Elijah said, plowing on.

"What's the second reason?" I said, not quite able to look directly at him.

"If a toll authority tried to go it alone, the whole burden of raising capital for the new toll road would fall on its shoulders."

"So?"

"Now obviously, an existing public authority can't sell equity shares to private investors. So all the capital it raises has to be debt capital. From the municipal market."

"Tax-exempt debt. That's cheaper, isn't it?"

"In terms of interest costs, yes. But the muni market's very conservative. And that creates a problem."

"How?"

"The muni market wants to lend against *existing* toll roads. Where there's already a revenue stream with a documented history. So the market's comfortable. But a new toll road's something else again. A Great Unknown as far as potential toll revenue's concerned. And all the consultant studies in the world aren't going to change that."

"So they won't lend?"

"Let's say you're better off in other debt markets. Worldwide markets where there's lots more capital looking for deals. And a commercial corporation can access those markets. So if the toll authority is one of the owners of that corporation...."

"Yeah, I see what you mean."

"It's actually an advantage if you look at it the right way. It allows Government to lay all the risks of a new toll road on the private sector. Financing risks. Construction risks. Market demand risks. Operating risks. And so on. The private sector's supposed to be better than Government in assessing and managing these risks. In theory."

"In theory?"

"Well, if you exclude General Motors. And Ford. And Chrysler. And...."

"I get the point. But there's still a price."

"Naturally. Everything comes with a price. But there may be ways you can offset that."

"Yeah? How?"

"Suppose the toll authority issues new debt in the muni market. Against its *existing* toll revenues, so it looks nice and safe. Then it uses the debt proceeds to buy more equity in the new corporation. Which means the new corporation doesn't have to issue so much expensive debt in worldwide markets. So in effect, the corporation's getting some cheap muni debt to help build the new toll road."

"The toll authority's allowed to do this?"

"If it makes the right deal with the Feds. Which can require some fast talking. Plus phone calls to the right people. Obviously, it'll have to give up any claim to pass-through tax deductions from the corporation."

"You've lost me on that."

"Let's go back a bit. Private investors buy equity in the corporation through limited partnership deals. So they get annual dividends. Plus the tax deductions the corporation generates from its interest payments on taxable debt and its depreciation on capital assets. All of which the corporation passes through to the investors. Which increases the value of their dividends. Clear so far?"

"I think so."

"Okay. But the toll authority's a state entity. Therefore, it has no federal tax liability. So the tax deduction pass-throughs have no value to the authority. It can waive all claim to them without losing any money. So they're left with the corporation. Which can pass them through to the private investors. Thereby further enhancing the after-tax value of their dividends. Meanwhile, the corporation gets the benefit of some cheap muni debt by the back door. You see?"

"Wheels within wheels."

"Why do you suppose investment bankers earn so much money?"

"Yeah, but it's so...."

"Look. The new toll road gets built, doesn't it? That's what really matters. A transportation facility gets built to provide lots of benefits to lots of people. Who cares about the financial shenanigans it took to accomplish that?"

"And if something goes wrong on the financial side?"

"Obviously, there's always that risk. But nobody's going to plow the road under if it materializes. You simply do a financial restructuring. Happens all the time with purely private deals like new commercial buildings. The main thing is what gets built. By hook or crook, if necessary."

"The ends justify the means, in other words."

"Of course. You think we human beings could have climbed out of our caves if we didn't come to terms with that reality? Someday, I'll tell you the real story of Abraham and you'll understand."

"Sounds like a story worth looking forward to."

"You'll see. When the time's right."

"Anyway, the bottom line's apparently more private partners seeking deals. Right?"

"Absolutely."

"And that presumably means greater competition."

"Which can lead to better deals for the public."

"So the thin-market risk disappears?"

"Let's say it's changing."

"Changing?"

"So far, we've been thinking in terms of Government creating projects that can be good candidates for public-private partnerships. Then beating the bushes for private-sector partners."

"Yeah."

"But now we're beginning to see investment bankers knocking on Government's door with project packages that look ready to go."

"Like what you did with the toll corridor project."

"Somebody had to get it started. But the point is, the initiative for coming up with potential public-private partnership deals is moving from Government to the private sector."

"That's good?"

"It can be. Even just as a source of ideas for Government about new ways to do big projects. Opens new doors, as it were."

"With new risks."

"Oh, naturally. Those investment bankers knocking on your door want to sell you one of their neatly wrapped packages. Which they designed to provide maximum benefits to their private-sector clients. So you have to know how to evaluate the details."

"And how do you do that?"

"You need the right kind of expertise. Something not normally found in Government."

"Yeah."

"But it can be gotten."

"How?"

"Suppose you're a state government. That means you've got a governor with a campaign financing apparatus behind him. Which can get you all the investment banking expertise you need."

"I still don't see.…"

"Look. Campaign financing for any governor, east or west, north or south, starts in New York City. Once New York's on board, Southern California automatically follows. Then the other political money centers join the party. But it starts in New York. That's one of Hamilton's gifts to us."

"Alexander Hamilton?"

"He made a very cagey deal with Thomas Jefferson."

"The colonial schnorrer."

"I see you remember."

"Who could forget after the way you described him?"

"Anyway, Hamilton agreed to back Jefferson's idea of building the nation's political capital on that swamp called Washington. Just so long as New York remained the commercial capital. But commerce means money. And money's always ruled politics. Today more than ever. Where do you think Washington gets its marching orders when the chips are really down?"

"Now I get it. And New York's investment bankers are.…"

"… Up to their eyebrows in the whole campaign financing megilla, a lot of them. Especially senior guys at big firms. So you're a governor who needs investment banking expertise for some deal his state's looking at? All it takes is a phone call, and the necessary mavens are on the next plane."

"Okay. All that's good for roads. But it does nothing for passenger rail projects."

"Who says?"

"But toll roads generate profits. Passenger rail operations have to be subsidized."

"So?"

"Your partnership concept can work for them?"

"Why not?"

"I'm not talking about your toll corridor project, where you've got revenue from the toll highway to subsidize the passenger rail line. . . . "

"Right. A stand-alone rail line."

"Okay. How?"

"Suppose a state government wants to see a high-speed passenger rail line built between two of its major cities. And for whatever reason, there's no way it can share a corridor with a toll highway. So it's strictly a stand-alone deal."

"Yeah."

"Now the rail line's going to have revenue from passenger fares. But obviously, that won't be enough to cover all its costs. So the state knows it'll have to provide operating subsidies. And it thinks subsidies are worth it because the rail line can help generate more economic activity in the state. Thereby adding to the state's tax revenue base. Clear so far?"

"I guess so."

"All right. And let's assume the state's financial advisors recommend the same kind of commercial corporation structure we've been talking about."

"The state sharing ownership of the corporation with private-sector partners?"

"Absolutely. So the state asks for bids from various consortiums of business firms and private investors. And how will it determine the winning bidder? The consortium offering a deal that requires the *smallest* operating subsidy from the state."

"That makes sense. Can it really work?"

"Why not? It's the same concept as for a traditional bond underwriting. In that case, the winning bidder's the banking syndicate offering the state the *lowest* borrowing cost."

"Yeah, I see the parallel. Is there any problem investment bankers can't solve?"

"Not if we're crazy enough."

* * *

"Give me two reasons why private firms can run service operations better than government agencies," Elijah said at the beginning of our next conversation.

"Only two?"

"That'll do for a start."

"How about giving me a hint?"

225

"Okay. What's the most important factor in running anything?"

"I don't know. Management maybe."

"Right. If the managers are good enough, they can overcome almost any disadvantage. If the managers are klutzes, then nothing else an enterprise has going for it matters. It'll still go down in flames."

"So you're saying private firms have better managers than public agencies."

"In general, yes. Do you know why?"

"Higher salaries?"

"Right again. You must have had Wheaties for breakfast."

"How'd you guess?"

"Shot in the dark. Sounds simple, doesn't it?"

"The salary difference?"

"If that's the only problem, shouldn't the solution be easy enough? Pay government agency managers as well as their counterparts in private firms. Then government agencies will be able to attract the same quality management talent as private firms."

"Maybe government agencies can't afford to match private-sector salaries."

"Come on, Wes. Do you know what percentage of a typical government agency's operating budget is devoted to manager salaries?"

"No."

"Guess."

"About 10 or 15 percent?"

"How about 1 percent."

"That little?"

"You bet. So you could increase manager salaries by four or five times without having any material impact on the agency's budget. And that's before making any allowance for the cost savings from better management. When you factor those in, you could be talking about a net budget impact of zero."

"Okay, I agree. It sounds too simple to be true."

"Right. Because it ignores the biggest reason why the salaries of government agency managers are too low to attract the talent they need."

"Which is?"

"The American public. And its irrational hang-up over paying competitive salaries to government managers. It's like the public thinks there's this big group of trust fund babies with superior management talent just dying to work for government. As a more interesting alternative to playing polo or taking up sailing."

"I've known people like that."

"At Harvard and Exeter, right?"

"Not in Bed-Stuy."

"Sure. Because the talented kid from Bed-Stuy who comes out of graduate school with an MBA is probably loaded down with a ton of student-loan debt. So he doesn't have any choice but to go where the money is. Which isn't Government."

"So unless you can change the American character...."

"Not likely."

"Then government salaries are destined to remain too low to attract good management talent."

"Which leaves us where?"

"Hiring private firms to run things, I guess."

"It's the only practical solution."

"But with Government still calling the shots?"

"Of course, Wes. Government defines goals. Sets performance standards. Then gets private firms to carry them out effectively. With their superior management talent. A logical partnership."

"While Government draws up clever contracts to ride herd on the inevitable cheating."

"That goes without saying. We're not living in a dream world."

"What about the second reason?"

"Second reason?"

"For hiring private firms to run things."

"Oh, that. It's because good private firms are always on the lookout for new and better way of doing things."

"Like new technology?"

"It can be technology. Or new procedures. Anything that promises to be more effective. Remember we didn't get out of the Stone Age because we ran out of stones."

"And Government doesn't do the same?"

"Not usually. Most government agencies are risk averse. They don't like to take chances. Safer to stick with what they know. Nobody gets pissed on for doing the same old things in the same old ways."

"But private firms are willing to take chances."

"Good ones are. It's like a competitive instinct. Their managers get paid bonus money for coming up with ways to produce something cheaper or better. But there aren't any bonuses for government managers."

"So the only practical way for government agencies to get things done in new and better ways is to hire private firms."

"For the most part. That way, private enterprise assumes the risk of failure."

"Then Government avoids things that are new and different until they've proven themselves."

"By which time they're usually obsolete because something newer and better has come along."

* * *

"Of course, there's a little matter of Acting Responsibly," Elijah said during one of our discussions about Privatization.

"In making deals with private firms?"

"Yes. And a talent for Acting Responsibly isn't exactly a strong point in the American character."

"I suppose not. God handed us such an enormous wealth of resources."

"So much of which takes the form of low-hanging fruit. Like existing toll roads that certain states or cities happen to own."

"You're referring to the Chicago Skyway deal?"

"That's as good example as any. You familiar with the details?"

"According to what I read on the Internet, Chicago's government awarded a lease to a private syndicate to operate the Skyway toll road for ninety-nine years and keep all the toll revenue. In exchange for an up-front cash payment of a billion eight."

"Right. And what's the City going to do with all that cash?

"Umm.... Let's see if I can remember."

"It's okay, Wes. Don't strain yourself. Susan sent me the numbers."

"I assumed you memorized them."

"Second nature for an investment banker. To start with, Chicago used $463 million to pay off existing debt it originally issued to build the Skyway. Plus another $392 million to reduce other City debt. That totals $855 million so far. To pump up the City's balance sheet."

"Okay."

"Then it squirreled away $875 million as a reserve for future City operating expenses. To minimize the need for tax increases. That makes the mayor and city council members look good for the next election. Smart?"

"Well, politically smart."

"Right. All of which left about $100 million from the original billion eight. And they put this into a fund to be drawn down over five years. For, quote, 'neighborhood and business infrastructure projects,' unquote."

"Preelection goodies?"

"What do you think?"

"Yeah."

"But nothing for better transportation in Chicago. Right?"

"I guess that's true."

"So in effect, what they did was to transfer the capital value of an important city transportation asset to other things. Is that Acting Responsibly?"

"I suppose it depends on your point of view."

"Come on, Wes. Isn't that like a guy selling off a safe income stream for up-front cash so he can buy a fifty-foot yacht with all the trimmings and cruise the Mediterranean? After he pays off the bookies he's in hock to for sports betting losses. Suppose you were that guy."

"Actually, I already am."

"Yeah?"

"I … I have a trust fund. My adoptive family set it up for me when I was at Exeter."

"The Upper East Side couple?"

"They wanted me to have a certain amount of financial freedom. So my choice of a career wouldn't have to depend entirely on the need to earn a living."

"It throws off a decent income?"

"Well, more than I make at the newspaper I work for. Which isn't saying much."

"Nice."

"One more goodie I've done nothing to deserve."

"It's never too late to start."

"That's why I want to do your book."

"Why do you keep calling it my book?"

"The ideas are yours. I'm not what you could call an original thinker. Very few journalists are. We just report what we see. And maybe try to make some sense out of it."

"That's not what the biblical scribes did."

"I'm not in their class. Except maybe when it comes to faking documentation for my stories."

"Don't sell yourself short. You seem to be responding well to my attempts to unlock your brain."

"To overcome my knee-jerk Ivy League liberal hang-ups?"

"At least to think them through independently."

"Well, I'm trying."

"So I notice. Anyway, back to the issue of Responsibility in Government."

"You mean, the Chicago Skyway deal?"

"The temptation to harvest low-hanging fruit. By privatizing a government income stream in exchange for a big up-front cash payment."

"But is that necessarily irresponsible, Elijah? I mean, suppose Government privatizes an existing toll road for cash to invest in better transportation."

"Exclusively?"

"Let's start by assuming exclusively."

"Okay. You can probably make a reasonable case for that. Depending on the circumstances. That's what Indiana did when it leased out its toll highway. On the other hand, you can also argue that new transportation facilities should pay their own way. Isn't that the acid test? Not what the public *claims* it wants, but what it's actually willing to pay for."

"That may make sense for highways, Elijah. But not for public transportation."

"Why not?"

"History shows it's not practical to cover the costs of public transportation solely from fare revenues."

"Right. It needs public subsidies. On the other hand, good public transportation in a crowded urban region can avoid the need to build more roads."

"Yeah, I suppose that's true."

"So maybe subsidies for public transportation come from the money you *don't* have to spend on roads. You might even come out ahead if you're clever enough."

"I guess so."

"It's like the portfolio-of-assets approach in well-managed private corporations. Didn't Susan tell you about that?"

Susan again. My gut responded by clenching into an agonizing knot. Why did he have to keep mentioning Susan?

"I guess she must have."

"Sure. You manage different product lines so they support each other

Joe Giglio

in the interest of greater total profits for the corporation. Even if that means some products don't meet the narrow accounting test of profitability."

"I remember now. The whole is more than the sum of its parts."

"Of course, there's always the Hong Kong approach."

"What's Hong Kong got to do with it?"

"Its government set up two commercial corporations for public transportation. One for its subway system. The other for its commuter rail system. And both corporations make nice profits from carrying passengers. No taxpayer subsidies needed, in other words."

"How's that possible? I thought...."

"Well, Hong Kong's a special case."

"Special how?"

"For one thing, all land development in Hong Kong is controlled by its government. Through its elaborate regional planning process. And the government's policy is to house nearly all of Hong Kong's residents and business firms on only about 15 percent of the metropolitan region's land."

"What's on the rest?"

"Wilderness mostly. Mountain wilderness that's not really practical to build on. But with that kind of government-guided development density, you can see why public transportation companies make out like bandits. Subways and buses and commuter rail lines and so on handle more than 80 percent of passenger trips each day. On average."

"Sounds like an environmentalist's dream world."

"Well, it shows there are other ways of doing things."

"But I thought Hong Kong was such a great paradise for private enterprise. Free markets and all that."

"Oh, it is, Wes. It definitely is. The government goes to great lengths to encourage private enterprise. As far as providing discretionary goods and services is concerned."

"Discretionary? You mean, where people have real choices about whether to buy or not?"

"Absolutely. So when you step back and look at the total picture, private enterprise works so well in Hong Kong because the government provides many nondiscretionary goods and services. Which usually come with all kinds of social welfare baggage attached that get in the way of private firms trying to maximize profits. Housing's a good example."

"The government's involved in housing?"

"Big time. Roughly 40 percent of Hong Kong residents live in some form of government housing. And their monthly housing costs are pegged at an average of less than 10 percent of their family incomes."

"That sounds pretty modest."

"Sure it is. Among the lowest anywhere. By First World standards, anyway. But you see the opportunities this creates for private real estate firms."

"In upscale markets for luxury housing?"

"Right. They can serve these discretionary markets on a purely profit-maximizing basis. Free-market capitalism in action. Because the government takes care of meeting the region's nondiscretionary housing needs."

"Where does the government get all the money to do this?"

"Well, one source is its tax monopoly."

"You're saying Hong Kong residents only pay taxes to their metropolitan government?"

"Right. Residents and business firms don't pay taxes to any federal or state government like in New York and other American metro regions. Just to Hong Kong's government."

"So the total tax burden may be smaller. But it all goes to the local government."

"One reason why the government's operating budget runs a surplus most of the time. Like a private firm making a profit. Which is unheard of for local governments in the U.S."

"Doesn't that mean the government's tax rates are too high?"

"That's one way to look at it. But you can also say the government imposes a relatively high savings rate on Hong Kong's private economy. To generate cash for new investments to help the economy grow."

"You're talking about those two government-owned transportation companies? For subways and commuter rail lines?"

"Among other things. Like land development, for instance."

"Because the government controls all the land?"

"Right. So it leases land parcels to private real estate firms for development purposes. Sometimes by negotiation. Mostly by competitive bidding. For big up-front payments, plus annual income streams. With the cash being used for new infrastructure projects to support Hong Kong's growth."

"So it doesn't need to issue so much debt."

"It doesn't need to borrow at all. Not with all that money flowing in from budget surpluses and land leases. It's called Pay-As-You-Go investing. Like a highly successful private corporation investing its profits in new business opportunities. You've heard about Hong Kong's new airport?"

"Just that they have one. It's supposed to be top-notch."

"Best in the world, probably. They built it during the 1990s. With all the trimmings. Including a new subway line to connect the airport with Hong Kong's downtown business centers. Where the stations have satellite airline terminals so you can check your bags through to JFK in New York, if that's where you're headed. Plus a new expressway between the airport and downtown Hong Kong. Which crosses an ocean inlet on a suspension bridge slightly longer than the Verrazano. Just to make things interesting."

"The whole program must have cost a fortune."

"About twenty-one billion dollars, in fact. That's in American dollars. With Hong Kong's government supplying nearly three-quarters of the total. Just by writing checks against its cash balances. Never borrowing a dime. While also funding twenty billion or so in other infrastructure projects during the six years it took to do the airport development program. Not to mention adding fifty billion to its cash reserve funds."

"All this from budget surpluses and land lease deals?"

"Right. Shows you what God might be able to do if he had that kind of money."

"I should have figured you'd find a way to bring God into it."

"Well, you have to admit Hong Kong almost sounds like a biblical miracle."

"I'll say."

"Except it's no miracle. It's real. Even today, Beijing knows that Hong Kong can produce lots of new wealth for China. If you keep hands off and let it go its own way. Not like here, where the federal and state governments think of metropolitan regions as cash cows to help them fund their antiquated Jeffersonian rural fantasies. You can hop on a plane and go there tonight. See for yourself that there really is another way."

"But would any of that work here?"

"No, probably not. We've gone too far in the wrong direction."

"So we're left with … what? Privatization? Public-private partnerships?"

"Yes. Clever financial engineering. Served up with a certain amount of con artistry. It's called Living By Your Wits. Something we kids from Brooklyn learn at an early age."

* * *

Elijah's talk about Acting Responsibly got me thinking. And I couldn't wait to lay my ideas on him at our next meeting.

"That business about low-hanging fruit from existing toll roads isn't the real issue," I said.

"Why not?"

"What we're actually talking about is converting *any* existing income stream into ready cash. And how we use that cash."

"Yeah, so?"

"Take the case of a guy who inherits a small bond portfolio from his father."

"Spoken like a real trust fund baby."

"No cracks, Elijah. This is a hypothetical case."

"Sorry. I couldn't resist."

"Anyway, the bond portfolio pays him a modest income each month. Not enough to mean anything as far as his lifestyle is concerned. Just steady and safe."

"Okay."

"But he and his wife just had another child. So he really needs another bedroom. By converting the attic, let's say. Which is going to cost a few dollars. More than he can pay for out of his current income."

"So he sells the bond portfolio?"

"Right. Converts that modest income stream into ready cash to build the new bedroom. Does that make sense? Is he Acting Responsibly?"

"Maybe."

"Maybe? Not certainly?"

"Depends. Suppose his house has a heating system that's a real antique. Always breaking down. And so inefficient when it runs his heating costs have been skyrocketing. Especially with the rise in oil prices. Shouldn't he replace the heating system before he thinks about a new bedroom?"

"I guess he has to make a choice."

"Sure. Maybe he's going to need that bond income to help pay his rising heating costs. Or maybe he cashes out the bonds and splits the proceeds between a new heating system and a bare-bones bedroom. Hoping to save enough on his heating costs to cover the cost of a home equity loan for the balance. See how complicated it can get."

"As I said, this is a hypothetical case."

"But not so hypothetical in the real world. A lot of states face problems like this. You've followed what's been going on in Jersey?"

"Just what comes over the AP ticker at the newspaper."

"It gets the AP news feed?"

"Well, we're not a total amateur-night operation. AP's a cheap way to get filler stories on national stuff."

"Okay. Then you're familiar with the governor's proposal to raise tolls on the Jersey Turnpike and the Garden State Parkway and the Atlantic City Expressway."

"That's a dead issue now, isn't it?"

"Sure. But it was still an interesting idea."

"To get money for new transportation improvements, the governor said."

"Among other things."

"What other things?"

"Like paying down existing state debt. A lot of which is from back-door borrowing to cover budget deficits in prior years. Because the legislature wouldn't agree to raise the ridiculously low state gas tax. Or the income tax."

"That I didn't see on the AP ticker. But I don't follow Jersey news very closely."

"Plus all those Jersey homeowners screaming about their high real estate taxes. So the governor figured he had to do something for them."

"I guess you're right. I wasn't thinking about the real estate tax problem."

"So what's a governor to do? All these people with their hands out saying 'gimme, gimme.' A mountain of debt that needs to be paid down. Big transportation projects up ahead, with the state's Transportation Trust Fund running on empty. And a state legislature that absolutely refuses to even think about raising taxes."

"And the governor saw the three toll roads as the only low-hanging fruit he could harvest."

"Right. Their existing toll rates are very modest. And it's been years since they were raised. But if they were moved up to realistic levels and indexed to future inflation, they'd generate an income stream that could cover a lot of financial holes."

"Higher toll rates was the whole basis for the Chicago Skyway deal, wasn't it?"

"Sure. Why else would a private syndicate pay the City a billion eight for a long-term lease?"

"So Jersey's governor was simply playing Follow the Leader."

"With a slight but important difference."

"Which was?"

"He knew he couldn't sell the concept of leasing the three toll roads to a private syndicate. Certainly not in Jersey. Too many people consider Private Enterprise a stepchild of the Mafia."

"So he repackaged the concept?"

"Right. Fold the toll roads into a new commercial entity that the state would own. An entity with enough political independence to reprice toll rates at more realistic levels and keep them indexed to inflation. But still a so-called state entity."

"With a big new income stream from the higher tolls. To fund solutions to the state's problems."

"And borrow against. Issue self-liquidating bonds for new transportation projects. You get the idea."

"Sounds like an act of desperation."

"Of course it is. But what's the alternative?"

"If Jersey's so poor. . . . "

"Believe it or not, Jersey happens to be a very rich state. But you wouldn't know it from the way they've fucked up their whole government structure."

"Fucked up how?"

"Look at it this way. The whole New York Metropolitan Region contains thirty-two counties in the three states it covers."

"Okay."

"Now the five biggest counties happen to be in New York City."

"You're talking about the boroughs."

"Right. Five boroughs, five counties. Home to eight and half million people. But with a single municipal government. That means one police department for eight and a half million people. One fire department. One public school system. One public hospital system. And so on. You know what smart people call that?"

"The Big Apple?"

238

"Come on, Wes. Don't get cute with me."

"I couldn't resist."

"Smart people call it Economies of Scale. Know what that means?"

"Bigger is better?"

"In terms of efficiency, yes. From the government efficiency perspective, bigger is definitely better. One government for eight and a half million people living in five counties."

"That makes sense."

"Sure it does. But how many local governments do you think there are in the rest of the metropolitan region outside New York City?"

"I don't know. Maybe fifty or so?"

"How about 779?"

"You're kidding."

"Seven hundred and seventy-nine local governments. One for each of the twenty-seven suburban counties outside New York City. Plus 752 for all the cities, towns, villages, townships, you name it, in those twenty-seven counties. Each with its own police department. Its own fire department. Its own public school system. And so on. Does that sound like efficiency to you?"

"More like waste on a grand scale."

"Right. Now maybe these people think there are benefits to having all these expensive little toy governments. And that's okay as long as they're willing to pay the higher costs through their taxes. But do they have any right to scream about taxes being too high when they get their bills?"

"Not if they're rational."

"Who said anything about rational? You want, you pay. To quote your Book Proposal. The American free market in action. The more you want, the more you pay. Take your choice."

"But the nature of the tax system makes things worse."

"How do you mean?"

"The taxes these people are screaming about are real estate taxes. Taxes on the homes they own, mostly. Which don't produce a cash income."

"Ah. Now you've hit on something, Wes."

"Have I?"

"Taxes on Wealth. As opposed to taxes on Income. Or Consumption."

"You're saying real estate taxes are actually Wealth Taxes. So?"

"There's nothing wrong with Wealth Taxes. If your goal is to redistribute wealth. Every junior grade Marxist will agree with that."

"Why do I get the idea that there's another side to the equation?"

"That's what you've hit on. If your goal is to raise revenue, you don't want to tax wealth. Too many problems. Like people screaming because their homes don't produce cash income. Out of which they can pay taxes levied on the value of their homes."

"What's the alternative?"

"You tax income or consumption."

"Consumption means sales taxes, doesn't it?"

"Right."

"I have a problem with that, Elijah."

"What problem?"

"With sales taxes, the less your income, the larger proportion of it you have to pay in taxes."

"Spoken like a classic knee-jerk liberal."

"Never mind being snide. It's true."

"Of course it is. That's why sales taxes usually exempt basics. Like food and housing. Even clothing below a certain price."

"But taxing income still makes more sense. After all, isn't your income the best measure of how much you benefit from living in a particular society?"

"Of course it is. So the higher your income, the larger proportion you should be willing to pay in taxes to help support that society. Right?"

"Ideally. But I can live with the same proportion for everybody."

"So can I, if it comes down to brass tacks."

"Wow. You mean, I've actually won an argument with you?"

"Let's say it's something we happen to agree on. Even if for different reasons."

"Then why don't local governments scrap real estate taxes and simply tax income?"

"It's a structural problem."

"What does that mean?"

"Most state constitutions give local governments the right to tax real estate pretty much as they please. Within broad limits. But they need the state legislature's approval to tax income. You know what it's like to get a local income tax bill passed by the state legislature?"

"Not very easy?"

"You wouldn't believe what you're up against. All the back-room bargaining that goes on. And most of the time, you fail. When I worked for New York City's Office of Management and Budget, I went through it more times than I can count. Like once a year, usually."

"But that's crazy. Why?"

"It has to do with an old theory. People can move to another town or county if they think their local income taxes are too high. But real estate can't move. It's supposed to make for a more stable local government tax base."

"Does it?"

"Not if you look at places like Camden in Jersey, or East Saint Louis in Illinois. Maybe the real estate can't move. But the *investment* in real estate certainly can. And does. That's what turned Camden and East Saint Louis into urban basket cases. Full of slums and abandoned buildings. It's more common than most people realize."

"So most local governments are stuck with real estate taxes. And the screaming they generate."

"It's the American way, Wes."

"That's what you meant by the country going down the wrong road?"

"One example. An important one."

"Can't anything be done to change that?"

"Probably too late. You want to try rewriting fifty state constitutions? Good luck."

"Then the country's doomed?"

"Well, 'doomed' is a pretty strong word. Let's say we have to be a lot smarter in coming up with clever solutions to our problems."

"You're talking about public-private partnerships. Privatization. Things like that."

"Among others."

"So America's fate is in the hands of its investment bankers."

"Always has been, if you think about it. We make fortunes coming up with clever solutions to problems."

"And packaging them with the right amount of con artistry."

"That goes without saying. Americans don't want to hear the truth, usually. They like fairy tales better."

"I've never heard you sound so grim."

"Maybe it's the effect of prison. You have a lot of time to think. Mainly about unpleasant things."

"But when you get out, you'll be able to go back to developing clever solutions to problems. More toll road projects."

"I don't think so."

"No?"

"Can you imagine an investment bank hiring an ex-con to drum up new business?"

"But it's not like you murdered anybody. I mean, Insider Trading. . . . "

"That might be okay if I was a securities trader, maybe. Almost like a badge of honor. But it's death for an investment banker."

"Jesus. . . . Then pleading guilty cost you more than you've let on."

"Come on, Wes. It's not like I need to earn a living. I'm financially independent. So are my wife and children. I can afford to do what I want."

"Which is what?"

"Oh, you know. Study the Talmud. Visit the Poker rooms in Atlantic

City. Try to figure out the various ways God plays dice with the Universe. I'm looking forward to it."

"And help me write my book?"

"Sure. If you want me to."

"Of course I do. It's your book. The ideas are, at least. I'm just the bystander who writes them down."

"How's it coming, by the way?"

"My agent in New York thinks he's got two offers pending. Informally. He's expecting something on paper soon."

"From decent publishers?"

"Middle-mainstream."

"That's good. At least one of us stands a chance of going on to fame and fortune."

"That comment can be taken several ways."

"Well, you know me."

"After a fashion, anyway."

* * *

"When did Japan lose the Pacific War?" I asked Elijah at our next meeting, hoping to mousetrap him with my own brand of cheese.

"What's this, another trick question based on you being a World War II history maven?"

"I thought trick questions were supposed to be part of the game. You're always asking them."

"Trick questions? Moi?"

"Come on, Elijah. When did Japan lose the Pacific War?"

"August 1945, wasn't it? After the U.S. dropped the two atomic bombs?"

"That's just when the Japanese government surrendered. But the basic issue had long since been decided by then. Try again."

"Okay, let's see.... The Battle of Midway. June 1942. When the U.S. Navy ambushed the Japanese fleet and sank its four best aircraft carriers."

243

"Not bad. Most Americans never heard of Midway."

"Who ever said I was an American?"

"I know. Just a barefoot boy from Brooklyn."

"Which is a lot different."

"Better."

"Sure. But don't let anybody west of the Hudson hear you say that. Is Midway the right answer?"

"No."

"Figures. Okay, you got me. When did Japan lose the War?"

"On December 7, 1941."

"The Pearl Harbor attack?"

"Yes."

"I thought Pearl Harbor was supposed to be a great Japanese victory."

"That's the common assumption. Shows how wrong common assumptions can be."

"Why do I get the sense there's a hidden agenda behind all this?"

"Isn't that why Talmudic scholars like to ask trick questions?"

"Okay, Wes. I've played your game. Now tell me what's on your mind."

"It's those Transportation Needs Studies I've been reading about on the Internet."

"Oh, them."

"They claim to be enlightened examples of 'Strategic Planning for American Transportation.' To establish parameters for the next round of congressional action on national transportation funding."

"You have problems with that?"

"To put it candidly, they make Japan's strategic planning for the Pacific War look good by comparison."

"That doesn't even sound like faint praise."

"Look. Anybody who wants to mess with Strategic Planning has to know World War II. Otherwise it's like trying to do Engineering without knowing Physics."

"Interesting analogy."

"World War II's filled with examples of the right way and wrong way to do Strategic Planning. Fortunately, the U.S. and its allies mostly did it right. While Germany and Japan mostly did it wrong. That's a big reason why our side won."

"So if a student of World War II reads those Transportation Needs Studies…?"

"Their flaws jump right out at you."

"That obvious?"

"They're full of all these numbers about the amount of money the country should spend on various aspects of transportation. Big numbers. These studies all have a fairly used feel to them—like paper that has lost it crispness by being handled too frequently. But you know what?"

"What."

"They unconsciously assume the future's going to be like the past. Just like Japan did in planning Pearl Harbor. They lacked a strategic understanding of the war they were fighting."

"Can you fill me in on Japan, so I can make the connection?"

"You mean, there's actually something you don't know? I'm astonished."

"Just so long as you keep my secret."

"Let me give you some background first. Japan's a resource-poor nation. Has to import a lot of its food. Most of its petroleum and other natural resources. And so on."

"A lot of nations are like that. So they trade."

"Right. Buy and sell commercially. Makes sense."

"Of course."

"But not if you're a Samurai general. Then your instinct is to take what you need by force."

"Oh, I get it. And the Samurai generals came to dominate Japan's government during the late 1930s."

"I thought you didn't know about Japan."

"Well, just a little."

"Anyway, you're right. The generals effectively took over the government. So they sent the army to invade Manchuria for its resources. Then China. But they still needed more. Like oil from Indonesia, which was then a Dutch colony. Tin and other metals from French Indo-China. In other words, military conquest throughout eastern Asia."

"Which annoyed the U.S. no end."

"Sure. Because of our colonies in the Philippines and Guam. Well, being annoyed is one thing. Being able to do something about it is another matter. Can you visualize a map of the Pacific Ocean?"

"More or less."

"Notice Pearl Harbor right out there near the middle?"

"Yes."

"A full-service naval base."

"Okay."

"So you can move the U.S. Pacific Fleet to Pearl Harbor. Now you've got a powerful naval force pointed like a dagger at the heart of Japan's military ambitions in East Asia."

"A meaningful deterrent."

"That's how the Samurai generals saw it. And they knew they had to neutralize that fleet before they could move against Indonesia and French Indo-China. So, logically enough, they turned the job over to the Imperial Japanese Navy."

"And that brought Admiral Yamamoto into the game?"

"Oh, you know about him."

"Well, I know he went to Harvard."

"Is that one of your cracks?"

"He's also supposed to have been a brilliant Poker player."

"I knew a lot of people at Harvard who were into Poker. So what?"

"Sorry, Wes. I didn't mean to interrupt your explanation. It's making very good sense."

"Okay. Now Yamamoto thought the whole idea of going to war with the U.S. was crazy. But he had his orders. So he came up what seemed like a brilliant strategy. Send a fleet of aircraft carriers to attack the Pacific Fleet on a weekend, while it was moored in Pearl Harbor. That's what he did. With great success."

"Causing all hell to break loose."

"Of course. But it still cost Japan the war."

"How?"

"Yamamoto chose the wrong targets at Pearl Harbor."

"What do you mean?"

"Think a minute, Elijah. There were *two* ways to neutralize the Pacific Fleet. Know what they were?"

"Obviously, one was to cripple its warships."

"Of course. And that's what Yamamoto did. But the U.S. was already building the world's largest and most modern navy. New battleships. New aircraft carriers. New cruisers. The works. And in great numbers. Due to start coming into service in less than a year. So how much time could Japan buy for itself by crippling the eight obsolete battleships moored at Pearl Harbor?"

"Not enough, apparently."

"Right. Now what was the second way to neutralize the Pacific Fleet?"

"You got me."

"How about crippling Pearl Harbor's ability to serve as a naval base in the middle of the Pacific?"

"Oh, I think I see. . . . "

"Sure you do. Warships are very fuel-hungry. So you bomb Pearl's fuel storage facilities. Also, warships need lots of maintenance. So you bomb Pearl's ship repair facilities. And where does that leave the Pacific Fleet?"

"Without a functioning navy base in the middle of the Pacific."

"Of course. So it has to retreat two thousand miles to the West Coast. Where it's no longer a meaningful deterrent to Japan's military expansion in the western Pacific."

247

"But the navy could rebuild Pearl Harbor."

"Sure. In time. Maybe a year or two. Meanwhile, Japan could run wild. And maybe, just maybe, negotiate some sort of settlement with the U.S. to give it free rein in the western Pacific. That's the best Japan could have hoped for. And it might have been enough."

"So Yamamoto chose the wrong targets at Pearl Harbor. And that choice cost Japan any hope of victory. Is that what you're saying?"

"Absolutely. Japan lost the war on December 7. And why did such a presumably brilliant Poker player like Yamamoto make such a bad choice?"

"I guess you're going to tell me."

"He automatically assumed that the future would be the same as the past. Just like the assumptions behind those Transportation Needs Studies."

"I need more detail than that, Wes."

"It's coming. It's coming."

"Okay."

"Now, the overriding model for everything the Imperial Japanese Navy did and thought was the British Royal Navy. It dominated everything. Young naval officers studied the history of the Royal Navy until they knew the details cold. And that certainly included Yamamoto. You know anything about the history of the Royal Navy?"

"No. I mean, naturally I've heard of the Battle of Trafalgar. . . . "

"Right. A sea battle. Royal Navy warships attacking enemy warships. That's the main focus of Royal Navy history. Its warships attack the other guy's. Is it any wonder Yamamoto never thought of anything else but attacking the Pacific Fleet's battleships?"

"An intellectual prisoner of the past. Which he instinctively thought was the shape of the future."

"Same problem with those Transportation Needs Studies. It jumps right out at you."

"Americans aren't into history, Wes."

"It's certainly not one of the more popular undergraduate majors. The other history majors I knew at Harvard mostly chose it because they thought it would look good on their law school applications."

"Not something they took very seriously, in other words."

"That's for sure. So where does that leave us?"

"Us?"

"In transportation. Do we simply throw the same old money at the same old concepts?"

"I think you're overlooking something, Wes."

"What?"

"A little thing called Reality. Very important in Strategic Planning."

"I'm all for Reality. What in particular do you have in mind?"

"The real audience for those Needs Studies."

"What real audience?"

"Congressional staffers."

"Not Senators and congressmen?"

"They have to spend too much of their time raising money for their campaign war chests. So they rely heavily on their staff guys. Especially for legislation full of technical stuff."

"To be honest, that wasn't part of my beat in Washington."

"As an investment banker, I had to get in bed with a lot of congressional staffers. Part of looking after my clients' interests."

"What are they like?"

"Staff guys? Very bright. Quick studies on technical stuff. Above all, very focused on doing deals."

"Legislative deals?"

"That's food and drink to them. The more deals they do, the more prestige they have. It's known in the trade as 'Carrying a Contract.'"

"Makes sense."

"So how do you position yourself to get deals done if you're an ambitious staff guy? Well, some lobbyist comes to you with a new funding proposal for a big-price-tag federal program. You automatically cut his dollar estimate in half, whatever it is. Now you're ready to start negotiating up with other staff guys. That's how you do business in Washington."

"Yeah, I guess so."

"Of course, lobbyists are no dummies. They know they're going to be cut. So what do they do?"

"Be generous in their cost estimates?"

"Right. Compute your cost estimates as accurately as you can. Then double them. And go to the staff guys with the higher numbers."

"But don't staff guys see through that?"

"Of course. That's the way the game's played. It's called Open Government, American style."

"Open Government? You're kidding."

"I said, American style. You know that I know that you know, etc. So we're all on the same page. What could be more open than that?"

"Forgive me for sounding like a hopeless innocent, but it seems … so cynical."

"Look, Wes. You want to do Strategic Planning in an ivory tower? That's okay. But unless you carry the results into the real world, all you end up with are fancy reports that nobody looks at. So what have you accomplished?"

"And the guys who did those Needs Studies?"

"They're obviously very savvy. Now comes the wheeling and dealing. You want big bucks from the Feds? Then you have to play the Poker game. With the staff guys starting out as the chip leaders."

"I thought you said God runs the Poker room."

"Oh, he does, Wes. He definitely does."

"And he stacks the decks."

"That's his nature."

"In whose favor?"

"Why do you suppose the staff guys start out as chip leaders?"

* * *

How could I betray a man like Elijah? Even in my dreams?

We seemed to disagree about so many things. Yet somehow ended up on the same wavelength when we talked. Was that what friendship really meant?

If so, it was a new experience for me. Except for Tim, I'd never really had friends before. Just people I knew and could manipulate. Because of that gold spoon I was born with. Or cursed with.

Was that why I couldn't resist the idea of illicit sex with Susan? Sure, only in my dreams, maybe. But that was beside the point. What mattered was my craving for her. Which I couldn't control. Didn't want to control. Was all too eager to let run wild in my imagination.

Passionate sex with Elijah's wife.

Wife of the friend I was betraying.

Who could forgive that?

251

Chapter Six

Where Is Abraham
Now That We Need Him?

There's an old myth in the newspaper business about Wednesday being the dullest weekday as far as hard news is concerned.

Maybe so.

But on that particular Wednesday, a thirty-two-year-old bicyclist named Henry Stone wearing a homemade bomb around his waist was struck and killed by an eighteen-wheeler on the street outside my newspaper's office at 10:05 in the morning.

I happened to be in the newsroom working on a story and heard the wild screech of brakes outside. So I rushed to the front window. Saw a crumpled figure in a leather jacket lying in the street about twenty feet ahead of the truck. Ran outside to get the details.

"He turned right in front of me," the distraught truck driver bellowed when I stuck my pocket tape recorder into his face. "What could I do? Who expects anybody to make a turn like that in the middle of the block?"

I ran over to the figure lying on his back in the street. His face was smeared with blood and his half-open eyes had a vacant stare. So I wasn't surprised when I checked the pulse point in his neck and felt nothing. You don't stand much of a chance against a truck that size.

"He turned right in front of me," I heard the truck driver shout to the people gathering around him. "I never even had a chance to hit the brakes."

I was dialing 911 on my cell phone when a city police car turned onto the block. It stopped next to the guy lying in the street and the lone cop got out from behind the wheel.

"He was apparently hit by that truck," I said, rushing over to the cop and making sure that he could see the press card hanging around my neck. "I think he's dead."

"All right. Thanks," the cop said. "I'll take it from here."

"He turned right in front of me," the truck driver kept insisting to anybody within earshot. "There was nothing I could do. Nothing."

I watched the cop kneel down next to the guy in the street. Saw him check for a pulse in the guy's neck. Then in his wrist.

Finally he unzipped the guy's jacket. And immediately froze at what he saw. Then leaped to his feet and ran towards us.

"Everybody back. He's wearing a bomb," the cop shouted. "Get back, all of you. Clear the block. Now."

"He turned right in front of me," the truck driver wailed to the cop.

"Never mind. Clear the block. Everybody off the block. You, too."

"Leave my truck?"

"Yes, yes. Now get the hell out of here. He's wearing a bomb."

I backed into the recessed front doorway of the newspaper building. It was far enough up the street for the angle to provide some protection in case the bomb went off but I could still take in the whole scene. The cop crouched behind the back of his car talking into his hand radio. The small crowd that had collected had moved beyond the back of the eighteen-wheeler but seemed reluctant to retreat any further.

"He turned right in front of me," the truck driver kept telling anyone in the crowd who would listen. "I swear there was nothing I could do."

I heard the distant sound of police sirens getting closer as I continued feeding disconnected scraps of information into my tape recorder. Waiting to see what would happen next.

The fact that the guy was wearing a bomb would automatically make this our front-page lead story in tomorrow's edition.

There was also the possibility of coverage by TV crews from Santa Barbara for the evening news. Maybe even from LA and San Francisco if it was the mythical slow-news Wednesday for them. That might encourage

253

the city and county police departments to release whatever details they came up with sooner rather than later. Which would make life easier for me, since I assumed that our editor would assign the lead story to me as the newspaper's only eyewitness.

* * *

When I met with Elijah that Sunday, he told me he'd read my newspaper stories about the guy with the bomb. But he wanted more details. So I gave him a complete rundown on everything I knew, including speculative stuff I couldn't put in my stories. He listened without saying a word. Then pursed his lips and nodded slowly.

"Okay," he said. "Let's see if I've got this straight. Sometime before ten o'clock Wednesday morning, a guy named Henry Stone, who happened to live in the apartment building next to yours near the university . . . ."

"I told you, that didn't mean I knew him. I don't even know the people who live in my own building. The cops agreed it was just a coincidence when they questioned me."

"But he had your name and email address on his computer."

"My *newspaper* email address. Not my personal one. He had names and newspaper email addresses for the other reporters, too. They're all on the newspaper's Web site."

"Then there's no evidence that he knew you personally."

"I'm glad we're clear about that."

"So sometime before ten o'clock, Henry Stone fastens a homemade bomb around his waist in his apartment. A bomb he'd apparently learned to assemble from one of those Internet Web sites."

"The cops found records on his hard drive. He'd accessed three such sites."

"Right."

"But according to the cops, he wired the bomb all wrong. It would never have gone off."

"Could he have done that deliberately?"

"Wired it wrong?"

"You know. Like a guy who's planning to rob a bank and wants to use a bomb around his waist to spook the tellers. But he wants to make sure the bomb can't explode. Even by accident."

"I suppose that's possible. We'll never know."

"Okay. So Henry Stone fastens the bomb around his waist. Puts on a leather jacket to hide it. Leaves his apartment. Gets on his bicycle. And starts riding downtown. Which happens to be in the opposite direction from the university. Where he works."

"His work shift didn't begin until noon."

"Maybe he wanted to stop someplace else first."

"Wearing a bomb?"

"Suppose the someplace else involved using the bomb."

"Like a bank he wanted to rob?"

"Maybe. Or your newspaper."

"My newspaper?"

"He had all the staff names and email addresses on his computer."

"What does that prove?"

"Maybe nothing. But one of your stories mentioned how his computer's hard drive showed he'd been accessing radical blog sites."

"So?"

"Including several blogs about how the news media is ruining the nation. Always supporting Big Business and so on."

"But we're scarcely the *Wall Street Journal*, Elijah. Our editorials are the usual mom and apple pie stuff."

"Supporting the local business community?"

"Naturally. That's where our advertising comes from."

"Including real estate firms?"

"Sure. Many of them are major advertisers."

"Any recent editorials or stories about new real estate projects?"

"We've had some coverage of a proposal to build a town house project out near the university. But the developer needs a zoning change to do it."

"Ah. And your newspaper's been supporting the developer?"

"He happens to be married to our publisher's niece."

"Any controversy about the project?"

"Not at the newspaper."

"Outside the newspaper?"

"I don't know of any."

"All right. Now I want you to assume three things. Purely for the sake of discussion."

"Where's this leading, Elijah?"

"Come on, Wes. Humor me."

"Okay, I'll humor you. What three things do you want me to assume?"

"First: you've stopped working at the newspaper. Never mind why. Maybe your book deal's come through. With a nice advance."

"I've still got my fingers crossed about that. What are the other two things?"

"Second: you're against the town house project. For whatever reason. You're against it and you want to stop it."

"Okay."

"Third: you think the best way to stop the project is to get the newspaper to oppose it. How would you proceed?"

"Hmm.... Maybe by privately contacting a few of the newspaper's big advertisers."

"Advertisers?"

"Like other real estate firms. Try to convince them that the town house project could be bad for their business. You know. New competition for housing sales."

"Would that be credible?"

"There's always a downside to anything new if you look for it. The idea would be to get other real estate firms thinking about the project's downside to them. Worry them a little."

"So they'll talk to the publisher?"

"Yes. And since the project needs a zoning change, maybe their angle would be to convince the publisher to run some editorials pushing for a detailed study first. Because the zoning change would be a radical action."

"And the right kind of study can take time."

"A few months at least. That slows down the town house project. Which is bad for any new real estate proposal."

"And the publisher has to listen to the real estate firms because they're big advertisers."

"Big and steady. And if I remember correctly, the town house developer is from Santa Barbara. Not a local guy."

"So even though he's married to the publisher's niece...."

"It's tough to fight the local real estate establishment, no matter who you're married to."

"Sounds like a very rational approach."

"I guess so."

"But if we assume that Henry Stone opposed the town house project, his approach could have been a lot less rational."

"Come on, Elijah. Are you suggesting he was planning to storm into the publisher's office on Wednesday wearing a bomb? Threatening to set it off if the publisher didn't promise to oppose the town house project?"

"Something like that. Maybe inspired by what he read on one of those radical blogs."

"But that's totally crazy."

"Certainly not very rational."

"It wouldn't even work. He'd never get to see the publisher."

"Probably. Being irrational seldom works."

"Where are you going with this? It doesn't make any sense."

"I'm just trying to make a point."

"I figured that. What point?"

"People do irrational things."

"But Henry Stone had to be a nut case, Elijah. I mean, leaving his house with a bomb around his waist.…"

"Even normal people do irrational things. A lot of the time, in fact."

"So?"

"But classical economics takes it for granted that people always behave rationally. That's the whole basis of free-market theory. Rational people making rational decisions about buying and selling. That's why free markets are supposed to be efficient."

"Yeah, but does anybody really believe that?"

"You'd be surprised. It's an element of faith throughout the economics profession. Has been ever since the days of Adam Smith."

"I meant normal people."

"Like those who went to Harvard?"

"Not just them."

"Anyway, you're right."

"That's quite an admission, coming from you."

"The point is, there's a new wind blowing though the economics profession. Ever hear of something called Behavioral Economics?"

"Sort of. I've never checked out the details."

"It's right up your alley. Small groups of younger faculty members in various universities. Conducting some interesting experiments."

"What kind of experiments?"

"Mostly among university students. Because they're handy and cooperative. They're given common situations to evaluate. Then asked to make choices. You know, like buying Product A that costs one price. Or Product B that costs a higher price. Or Product C that costs a lower price. And so on. To measure how rational their choices are."

"So everybody chooses Product C. What does that prove?"

"There's more to it than that. Only the control group gets offered simple choices based on price alone. The other groups are offered more complicated choices. For example, Product A comes with the right to buy another product at a 25 percent discount. But the higher-priced Product B gives you the other product at no cost. Do you see what I'm getting at?"

"I think so."

"Now assume that the three products are identical soft drinks. For one group, the extra product is something food-related. Like an order of french fries. For another group, the extra product has nothing to do with food. A ballpoint pen, for example. For a third group, the extra product is a coupon entitling them to a free soft drink the next time they come in. In other words, the choices become increasingly complicated."

"Sounds like a standard consumer survey."

"This particular experiment was adapted from such a survey. But the goal was to measure how rational the students were in their choices."

"You're describing an actual experiment?"

"I ran across it on the Internet."

"What were the results?"

"Some interesting choice patterns. The control group overwhelmingly chose Product C—the soft drink at the lowest price. That's the most rational choice. But the results for the other groups showed choice patterns that were anything but rational. And the degree of irrationality depended on how the choices were packaged."

"So you're talking about one experiment."

"But you can multiply that by a few hundred. Maybe even a thousand."

"A thousand?"

"Give or take."

"With all the results on the Internet?"

"Many of them. Or in professional journals. That's what Behavioral Economists do. Run experiments and report the results. Without getting into a lot of theory. Because they don't have to. Their empirical evidence makes the point for them."

"And the point is?"

"Adam Smith's so-called rational man seems to be a myth. Real people don't behave that way."

"So what does that mean for free-market economics?"

"Well, at a minimum, the free market can be manipulated."

"Including the stock market?"

"That's one of the best examples. How do you think price bubbles get started?"

"People buying because everybody else seems to be buying?"

"Right. Goaded on by insiders who are looking to unload when the price gets high enough. Ever hear the shoeshine story?"

"No, but I bet I'm going to."

"One morning, a normally intelligent businessman gets a phone call from his broker recommending a particular stock. A hot company called XYZ. Everybody's buying it, the broker claims. The price has doubled in the last month. Going up like mad. Now's the time to get in on it."

"So the businessman buys?"

"He's tempted to. But he's late for a meeting and tells the broker he'll have to call him back. Got the picture?"

"So far."

"Anyway, after his meeting, the businessman goes out to lunch. On the way back, he stops at the shoeshine stand in his building's lobby to have his shoes shined. And the shoeshine guy's talking about the stock market to the customer sitting next to him. So on a hunch, the businessman asks the shoeshine guy about the XYZ company. 'Oh I'd stay away from that one,' the shoeshine guy says. 'The insiders are already bailing out. Its price should tank in another few days.' So what's the businessman's next move?"

"He calls his broker back and tells him what his shoeshine guy said."

"Right. And there's a long silence on the other end of the line. Then his broker says: 'That's odd. My shoeshine guy says insiders are buying XYZ like there's no tomorrow.'"

"Yeah, very funny. But how often does that really happen?"

"You'd be surprised. Why do you think we have bubbles?"

"Okay. So the stock market is irrational."

"Like all so-called free markets. Because people are mostly irrational."

"As bad as Henry Stone?"

"Fastening a homemade bomb around your waist isn't the only way to act irrational."

"But if people are irrational, doesn't that undercut everything you've been saying about the benefits of privatization and public-private partnerships?"

"Not necessarily."

"No?"

"It simply means that markets can be manipulated, if we're clever enough."

"But...."

"Remember when we talked about negotiating supplier contracts?"

"Yeah. We had to assume the vendor was going to cheat."

"And build that into the contract."

"Con the vendor, in other words."

"While he thinks he's conning us. But he knows that we know that he knows, etc. So it all works out."

"In other words, the whole world's a con game."

"Is that surprising to anybody who grew up in Brooklyn?"

* * *

"I've come to an interesting conclusion," I said to Elijah the next time we met.

"Yeah?"

"The world's neither round nor flat."

"So what is it?"

"Crooked."

"I'm assuming you don't mean physically crooked."

"That's right."

"So it's morally crooked. You're surprised?"

"Not after what you've been telling me. Plus what I've been reading on the Internet."

261

"That sounds ominous. What in particular have you been reading?"

"About the privatization of British Rail."

"Oh, that."

"It's quite a story."

"Did you read the part about how the whole thing was a secret plot by the Labour Party to trick the Tories into doing something that would discredit the whole concept of Privatization?"

"What are you talking about?"

"So you didn't read that part."

"Come on, Elijah. You're trying to con me again."

"Naturally. British Rail's a major embarrassment to anybody who believes in Privatization."

"I can imagine. But you know what struck me most?"

"What."

"How complicated the Tory government made it. You know, splitting up British Rail into something like a hundred individual pieces and selling each one separately to private-sector buyers. And the question is, Why?"

"Depends on who you're asking."

"Was British Rail really too large to privatize in a single deal?"

"That's one answer."

"But you don't agree."

"Well, I can see how you could've put together a single consortium to be the buyer. After all, you had the whole world to draw on for partners. Not just the UK."

"That's how you would have done it?"

"I like to keep things simple. If possible."

"Since when?"

"Well naturally, complicated can have advantages sometimes. Depends where you're coming from."

"Could you be saying there were … certain forces pushing for the split-up?"

"Seems reasonable, doesn't it?"

"What forces?"

"Who stands to profit most from a hundred medium-sized sales rather than one gigantic sale?"

"You seem to be implying that London's investment banking industry was behind the split-up."

"Obviously, more sales would mean more fees for more firms. Figure it out."

"But that would mean the British government was dealing with what amounted to a cartel. A self-serving cartel."

"Aren't all cartels self-serving?"

"So the public interest inevitably gets lost in the shuffle."

"Been known to happen. Especially in London."

"But less so in New York?"

"Well, New York investment bankers tend to be liberal Democrats. Closet or otherwise."

"You're including yourself?"

"If you want to think of it as a Jewish thing. The goal of most New York investment bankers is to make yourself independently rich before you're fifty. So you can devote the rest of your life to Good Works. Charities. Cultural enterprises. Saving the Environment. The right kind of appointive posts in Government. That sort of thing."

"But London's different?"

"Investment banking's more a class thing in London. Or so I'm told. You want to become rich enough to buy a baronial estate in Scotland. Maybe get named a Peer of the Realm and sit in the House of Lords."

"I get the picture. But from what I read, even the Tories now believe that splitting up British Rail was a mistake. A major reason why Privatization turned out to be a disaster."

"Pretty safe position for the Tories to take these days."

"So what's the answer?"

"You mean, in terms of paying off for the public?"

"Yes."

"Depends how you set up the deal."

"By including plenty of oversight?"

"Come on, Wes. You know I hate that word."

"But in terms of protecting the public...."

"Everybody assumes oversight means some sort of government commission. With lots of bureaucracy and external regulations."

"I was actually thinking about your toll road project."

"That's different."

"As you described it, the state government establishes a corporation to build and operate the toll corridor. The corporation sells equity shares to private investors for up-front cash. But it also gives equity shares to the state government and local governments in the corridor. In exchange for the necessary permits and so on needed to build the toll road. That's how the public interest gets protected."

"Don't forget the third class of owners."

"The private companies whose sales revenue depends on economic activity in the region?"

"Right. They buy equity shares in the corporation because they believe the toll corridor will boost economic activity. If it's run properly."

"So their interests coincide with the interests of the public."

"By a fortunate coincidence. Which is the best way, if you can swing it. And together with the government owners, that gives you all the oversight you need. Operating from the inside. At the board of directors level. Where it's most effective."

"I guess that's true."

"Sure it is. What better way to manage the Monopoly Risk, for example?"

"Yeah, monopoly's something the public's bound to be uneasy about."

"Of course. But the corporation has to have what amounts to a transportation monopoly in the corridor. To give it real pricing power."

"So it can implement Value Pricing?"

"Right. Yet any outside regulatory commission's going to insist that the corporation's toll rates be based solely on its costs. There's no way it'll sit still for letting rates reflect the customer's perception of the value to him of making faster trips."

"And I guess the flip side of that is using variable rates to manage roadway demand."

"Can you imagine a bunch of commission bureaucrats trying to figure their way around that one? When their every instinct tells them that Economic Rent can only mean a rip-off of the public?"

"So an all-private corporation's bound to be hamstrung."

"Inevitably. And without meaningful pricing power so it can generate Economic Rent with good service to customers, its equity shares are bound to be worth less to buyers in the private investor community. Maybe a lot less. So it has to issue more debt."

"Adding to its costs."

"Of course. On the other hand, if the corporation has some owners whose mandate is to represent the public, and some other owners whose private interests just happen to be the same as the public's...."

"Then it can manage Monopoly Risk in ways that pay off for society as a whole."

"Also inevitable."

"Okay. Now tell me something, Elijah."

"What."

"Why couldn't the British government have done this with British Rail?"

"Something got in the way."

"Yeah? What?"

"Ideology."

"Ideology?"

"Remember the historical context. The Tories under Margaret Thatcher got hung up on the ideological concept of Privatization. Sell off government corporations to the private sector in the name of greater efficiency and so on. You know why that happened?"

"Why?"

"Margaret got seduced by Frederick Hayek, the Austrian free-market economist."

"I assume you mean seduced in the intellectual sense."

"That's probably what Margaret thought. But Frederick may have had other ideas."

"You're kidding."

"You think economists are totally bloodless because of how they talk? Look at Lord Keynes."

"I thought he was gay."

"More like bisexual. Oh, he had gay affairs in his younger days when he was running with the Bloomsbury crowd. But then he married that beautiful Russian ballerina, and everything changed."

"You're really serious about Hayek having a thing for Margaret Thatcher?"

"According to the story, they had a lengthy private meeting together. Back when she was Leader of the Tory Opposition in Parliament. She'd already read some of his books and thought his free-market ideas made sense. At least as a political shtick for beating Labour in the next General Election."

"So they had an intellectual conversation about free-market capitalism. But that doesn't mean...."

"After their meeting, Hayek's associates tried to sound him out about what he thought of her. You know, as Tory leader and potential Prime Minister. But all he did was sit there starry-eyed mumbling about how beautiful she was. I'll leave the rest to your imagination."

But that was the last thing I wanted my imagination to contemplate. It hit too close to home.

"He could have meant it metaphorically," I said hurriedly.

"Come on, Wes. What do you think Lord Keynes meant when he

talked about Animal Spirits? Just human greed? Of course not. He meant sex, too."

"But...."

"Sex. With a big capital 'S.' It makes the world go round. Even more than money. Hayek was no different from the rest of us guys, even if he did win the Nobel Prize."

"I guess that's really not so far-out when you think about it."

"Of course not."

"To be perfectly candid, I always thought Thatcher was an attractive woman."

"You see?"

"She reminded me of a teacher I had in grade school. Mrs. Bernstein. Very prim and strict, and ... sort of terrifying. But she had the greatest legs."

"I'm glad you started noticing such things at an early age."

"Part of my ethnic culture."

"You and the Italians."

"Anyway, so Thatcher started something that led to the Privatization of British Rail."

"Right."

"Except she wasn't the one who actually did it. It was John Majors."

"Right again. Her successor as Prime Minister. Margaret was too smart to get caught up in the minefield of British Rail. But all Majors cared about was winning the next election. So he fell back on Thatcher's free-market ideology. You know how it is. A shtick in time...."

"Fine. But what about the Chicago deal?"

"The Skyway lease?"

"Yes. Couldn't Chicago have made out better with something like your toll corridor approach? Selling some equity shares to the private sector but still keeping its hand in?"

"Sure. But once again, something got in the way."

"Ideology?"

"In Chicago? You must be kidding."

"Then what?"

"Something bigger than ideology. Simple greed."

"That big up-front payment for the lease?"

"A billion eight in ready cash. So they burned their bridges behind them."

"What bridges?"

"Think of it this way. By signing that lease, the City of Chicago lost control of the Skyway for the rest of this century."

"Yeah."

"Now fast-forward ahead by ten or fifteen years. Somebody comes up with a super whiz-bang plan to integrate the whole portfolio of transportation assets in Chicago. Financially and operationally. In the interests of greater efficiency and better overall performance."

"Is that very likely?"

"It's probably the best possible future for transportation in metropolitan regions. Transportation facilities aren't like a collection of kiddie rides in some amusement park, after all. Sooner or later, they have to be managed as an integrated system. Just like a portfolio of different businesses in a big corporation like GE."

"But the Skyway can't be part of such a system."

"Not without an expensive buyback of the lease. Which might make the whole plan too costly to manage. So who loses? The people of Chicago."

"Okay. But keeping some control over the Skyway would mean a smaller up-front cash payment, wouldn't it?"

"Not necessarily."

"No?"

"Depends on how you package the whole deal. Want an example?"

"What do you think?"

"Then assume the following alternative. Chicago establishes a commercial corporation to lease the Skyway. But it keeps a share of equity ownership in the corporation. Which means it retains some control over the Skyway. Including the possibility of making the Skyway part of some future integrated transportation complex."

"Sounds like your toll corridor project."

"A variation of it. Now as an equity owner, Chicago receives annual dividends from the Skyway's toll revenues. Just like the private-sector investors. Okay?"

"I follow."

"Those dividends are an income stream. And if the government wants ready cash, it may have the possibility of issuing debt secured by those dividends. Which is known in the trade as 'capitalizing an income stream.' Clear enough?"

"Yes."

"Now by packaging the whole deal properly, the proceeds from that bond sale might bring Chicago's total up-front cash from the Skyway back up to the billion eight level. Maybe higher. You see?"

"So it wouldn't have cost Chicago's government any money to keep some control over the Skyway."

"Doesn't have to."

"Including making it part of some future integrated transportation system."

"Absolutely. That comes under the heading of managing System Distortion Risk in the most effective way."

"I see what you mean. That's … very elegant."

"Sure it is. And in this business, elegance can pay off big-time. Especially these days."

"These days?"

"Look, Wes. You read the papers. You think there's any realistic possibility of the Federal Government coming through with the kind of serious money needed to overhaul our transportation systems?"

"I guess not."

"So what's the alternative?"

"The states going it alone?"

"Right. State governments have to get up on their hind legs and look for the kind of deals that can bring major dollars to their pieces of the nation's transportation complex. I mean, forget federal grants. Forget fuel taxes. That's all horseshit now. They have to learn how to do the right kind of deals with Private Enterprise. Once again, open up the doors of cooperation with the private sector to improve the transportation system.

"Like your toll corridor project."

"That's a start. If enough states do enough deals like that one, you know what we'll have?"

"What."

"A nice example of Economics trumping Politics. With big payoffs."

"Even for the public?"

"If that's what you want."

"I guess it depends on what your agenda is."

"Doesn't it always? British Rail certainly demonstrates that."

* * *

The next time we met, Elijah started rambling on about the Maintenance issue.

How the nation has developed a bad habit of cutting corners on the money it spends each year to keep transportation facilities in proper condition.

How this causes them to wear out faster than they should.

How this creates a huge backlog of restoration needs, especially for public roads. Not to mention worse service for people who depend on them.

And so on and so forth.

"Come on, Elijah," I said after letting him go on for a while. "I know about this. I got the facts and figures from the Internet. Yes, it's a terrible problem. But what's your point?"

"Haven't you wondered why?"

"Sure. But aren't the answers obvious?"

"Maybe. Tell me which answers you mean."

"Well, in the case of roads, maintenance spending comes out of state and county and municipal operating budgets. Where it has to compete with spending for schools and cops and other items that have more sex appeal to the public."

"So it's left sucking the hind tit?"

"If you want to put it that way."

"And when a road deteriorates to a point where it's ready to fall apart?"

"Then it has to be completely rebuilt."

"And that's a capital project, isn't it? Nothing to do with the operating budget."

"So maybe you issue debt to fund the rebuilding."

"Or even get a federal grant."

"Yeah. That too."

"Okay, Wes. Now assume you're a city budget director facing that kind of warped incentive system. How do you allocate your scarce operating budget dollars?"

"I guess road maintenance isn't very high on my list."

"Not when enough neglect can convert maintaining the road into a big capital project down the line. Funded by bonds, and maybe even a federal grant. No direct impact on your operating budget."

"And the mayor and city council will probably back me up."

"Oh, definitely. It falls under one of their favorite mottos. Benefits Now, Costs Later. Which fits neatly into the standard four-year election cycle for so many public officials."

"I see what you mean. But can't there be … problems?"

"With what?"

"You know…. Accounting standards and so on."

"Ah. Now you've hit on something really interesting. You better sit down for this."

271

"That bad?"

"Wait'll you hear."

We sat down on a convenient bench and Elijah got right to it.

"Suppose you run a private company," he said. "Sales were good last year and you've been keeping costs under control. So you want to declare a profit for the year."

"Okay."

"Now in simple terms, a profit means your Revenues were more than your Costs."

"If I'm not playing accounting tricks."

"We'll assume your books are completely kosher."

"I'm relieved to hear that."

"Good. Now if your Revenues were more than your Costs, that means you've counted all your costs."

"Yeah. So?"

"And since you run a private company, one of the costs you have to count is Depreciation. You know what that is?"

"Tell me, so I'll be sure."

"Depreciation is the estimated annual cost of wear and tear on the tangible assets you use to produce whatever it is you sell. Assets like your factory, the production equipment inside it, and so on."

"Estimated cost?"

"Right. Take your factory, for example. You know how much it cost you to buy it or build it. And you know how many years of useful life it should have before you have to spend major dollars to overcome accumulated wear and tear. Like putting on a new roof."

"Okay."

"So you take your factory's original cost and divide it by the number of years of useful life. The result is the estimated cost of Depreciation per year for the factory. And that goes on your Income Statement as an operating cost. Same thing for all your production assets."

"Wait a minute. Suppose I paid all cash for the factory."

"Doesn't matter. It simply means you exchanged cash you had on hand for the factory. In other words, you exchanged one asset for another. As far as your balance sheet's concerned, your Total Assets remain the same. So acquiring the factory has no impact on your Income Statement."

"And if I took out a mortgage to buy the factory?"

"Then you increased your Total Assets by the cost of the factory, and increased your Total Liabilities by the amount of the mortgage. One offsets the other. And neither affects your Income Statement."

"Wait, wait. Let's see if I've got this."

"Take your time. These aren't exactly easy concepts."

"You're telling me that buying the factory is ancient history as far as last year's Income Statement is concerned. Right?"

"Absolutely."

"But I have to show the average annual cost of the factory's wear and tear as an expense item on last year's Income Statement. Under a cost category called Depreciation. Which has to be covered by last year's revenues before I can declare a profit."

"That's it exactly. You're doing very well."

"Chalk it up to my Harvard education."

"Now, don't be snide."

"Oh, but wait."

"What."

"Do I have to write checks to somebody for Depreciation?"

"No. It's what accountants call a 'Non-Cash Cost.'"

"Sounds good to me."

"But you see the implications, don't you?"

"Damn. I was afraid you'd ask something like that. You better tell me."

"You have to list Depreciation as a cost on your Income Statement. And you have to cover that cost with revenues before you can declare a profit."

"Right."

"But because you don't have to write checks to anybody for Depreciation, the revenues you cover it with effectively fall out of the bottom of your Income Statement as extra cash. Over and above your profit."

"Like free cash? That I can put in my pocket and walk away with?"

"Well, not if you're a responsible manager."

"So what do I do with it?"

"You use it as a source of Capital Dollars to replace worn-out production assets."

"Oh, now I get the picture."

"Do you? Sketch it out for me."

"Let's see if I can phrase this properly. Profitable operations for a company mean it has to have enough revenues to cover normal costs like employee salaries and buying raw materials. Plus a noncash cost called Depreciation. The effect of which is to generate Capital Dollars to spend replacing worn-out production assets."

"That's very good, Wes."

"I got it right?"

"Absolutely."

"So the whole thing's sort of like a circular process. I buy production assets and put them to work making products I can sell. If I'm successful, my revenues cover all my costs. Including the estimated cost of wear and tear on my production assets. Which generates cash I can use to replace these assets when they wear out. Thereby starting the Depreciation process all over again. And so on. Round and round forever."

"You certainly have a way with words. I'm impressed."

"Everybody has to have a way with something. But listen."

"What?"

"You taught me something new again. But I've got believe you had an ulterior motive."

"Of course."

"Okay. So let's hear."

"You buy a factory and equipment to produce products. You manage things so the sale of those products covers, among other things, Depreciation of those assets. Which generates cash you spend to replace those assets when they wear out."

"Just what I said."

"And suppose you build a road leading to the factory so trucks can make deliveries. Same thing?"

"Sure. The road's an asset. So I depreciate that too."

"Right. And the public highway that your road connects to?"

"Wait, Elijah. You're leading up to something, aren't you? Just like always?"

"You know me too well."

"Practice makes perfect."

"Okay. Now so far, we've been talking about the accounting rules that apply to private-sector companies. With emphasis on the rules involving Depreciation."

"Yeah."

"But the public sector in the U.S. is allowed to play by different accounting rules. For example. governments can ignore Depreciation."

"Ignore it?"

"Pretend it doesn't exist. Act like that public highway running past your factory will last forever. Never wears out, no matter how much traffic it carries."

"But ... that's crazy."

"Tell me about it."

"And what happens when the highway does wear out?"

"Then the government that owns it may have to issue new debt to rebuild it."

"And when the rebuilt highway wears out?"

"The government issues another round of debt. So it goes."

"Jesus.... "

"It's the American Way, Wes. Part of what supposedly made us great."

"Governments all over the world do this?"

"Oh, no. Most of them recognize Depreciation as a cost. Just like private companies do. Take Sweden, for example."

"But Sweden's into Socialism, isn't it?"

"Are you suggesting Socialism makes for more responsible financial management by Government?"

"Well, if what you say is true.... Oh, wait. What about the Balanced Budget concept elected officials fuss over?"

"It's a con job."

"Con job?"

"Elected officials point with pride when they produce an operating budget where Revenues balance Costs. But they do that by leaving out the cost of Depreciation. So they're just conning the public. With the blessings of the accounting profession."

"And if private companies tried to do that?"

"Well, if they're publicly traded and the SEC finds out, they could be prosecuted for Accounting Fraud. If it's big enough, some of their top managers could end up here."

"So what many elected officials are doing is nothing short of ... disgraceful."

"Disgraceful? There's a mid-Victorian term I haven't heard in a while. Wake up, Wes. Do you know what century we're living in?"

"Then the bottom line's really depressing. As far as expecting Government to manage transportation facilities responsibly for the long haul.... "

"Remember the motto when your time horizon's bounded by the next election. Benefits Now, Costs Later. All with the blessings of the accounting profession."

"Sounds like a great argument for privatizing everything and be done with it."

"You think so?"

"Well, much as I hate to admit it, at least private-sector managers have an incentive to maintain things properly."

"Because they supposedly have skin in the game?"

"That's the phrase I keep running across in the stuff I've read about privatization."

"You know what that means?"

"Having skin in the game? I suppose it means their own money's at risk. Concentrated ownership rather than diversified ownership. Which obviously isn't possible with public-sector managers."

"Sure. The old concept of managers owning the firm. So naturally they have an incentive to take good care of the firm's plant and equipment. Which is mostly bullshit these days."

"It is?"

"Look, Wes. In practical terms, privatization means turning over responsibility for properly maintaining public assets like transportation facilities to top managers in the private sector. Whose time horizons are at least as short as elected officials.'"

"You're talking about companies hung up on Wall Street's passion for quarterly results?"

"It's worse than that, Wes."

"Worse?"

"The American economy's basically dominated by large corporations owned by stockholders and run by hired-gun managers. And never do the twain meet. So in practice, these corporations really belong to their top managers. Who run them to 'Maximize Their Own Welfare,' as academic types like to put it. And if the stockholders don't like it, they can sell their shares. That's the reality."

"Yeah, but those managers who are in it for the long haul...."

"What long haul? Do you know the average job tenure for top managers in these corporations, Wes? Three or four years, tops. They don't expect to be around any longer. Don't even want to be around any longer."

"I ... I never realized...."

"So with that short a time horizon, you expect them to spend any time on intelligent life-cycle management of capital assets with productive lives running ten or twenty years? Not likely. Too busy positioning themselves for the maximum payout when they leave. Let the next guy worry about the factory in Ohio whose leaky roof should have been replaced three years ago."

"As bad as public agencies, in other words."

"In effect. Nobody has any incentive to manage for the future."

"You make it sound totally hopeless."

"Not totally. Not if we're smart."

"There's a solution?"

"Remember the toll corridor project?"

"Right. The true Messiah of our Salvation."

"Don't kid yourself, Wes. In its own way, it contains all the answers."

"Why would I ever imagine otherwise?"

"The corridor's owned and operated by a commercial corporation. Whose top managers are prohibited from owning any of its equity. Just like professional athletes are prohibited from betting on any games they play in. You remember—we talked about that."

"Right. So these hired-gun managers get paid good salaries plus cash bonuses."

"Performance-based bonuses. Paid out over a period of years after they leave. With each year's payment reflecting how well the corporation's been doing over the last five years or so. That's a meaningful incentive for them to manage for the long haul when they're running the corporation."

"And the issue of maintenance? Reflecting true life-cycle costs?"

"All part of the long haul. If they do well as managers, they can end up very rich. And they'll have earned it."

"But can't you do the same thing in public agencies?"

"Of course you can. We're talking about major enterprises that produce essential services for the public. In transportation or whatever. It doesn't matter whether they're owned by Government or Private

Enterprise. Or whether ownership is shared through some sort of pub-lic-private partnership. Whatever works best under the circumstances. The important thing is making sure their top managers have the right kind of incentives to manage for the long haul."

*   *   *

When I reached the prison for next Sunday's meeting with Elijah, there were only three cars in the parking lot. And there was a hand-lettered sign taped to the front door of the Visitors Building.

It stated that visiting hours for that Sunday had been canceled due to circumstances beyond the prison's control.

Since the front door was locked and nobody was in the parking lot, there was no way I could get any further information. So I drove back to the newspaper to see if we had any stories that might explain things. But there was nothing about the prison. The only story mentioning the prison's town was a one-paragraph piece on an inside page of our Sunday edition about a demonstration on Saturday by local farm workers who marched through the downtown area. Period. No further details.

I hung around until the regular Sunday crew started drifting in to begin work on Monday morning's edition, hoping one of them would know something. But the only responses I got to my questions were blank shrugs. Until I asked a grizzled veteran reporter named Charlie Harris if he had any idea why the prison might have cancelled regular Sunday visiting hours.

At first he just stared at me. Then he rolled his chair closer to me.

"So the prison's shut down, too?" he said quietly.

"Too? What do you mean?"

"You said it cancelled visiting hours?"

"There was a hand-lettered sign on the Visitors Building door."

"What did it say?"

"Just that visiting hours were cancelled for today due to circumstances beyond their control."

He immediately spun back to his desk and began typing rapidly on his computer keyboard.

"Charlie…?" I said.

"Wait."

He typed a few more words. Then hit his Save button and turned back to me.

"The whole town's shut down. Not just the prison. You didn't notice?"

"No. What's going on?"

"I'm not supposed to talk about it."

"Who says?"

"The publisher. I'm to collect all the information I can and send it upstairs to his office. But not prepare any stories."

"Why not?"

"Orders from on high."

"Come on, Charlie…."

"It involves yesterday's farm workers' demonstration."

"Yeah, I read the piece about that. But…."

"Don't ask any more questions, Wes. I'll tell you more when I can. You're sure the prison was shut down?"

"All I know is it cancelled today's visiting hours."

"Okay. Let me get back to work."

"But…."

"Bye, Wes."

On Monday night when I got back to my apartment, there was an email from Susan waiting for me on my computer. She apologized for the unexpected cancellation of visiting hours at the prison but said that Elijah would explain everything when we met next Sunday. That was all.

I emailed her a reply confirming that I'd be at the prison at the usual time next Sunday. And also asked if she knew why visiting hours had been cancelled. Her one-sentence answer fifteen minutes later said that Elijah would explain everything.

Why was everybody being so mysterious?

I suppose it might have been something to obsess about if I hadn't gotten distracted by what happened at Wednesday's Kiwanas Club luncheon.

The featured speaker was one of the local business community's Grand Old Men. He seemed to have consumed too much wine during lunch and insisted on telling us a rambling, half-coherent joke with virulent anti-Mexican overtones that he apparently thought was hilarious. And as he exploded with laughter at the end, he suffered a major heart attack and collapsed dead behind the rostrum.

Since I was covering the luncheon, our editor assigned me to write Thursday's front-page lead story about "Our Shocking Loss." Plus two follow-up stories for the Friday and Sunday editions. One about the Grand Old Man's elaborate funeral and all the local dignitaries present. The other about the details of his "distinguished career of service to the community." Which seemed to consist of making lots of money in a large number of local businesses and giving much of it away to fashionable local charities.

All in all, it was enough to distract anybody from almost anything. But Elijah quickly brought me back to earth on Sunday when we met.

"We had a Police Riot last Saturday," he announced in a conspiratorial tone.

"A Police Riot? Is that why visiting hours were cancelled last Sunday?"

"Sure. Apparently, everything in the town was shut down except for church services. Even the movie house was closed."

"What happened?"

"It seems to have started with the demonstration Saturday morning by the farm workers. You know about that?"

"Just what was in the one-paragraph story my newspaper ran Sunday. No details."

"Yeah, that figures. They're trying to keep it as quiet as possible."

"Who's 'they'?"

"The Powers That Be. Translated, that means the county's business community. Police Riots are assumed to be bad for business."

"How do you know all this?"

"Most of our guards live in town. Between them, they know a lot of people. Including so-called eye witnesses."

"And they told the inmates?"

"A few of us, anyway. I happen to be on close terms with some of guards. They seem to like talking to me."

"When they can find a translator."

"Come on, Wes. My Brooklyn accent isn't that bad."

"Yes, it is."

"Not if I talk slowly and avoid Yiddish words."

"And stay away from Religion."

"I don't talk to them about Financial Economics either. What would be the point?"

"So fill me in on the details."

"I'd better start at the beginning."

"By all means."

"The Farm Workers Union has a labor contract with the local Growers Association. Among other things, it requires the association to make monthly payments to the union's Health and Welfare Fund. You know, to cover medical benefits and so on."

"Okay."

"Well, several months ago the association stopped making payments. Claimed it couldn't afford them any longer. Naturally, the union insisted that the Association didn't have any choice. The contract said it had to make them."

"So the two parties sit down and discuss it."

"Yeah, but remember. This isn't Brooklyn where everything's open to discussion as a matter of course."

"Then the union files suit and waves its contract in front of the judge."

"Of course. But some firebrands in the union wanted to have a public demonstration. March through downtown, blocking traffic. On Saturday morning, the week's biggest shopping day. To show everybody they couldn't be pushed around."

"That's easy to understand."

"Needless to say, the local cops aren't exactly the NYPD when it comes to handling things like large demonstrations. So when they found themselves confronted by all those marching farm workers, they panicked."

"Panicked?"

"Started macing the demonstrators."

"Oh, great."

"Which led to understandable chaos. Store windows broken accidently. Fights between cops and demonstrators. People injured. Everything suddenly out of control."

"Sounds like a real mess."

"That's what the guards told us. Bigger than anything the local cops ever experienced before. So they called for reinforcements."

"The National Guard?"

"No, the county police."

"Yeah, that makes sense. They could get here faster."

"Plus they had larger numbers. And were better armed. But still lacked the training to handle anything of this magnitude. Except with brute force."

"So they broke up the demonstration."

"Eventually. It took most of the day, but they finally got the town shut down. Carted most of the demonstrators off to County Jail. Except for those who needed emergency room care. And they imposed a curfew lasting through Sunday night. That's why the prison officials canceled visiting hours."

"No wonder the Powers That Be put a lid on all information."

"Sure. They needed to get their bearings. But you see the larger significance."

"What larger significance?"

"The farm workers had Law on their side. Except among law enforcement types, of course. They had a solid contract with the Growers Association and saw no reason to take any shit. So they ended up shutting down the town. On the week's biggest shopping day."

"Where's the larger significance in that?"

"Think about the same thing multiplied by millions."

"Millions?"

"I'm talking about retired people, Wes."

"Oh. Right."

"Know how many there are today?"

"I don't have the numbers at my fingertips."

"Figure 39 million. Give or take. That's roughly 13 percent of the population. Real voting clout, apart from anything else."

"Like the Midwest farmers."

"Even bigger when you consider how fast their numbers are growing as Baby Boomers retire. By 2020, retired people will amount to 16 percent of the population. Can you imagine the implications of that?"

"I guess there are some interesting scenarios."

"You bet. Let me give you one."

"Okay."

"Assume some very aggressive political types with kingmaker ambitions get control of the groups representing retired people. AARP and so on. Think what they're going to be telling members of Congress."

"Yeah, I can imagine. Vote our way on elderly issues and you'll have long political careers. We guarantee it."

"Right. But vote against us and it's goodbye Washington come the next election. We can guarantee that, too."

"So I guess that means more generous pensions."

"Inevitably. Through the kind of national pension system you talked about in those notes you did on transportation. Remember?"

"I remember."

"Stamped and delivered by a docile Congress. Pensions that preserve the living standards of retired people after their working years. After all, their aggressive leaders will insist, didn't they work hard all their lives to build this country? Doesn't that entitle them to comfortable retirements? Who's to say no?"

"Obviously not members of Congress who want to stay in Washington."

"Of course not. So just like those demonstrating farm workers, retired people have the power of Law on their side. In this case, because of their huge voting clout."

"And paying for all this…?"

"Retired people don't have to care. It's not their problem. Congress has to work that out. Raise income tax rates on people who work? Fine. Tax the profits of big corporations? Okay. Cut other federal programs that don't effect retired people? Why not?"

"Or grow the economy faster."

"If that's what the rest of the country wants to do. In any case, it's not their problem."

"Yeah."

"But you see the implications, Wes? Once retired people wake up to the fact that they have the rest of us by the short hairs…. "

"So the country really doesn't have a choice. It has to grow the economy."

"Unless it wants to see retired people shut everything down. Like the Farm Workers ended up doing in this town."

"Then it's not a matter of Whether, but How."

"And the How is what we've been talking about all these Sundays. You and me, Wes. Here in this prison yard."

"So which way are you betting?"

"Me?"

"Can the country do it?"

"Oh, my family's protected by walls of money either way. That gives me the luxury of being cynical."

"You mean realistic?"

"That too!"

"Well, I can't afford that. It's too late for me to go into investment banking."

"Then let's hope you can do your book. And the right people read it."

* * *

"Abraham's the key," Elijah said at our next meeting.

"Abraham who?"

"Abraham Konigsberg from Midwood. Woody's uncle. Who do you think?"

"What?"

"Come on, Wes. You seem really obtuse this morning."

"I must be getting my period."

"I'm talking about Abraham of the Bible. Spiritual father of three major religions. The original Hat Trick guy."

"Oh, him."

"A very big Him. Maybe the biggest."

"So what's he the key to?"

"Lots of things. Like, what do you do when your back's really against the wall? A wall with no cracks you can slip through?"

"Why do I get the suspicion you're trying to link Abraham to your favorite subject?"

"Which favorite subject did you have in mind?"

"You know. Transportation."

"You don't think our backs are really against the wall when it comes to transportation?"

"That's what a lot of transportation fanatics claim."

"You going to argue with them?"

"Not today. I just want to know where Abraham comes in."

"Remember the Bible story?"

"There are lots of stories about him in the Bible."

"The one that matters most is where God tells him to sacrifice his son Isaac."

"No doubt while wearing his Gestapo uniform."

"What are you trying to do, humor me?"

"Just want to cooperate."

"Anyway, no Gestapo uniform this time. God was all decked out in a full set of evening clothes when he told Abraham to sacrifice Isaac."

"Evening clothes?"

"You know. Top hat. White tie. Black tailcoat. Ivory-handled cane. White gloves. The works."

"Sounds like Fred Astaire."

"Better. He was even wearing a black opera cape with a red lining. Just so Abraham wouldn't have any doubts."

"Must have been quite a sight."

"Obviously. That was the whole point. But you can imagine why the scribes who wrote the Bible had such problems with this story. I mean, if God's so great and benevolent and everything, how could he tell Abraham to sacrifice his own son? And why was Abraham so quick to agree?"

"Yeah, I can see what you mean."

"That's why the scribes tacked on that ridiculous happy ending. You know, God stays Abraham's hand at the last minute. Pretty lame. But it was the only thing they could come up with."

"You've got a better version?"

"Sure. One that's consistent with the spirit of Midrash."

"Midrash?"

"Hebrew word. With two meanings. The one most people think of is the title of an important section of the Talmud. But the less common meaning is more interesting."

"Yeah?"

"It has to do with Midrash as an intellectual discipline. The process of interpreting old myths and legends in terms of what we've learned about reality since they were written down."

"You do that a lot, don't you. I'm thinking about your Genesis story. Eve as the real mother of us all. "

"Of course. That's what studying the Talmud's really all about. Not a lot of ivory tower jerking off over linguistic minutiae. It engages the real world around us. Even the parts that may seem mundane."

"Like transportation?"

"Well, some people may think so. Obviously, I don't. Not when it affects our daily lives so profoundly."

"And Abraham is the key to all this?"

"You bet. Want to hear why?"

"What do you think?"

"Okay. Now, naturally Abraham was shocked when God told him to sacrifice Isaac. But not necessarily surprised. After all, he'd dealt with God before. If you believe the Bible."

"Yeah."

"So he looked at God and said: 'Oh, gee, I don't know. We haven't done anything like that in a long time.'

"'I'm aware of that,' God said.

"'Some of the other tribes still do child sacrifice. Maybe you should talk to them.'

"'Obviously I would have if I wanted to. But I'm talking to you.'

"'My son's almost completely grown up, you know.'

"'Does he have a wife?'

"'Not yet. But he's....'

"'Then technically he's still an adolescent. That makes him eligible.'

"'Isn't there something else I can do?'

"'Not today. I want you to sacrifice Isaac. And I can make it worth your while.'

"'How?'

"'By making you King of the World, for instance.'

"'Yeah?'

"'Wouldn't you like to be my duly appointed Number One emissary here on earth?'

"'You'd do that?'

"'Of course. With a snap of my fingers.'

"'The thing is....'

"'What.'

"'Well, it's the leaders of the individual sects who make all the money.'

"'I can change that in a second. I'll have them pay you license fees.'

"'Yeah?'

"'Then all you have to do is sit back and collect their payments. You'll be the richest man on earth.'

"'Can I get that in writing?'

"'What's the matter, don't you trust me?'

"'Oh, I trust you. But I need something to show the others. How can I make them believe me otherwise?'

"'Very well. I have some angels who went to law school. I'll have them draw up a New Covenant tonight. And sign it in your presence. After you sacrifice your son.'

"Okay.'

"'Shall we plan to do it first thing tomorrow morning? That hill over there looks good.'

"'Fine by me.'

"'You'll bring everything?'

"'Sure. But look.'

"'What now?'

"'If this deal's going to work as far as the others are concerned, I can't be the only one who benefits. I have to deliver a few things for them.'

"'You mean money?'

"'Nothing like that. Little things. Favors.'

"'What did you have in mind?'

"'For example, our local choral society has this great new boy soprano. With a voice like you wouldn't believe.'

"'So?'

"'But the thing is, the Music Director's been hitting on him. You know how those guys can be. And it's got the kid's mother all upset.'

"'All right. I'll speak to the Music Director.'

"'Then there's this friend of mine whose wife is....'

"'There's more?'

"'Look. I've been going to bat for you every day. Convincing the others to accept you as the One True God. And believe me, that's taken a lot of work. You think Circumcision was an easy sell? I need some favors to spread around.'

"'Well, don't overdo it. Now what's the problem with your friend's wife?'"

"Wait a second, Elijah," I finally managed to break in. "Just wait a short second."

"What?"

"You want me to believe Abraham tried to con God?"

"Not just tried. Wait till you hear the rest of the story."

"But...."

"So what did you expect Abraham to do? Tell God to get lost? If you've read the Bible, you know how bad-tempered and vengeful God can be. Remember what happened to Prometheus when he stole fire?"

"That's not in the Bible."

"Not everything important is."

"I see what you mean."

"Look, all four of my grandparents survived the Death Camps. You know how? Not by giving every German in sight the finger. They had to learn the right way to Make Nice. Just like Abraham."

"I must admit, your Death Camp metaphor's very compelling."

"Glad you think so. But you see why Abraham faced a really big-time back-to-the-wall problem."

"I guess so. Tell me the rest of the story."

"Okay. Now the scene changes to early the next morning. Abraham's waiting on top of that hill. And soon God arrives. In a golden chariot drawn by the usual fourteen angels."

"Still wearing evening clothes, I assume."

"Oh, absolutely. That's part of the show."

"Naturally."

"So Abraham immediately says: 'You brought the New Covenant?'

"'In my pocket.' God says. 'Where's your son?'

"'He's going to meet us here.'

"'Meet us here? Why didn't you bring him yourself?'

"'I didn't want him to get suspicious. You know how these kids are. You make a big deal out of something and right away they start asking all kinds of questions. Why this and why that. I figured it was better to act sort of casual.'

"'Well, he damn well better show.'

"'Oh he will. I'm sure of it.'

"So Abraham and God stood there on the hilltop waiting. And time passed, but there was no sign of Isaac. Meanwhile, God paced around becoming increasingly impatient. Finally he couldn't stand it anymore and turned to Abraham.

"'Where the hell is your son?' God said angrily.

"'I don't understand it. He promised to meet me here.'

"'Well, I can't wait around forever. I'm already running late.'

"'Okay, look. Tomorrow I'll bring him myself.'

"'Tomorrow?'

"'Come on. Give me another chance. Haven't I always come through for you in the past?'

"'Very well, tomorrow. But no more slipups. Understand?'

"'No, no. I'll bring him myself. I promise.'

"So early the next morning, Abraham brings Isaac to the hilltop and they wait for God to arrive. Which he does about ten minutes later."

"In the usual golden chariot, I suppose," I said.

"Of course, Wes. I'm not changing any of the details. Just reporting the facts. You know about facts."

"Yeah, sure."

"Anyway, God takes one look at Isaac and explodes with rage."

"Rage? Why?"

"Well, for one thing, Isaac's wearing earphones. Obviously listening to rock music. Snapping his fingers to the rhythm and dancing around. With an extremely spaced-out look in his eyes.

"'Oh, hell,' God screamed. 'The damn kid's stoned out of his mind.'

"'I wanted to make sure he'd be cooperative,' Abraham said.

"'You had him smoke grass?'

"'Just a little. So he'd be easy to control.'

"'You dumb idiot. Don't you get it? He has to be fully alert for the sacrifice. Otherwise, what's the point?'

"'Sorry. I didn't know. As I told you, it's been a long time since we've done anything like this.'

"'That's obvious.'

"'So what should I have done?'

"'Tie him up, moron.'

"'Tie him up?'

"'Yes, yes. Do I have to draw you pictures? Tie him up good and tight. But make sure he's fully conscious and alert. I want to hear him scream and beg and plead when it happens.'

"'Oh. Now I get it.'

"'Now you get it? You miserable incompetent. . . .'

"'Okay, look. Now that I'm clear about what you want, we can do it tomorrow. . . .'

"'Tomorrow? You can forget tomorrow, as far as I'm concerned.'

"'No, listen. I'm trying to do what you want. Just like always. But the details were too vague. Now come on. Be fair.'

"'Me? Fair? Who do you think you're talking to?'

"'The One True God. Great and All-Powerful. Before Whom All Nations Must Bow. Like I've been telling the others for years. . . .'

"'All right, tomorrow.'

"'Believe me, you won't regret it. Now that I know exactly what you. . . .'

"'Well, just get it done.'

"'Yes, I promise. . . .'"

"Jesus, Elijah...." I managed to break in.

"What? You think I'm making God sound too dictatorial?"

"No, that I can buy. I can even buy you calling him a Nazi. But to suggest he's also a...."

"It's a metaphor."

"Metaphor? For what?"

"God as the Ultimate Child Abuser."

"That's ... monstrous."

"Of course. That's the whole point."

"Where did you get such a crazy idea?"

"The evidence is all around us, if you're willing to look. In my case...."

"Don't tell me. You've had direct experience?"

"You might call it that."

"This had better be good."

"Well, listen and decide. Now, you know how exotic Brooklyn is."

"Sure."

"Probably the most exotic place on earth. Because it's full of the whole world. But not just nice exotic. You know, quirky and colorful and over-flowing with life. It's also got plenty of bad exotic. Monstrous and evil exotic. God's bile, if you will."

"Yeah, I guess there's no shortage of that."

"Well, a few years ago I was having a back problem. So my doctor sent me to this therapy place he thought might do me some good. It was in Sheepshead Bay. Way the hell over on Nostrand Avenue. The bus let me off about a block away, so I had to walk a short distance. And I came upon this building with a line of school buses in front."

"A school?"

"Actually, it turned out to be like a day care center for mentally disabled people. Kids mostly. Where they could get medical care and training and so on. The school buses were waiting to take them home."

"You saw the kids?"

"The attendants were bringing them out to the buses when I got there.

Some of them could walk more or less okay. But when you looked at their faces.... "

"Yeah, you see a lot of people like that in Brooklyn. Walking the streets and in the subway."

"They're the lucky ones. They can make it on their own, with a little help. But so many were in wheelchairs. All twisted up from birth defects and so on. Writhing and drooling and moaning. But we don't give up on them. We don't put them to death like the Germans did. Not in Brooklyn. We do what we can for them."

"Yeah.... "

"And who did such terrible things to those kids, Wes? Who abused them that way? Was it Adolph Hitler? Joseph Stalin? Pol Pot? Idi Amin? No, none of those bastards ever had imaginations that vicious."

"I see what you're getting at."

"Why couldn't he pick on somebody his own size? That's what I kept asking myself as that parade of abused kids passed before me. Over and over. Why couldn't he pick on somebody his own size? Until I was so filled with rage I wanted to grab that miserable putz by the throat and choke the living shit out of him.... "

"You and Captain Ahab."

"Melville's Ahab?"

"Well, some literary critics think *Moby Dick*'s the story of a man who wanted to kill God."

"But don't they assume Melville was a little crazy?"

"Look who's talking."

"All part of being a successful investment banker. Anyway, that doesn't mean Melville wasn't right. But you can see why the biblical scribes had such a problem with Abraham's story."

"Why didn't they just leave it out?"

"I'm sure a lot of them wanted to. But apparently it was too deep a part of the folklore. So they prettied it up as much as they could and tacked on that happy ending. Even so, many theologians find the story very disturbing. They can't help reading between the lines. And find the implications terrifying."

"So how does your version end?"

"Oh, you'll like this."

"I'm sure."

"On the third morning, Abraham and Isaac were waiting on the hill-top as agreed. Abraham had bound Isaac with a rope from the waist up. So tightly he couldn't move his arms. And pretty soon, God arrived in the usual manner."

"'I did everything you told me to,' Abraham said to God. 'See how he's all tied up?'

"'Why didn't you tie his legs, too?' God said.

"'Then he wouldn't be able to walk. How could I have gotten him up here?'

"'You could have carried him.'

"'Come on, be reasonable. I'm an old man. I've got a bad back.'

"'Oh, all right. Let's get to it. Now make him kneel in front of me.'

"'Okay, Isaac. You heard what the man said. Here, I'll help you so you don't lose your balance.'

"Abraham moved close to Isaac. But Isaac abruptly shoved him to the ground. Then turned and started running.

"'Grab him.' God yelled. 'He's trying to get away.'

"'You grab him. You're closer. Oh, my back....'

"So God made a quick lunge for Isaac. But tripped over some rocks and sprawled face down on the ground. Tearing his pants in the process. Breaking his cane and crushing his top hat. Getting mud all over his clothes. While Isaac ran down the hill to safety.

"'Damn, damn, damn!' God screamed as he struggled to his feet. 'Of all the....'

"'I'm sorry as hell. Believe me.'

"'The kid got away. And it's your fault.'

"'How is it my fault? I did everything you told me to.'

"'Damn, look at me. Do you know what this outfit cost?'

"'Don't worry. I know a tailor who can do wonders with things like this. He can have it ready for tomorrow.'

"'The hell with tomorrow.'

"'But we can try again. I'll tie his legs this time.'

"'Never mind. The deal's off. I've wasted enough time.'

"'Oh, come on. I know you're upset, but. . . .'

"'I told you, the deal's off.'

"'But I did my best. Everything you told me to.'

"'I don't care. The deal's off. I should have known better than to try to do business with an idiot like you.'

"'You're still going to sign the New Covenant, aren't you?'

"'Yeah, sure. As far as I'm concerned. . . .'

"'Come on. I kept my part of the deal. I did everything you. . . .'

"'Go to hell.'

"'But what am I going to tell the others?'

"'What others?'

"'You know. My people.'

"'You told them about our deal?'

"'I had to. So they'd believe me when I showed them the New Covenant.'

"'What are you going to tell them now?'

"'If you sign the New Covenant, I can tell them you stayed my hand at the last minute. As a sign of your Blessed Mercy. That'll really impress them.'

"'The hell with them. I can wipe out this whole damn valley with an earthquake. Just like that.'

"'Of course you can. But what'll that get you in the long run? It'll only make things easier for those guys who want to bring back the pagan gods. Then where will we be?'

"'I suppose that makes sense.'

"'Sure it does. Okay, so maybe things didn't turn out the way we planned. But let's salvage what we can.'

"'You're sure you can cover with the others?'

"'I'm highly confident. With the New Covenant signed by you. Plus my story about how you stayed my hand at the last minute. As a sign of your Blessed Mercy as the One True God. I mean, what can those guys pushing the pagan gods possibly do against that?'

"'Very well.'

"'You'll sign?'

"'Yes.'

"'Great. Believe me, you won't regret this.'

"'I'd better not.'

"'I understand completely. And while you're at it, can you sign each page? It'll look better that way.'

"'Yes, yes.'

"So God signed each page and gave the New Covenant to Abraham. Then vanished in a pillar of fire that also consumed the golden coach with its angels. After which, Abraham walked down the hill and found Isaac sitting on a rock at the bottom.

"'You got the New Covenant, Dad?" Isaac said.

"'Yeah.'

"'That's great. Your plan worked like a charm.'

"'Seems to. For what it's worth. You did a great job on your end.'

"'You expect God to keep his word?'

"'Maybe on a few things.'

"'He's that bad?'

"'Well, you heard how he carried on up there.'

"'A real shmuck, in other words.'

"'You got that right. Anyway, let me untie your ropes.'

"'Be careful. I don't want you to hurt your back.'

"'What back.'

"'I heard what you said up there about your back.'

"'Well, at my age, a bad back's a good excuse for a lot of things. And everybody believes you. Now, come on. Let's get these ropes off you and go home. Maybe Sarah can make us a decent brunch. I'm starved.'"

When Elijah finished this story, I could see by the glow in his eyes how proud he was of it.

"One of these days, you're going to be struck by lightning," I told him.

"Oh, I already have."

"Yeah? When?"

"The first night I met Susan at Baruch."

"Oh."

"Someday, the same thing will happen to you. If you're as lucky as I've been."

I suppose I should have expected something like that. And it filled me with a terrible sense of dread. But what could I do?

"You make Abraham seem like a major hero," I finally managed to say.

"When your back's against a wall, what other choice do you have?"

"Maybe we should make him our spokesman for transportation."

"Wouldn't hurt. If we're smart about it."

* * *

Another dream about Susan.

She and I were sitting at a table for four in what seemed like an elaborate ballroom. Very Art Deco. With lots of other people seated around us at similar tables.

Apparently this was some sort of professional conference. Elijah was standing behind the rostrum at the far end of the room addressing the audience. Occasionally using his laser pointer to indicate something on a multicolored diagram projected on the large screen behind him and slightly to his right. The audience seemed to be hanging on his every word.

Then I realized where we were. In the vast First Class dining salon of the ocean liner *Queen Mary*. Permanently moored in Long Beach as a combination tourist attraction, upscale hotel, and conference center.

I'd been here twice before. Once to cover a real estate convention for my newspaper. The second time on my own a few months later. To wander around the huge ship, soaking up its museum-like atmosphere of the 1930s. Which made a deep impression on me. Almost like a time machine.

"Isn't this a great room?" I said to Susan in a low tone.

She smiled back agreeably.

"Imagine sailing across the Atlantic on this ship in the good old days of the 1930s."

"Shh," a middle-aged man at the next table hissed at me with obvious annoyance.

I mouthed a contrite "Sorry" to him. Susan covered my hand with hers and indicated that I should pay attention to what Elijah was saying.

He was going on at great length about accounting and how screwed up it was. The sins of accrualism and so on.

I remembered our discussions about accounting and the strong opinions he'd expressed. On the other hand, he had strong opinions about almost everything and wanted to make sure you knew exactly what they were. But I was used to that, so I didn't take it too seriously.

Except now he was going on about accounting in much greater detail and with real passion. As if it was one of his major obsessions. Right up there with transportation and free-market capitalism. Something much too important for the rest of the world to keep on ignoring.

And the audience seemed to love it. They were leaning forward eagerly so as not to miss a word. Periodically nodding in agreement. Smiling with satisfaction. As if some long-overdue truths about the world were finally being given voice.

None of which made much sense to me. Too technical and esoteric. But at least I didn't have to cover his speech for my newspaper. I was just a patient spectator. Sitting with Susan.

Finally his speech was over. The audience responded with enthusiastic applause as Elijah stood there smiling. And when the applause died away, the audience began shouting questions from the floor. Which caused a middle-aged man in a dark blue suit to rise quickly from his table near the rostrum and stride to Elijah's side.

"We're running a little late, folks," the man said into the microphone. "Please save your questions for the panel discussion after dinner."

Members of the audience began mumbling to each other as Elijah and the man in the blue suit left the rostrum. They were joined by half a dozen similar looking men, all of whom made polite comments to Elijah. And the whole group headed for a door beyond the rostrum.

"Where's he going?" I asked Susan.

"They have a meeting of the association's board of directors."

"Oh."

"He's trying to get them to adopt a formal policy on accounting."

"I didn't realize he had such an obsession about it."

"He has lots of obsessions. Some of them change from day to day."

"I guess so."

"In any case, it's likely to be a long meeting. So we'll have plenty of time."

"Great."

Suddenly there was an abrupt change in the room's lighting. It became dimmer. More like an old-fashioned nightclub.

Then I heard a dance band strike up a Gershwin tune and noticed that the rostrum and projection screen had been replaced by a bandstand filled with tuxedo-clad musicians. A slender male singer was holding onto the microphone stand as he crooned the tune's familiar words in a reedy Fred Astaire voice.

> *The way you wear your hat*
> *The way you sip your tea*
> *The memory of all that*
> *No, no, they can't take that away from me....*

I glanced at Susan. She was wearing a stunning black gown, and she smiled enigmatically at me. And I realized I was wearing a tuxedo with all the trimmings. Just like the other men in the room.

Then I noticed the two half-filled glasses of champagne that had suddenly appeared on our snow white linen table cloth. Saw how the surface of the champagne was tilting slightly with the easy roll of the ship. And it all became clear to me.

We were sailing across the Atlantic on a late summer night in 1939.

Trying to banish the looming clouds of onrushing War by surrounding ourselves with the Art Deco elegance of the *Queen Mary's* nightclub glitter.

Clinging to the last vestiges of dreams that were destined to vanish all too soon. Like the sad incandescence of Gershwin's music.

> *The way your smile just beams*
> *The way you sing off key*
> *They way you haunt my dreams*
> *No, no, they can't take that away from me....*

"Shall we dance?" I said to Susan.

"I'd be delighted."

The dance floor was already filling with other couples, and I took Susan in my arms as soon as we slipped between the last circle of tables.

"They're saying War will break out any day," I murmured idly to her as we began dancing.

"Let's not talk about that now. We should enjoy whatever time we have left."

"I guess you're right."

"If the man is handsome, the lady is lovely, the night is drenched with moonlight, and each is thrilled with the warmth of the other's arms...."

I recognized the Dragon Lady's words from that sequence where she was teaching Terry to dance. In Hong Kong during that same summer in 1939. On the other side of the world. Where War had already spread its devastation.

"My love...." I whispered and held her closer.

She rested her cheek against my shoulder as we whirled slowly among the other couples. And as my heart swelled with passion, I heard myself murmuring words that came from deep within my memory.

"I never knew anyone could be as completely graceful as you are," I said, imagining I was Terry once again.

"Why, thank you, sir."

"It seems that the time and the place and the music have combined to form a setting for the precious jewel that is you."

"Ah, you are adept at the pretty speech."

And she was repeating the Dragon Lady's words. As if she knew the sequence in the comic strip as well as I did.

"I didn't think life could ever hold a moment as exquisite as this," I heard myself say, unable to stop myself from repeating Terry's words.

"Aren't you being a bit flattering?"

"Oh, darling, you're too beautiful to share with other people. Let's get away, where we can really be alone."

Gershwin's music swelled to a romantic climax as we embraced each other passionately. And my hands slid up her body to cup her breasts. Naked and heaving beneath her evening dress.

> *The way you hold your knife*
> *The way we danced till three*
> *The way you changed my life*
> *No, no, they can't take that away from me*
> *No, they can't take that away from me*
> *Can't take that away*
> *Can't take that away from me....*

An instant later, we were sprawled naked together on the bed in our First Class cabin.

But suddenly a deep, male, English-accented voice boomed from our cabin's loudspeaker.

"Attention, passengers and crew. Attention. This is the captain speaking. I have just been informed by the office of the British Prime Minister that German tanks and warplanes attacked Poland early this morning at several points along their common border. Information is limited, but this appears to be a full-scale invasion of Polish territory by Germany. I will keep you informed of further details as they are received. Meanwhile, all members of the crew are directed to report to their emergency stations immediately. Passengers are to remain in their cabins until further notice. That is all for now."

So it had come at last. The new European war feared by so many. And I had an uneasy feeling that nothing would ever be the same again.

I turned toward Susan.

But the bed was empty. She was gone. Vanished into the hopeless maw of a world gone mad.

All I saw was my copy of Volume Nine of the comic strip lying on her pillow. Open to the sequence where she was teaching Terry to dance.

I snatched it up and stared at her face in the panels. It was all that remained of her.

And I realized with a throb of dismay that I'd been making love to a cartoon all along. Not to Susan. Not to any real-life incarnation of the Dragon Lady at all. Only to a bloodless two-dimensional cartoon. A figment of the artist's imagination. Which, by some black magic, had come to vivid life inside my brain.

Now gone. All gone. Taking a vital piece of me with it.

> *The way you hold your knife*
> *The way we danced till three*
> *The way you changed my life*
> *No, no, they can't take that away from me....*

But they had taken it away.

For better or worse.

* * *

I awoke from this dream to astonishingly bright morning sunshine. Sat on the edge of my bed and waited for the familiar pain to grab me by the gut. I'd been living with it for so many weeks that I more or less took it for granted.

But all I felt was an eerie sense of peace. Calmness. Even tranquility.

It was so pervasive I actually stood up and strode over to my bedroom window. Flung it wide open. Took a deep breath of fresh air. And became aware of a faint ocean tang filling my nostrils. As if Coney Island's boardwalk lay just beyond the western hills.

Finally I took a shower and shaved. Got dressed. Headed downtown to the newspaper. Stopped on the way at a Real McCoy diner for the first solid breakfast I'd eaten in a good many weeks. Three eggs scrambled with bacon chips. Two oversized sausage patties. Crispy home fries. Double order of English muffins with sweet grape jelly. Lots of hot black coffee brewed the old fashioned way.

Aware as I ate, with a growing sense of wonder, that my whole world had just been turned right-side up again.

What did it mean?

Chapter Seven

Who Says You Can't
Go Home Again?

My *Queen Mary* dream and its immediate impact obviously raised lots of questions that I could have spent a good deal of time thinking about.

And I certainly would have if it hadn't been for the email waiting on my apartment computer when I got back from work early the next evening after treating myself to a hearty steak dinner and a decent bottle of red wine.

It was from my literary agent in New York. He'd finally gotten me a book deal with one of the publishers he'd been romancing.

His email was very brief. But it had two attachments explaining everything. One was his point-by-point summary of the contract the publisher was offering. The other was a scan of the contract itself, written in the usual tormented legalese that was barely comprehensible.

But the bottom line was clear enough. I had scored with my best hook shot ever. With the coach from Lincoln High School watching in the stands. Three cheers.

I got up at the crack of dawn the next morning and took advantage of the time difference to phone my agent at his office half an hour before he was supposed to leave for a lunch date. He confirmed everything. Said he'd just overnighted me three copies of the contract itself. Told me it was pretty standard. Recommended that I sign it. But encouraged me to phone him anytime if I had questions.

We had two more crack-of-drawn phone conversations later that week. About minor questions. More in the nature of my going through the motions. Just to convince myself it really was true. And because it was all I could think about.

I told Elijah everything when we met on Sunday.

"That's great," he said with a big grin. "So the Good Guys win after all."

"Once in a while, anyway. I guess I should feel humble."

"Yeah, well don't overdo it. Humble doesn't play well in New York. Unless they know you're faking it."

"Don't worry."

"They give you a decent advance?"

"Not bad."

"Decent enough so you can work full-time on the book?"

"Oh, sure. With my trust fund income, I won't have to do anything else for the next year."

"So you'll leave the newspaper."

"Heartbreaking, isn't it."

"Where will you go?"

"I don't know yet."

"But you won't stay here."

"No, I'll probably go to New York. But I haven't figured out where yet. I don't really have a home anywhere."

"Yes, you do."

"Yeah? Where."

"Brooklyn."

"Come on, Elijah...."

"I'm serious. I've gotten to know you pretty well these last few months. Down deep, you're still a Brooklyn street kid. That's something you never get over."

"I couldn't go back to my old neighborhood in Bed-Stuy. It's become very gentrified now. Full of upscale African-American families restoring the brownstones."

"What about Park Slope? The north end. Short walk across Grand Army

Plaza to the Central Brooklyn Library with its great research facilities."

"Maybe. Actually, though...."

"What?"

"I always thought it'd be kind of interesting to live in Coney Island."

"Now you're talking. Stroll over to Gargiulo's for linguini with white clam sauce."

"Or the other way, to the Russian restaurants in Brighton Beach. Borsht and Chicken Kiev."

"Stop it, Wes. You've got me starving."

"You and me both."

"So I guess you'll work it out."

"I guess so."

"Well, I have my own news."

"Yeah?"

"They're moving me to a halfway house in Manhattan for the last few months of my sentence."

"My God...."

"It's the usual routine. I'll have to sleep nights at the halfway house. But I'll be free to come and go during the day."

"When?"

"The move? End of the week."

"So soon?"

"That's the way these things work. So this'll have to be our last meeting here."

"Guess I'd better hurry up and move back to Brooklyn."

"That's my hope. Then we can resume our meetings over pastrami at the Carnegie Deli."

"Or cheese cake at Junior's."

"God, a person can starve to death out here."

"In more ways than one.

"By the way, Wes, Susan's going to be joining us soon."

"Susan?"

"She flew out to help me get things ready. You know, for my move. Hope you don't mind."

"No, no. That's fine. When's she joining us?"

"Now."

"Now?"

"Look."

I looked in the direction he was pointing and saw Susan walking towards us across the lawn. Already close enough so I could see her big smile of greeting.

"Hey, guys," she said cheerily. "Are you plotting another intellectual takeover of the world?"

"When was the last one?" Elijah asked. They kissed each other heartily. "I forget."

As I stood there feeling slightly awkward, she turned to me.

"Come on, Wesley," she said. "Don't I get a hug from my favorite journalist?"

"You bet."

We hugged like old friends running into each other on Fifth Avenue. And I was relieved that she didn't seem to be wearing any perfume.

"Wes has great news, sweetheart," Elijah said. "He got a book deal."

"That's wonderful, Wesley."

"And he's going to write the book in Brooklyn."

"Really? You're moving back?"

"Seems so. I have a few things out here to take care of first."

"Well, don't be a stranger when you get settled."

"Not a chance. I need a lot of input from Elijah for the book."

Susan abruptly sat down on the shaded bench next to us and leaned back.

"Go to it, guys," she said. "Don't mind me."

"Gee, Elijah," I said. "We never had an audience before. I guess we'd better be careful what we talk about."

"How about the Morality of Capitalism?" he said.

"That sounds suitably grandiose. You start."

"Okay. All our decent human instincts tell us that Capitalism is nothing less than a Great Scourge."

"Not that I necessarily disagree. But what brought you to that conclusion?"

"Look at the historical record. Is there anything that's been more effective in bringing out the worst in people than Capitalism?"

"Organized religion maybe?"

"Good point. Each one runs the other a close second. But which is Number One remains a matter of debate."

"I guess so."

"This place is full of examples of how Capitalism can corrupt the most decent people you could imagine."

"Because it's a Minimum Security institution?"

"Right. So most of the inmates are here for White Collar Crimes. Which basically means they've been led into perdition by the scarlet woman we call Capitalism."

"Are you including yourself?"

"No, I'm different. I'm the only one who studies the Talmud. That helps me see the difference between what's morally wrong and what's merely illegal."

"Like Insider Trading."

"I already explained about that."

"I know."

"But these other poor schnooks don't have that advantage. So they didn't realize when they were walking into moral minefields."

"Are you saying they're different from Mad Max Bloom?"

"Oh, definitely. I mean, guys like Uncle Max have their heads wired all wrong. They don't make moral choices. Just follow their instincts."

"Like the scorpion."

"Exactly. But not like most guys in places like this. Andrew's a good example."

"Andrew who?"

"Just Andrew. I got to know him when I first came here. He was released last year."

"What was he in for?"

"Securities fraud. He was an accountant by training. Chief financial officer of a middle-size manufacturing company in Indiana. Pleaded to three counts of cooking his company's books prior to a common stock offering. The stock tanked six months later. Leaving some politically connected local investors screaming to their congressmen. Leading to an SEC investigation that opened up a real can of worms. You know. Off-the-books shell companies to hide losses. Revenue sources that didn't actually exist. The whole megilla. Old Andrew was having himself quite a time."

"Sounds like a real lascivine."

"A what?"

"Lascivine."

"Sorry. That's a word I don't know."

"I learned it from a guy at Columbia. It's adapted from the word 'lascivious.' But with a much broader meaning."

"Sounds worth remembering."

"Does it fit Andrew?"

"Sure. In terms of what he did. But you wouldn't know it to look at him."

"What do you mean?"

"He looked like a total schlub. You know. Middle-aged. Overweight. Klutzy. Hair combed just so over his bald spot. Glasses with wire frames. Slightly high-pitched voice. Always at a loss for words.... "

"The last guy you'd expect to find playing elaborate accounting tricks."

"Right."

"A Boy Scout leader too, I'll bet."

"As a matter of fact, yes. Not to mention a wife and two children. Plus a split-level house in Evansville, Indiana. Where he grew up."

"The polar opposite of Mad Max."

"Absolutely."

"So what sent him down the garden path?"

"A scarlet woman named Capitalism."

"That's a nice metaphor."

"But in Andrew's case, there really was a woman."

"Oh come on, Elijah. That's such a cliché."

"I know it sounds hard to believe. But it's true. Her name was Monica. She paid for her MBA from NYU by working for an upscale escort service owned by some Russian guys in Sheepshead Bay."

"Not Brighton Beach?"

"They'd moved up in the world. But not as far as Manhattan Beach."

"I can imagine."

"Actually, the escort service was just a side business. Their main shtick was taking nowhere companies private. Inflating their balance sheets and income statements with accounting tricks. Then selling them off to the suckers in the investing crowd for big bucks. Very profitable."

"They took over Andrew's company?"

"And made him CFO. Because he was a local boy who looked too schlubby to play any tricks."

"Nice, safe Front Man."

"That's what they thought. But then they discovered they had a secret financial genius on their hands."

"Andrew was that good?"

"He had a super-brilliant accounting mind. And didn't even know it. I mean, he'd talk to me about things I never dreamed existed. And I thought I'd heard everything."

"More than just accrual tricks."

"You wouldn't believe. And when the Russians found out, they changed their game plan to make him the point man in their scenario. Promising him millions in the bargain. Of course, he was such a straight arrow they had to soften him up first."

"That's where Monica came in, I suppose."

"Right. She'd just gotten her MBA, so they sent her out to Evansville to be Andrew's executive assistant. You can guess the rest."

"She seduced him."

"Did she ever. He couldn't stop talking about it. Gave him orgasms like he never thought possible. Even after three years in here, sex with her was still the most memorable thing in his life. Everything else was secondary."

"You make it sound like *Double Indemnity*."

"The movie?"

"Barbara Stanwyck luring Fred MacMurray into killing her husband as part of an insurance scam."

"Right. In this case, with Monica playing the Stanwyck character to the hilt. Luring Andrew into killing the company he'd devoted his life to. Driving him crazy with dreams of lifetime orgasms. After they ran away to Rio together with their ill-gotten millions."

"Nice touch. Killing companies beats killing husbands any day."

"The really pathetic thing was that Andrew was still hung up on her."

"Monica?"

"He was convinced she was 'waiting for him.'"

"What about his wife and kids?"

"Oh, long gone. His wife divorced him and moved somewhere else with the kids. Changed her name and so on. But that was just a technicality as far as he was concerned."

"Technicality?"

"It meant nothing to him emotionally. Because he was so hung up on Monica."

"And his ill-gotten millions?"

"All part of the same package. As far as I could tell, Monica and the money had become two sides of the same coin in his mind. I don't think he could separate one from the other."

"Interesting how sex and money almost become the same thing in cases like this."

"Maybe they really are the same thing, Wes. For guys, at least."

"Metaphorically?"

"More than that."

"You're saying they're both related to greed?"

"Isn't greed the father of each? Think about it."

"With Capitalism as the midwife."

"Could be."

"Whatever happened to Andrew?"

"As I said, he was released about a year ago."

"Was Monica waiting at the gate for him? Behind the wheel of a brand new BMW?"

"What do you think?"

"Yeah, I guess that figures. So all he had left was the money."

"Not even that, probably."

"No?"

"A few times, he mentioned being the plaintiff in some civil suits. You know, from defrauded local investors."

"They got it all?"

"Seems reasonable, don't you think? He was the obvious target, being a local boy. The Russians were probably shielded by the various shell companies Andrew had set up for them."

"So he was left with nothing."

"That's my guess. Just another technicality, as far as he was concerned."

"You seem very well informed about Andrew and Monica."

"Of course. I had them checked out."

"Checked out?"

"There are services for that."

"Oh."

"It's routine. I do it with everybody."

"Including me?"

"Right after you sent me that first letter."

313

"Jesus...."

"You'd rather I beat around the bush wondering if I could trust you?"

"It's still ... unsettling."

"There are worse things."

"Yeah.... Did you ever hear from Andrew after he got out?"

"Not a word. But I didn't expect to."

"So he could be dead."

"For all practical purposes. The history of Capitalism's littered with dead bodies. Literally or otherwise."

"So you agree with me, in other words."

"We agree about a lot of things. But in different ways."

"What's that supposed to mean?"

"In this case, it means that Capitalism may well be a Great Scourge. With a long history of bringing out the worst in people. Even straight arrow Boy Scout leader types like Andrew. Because of its unmatched ability to exploit human greed. And yet...."

"And yet?"

"Has anything else been a greater source of prosperity than Capitalism? Has anything else been able to marshal the incredible resources of human creativity to produce riches beyond our wildest dreams? If it has, I haven't been able to find it."

"But think of the cost."

"Oh, there's no question the cost's been high. Because there's no free lunch, supposedly. Right, Susan?"

"Depends on who has to pay the bill," she said quickly.

"Spoken like a true economist," Elijah said with a grin. "Anyway, the real issue is whether the cost of Capitalism can be worth its benefits. Or whether we can make it so if we're clever enough."

"Is that another of your ironies?" I said.

"We're surrounded by ironies. It's part of the human condition. Let me give you an example."

"I was waiting for that."

"Back in 2001, Susan and I attended a Saturday matinee performance of Wagner's *Die Meistersinger* at the Metropolitan Opera. Remember, sweetheart?"

"How could I forget?"

"You know about opera, Wes?"

"Not really."

"Most operas are like circuses. Big lavish circuses that can sweep you off your feet if you give them half a chance. Great fun, in other words. But you don't take them seriously."

"Sort of like sex without commitment."

"Exactly. But *Meistersinger* is something more. Still a great circus. But also a great work of art. One of the towering masterpieces of Western culture. Saluting the glory of being human with some of the most incandescent music imaginable. Gives you an idea of what God might be able to do if he had the talent. And in an uncut performance like the Met does, it goes on for six hours."

"Six hours? You've got to be kidding."

"Not at all. This is no glitzy Broadway musical, after all. No two-and-a-half hours and you're back out on the street wondering where to go next. Six fabulous hours. That go by like a whirlwind. I mean, you may happen to glance at your watch and realize that you've already passed the five hour mark. But you find yourself wishing it would go on forever."

"The audience must be half-dead by the end."

"Anything but. They're like rejuvenated. Their very souls have been charged up with the spirit of life. At the end of the performance we attended, all four thousand people in the opera house stood up and cheered. Cheered. At the top of their lungs. Like their team had just won the Super Bowl. On and on. Until the ushers had to shoo us out, so the Met could get ready for its performance of *La Traviata* at eight o'clock."

"Two operas in one day?"

"That's New York, Wes. The ultimate cornucopia of life's richness. And because that performance of *Meistersinger* was the regular Saturday matinee, it was broadcast live on radio to the entire world. Three months after 9/11, as it happened. Showing everybody that we were still alive and kicking, despite the wounds we had suffered. New York resurgent."

"Wow."

"Fortunately, the Met videotaped that performance. It's available on DVD. Sort of the world's longest and most exciting music video."

"You're suggesting that I buy it?"

"Only if you want to enlarge your life in some cosmic ways."

"I get the point."

"Anyway, Susan and I finally left the opera house. Walked across Lincoln Plaza towards Broadway. Feeling like we were floating three feet above the ground, with that music still ringing in our ears. And as we passed the fountain, I had what you might call an epiphany."

"An epiphany?"

"I can't think of any other word for it. There I stood next to the fountain. Looking back at the opera house. All lit up against the western sky. And it suddenly hit me that maybe God was laughing at us."

"Laughing?"

"It took an enormous creative gift to write *Meistersinger*. And who did God give that gift to? Not some mensch like Felix Mendelssohn, who was as decent a guy as you could imagine. He gave it to Richard Wagner. A world class schmuck if there ever was one."

"Anti-Semitic, wasn't he?"

"That was the least of his shortcomings. He was a total monster in every conceivable way. Devoid of any redeeming virtues. Except for his ability to write great music like *Meistersinger*. Because God gave him a monumental gift that, by any justice, should have gone to somebody like Mendelssohn. God took that gift to humanity, then wrapped it in shit and gave it to a total schmuck. How do we come to terms with that?"

"You tell me."

"Did God simply want to laugh at us? Was it part of his vengeance because Abraham had conned him? What?"

"Like you say, maybe God's a Nazi."

"Interesting you should mention that. Because the Nazis embraced Wagner as one of their own. The official Nazi composer, as it were. And how do we respond to that in New York? Which is, among other things, the world's preeminent Jewish city. Do we ban his music?"

"Not so you'd notice, I guess."

"Right. We take him for what he is. A world champion schmuck who happened to write *Meistersinger*. So we embrace the music and piss on the man. Make it all work for us. On our terms. Does that suggest something?"

"About operas?"

"About Capitalism."

"What?"

"Come on, Wes. Put your arms around it."

"Can you possibly be suggesting that Wagner and Capitalism are the same?"

"Not the same. Just alike. Both of them scourges. But each containing something that can make us infinitely richer if we can figure out how to use it. So let's start figuring."

"This was your epiphany?"

"You were expecting maybe something like a Second Coming? Tell him, Susan."

"The expression on his face was like nothing I've ever seen, Wesley. It made me realize that I was married to a true prophet."

"So you lived up to your name in the eyes of your wife."

"Always tried to."

"Is that what gave you the idea for the toll road project?"

"Can you think of a better way to demolish pagan gods?"

"I guess it'll do for now."

"What a pair you two are," Susan said, rising from her bench. "Like judges of a secret court here in this prison. Passing down verdicts about some of the basic aspects of human society."

"Somebody has to," I said.

"Who better than a pair of rogues like us?" Elijah said. "Right, Wes?"

"Oy veh."

"My goodness," she said. "What's the world coming to?"

"You should know," I said, not exactly sure what I meant.

Maybe that was why something told me it was time to leave.

"Look," I said, facing them. "You two must have a lot of things to do, with Elijah moving and everything. I'd better be on my way."

"Stay in touch, Wesley," Susan said.

"I'll be able to talk to you on the phone once I'm in the halfway house," Elijah said. "And send you emails."

"Yeah. Good."

I turned and walked away from them. Not exactly sure where I was going. But that didn't matter now. Just away....

*   *   *

I took the back road because I wasn't in any hurry. Enough was coming to an end as it was.

But as I neared the summit of the ragged mountains north of town, the music on my car radio abruptly faded out. I absently hit the scan button. And a moment later, heard a song I knew all too well.

> *Thanks for the memory*
> *Of candle light and wine,*
> *Castles on the Rhine,*
> *The Parthenon*
> *And moments on*
> *The Hudson River Line.*
> *How lovely it was.*

It was Bob Hope, singing his well-known signature song with Shirley Ross.

They had first performed it in an otherwise forgettable 1937 movie I'd seen recently on a cable TV station as part of a Bob Hope retrospective. Where the Hope character runs into his ex-wife at the bar on a super-glitzy ocean liner crossing the Atlantic. And they can't help singing about their former life together.

> *Thanks for the memory*
> *Of rainy afternoons,*
> *Swingy Harlem tunes,*
> *And motor trips*
> *And burning lips*
> *And burning toast and prunes.*
> *How lovely it was.*

The sadness and regret in their voices stabbed me in the chest. Made me gulp with anguish. Flooded my eyes with tears.

I had to pull off the road and stop the car. Sit there trembling as their song washed over me. Staring half blind with tears of emotion at the empty mountain valley beyond the edge of the road.

She wasn't just a two-dimensional cartoon. A figment of someone else's imagination who had become an obsession to me.

She had her own reality that was completely unconnected to any pen-and-ink cartoon image. A light in her eyes and smile that only a poet or some other mystic could possibly understand. Firing my dreams beyond all imagining.

Yeah, what foolishness....

But what magic. Sublime in a way that I guess you had to be an idiot like me to appreciate.

After all, how many other guys had ever been lucky enough to love such a woman? And have her leave such a glorious piece of herself behind? To make me a better person, hopefully.

So thanks for the memory.
And strictly entre nous,
Darling, how are you?
And how are all the little dreams
That never did come true?
Awfully glad I met you.
Cheerio and toodeloo....
And thank you so much.

Finally my eyes cleared. My breathing became normal again. So I shifted into Drive and pulled back onto the empty road. Heading for my apartment to start packing.

After all, I had a book to write.

Back in Brooklyn where I belonged. Scars and all.

With Elijah standing by to keep my back straight.

And Abraham grinning proudly from the shadow.

I took a deep breath and let it out slowly as my car raced eagerly down the roller coaster grade towards the long valley.

My exile was ending. ■

Endnotes

CHAPTER 3

Pages 145–156   The discussions of the Dragon Lady's significance as a major American literary character are taken from an unpublished, privately circulated essay by an anonymous literary critic. A copy of this essay is in the author's private library.

Pages 145–156   As noted in the text, Wes acquired a complete set of reprints of Milton Caniff's *Terry and the Pirates* comic strip back in the mid-1990s while he was attending Columbia University's Graduate School of Journalism. These reprints were published in softcover volumes between 1990 and 1992 by the Nantier-Beall-Minoustchine Publishing Company (known as NBM) of New York City under its Flying Buttress Classics Library imprint. These are the volumes Wes refers to in the text.

The NBM reprints are long out of print and very difficult to find. But beginning in 2007, a new set of *Terry and the Pirates* reprints began appearing in quality hardcover volumes under the general title *The Complete Terry and the Pirates*. They are being published by IDW Publishing, a division of Idea and Design Works LLC of San Diego (www.idwpublishing.com) and are available from such online sites as Amazon and Barnes and Noble Online. So far, four volumes have appeared; these carry the comic strip from its beginning in 1934 through 1942. The remaining two volumes are scheduled to appear by the end of 2009 and will carry the comic strip through the end of Caniff's authorship in 1946.

For the convenience of this novel's readers, the references below to specific sequences in the comic strip are to the current volumes of the IDW series and the page numbers cited are for these volumes.

Pages 148–151   (First appearance of the Dragon Lady.)
The Complete Terry and the Pirates: Volume One, pages 24–37. As was common practice at the time, the original newspaper publication of *Terry* told one story in its daily (Monday through Saturday) black-and-white strips and an entirely different story in its Sunday-only color strips. This practice ended in August 1936, when the two story lines

were merged and *Terry* became a full Monday through Sunday strip telling a single ongoing story. This sequence first appeared in the Sunday-only strips.

Pages 152–153   (The Dragon Lady inspires Klang's bandit gang to become a guerrilla militia under her leadership and fight the Japanese invaders.)
The Complete Terry and the Pirates: Volume Two, pages 226–227.

Pages 155–156   (The Dragon Lady teaches Terry to dance.)
The Complete Terry and the Pirates: Volume Three, pages 89–95.

CHAPTER 5
Page 204

William Blake's *The Tyger* is one of the most famous—and disturbing—poems in the English language. It was first published in *Songs of Experience* in 1794 and appears in many collections. The final verse used here is taken from page 37 of *William Blake: Selected Poetry*, edited by W. H. Stevenson and published in 1988 by Penguin Books Ltd. of London and New York. Contemporary spelling is used for the convenience of readers.

CHAPTER 6
Pages 300–303

"They Can't Take That Away From Me" is a 1937 song by George and Ira Gershwin. It was first performed by Fred Astaire in the 1937 RKO film *Shall We Dance*. Fred sings it (but does not dance it) to Ginger Rogers on the deck of a ferry crossing the Hudson River between New Jersey and Manhattan. The song was nominated for the 1937 Oscar as Best Original Song.

CHAPTER 7
Pages 318–320

"Thanks for the Memory" is a 1937 song by Ralph Rainger and Leo Robin. It was first performed by Bob Hope and Shirley Ross in the 1938 Paramount film *The Big Broadcast of 1938*. Hope and Ross play a long divorced couple who meet by accident on an ocean liner and sing a duet about the bittersweet joys of their failed marriage. The song won the 1938 Oscar for Best Original Song, and Hope later made it his signature tune.